The SECRET CASEBOOK *of* SHERLOCK HOLMES

DONALD THOMAS

JAICO PUBLISHING HOUSE

Ahmedabad Bangalore Bhopal Bhubaneswar Chennai
Delhi Hyderabad Kolkata Lucknow Mumbai

Published by Jaico Publishing House
A-2 Jash Chambers, 7-A Sir Phirozshah Mehta Road
Fort, Mumbai - 400 001
jaicopub@jaicobooks.com
www.jaicobooks.com

Published in arrangement with
A. M. Heath & Co. Ltd.
6 Warwick Court, Holborn
London, WC1R 5DJ

To be sold only in India, Bangladesh, Bhutan,
Pakistan, Nepal, Sri Lanka and the Maldives.

THE SECRET CASEBOOK OF SHERLOCK HOLMES
ISBN 978-81-8495-500-2

First Jaico Impression: 2014
Second Jaico Impression: 2015

Printed by
Repro India Limited, Navi Mumbai

To Ben and Pet

In gratitude for Mrs Carew

Contents

A Letter to Posterity
from John H. Watson, MD

I

Those who have read my narrative of the Brixton Road murder, made public under the somewhat sensational title of *A Study in Scarlet,* will recall the events which led to my first meeting with the late Sherlock Holmes. For any who come new to this story, let me recapitulate the circumstances as briefly as I may. Having taken my medical degree at the University of London in 1878, I had attended the required course of the Army Medical Department at Netley. When my time at Netley was over, I was attached as Assistant Surgeon to the Fifth Northumberland Fusiliers. I will not repeat in detail how I landed in Bombay when my regiment was already in action in the Second Afghan War; how I joined it at Candahar only to be wounded in the shoulder, my active service career terminated by a Jazail bullet at the battle of Maiwand.

It was not the wound received in battle that alone decided my fate. Enteric fever contracted at the base hospital of Peshawar so weakened and emaciated me that the medical board had not the least hesitation in ordering my return to England. A few months later I was endeavouring without success to lead a comfortless existence at a private hotel in the Strand upon my invalid allowance of eleven shillings and sixpence a day.

The weeks of summer passed in 1880, and I watched with dismay as my little stock of capital ran lower. I had no family in England, no expectations, no one to whom I could turn for immediate assistance. My state of mind may easily be imagined, as I contemplated the loss of both health and independence.

In such gloomy circumstances I had taken a turn down Piccadilly one morning in July. That fashionable avenue was busy with swan's-neck pilentum carriages drawn by glossy bay geldings, here and there a coach with armorial bearings upon its door and a hundred hansom cabs. Among these symbols of imperial prosperity, I reflected that walking costs a man nothing. The clocks had struck twelve as I began to make my way back from the trees and carriages of Hyde Park Corner, where the pretty horse-breakers and their escorts rode under the leafy branches of Rotten Row.

In the course of this stroll, I had decided that my first economy must be to leave the private hotel where I had been living. I would seek cheaper lodgings. With that, I felt a little richer and entered the old Criterion Bar in Coventry Street. It was a chance in ten thousand that, as I stood at the bar, I should have been tapped on the shoulder by young Stamford, who had been a surgical dresser under me at Bart's Hospital. To him I described my situation and my new resolve as to where I should live. He it was who mentioned his acquaintance Sherlock Holmes, a man also in search of diggings. That very day Holmes had been bemoaning to Stamford that he could not get someone to go halves with him in a nice set of rooms which he had found but which were too much for his purse.

I recall, as if it were only a week ago, my excitement at this chance of solving my own problem so easily. I turned to Stamford and exclaimed, 'By Jove! If your friend really wants someone to share the rooms and the expense, I am the very man for him. I should prefer going halves to living alone!'

As yet, I had not set eyes upon my unwitting partner.

This is not the place to draw a complete portrait of him who was to be my friend and companion for so many years. I must say, however, that in all the time I knew him the appearance of

Sherlock Holmes seemed to alter no more than his demeanour. He was a little over six feet in height and throughout his life he remained so lean that he looked, if anything, taller. His eyes were sharp and his gaze penetrating, his nose was thin and hawk-like, making him seem always alert and decisive. His jaw was firmly set, square and prominent with a look of resolve and determination. If I were to compare his features and behaviour to those of public figures, he had the stance and manner of Sir Edward Carson QC, that most vigorous and astute of prosecuting lawyers. In his style, he had something of the combative and self-assured manner of Lord Birkenhead, the former Mr F. E. Smith. Perhaps I do him and them a disservice by such comparisons. There was never any man who was a twin for Sherlock Holmes.

My first meeting with him, when Stamford introduced us later that day, was in the chemical laboratory of Bart's. His fingers were blotched with acid and stained a little by ink. Surrounded by broad low tables, shelves of bottles, retorts, test-tubes, and Bunsen burners with their blue flickering flames, Holmes seemed in his element. He quite ignored me in his excitement at explaining to Stamford the success of an experiment on which he had been engaged. He had discovered a reagent which was precipitated by haemoglobin and by nothing else. In plain terms, it would now be possible for the first time to identify blood stains long after the blood had dried.

I was soon to see for myself a curious antithesis in my new friend's character. He alternated between periods of fierce intellectual excitement and moods of brooding contemplation. There were days of torpor in which he appeared to see little or nothing of the world about him. I had yet to discover that the last of these states was often produced by his use of narcotics. Life cannot always be lived at a pitch of fierce excitement. There are days, weeks, and months of tedium. Other men might have turned to drink or sexual vice. Sherlock Holmes preferred the less complicated palliative of cocaine. I deplored his use of it and protested to him—but in vain. I came to see that the drug was not his true addiction, merely a substitute for a more powerful enchantment. Cocaine, he said, was his protest against the tedium of existence. When his powers were fully occupied, he showed not the least need of it. The excitement of discovery, detection, activity, was everything to him. I firmly believe that cocaine was a make-do for the greater stimulant of adrenalin. The syringe provided for his needs when his adrenal gland failed to do so.

The world knows so much about the reputation of Sherlock Holmes that I need add little here. He pretended to be the dedicated student of science, yet from time to time one caught a glimpse of the great romantic. When I first met him, I noted that he had a profound knowledge of chemistry, an adequate but unsystematic acquaintance with anatomy. He had a good practical knowledge of the English law and was unrivalled in his reading of the literature of crime. From botany and geology he took just such information as seemed useful to him. Whenever necessary, he could make himself expert at a new subject in an astonishingly short time. When the new science of morbid psychology came into its own after 1880, he mastered it with such skill that neither Krafft-Ebing nor Charcot could tell you more of his own works than could Holmes.

At first I noted that he appeared to have little knowledge or interest in literature or philosophy. I was to discover that, when it suited him, he could show a degree of familiarity with writers like Edgar Allan Poe, Charles Baudelaire, or Robert Browning, the analysts of human darkness, which lifelong students of literature might envy. There were days when he exercised his brain as other men would have used a chest-expander or a set of dumb-bells. In such times of idleness he set himself the task of confronting the great unsolved problems of mathematics. If he did not find solutions to Fermat's Last Theorem or the Goldbach Conjecture, I believe that he understood at length the nature of those abstract impossibilities better than any man living.

There was something not quite English about Sherlock Holmes. Having played rugger for Blackheath in my younger days, I found he had no sense of sport in his physical activities. You could not imagine him among 'the flannelled fools at the wicket and the muddied oafs in the goal'. His physical exercise was Continental rather than Anglo-Saxon. Like a French or German student, he was an expert swordsman, boxer, and single-stick player. Though far from burly in his build, he demonstrated a grip that was the strongest of any man I have ever known.

He cared very little for society, let alone for politics or public men. Early in our friendship he assured me that a nation was better led by a rogue than by a reformer. In more recent years, he abominated Mr Asquith as leader of the government but openly admired the style and complicity of Mr Lloyd George. As the result of services which he had rendered to the Crown in the years before the German war, I was with him once at the Reform Club, when Mr Asquith spoke after dinner. Sherlock Holmes had attended the function reluctantly and sat with eyelids drooping and an air of ineffable boredom. Intending to compliment or instruct his audience, the late Prime Minister remarked that he owed much of his success in life to an endeavour to associate only with those who were his intellectual superiors. To my dismay, I heard Holmes rouse himself and say loudly enough for all those around him to hear, 'By God, that wouldn't be difficult!'

He was once at a soirée of the late Mr Oscar Wilde, an occasion which he would have avoided if he could. The unfortunate playwright was at his most self-satisfied and paradoxical, preening, praising his own works and genius in every nuance, while his sycophants chortled and encouraged him. As the guests prepared to depart, Sherlock Holmes stood up and the faces of the company turned towards him. He fixed Mr Wilde, the serene egotist, with those glittering eyes and seemed to bow a little towards him. The breath hissed slightly between his teeth.

'Master,' he said with expressionless irony, 'before we leave, could you not perhaps tell us a little about yourself?'

It was cruel and it was deadly. For more than an hour, Mr Wilde had seemed to talk of nothing but himself. This egotism would have justified Holmes's sardonic reprimand. Yet there was something more about the playwright which Wilde knew and Holmes had guessed, but which remained hidden from the others. Holmes, as I have said, was well read in the literature of morbid psychology. From this knowledge he had divined a pathological truth behind the mask of the *poseur* and he let the unhappy victim know it. A smile touched Wilde's lips, the worse for its ghastliness. The truth which Holmes inferred was one that the rest of the world was soon to hear in three trials at the Central Criminal Court.

I believe it was as well that Sherlock Holmes remained a private and secretive man. His tongue would have destroyed him in public life, though not before it had destroyed a good many other men. Among several instances of his savagery, his brother Mycroft told me, after the funeral, of young Sherlock Holmes's first brief acquaintance with formal education at a great Oxford college, whose master was something of a household name. It was the master's custom to take each of the new men out for a walk alone, from Oxford into the countryside and back again. The great scholar would keep an absolute silence as the pair walked to Headington or Godstow. The hapless undergraduate would feel the strain of this and would compel himself at last to make some nervous and banal remark, often about the weather or the meadow scenery. The master would either crush this by his retort or would continue the walk without reply, as if the observation were beneath notice. In either event, the poor young man would have been put securely in his place for the next three or four years. The stratagem had not been known to fail.

When Holmes was taken on this solitary freshman exercise, it was he who maintained a silence. Keeping step with the master of the college, he walked over Magdalen Bridge, through Headington and up Shotover Hill. Unused to this resolute behaviour but enjoying a natural position of superiority and eminence, the master himself broke the silence at last. It was a laconic and patronising inquiry.

'They tell me, Holmes,' he said, 'they tell me that you are very clever. Are you?'

'Yes,' said Holmes ungraciously.

Silence returned, unbroken, as they walked grimly back into Oxford and at last reached the college gates. Holmes turned to face the offended master with a slight bow, expressionless otherwise.

'Goodbye, sir,' he said courteously. 'I have so much enjoyed our talk.'

Mycroft Holmes assured me that his younger brother thereupon shook the illustrious dust of that college off his feet and found a humbler institution, where he was left to live pretty much as he chose. Sherlock Holmes himself had told me that Victor Trevor, son of a Norfolk squire, was the only friend he made during the two years he remained at college. Holmes was never a very sociable man. By his own account, he was always rather fond of moping in his rooms and working out his own methods of thought. His line of study was quite distinct from that of the other fellows, so that they had no points of contact at all.

In the long vacation he would go up to his London rooms, where he would spend the summer weeks working out a few experiments in organic chemistry. At first he had rooms in Montagu Street, just round the corner from the British Museum. Then, as he spent more time in the chemical laboratories of the great hospitals, he crossed the river and found lodgings in Lambeth Palace Road.

II

Those who have followed the published adventures of Sherlock Holmes in the past thirty years will know something of these matters. Let me now explain how this further collection of narratives has been compiled.

From time to time, during the years when I shared rooms with him, he would lug from his bedroom the famous tin box which was half filled with bundles of papers tied separately with ribbon, each bundle representing a case now closed. Some of these which occurred before our meeting, like the case of the Gloria Scott or the Musgrave Ritual, have already been published from the documents and my friend's own recollection of them. Others were not so readily given to the world.

They included services to the state, matters of personal confidence, and investigations upon which Sherlock Holmes had been engaged before our meeting in the chemical laboratory of Bart's in 1880. In almost every instance, a delay was necessary before the facts of the case could be published. I may safely say that by the time you read these pages, Sherlock Holmes and I, as well as every other person mentioned in them, will have been dust for a good many years.

I have written often in the past of my friend's success as a 'consulting detective' to private individuals. Once or twice, in writing of the Naval Treaty or the Bruce-Partington Plans, I have hinted at something more. The reputation of Sherlock Holmes was such that his services were increasingly in demand by officers of the state. The Fenian dynamite outrages, the blowing up of post offices and the Metropolitan Railway in the 1880s, led to the setting up of the Special Branch at Scotland Yard. The safety of the Crown and its representatives was no longer a matter which could be left to an amateur police force and the good sense of all the people. Later still, as the threat of war with the German Empire approached in 1914, the Crown and government gave authority to the organisation of Military Intelligence. From Queen Anne's Gate, almost in the shadow of Parliament itself, such operations were undertaken by various divisions of this service. Two of its branches were of paramount importance. The fifth division of Military Intelligence was to supervise security at home against intrusion by our enemies, and a sixth division was to control our espionage against foreign powers.

It would have been astonishing if the skills of Sherlock Holmes, though he was well in his middle years, had not been employed by those at Scotland Yard and in the government who were already indebted to him for his assistance in other matters. The question is whether the history of these operations is to remain, for ever and literally, a closed book. That secrets of this kind should be revealed immediately after the events is unthinkable. There are men and women alive now whose reputations and safety would be compromised. The security of the realm itself might be undermined. In the present decade, it is by no means likely that even the great war with Germany will prove to be the last conflict of its kind. Enemies to our way of life may easily be identified in other quarters. A lifetime must pass before such narratives as mine can be made public.

I confess I find it a relief that the decision of publication or suppression is not mine alone. After the death of Sherlock Holmes, the question of his unpublished papers was immediately raised by Sir Ernie Backwell, Permanent Secretary at the Home Office. Sir Ernie would, I believe, have been happy to make a bonfire of them. Such a measure was out of the question. Moreover, the papers were not all in the Permanent Secretary's hands, so that he was obliged to barter a little. After long discussion with Mycroft Holmes and the legal representatives of the estate, a compromise was reached.

The private papers of Sherlock Holmes were to be deposited with the MEPO files of Scotland Yard in the Public Record Office at Chancery Lane. Files in this category remain sealed for fifty or a hundred years or even for ever, at the discretion of the government. Their very existence may be denied. However, before they passed into limbo, I as his literary executor was to have access to them in a special annexe of the Home Office library, overlooking Whitehall. Drawing upon these papers, I was to compile a narrative of the events described in them, taking much the form of the earlier adventures. The narrative was to be read and approved by Sir Ernie Backwell with his legal advisers.

It was not, of course, to be approved for immediate publication. When the manuscript was complete, it was to be deposited in the public records of domestic state papers. I asked that it should be released after fifty years. Sir Ernie assured me that His Majesty's ministers would not settle for less than a hundred. So it would have been had not Mycroft Holmes and the Attorney-General both been members of the committee of the Diogenes Club. After further argument, a period of seventy years was agreed. This would amply cover the probable remaining lifetime of any person mentioned in the narratives. It would remove any risk of exposing secret matters to a possible enemy of the state. Of what possible use can the confidences of a previous century be to present adversaries?

By this means stories are preserved of the fateful visit of King Edward VII to Dublin in 1907 and the truth attending the disappearance of the Crown Jewels from Dublin Castle; of the mysterious death of Herr Diesel in 1913 as the secrets of his famous engine were about to pass into British hands.

Other confidential matters may now be revealed which, though they do not threaten the safety of the state, could not have been made public at the time of the events without a great breach of private trust. Even in the volumes already published a certain latitude has been taken with names. If you have read the adventure of Holmes and the blackmailer 'Charles Augustus Milverton', for example, you will recall my caveat that the story could not have been told in any form without disguising the events and persons to an extent which gave the narrative more fiction than fact.

It can do no harm now to reveal the fictional character of Milverton as in reality that of the blackmailer and thief Charles Augustus Howell, born in Lisbon of Anglo-Portuguese parentage in 1839. He was secretary to Mr John Ruskin and agent to Mr Dante Gabriel Rossetti, the artist. You may read, in Mr Thomas Wise's *Swinburne Bibliography*, as you might have heard it from Mr Oscar Wilde, the manner of Howell's death in 1890, his throat cut outside a public house, a half-sovereign wedged in his teeth, the slanderer's reward.

Mr Howell's customary method of extortion was to obtain indiscreet or confidential letters from his dupes, paste them into a large album and pledge this volume to a pawnbroker on a plea of poverty. The dupes would be informed that the compromising letters had been pledged, that Mr Howell had not the money to redeem them, and that they must be publicly sold unless their authors would buy them back. Victims and their families hastened to retrieve these items only to be met with bills for many hundreds of pounds, divided afterwards between Mr Howell and the confederate pawnbroker.

It was so neatly done that, though the act was blackmail in fact, it was hard to establish the crime within the law, even had the victims been prepared to endure the threat of disgrace. The Rossetti family, Mr Swinburne the poet, and Mr Whistler the painter were among those ensnared by Howell's craft. To this catalogue might be added Mr Ruskin and the Reverend Charles Dodgson of Christ Church, known as 'Lewis Carroll' the world over. Such investigations carried out by Sherlock Holmes were sensitive in the extreme. They could be related only in a most indirect manner at the time.

State secrets and private confidences were not quite all that awaited me when I listed my late friend's papers as his literary executor. If you have read my account of our first meeting, you will recall that Holmes had been what he called 'a consulting detective' for some while. As he said, his services had already been of assistance to Inspector Lestrade of Scotland Yard when that officer had 'got himself into a fog over a forgery case'. The reference was to the so-called Bank of England forgeries in 1873, when the Bidwell brothers came within a hair's breadth of having the Bank's funds at their mercy.

Among the papers left by Sherlock Holmes were several of his 'reports' upon these investigations which preceded our first meeting. Yet a story-teller's narrative is far preferable to a mere report and I make no apology for attempting to interpret the nuances of the original. If I speak of Holmes as a student of analytical chemistry or human conduct, it is merely that he was a student of such things all his life. When I first met him, he was certainly far past the age at which a man normally walks the wards or reads for the bar.

At the time of the 'Smethurst Case', with which I shall deal first, he had his rooms—'consulting rooms', as he grandly called them—in Lambeth Palace Road, just south of Westminster Bridge. These lodgings were convenient for the chemical laboratory of St Thomas's Hospital, to which he had occasional access on the basis of grace-and-favour. I have written elsewhere that his origins lay among the English squirearchy. The indulgence shown him by the governors of the hospital stemmed from a bequest made by one of these kinsmen.

Those who know London at all well may recognise the handsome terraces and tree-lined vistas of Lambeth Palace Road as a favourite abode of our young medical men and students. Here it was that Holmes returned each evening from his methodical labours among test-tubes and Bunsen burners. All day he gathered information and much of the night he passed in restless calculation. How often did the night traveller or the policeman on his beat glance up and see the familiar silhouette against the drawn blind of the first-floor room? It was the shadow of a man pacing rapidly to and fro, his hands clasped behind his back, his sharp profile bowed by a weight of thought.

On other evenings he would venture out to eat his supper and then walk the streets of the great city until he seemed to know the landscape of London as accurately as the mirrored image of his own face. The young Sherlock Holmes was a lone observer as the hum of day ceased, the shops darkened, and the gin palaces thrust out their ragged and squalid crowds to pace the streets. The homeless and the destitute grew familiar with his passing as they huddled in the niches of the bridges and the litter of the markets. The wretched women shivering in their finery, waiting to catch the drunkard who went shouting homewards, watched him from a distance.

Sometimes this young student of humanity would stop to speak to a shoeless child crouching on a doorstep. Then his strange apprenticeship led him to join the conversations of a ragged crowd smoking or dozing through the night beside the glow of a coke fire, where the stones had been taken up and the gas streamed from a pipe in the centre of the street in a flag of flame. On summer nights, as he turned for home, the streets were already growing blue with the coming day. Church spires and chimney pots stood out against the sky with a sharpness seen only before a million fires cast their pall of smoke across the city. The early workers were gathered at the street corners, round the breakfast stall, blowing on their saucers of steaming coffee drawn from tall tin cans with the fire crimson beneath. As he crossed the river by London Bridge, the first ragged girl with her basket slung before her screamed watercresses through the sleeping streets.

Such was the practical education of Sherlock Holmes. Small wonder that in later years he could assume the appearance or speech of common men, so that even his friends did not penetrate the disguise. On other nights he would turn to his books, threading some obscure avenue of research whose result would bring success to an investigation in a manner that astonished all who heard of it.

No man had so curious a library as Sherlock Holmes. You might look in vain for volumes that were in half the families of England. But if you sought industries peculiar to a small town in Bohemia, or unique chemical constituents of Sumatran or Virginian tobacco leaf, or the alienist's account of morbid individual psychology, or the methods by which a Ming is to be distinguished from a skilful imitation, he had only to reach out his hand for the answer. In far more cases, however, that answer was carried in his head.

On a shelf of the break-front bookcase, between works on the manufacture of paper and a set of the Newgate Calendar, I noticed that a number of volumes and two finely bound essays lay on their sides. They had been disregarded and gathering dust for some years. Their contents had been abstracted and stored in that precise and ordered mind. The slimmest volume was by Dr David Hutchinson and it had won the Fiske Fund Prize of the Rhode Island Medical Society in 1857: 'What are the Causes of that Disease incident to Pregnancy, characterised by Inflammation of the Mouth and Fauces, accompanied by Anorexia and Emaciation?' Next to it were works of a similar kind by Abercrombie and by Professor Stoltz of Vienna, as well as fifty-eight accounts of related fatalities in Cartaya's 'Vomissements incoercibles pendant la grossesse'.

In these volumes lay the clue to what Holmes called his first investigation, whose outcome meant life or death for its subject. By his pursuit of that inquiry, he brought his skill in scientific analysis to the notice of Scotland Yard. You may read a fuller account of Dr Smethurst's ordeal in the Notable British Trials volumes and in the newspapers of the day. Holmes, however, shunned the limelight. He preferred to remain 'behind the scenes', for fear of embarrassing his patrons or revealing too much of himself.

His report, as I read it, had been drawn up for Mr Hardinge Giffard, whom history now knows as the great Lord Chancellor Halsbury. If that investigation of Dr Smethurst's crime did not bring public fame to Sherlock Holmes, it surely placed his skills before the nation's rulers. To that first case I now turn.

The Ghost in the Machine

I

As Holmes described the scene to me, it was a blazing Sunday afternoon at the end of May, a high sun beating hard on the still and empty length of Lambeth Palace Road. He readily confessed that business had been poor. After lunch on Saturday, he had shut himself in his room and set himself to work there until Monday morning, when he might have access to the laboratory again. The idleness of 'Sunday observance' always made his active mind fretful and the time of which I write was one when a rigorous Sabbath was much in fashion. Among such pieties in the homes of Westminster, Holmes was pursuing the subtleties of murder by poisonous perfumes at the court of Louis XIV.

He was just then absorbed in the fate of the young Madame de Brinvilliers, who had not been permitted execution until she had first undergone the ordeal of the water-torture. Such vindictive aberrations of the human mind were irresistible to him. Yet he was not, as the phrase has it, lost to the world. Standing at his oak reading-desk, turning the crisp pages of a seventeenth-century folio volume, Holmes nonetheless heard the wheels of a solitary hansom cab in the quiet sunlit street outside. Without ceasing to read of Madame de Brinvilliers, he heard the same wheels stop beneath his window.

There came the jangle of the bell and the voice of his landlady, Mrs Harris, in conversation with a female visitor. There were words of surprised recognition.

A door opened and closed on the lower floor. Ten minutes later it opened again and footsteps sounded on the stairs. There was a knock at Holmes's sitting-room door and Mrs Harris entered in response to his summons.

The good lady was flushed with apology at disturbing her lodger on a Sunday afternoon. Only the assurance that this was a matter of life and death, that it concerned her oldest and dearest friend, that speed was of the essence, could be offered in excuse. Her friend, Miss Louisa Bankes, would see Mr Holmes—and would see no one else.

Holmes listened, laid a silk marker in his folio volume, and closed the cover.

'Dear me,' he said gently. 'At all events one can't refuse a lady, and such a positive one at that. If she will take me as she finds me, I am at her service.'

'She had heard of you from your notice in the column of the paper and, seeing your address was here, must have your opinion,' Mrs Harris assured him.

'And no doubt she has heard a little from you, Mrs Harris,' Holmes said kindly. 'Well, we must not keep her waiting. Will you not show your friend up?'

It had seemed to him better that their interview should take place in his sitting-room, where he might more easily discuss the troubles of Miss Louisa Bankes without inviting Mrs Harris's presence.

The landlady returned a moment later in company with a slight but pretty woman, auburn-haired and about thirty-five years old. Her high-boned face was animated by the glance of quick grey eyes, though she looked at that moment flustered rather than animated.

'Thank you, Mrs Harris,' Holmes said courteously, in just such a manner as gave the landlady no alternative but to withdraw. He looked again at Miss Bankes and thought that she was possessed of the prettiest face he had seen under a bonnet for many a month.

'Mr Holmes?' she said before he could offer her a seat, 'I beg you to excuse my arrival in this fashion. I have read your notice in *The Times* on several occasions and had half persuaded myself to communicate with you some weeks ago. Now I fear it may be too late. It would have been more proper, I know, to write to you. But a letter could not reach you until Tuesday and the matter cannot wait. I knew I could reach you by way of Waterloo or the White Horse Cellar every half-hour and that I must do so at once.'

'By all means,' Holmes said gently. 'Pray sit down, Miss Bankes. Try the sofa, and tell me what it is that cannot wait until Tuesday. Pray, take your time.'

Louisa Bankes swept across the room. The sofa was the only article of furniture that would comfortably accommodate such full, cream skirts, a tribute to the crinoline still somewhat in fashion. The day was warm and yet she shivered as she drew about her the rose mantle edged in crimson. She faced Holmes, as if undecided how to begin, sitting with her back to the window.

'Mr Holmes,' she said at last, 'you will think me melodramatic, I know. You may even think me hysterical. I have come here because I must have your help on behalf of my sister. I believe she is being murdered.'

She paused and Holmes looked at her keenly but not unkindly. He crossed to the window and stared down at the hansom cab, which still waited outside. For a moment he said nothing. Then he turned to her.

'I take it,' he said gently, 'that your sister is living with her husband at Richmond or thereabouts. You believe that for some time he has been poisoning her. She is, I assume, married to a doctor.'

Louisa Bankes looked up at him with something like fear in her eyes.

'Then you know!' she cried.

'I do not know, Miss Bankes. I deduce certain possibilities from what you have just told me.'

'But I have told you nothing!' she protested.

Holmes settled himself in the chair on the opposite side of the fireplace.

'On the contrary,' he said, 'you informed me that you might have come at any half-hour to Waterloo or the White Horse Cellar in Piccadilly. The Richmond bus comes at the half-hour to the White Horse and the Richmond train every half-hour to Waterloo. Their routes do not cross elsewhere, except Richmond. Your demeanour suggests that you have come directly from a scene of great distress. You do not tell me that your sister has been murdered or is *going* to be murdered. You say that she *is* being murdered. A murder which is part accomplished surely suggests poison. When a woman is being poisoned and even her own sister is unable to prevent it, the guilty hand is very close to her indeed and is in all probability her husband's. It is true, of course, I cannot swear that your sister's husband is a doctor, but that is far the most common profession in such cases.'

The poor young woman bit her lip and then looked up.

'You are right, though, Mr Holmes. He is a doctor.'

'You had best tell me the circumstances,' Holmes said quietly.

Louisa Bankes kept her eyes steadfastly upon him, as if to convince him of her sincerity and, indeed, her sanity.

'My sister Isabella is a little older than I, Mr Holmes, but was also unmarried until December. Up to September, we had lived together in Notting Hill. The house was mine. Then she suggested that it would be better for us to live apart. There was no quarrel between us. I made no objection, though I feared there might be an association of which she was ashamed and wished to keep from her family. From September until November she lived at a boarding-house in Rifle Terrace, Bayswater. Among the other guests was a medical man of about fifty, Dr Smethurst. I cannot tell you whether his presence was the reason for her moving there. After some weeks, the familiarity between them grew so scandalous that the landlady, Mrs Smith, asked my sister to find other accommodation. Bella moved to Kildare Terrace, nearby. On the twelfth of December, she married Dr Smethurst at Battersea Church and they set up home at Alma Villas, Richmond, in furnished rooms. Bella became ill soon afterwards, first with biliousness and then with dysentery. It is his doing, Mr Holmes.'

As she paused, Holmes asked, 'May I ask, Miss Bankes, whether your sister is a wealthy woman?'

'Not wealthy, Mr Holmes, but she has a comfortable income on capital of eighteen hundred pounds. It is the interest on a mortgage.'

'I see,' Holmes said. 'Pray continue. What of your sister's health in the past?'

Louisa Bankes shivered once more and then composed herself.

'My sister had been in good health before her marriage, except that she sometimes suffered from bilious attacks. They were not frequent and never severe. I had no suspicions of Dr Smethurst until last month. Then, on the eighteenth of April, I received a letter from him telling me that Bella was really very ill and that she had asked for me to come to her. See here.'

She opened her bag and drew out a folded sheet of notepaper. She handed it to Holmes. He glanced at it, repeating aloud the phrases which caught his attention.

'"You will greatly oblige by coming alone . . . breathe not a word of this note to anyone . . ." Curious instructions, Miss Bankes. Did you visit your sister?'

The woman gave a half-sob at the recollection.

'I did, Mr Holmes, on the very same day. She was lying in bed, looking so pale and weak, scarcely able to move. She saw that I was alarmed at the sight of her and she said to me, "Oh, don't say anything about it to anyone. It will be all right when I get better." '

Holmes frowned. 'A very singular caution, Miss Bankes. And have you seen her since?'

Louisa Bankes shook her head and drew several more folded sheets of notepaper from her bag.

'Everything I received afterwards was written by Thomas Smethurst,' she continued. 'In the next letter, on the following day, he tells me that Bella passed a very bad night. The excitement of seeing me had brought back the vomiting and purging. A doctor had been called and had forbidden any further visits. A few more days passed and then he wrote again, saying that I might see her in a week's time. But, when that week had passed, he sent me these.'

She handed the other letters to Holmes, who once again read out the ominous phrases.

' "Dearest Bella begs of you to wait a little longer before calling upon her . . ."; "I much regret the state of the case will not yet admit of your seeing her . . ." '

Louisa Bankes broke in upon the reading.

'How can it not admit of my seeing her, Mr Holmes? Until last autumn, when this wretch stole his way into her affections, we had lived together. Sickness or health was all one in our sisterhood. Today he writes again and warns me that I had best take lodgings close to them but must not come to the house. What does it mean, except that she is to die and I am not to see her until the end?'

Holmes studied this last letter, a look of concern in his sharp eyes. Then he handed back the pages.

'You have reason for suspicion, Miss Bankes. However—'

' "However", Mr Holmes? Before you say "however", let me add this. I myself have done everything to see my sister, without avail. Then I begged him at least to let our family physician, Dr Lane, examine her. He refused to have Dr Lane in the house. In desperation, two days ago, I lay in wait and spoke to Susannah Wheatley, the daughter of the landlady at Alma Villas. I asked her how Bella was. She told me that she feared for my sister and that Bella had signed a will drawn up by Dr Smethurst. Miss Wheatley had witnessed it. Surely, Mr Holmes, he has imprisoned her there to take her life as a means of possessing himself of her money.'

Holmes said nothing for a moment, then he looked up at his visitor.

'During an illness of such length and gravity, your sister has been seen by other medical men?'

Louisa Bankes looked back at him wide-eyed in her despair, 'Dr Julius and his partner Dr Bird have both seen her. But Thomas Smethurst is a doctor too. Do you not think he could make poison appear as some disease? Dr Bird and Dr Julius are both led to believe that she has dysentery.'

Holmes said nothing for a moment, then the keen eyes settled upon her again.

'Answer me one question, if you please, Miss Bankes. If all is as you say, why have you come to me?'

'Where else should I go?' she cried.

For the first time there was scepticism in his eyes as he studied her. Yet he was still gentle with her.

'Come, now,' he said. 'You would surely have done better to take your story directly to Scotland Yard. The Metropolitan Police can do more for you than I may. They have powers of investigation far beyond mine. You may walk there in fifteen minutes from here. I will give you the name of the very man whom you must see. Ah, there is something more, is there not? What is it that you cannot tell them?'

For a moment the young woman looked at her hands and said nothing. Then she breathed deeply and spoke. It was, Holmes later told me, as if she had expected to have the secret forced from her but knew not how to yield it.

'Mr Holmes, when my sister met Dr Smethurst, he was already a married man.'

'Do you mean that he deceived her by committing bigamy?'

Louisa Bankes shook her head.

'No, Mr Holmes. He did not deceive her. When Bella lived at Rifle Terrace last autumn, Dr Smethurst and his wife were guests in the same boarding-house. They have been married many years, and Mrs Smethurst is quite twenty years older than her husband. She is now a woman of seventy and more. My sister knew all this, knew that he was already married.'

Holmes's keen eyes narrowed a little and he now stared at his visitor with fascination.

'What possessed your sister to abet a wilful act of bigamy? It was almost certain to have been discovered before long.'

Louisa Bankes lowered her head until the frame of her bonnet almost concealed her face. Her words were now punctuated by sobs.

'He told her it was to be their secret marriage and that there could be no harm in that . . . When old Mrs Smethurst died they would be man and wife in fact and law. Until then, if he and Bella should live together, a married name would protect her reputation. She believed him, Mr Holmes, and now she pays the price. You ask me to go to the police? The law would condemn the scoundrel who has ruined her but it would condemn my sister as well. If I could save her life in no other way, I would do it. You, Mr Holmes, are my hope that there is some other way.'

It was not a matter to which Holmes gave long thought. He stood up, as if to indicate that his mind was made up and the consultation at an end.

'Very well, Miss Bankes. You may rely upon me to do everything I can. I must tell you that I can do little for your sister's reputation. However, if all is as you say it is, I will go down to Richmond at the first opportunity and call upon Dr Smethurst. I, at least, have no reason to spare your sister's feelings or his and he will know it. I shall give him the choice of leaving your sister at once and never seeing her again, or of being exposed as a bigamist. The law may or may not proceed against your sister; I think it may not. It is Dr Smethurst who is twice married. Against him, the courts are empowered to pronounce a sentence of fourteen years in a convict settlement. If what you tell me is correct, we may yet have him on the hip.'

II

Despite the urgency of Miss Bankes, Holmes did not go down to Richmond until he had satisfied himself of certain facts. On Monday, he walked as far as Battersea Church and there paid the clerk a shilling to read an entry in the parish register for the previous year. It recorded the marriage of Thomas Smethurst and Isabella

Bankes on 12 December. Next morning, after a visit to Rifle Terrace, Bayswater, he summoned a cab for St Mark's Church, Kennington. Another shilling won him access to the parish register for twenty years earlier, from which he copied the record of a marriage between Thomas Smethurst and Mary Durham, now an elderly lady whom Holmes had seen an hour or two before at Rifle Terrace.

With copies of these two entries in his note-case, he took the half-hourly bus to Richmond from the White Horse Cellar, Piccadilly.

Dr Smethurst and Miss Isabella Bankes had set up their home in Mrs Wheatley's rooms at 10, Alma Villas, Richmond. Holmes had gathered from his visitor that theirs was a modest apartment of bedroom and sitting-room, in the latter of which the meals were served by the daughter of the family.

In answer to his knock, the door was opened by an aproned maid-of-all-work. Holmes handed her his card.

'Dr Thomas Smethurst, if you please,' he said. 'It is a matter of the greatest urgency.'

Holmes was taken aback to see that, when Dr Smethurst's name was mentioned, a look of consternation bordering on terror convulsed the girl's face.

'You can't see Dr Smethurst,' she blurted out presently, 'E've gone.'

'Gone?' said Holmes, 'And what of Mrs Smethurst?'

'You can't see her,' the girl said hastily. 'She's better since he went but the poor soul's still very weakly.'

'And who is looking after her?'

'I am,' the girl said proudly. 'And Mrs Wheatley and Miss Wheatley, of course, and Miss Bankes—that's Mrs Smethurst's sister. And Dr Julius and Dr Bird both been and left.'

From the shadows of the hall behind the girl, a man's voice called, 'Mr Holmes!'

The man appeared, a well-built ginger-headed policeman with a broad-boned face and a clipped moustache. Robert M'Intyre, Inspector of the Richmond Constabulary, was just then in his 'private clothes' of frock-coat and sponge-bag trousers, a pearl-grey stock at his throat. Holmes recognised him from an earlier confidential inquiry, a matter of domestic robbery.

'M'Intyre?'

The inspector waved the girl away.

'What brings you down to Richmond, Mr Holmes?'

'Miss Louisa Bankes is my client. Where is Dr Smethurst?'

M'Intyre cleared his throat discreetly and stepped out into the May sunlight.

'We may talk outside, if it's all the same to you, Mr Holmes. It's not convenient indoors with only two rooms and the poor lady in the state she is. Just down here a little way, if you wouldn't mind.'

The two men walked a short distance along the pavement of Alma Villas.

'Where is Smethurst?' Holmes demanded.

'In a police cell, Mr Holmes, where he ought to have been weeks ago. He stands charged with the attempted murder of his wife. I think Dr Bird half suspected it last week. Yesterday they took samples of what she brought up in her sickness. They sent them to be analysed by Professor Taylor. He found arsenic, Mr Holmes. No two ways about that. Arsenic enough to kill her, if that sample was repeated throughout the vital organs. Dr Smethurst was arrested last night to appear at the police court this morning. Since he's been out of the way, I hear she's improved a bit.'

Holmes stood tall and gaunt in the sunlight for a moment.

'Indeed?' he said thoughtfully.

M'Intyre turned back towards the house.

'You know your own business best, Mr Holmes, but if your interest in this case is what I think it must be, you'd be wasting your time down here. We've got him, sir, and the lady is in the hands of doctors who will do all that can be done for her. And that's all about that.'

III

If ever Sherlock Holmes had reason to feel that a case had escaped him, it was during the hours which followed his return to Lambeth

Palace Road. Thomas Smethurst had been removed from his investigation, or so it seemed. Mrs Smethurst—Isabella Bankes, as she was in truth—would recover or not, as the strength of her constitution and the skill of her physicians decreed. Whether the crime of bigamy would come to light, and whether Isabella Bankes would face prosecution as well as disgrace, were matters for others.

The best cure for his disappointments in life was always to be found in work. Holmes returned to the curious affair of the poisonous perfumes at the Court of the Sun King. He proposed a monograph upon this macabre subject. History records that the monograph was never written. He was meditating its contents on Thursday evening, two days later, as he walked back from the chemical laboratory of St Thomas's Hospital. Letting himself in at the front door, he sensed a chill silence about the house in Lambeth Palace Road. Having gone up the stairs, he had scarcely closed the door of his sitting-room and removed his coat and gloves when there was a knock. It was Mrs Harris. Her face was pale and, though the tears were now dry, their recent passage showed in her reddened eyes and haggard cheeks.

'She's dead, Mr Holmes,' the landlady said abruptly, 'Mrs Smethurst—Miss Bankes, that was. Passed away this morning. I heard from her poor sister just now.'

'Then Dr Smethurst must stand trial for murder,' Holmes said softly.

'They let him go back to her before she died, Mr Holmes.'

'Let him go?' The tall sharp-profiled figure advanced a step towards Mrs Harris, as though he might seize her and hold her accountable for such judicial stupidity. 'Let him go?'

'At the police court, Mr Holmes. Dr Smethurst swore his wife was so poorly she might die that very day. He vowed it was inhuman to keep him from her in what might be her last hours. They bailed him to go back to her. She was better after he'd been taken away. They all said so. The doctors, Miss Louisa . . . And the day after they let him back, the poor soul was dead. They caught him again—but too late for her.'

Seldom, perhaps on no other occasion, had Sherlock Holmes been at a loss for words. That a man accused of attempting to murder his wife should be released to go back to her was beyond belief. Yet it had happened.

'So now he faces the gallows in earnest,' he murmured.

'And no worse than he deserves, the devil!' said Mrs Harris bitterly.

The letter that Holmes was now obliged to write to Miss Louisa Bankes was, he always maintained, the most difficult of his life. He had failed her and would accept no fee, of course. She had come to him very late. To prevent the tragedy which occurred had been well-nigh impossible. But it was his profession to triumph over impossibilities—or rather it was his temperament. 'Failure' was the word that now sat heavily in his thoughts during the warm summer, like a raven on his shoulder. He did not, as in the tedium of inactivity, resort to cocaine. In his gloom, he spent a week or more confined to his rooms, sometimes brooding, sometimes stirring the air with passages of Haydn or Mendelssohn on his beloved violin.

IV

London's summer season with all its frivolities had come and gone by the time that Dr Smethurst stood trial at the Old Bailey for the murder of Isabella Bankes. Sherlock Holmes could give no simple reason for his determination to witness the proceedings. He had, of course, never set eyes on Thomas Smethurst and was fired by a curiosity to see what manner of man this might be. There was, however, a less commendable reason. Holmes was a 'gourmet'—I think the word is not too strong—for the sight of human beings in bizarre and desperate straits. To see the prey struggling in the toils of the law, a law that would surely tighten a noose round the man's neck, was a stimulation of his nerves to rival music or opium.

Better for him, perhaps, had he stayed away. What Holmes found in that courtroom was not at all what he had expected.

Smethurst himself was an unprepossessing man in his early fifties, square-set with ragged brown hair and a moustache. How any woman could have contemplated such a wretch, except with feelings of compassion for his shabbiness, was beyond comprehension.

Those who remember the Central Criminal Court before Newgate was pulled down and the area rebuilt may recall how like a theatre it seemed. The jury sat in an opera-box on one side, the defendants on the other. The stage was occupied by the judge, his chaplain and the sheriffs. Where the orchestra might have been in a theatre were benches for counsel and spectators. Here it was that Holmes, with a keen appetite for such living spectacles, watched hour by hour the destruction of the man in the dock. In those days, a defendant was still not permitted to give evidence in his own case. Smethurst stood at the dock-rail, wild-eyed, and watched his own death meticulously prepared.

Holmes never denied that he had gone there relishing the prospect of sport. Minute by minute the presumption of guilt grew stronger. Smethurst had bigamously married the dead woman. No sooner were they lodged at Alma Villas than her violent sickness began. He had refused the assistance of any other doctor until he could hold out no longer. In his own hand, he wrote out her will, summoned a lawyer, and stood over his victim while she signed it. Of that will he was the sole beneficiary. He then found repeated reasons for preventing her sister coming to see her. It was reported that 'Mrs Smethurst' was seen to look at her husband in terror.

There was a murmur of disgust in the court when Dr Bird described seeing Smethurst place small quantities of prussic acid on scraps of bread, throwing them out for the sparrows, seeing what quantity was enough to kill them and what was not. Dr Bird, who had been summoned by Dr Julius for a second opinion on the ailing woman, concluded after a few days that the patient was not suffering from biliousness nor from dysentery. Her symptoms were not those of any natural disease but of slow irritant poisoning. Three days before her death, samples were taken. Analysis by means of the Reinsch Test showed quantities of arsenic in her body sufficient to kill her.

Worse still, at the post-mortem, Dr Todd discovered the presence of the corrosive poison antimony in the kidneys. True, the quantity was not great but it could not be explained by any medicine that had been prescribed. For good measure, Dr Todd swore that he had never before seen on the face of a corpse such an expression of terror as that in which the features of Isabella Bankes had frozen during her death agony. Her entrails had been in an advanced state of inflammation and ulceration. Death had been brought on by exhaustion from vomiting, and from starvation caused by inability to keep a mouthful of food in her stomach, so long as Dr Smethurst tended her.

By his own admission, Smethurst alone had administered food and medicine to the deceased. When he was first arrested, she had improved in his absence and was even able to retain a little food in her stomach. When he returned, she died. At the post-mortem, it was also discovered that the woman was between five and seven weeks pregnant. He had killed not only his 'wife' but their unborn child.

Holmes watched keenly the examination and cross-examination of the witnesses. Smethurst was defended by Mr Parry, of a famous Welsh legal family. Parry was a well-fleshed man whose wig sat as tight on his head as a soldier's cap. He was eloquent in speech but failed everywhere in his attempts to pierce the armour of evidence against his client. When Dr Todd said that there was no arsenic found in the body at the autopsy, Parry thought he had him. But Dr Todd retorted that there was no arsenic because the organs were heavy with chlorate of potass, given by the murderer deliberately to flush the poison from the body once it had done its work. The unfortunate defence counsel was now left with the charge that Smethurst had not only killed Isabella Bankes, but had done it in the most devilishly cruel and cunning manner. Mr Parry, as Holmes remarked, had sewn up his client tighter still.

The damage inflicted by the witnesses for the Crown was made infinitely worse by those whom Mr Parry called for the defence.

Dr Richardson and Dr Rodger swore that, if Isabella Bankes had died of the poison, arsenic would have been found at the post-mortem. Unfortunately, as the Crown proved at once, Rodger and Richardson gave such evidence as a paid profession and had both testified in similar terms on behalf of Palmer, the notorious 'Rugeley Poisoner'. Dr Richardson, indeed, had once inadvertently poisoned one of his own patients.

The sight of Thomas Smethurst's destruction was more ghastly than any melodrama at the Hoxton Britannia. The Lord Chief Baron informed the jury that the case against Dr Smethurst was circumstantial. They were not to convict him on one piece of it alone. They must add one at a time to the scales of proof and see on which side they came down. Yet, after such a trial, there was no doubt that they must come down on the side of guilt with a crash like the gallows trap falling open under the accused man's feet. The jurors brought him in guilty half an hour later.

Smethurst made a long rambling plea for his life, only to hear the Lord Chief Baron tell him that he would be taken to the roof of Horsemonger Lane Gaol in a week or two, where all the world might see him, and there be hanged by the neck until he was dead. The wild, unkempt figure in the dock, broken by the ordeal of his trial, cried, 'I declare Dr Julius to be my murderer! I am innocent before God!'

Such fierce moments were like the finest brandy to the soul of Sherlock Holmes. All this time, however, he had been watching another man who spoke not a word in the proceedings. Mr Hardinge Giffard was junior counsel for Smethurst, behind his leader Mr Parry. His face was gentle and pale, trimmed by a line of dark whiskers. The future Lord Chancellor Halsbury had yet to make his way at the English bar. Yet Holmes already knew something of him and divined the massive intelligence that would one day fill library shelves with successive volumes of *Halsbury's Laws of England*. As the court rose, Holmes took a card and wrote upon it, 'Your client is plainly innocent. If you will allow me, I believe I can prove it.'

V

It is no disparagement of Mr Hardinge Giffard to say that, for all his forensic skill, he was mystified by the note. Though he was for the defence, he once told me that he thought at first the case against his client was as conclusive as any he had known. Dr Smethurst had seduced Isabella Bankes and bigamously married her. By his own account he had administered all food and medicine to her in her sickness. No other hand than his could have held the arsenic and antimony revealed by the analyst's reports just before the victim's death. Neither substance was present in any medicine prescribed for her. Smethurst had been seen by another physician, experimenting with poison upon the sparrows. He had prevented the woman from being seen by her own sister and by her family doctor. He had obliged her to sign a will, leaving everything to him, a will written in his own hand. When Miss Wheatley came to witness it he pretended to her it was some other legal document to which her name was to be affixed. The attorney, Mr Senior, intervened, telling him it was most improper to let the witness sign the paper thinking it was something else. Everything about Thomas Smethurst stank of fraud, connivance—and murder.

'Your client is plainly innocent. If you will allow me, I believe I can prove it.'

Mr Hardinge Giffard might have dismissed the offer as preposterous. That he did not shows the glimmer of the great Lord Chancellor of our own times in the young and penniless barrister of those days. Next evening, he called upon Sherlock Holmes in his rooms. No appointment had been made and Holmes was at his reading-desk with the gaslight white above him when his visitor was announced.

'Mr Giffard,' he said softly, shaking the young lawyer's hand, 'I had been expecting you.'

He took the visitor's hat and coat, laying them on a table at one end of the sitting-room. Then he gestured him to a chair, beside which on a small table lay a cigar box, a spirit case, and a supply of soda water in a gasoque.

Mr Giffard lowered himself into the chair.

'Mr Holmes, time is very short. The law now holds Dr Smethurst guilty of murder and will proceed to execution at once.'

'Your client's guilt is a proposition which I take the liberty to doubt,' Holmes said smoothly.

'Nevertheless, in a week or two he will die as a felon. You tell me that you believe you can prove his innocence . . .'

'I have not the least doubt that I shall.'

At that moment, Mr Giffard changed tack, as he might have done with a witness under cross-examination.

'Why should you take such interest in his innocence or guilt?'

There was a quick movement of Holmes's face, an impatience which many, who knew him only a little, thought was a smile or humorous quirk.

'I was engaged upon an inquiry into Dr Smethurst's treatment of Isabella Bankes, at the request of her sister. It was too late. The *soi-disante* Mrs Smethurst died before I could properly begin.'

'So I am told.'

Holmes stood up, poured his guest a glass of brandy, preferred the cigar box and left Mr Giffard to judge the gasoque for himself.

'When I began, Mr Giffard, I first established the facts. After all, one does not care to make libellous accusations. I verified the two marriages of Dr Smethurst, one valid and one bigamous. I consulted the copy of the will deposited at Doctors Commons.'

Hardinge Giffard put his glass down.

'Impossible, Mr Holmes. Miss Isabella Bankes's will is not proved yet, let alone registered.'

The same impatience tweaked Holmes's lips.

'Her father's will, Mr Giffard. By that will, Miss Bankes had eighteen hundred pounds, on the interest of which she might live. It was hers to do with as she pleased. She also held a life interest in five thousand pounds, which at her death would pass to other members of her family: a brother and several sisters. The income from it died with her. Curious, is it not, Mr Giffard? A man may be the blackest rascal but will he destroy a woman who is worth four times as much to him alive as she is dead?'

'Perhaps he did not know of her father's will,' Mr Giffard said quietly.

'Perhaps he did not,' Holmes said. 'But if he did not kill her for money, what else? Bigamy? He had only to run off, back to his first wife, if necessary. He had only to avoid marriage to Miss Bankes in the first place by sweet promises. Did he kill her because she was carrying his child? He had only to desert her, as men desert women in such circumstances a thousand times a day. No, Mr Giffard. There is no good nor sufficient reason why Thomas Smethurst should murder Isabella Bankes. No reason whatever why he should run his head into the hangman's noose on that account.'

Holmes paused and a look of dismay darkened his visitor's face.

'And is that all of it, Mr Holmes? If it is, then you will not save him. Supposition will no longer do. There must be irrefutable proof of his innocence.'

Holmes leaned back in his chair, his long legs stretched out, and touched the tips of his fingers together.

'Suppose, Mr Giffard, suppose there was no arsenic in her body, at any time.'

As Holmes relaxed, Hardinge Giffard sat upright.

'There *was* arsenic, Mr Holmes. Professor Taylor found arsenic. Dr Todd tested the substance and confirmed that it was arsenic. Mr Barwell tested it and agreed that it was arsenic. What good will it do to pretend that it was not?'

Holmes shrugged. 'Very well,' he said, as if resigning himself to defeat. 'Let us agree that it was arsenic. I never doubted it for a moment.'

There was a pause while Mr Hardinge Giffard sought words to extricate himself with the least possible discourtesy and find his way to the street outside.

'What more have you discovered, Mr Holmes?'

'Beyond the obvious fact that your client is innocent, very little,' Holmes remarked. 'I can prove it but not without your assistance.'

'What would you have me do?'

'The samples that were taken from Miss Bankes before her death, those in which arsenic was found—I take it that the untested portion of the specimens is still available?'

'No doubt it is.'

'I should like it brought to the chemical laboratory of St Thomas's Hospital. It will be made up into solution, under supervision. I will show you your client's innocence in the presence of anyone who cares to be there. Professor Taylor, if you wish, Dr Todd, the Lord Chief Baron himself.'

'When is this to be?'

'Dear me,' said Holmes. 'On any day before your client is hanged, I suppose.'

VI

Three days later, on an afternoon in late August, a distinguished company had assembled in the Chemical Laboratory of St Thomas's Hospital. Holmes was on familiar territory and was master of the scene. So many of his days had been spent in this lofty riverside room, lined and littered with countless bottles and apparatus. Though he was a hunter all his life, most of his quests so far had been among these broad low tables with their retorts, test-tubes and the blue flames of the little Bunsen lamps.

Like a host greeting his guests, he led the visitors to a table on which apparatus had been set up for the Reinsch Test. A quantity of solution from a sealed bottle, in which the specimens taken from Isabella Bankes had been dissolved, was poured into a glass vessel. The liquid was pale blue in colour.

'Gentlemen,' said Holmes, introducing the apparatus to his onlookers like a stage magician at the Egyptian Hall, 'the Reinsch Test is simplicity itself. Our solution of the specimen is boiled in a vessel which contains copper gauze. If arsenic is present in any quantity, it will collect as a grey substance upon the gauze. If it appears, simple treatment with nitric acid will confirm that it is, indeed, arsenic. That, Dr Taylor, is a fair summary I believe.'

'It is, Mr Holmes,' the professor said. 'In this case, however, you have also considerable quantities of chlorate of potass. This will tend to damage the copper gauze. However, after two or three pieces of copper gauze have been used, the chlorate of potass will have been exhausted. Then you will see whether you have arsenic or not.'

The light blue liquid was heated three times in all, a separate piece of copper gauze being used on each occasion. The first two pieces of copper gauze were corroded by the chlorate and no sign of a dark-grey substance appeared on them. A third time, Holmes took a new piece of gauze and applied the flame of the lamp. In the quiet room above the Thames it was hard to imagine that whether a man was to be strangled by a rope noose in a few days' time depended upon the outcome of such an academic test.

For a few minutes, the pale blue liquid shimmered and then boiled. Holmes drew the flame away. The bubbling ceased and the copper gauze was clearly seen again. It was almost completely coated with a dark-grey sludge. The sense of doom, for Thomas Smethurst, hung heavy in the air. It was Dr Taylor who broke the silence. He spoke courteously but emphatically.

'When you test that substance with nitric acid, Mr Holmes, you will find that it is arsenic. Enough arsenic to kill the poor woman twice over. There can be no doubt.'

'No doubt at all,' Holmes agreed.

'Then there is an end of the matter,' Mr Hardinge Giffard said, astonished at the speed of Holmes's apparent failure. 'There is no more to be done.'

It was an awkward moment, some of those present feeling sorry for Sherlock Holmes in his disappointment, others resentful at having their time wasted by a trick that failed. They seemed about to turn and leave without another word.

'One moment, if you please!' said Holmes and they turned back to him again. He addressed Dr Taylor. 'Did you attempt to establish the presence of arsenic by the Marsh Test?'

Dr Taylor frowned. 'Mr Holmes, there is arsenic on the copper gauze. You may see it for yourself. You acknowledge it is there in quantity enough to commit murder. What need is there of the Marsh Test or any other experiment?'

'There is the greatest of all needs, Dr Taylor. The need of a man who will in a few days be hanged for a murder he did not commit, for a murder that was never committed by anyone.'

Dr Taylor could not quite bring himself to leave. 'Next you will tell us that she died of natural causes,' he said irritably.

'Oh, I think it very likely that I shall, doctor,' Holmes said imperturbably. 'Indeed, I may tell you that now.'

'And that she never consumed arsenic?'

Holmes gave a quick, impatient smile. 'I should wager that Isabella Bankes never consumed arsenic in her life.'

There was a murmur of laughter at the absurdity of his claim. I would have given a good deal to have been in that chemical laboratory during the next few minutes. Holmes had set up the apparatus for the Marsh Test on the next bench in the laboratory. Like the Reinsch process, the Marsh Test is essentially simple. Arsenic is the easiest poison to detect in a body because it vaporises readily. A white fragment may be dried and tested simply by a detective officer. Placed in a sealed tube and heated, it will vaporise and then condense on the inner surface of the tube. In nine times out of ten, when this occurs with a suspect specimen, it will prove to be arsenic.

In the Marsh Test, which Holmes now conducted, the pale blue solution taken from the dead woman's specimens was diluted with a chemical base in a retort and heated until hydrogen was given off. The gas passed into a sealed tube that was warmed—a 'mirror', as it was called. If arsenic was present in the gas, it would collect as a greyish substance on the inner surface of the tube. When all the hydrogen was given off, Holmes turned down the flame of the Bunsen lamp. The 'mirror' tube was still perfectly clean. The same solution which had just before shown enough arsenic to kill Isabella Bankes twice over now showed none at all.

Imagine the consternation at this! Among those who watched Sherlock Holmes at work with his apparatus, there was relief and expectation among the defenders of Thomas Smethurst, dismay among those whose evidence had helped to cast upon him the shadow of the hangman's noose.

How could it be that one time-honoured and infallible test showed no arsenic and the other, equally honoured and infallible, enough poison to hang a man? You may be sure that Dr Taylor and his colleagues hastened to repeat these experiments, only to come to the same conclusion as Holmes. Yet one thing could not be denied. There was arsenic in the Reinsch Test, enough to bring Smethurst to the gallows.

Rumours spread of the strange discovery and, as the world knows, there was agitation for a reprieve. The Home Secretary of the Liberal government, Sir George Cornewall Lewis, found himself caught between the process of law and an opposing clamour of the scientific world. Physicians, lawyers, public men all protested against the hanging of Thomas Smethurst on such evidence as this. There was a petition to the Home Office and another to Her Majesty the Queen for a free pardon. Sir George, caught in this fix, summoned the one man in England who could explain the predicament in which he found himself, Mr Sherlock Holmes.

VII

It was the first time that my friend had ever visited the Home Office but it was by no means the last. The day appointed for the execution of Thomas Smethurst was little more than a weekend away. Indeed, it was very nearly too late to save him. Men were customarily hanged in public on a Monday morning but just then a new law of Sabbath-day observance was being debated. It was objected that the men who erected the gallows on the roof of Horsemonger Lane gaol would have to work on Sunday. The question was whether Thomas Smethurst should be hanged early, on Friday, or late, on Tuesday. They gave him until Tuesday and so saved his neck.

Sir George Lewis was a grave scholarly man, a former editor of the famous *Edinburgh Review* and author of *Observation and Reasoning in Politics*. There was never a Home Secretary more ready to be persuaded by logic and rational argument. On that summer evening he sat with his back to the Venetian window of his office, a view of the colliers and penny steamers on the Thames behind him, facing his visitor across the desk. The conversation had reached that point where Holmes felt confident enough to reveal his secret.

'I have always preferred to shave with Occam's Razor,' he said equably. 'The precept that when you have discarded all impossibilities, whatever is left, however unexpected, must be true. In the case of Thomas Smethurst, I confess I was also troubled by an absence of sufficient motive. He is a rogue, a cheat, a seducer. But, while I have known of men who have killed for gain, I have never known such a man who killed a woman when she was worth several times more to him alive than dead.'

'All that has been accounted for, Mr Holmes. It is only the matter of arsenic which remains at issue.'

'Very well,' Holmes said, 'I listened to the evidence that was given in court. When Dr Taylor tested the solution he looked only for arsenic. He did not need to test for chlorate of potass. He assumed that, if it was there, it had been used to flush out any trace of noxious substance from the poor woman's body. If he had any doubts, of course, they were soon settled. The chlorate of potass attached itself first to the copper gauze, corroding it. By using three pieces of the wire gauze, he was able to exhaust the chlorate. On the third piece, he collected a good deal of arsenic.'

'And this would happen if there was arsenic in the body?' Sir George said sympathetically.

'Indeed,' said Holmes, 'and it would happen even if there was no arsenic in the body.'

The Home Secretary shifted uncomfortably in his leather chair. 'I think you had better explain that.'

'When there is merely arsenic, Sir George, the experiment is infallible. That is the case ninety-nine times out of every hundred. Dr Taylor had never encountered one that was otherwise. This time there was also chlorate of potass. He was right in thinking that the chlorate of potass must be exhausted before arsenic would gather on the copper gauze. It was after this that he made his error.'

'Dr Taylor's reputation stands high, Mr Holmes. He is one of our foremost chemical analysts.'

Holmes inclined his head. 'Dr Taylor is all that you say. However, as students, our paths diverge. He is the scholar, I am merely an inquisitive amateur. For some months I pursued researches into mineralogy with a view to improving the apparatus used in detecting murder by poison. I studied not only the chemicals that were tested but the constituents of the materials used to test them.'

'Do you say, Mr Holmes, that the Reinsch Test is unreliable?'

'Entirely reliable,' Holmes said, 'provided that one tests only for arsenic. Copper gauze, however, is a curious substance. It is copper, to be sure, but it cannot be refined to a state of absolute purity. There is seldom any necessity for it. It contains, among other impurities, quantities of arsenic.'

The colour began to flow from Sir George's face. He thought, no doubt, of men hanged in the past who might have been innocent. Holmes waved away his anxieties.

'This does not invalidate the test, as a rule,' he said quickly. 'Usually there is no corrosion and arsenical impurity is not released from the copper gauze. In this rare case, the chlorate of potass corroded the metal gauze, releasing the arsenical impurity from the metal into the very solution being tested. Dr Taylor is a fine chemical analyst but he is no mineralogist. The Reinsch Test should never be used, where there is chlorate of potass in the solution tested. The Marsh Test would have shown no arsenic in Miss Bankes.'

Sir George Lewis cleared his throat and seemed as if he was trying to gain time for his reply. But there could be no reply save one.

'Then you insist, Mr Holmes, that the arsenic came not from the dead woman but all of it from the copper gauze? It is beyond question?'

'There can be no question,' Holmes said, 'I had already tested a solution that contained only chlorate of potass—no arsenic whatever. Yet the third piece of copper gauze was coated with as much arsenic as Dr Taylor found. It was little enough, but remember that the specimen from Miss Bankes, in solution, was tiny in itself. Had this amount of arsenic come from such a minute sample, when multiplied by the total amount taken from her, it was enough to have killed the poor woman twice over.'

The bombshell that his visitor exploded in this manner was not yet enough to alter the Home Secretary's mind. Sir George Lewis stood up and gazed from his window across the coal wharves and the masts of the collier brigs, the slow barges under rust-coloured sails and the smoke-trails from the tall funnels of the little steamers.

'He put prussic acid on the bread, Mr Holmes, and tested its strength by feeding it to the sparrows.'

'Prussic acid, sir, is a constituent of effervescent medicine given to ease the type of vomiting from which Miss Bankes suffered. It proves nothing.'

The Home Secretary turned round again.

'And he surely gave her the chlorate of potass. What reason for that, unless to flush from her kidneys before death all trace of arsenical poison?'

'It was that, sir, which made the use of arsenic still more plausible. However, I took the liberty of testing for substances which were beyond the purview of Dr Taylor. Though the results were not conclusive, I believe that elaterium and veratrine were both present in the specimens taken from Isabella Bankes. They are not mineral irritants, like arsenic, but vegetable irritants. Their effect is to produce symptoms of vomiting and dysentery, very similar to those shown in this case.'

'Then he killed her, whether by arsenic or not?'

Holmes shook his head.

'Veratrine and elaterium are not the weapons of the poisoner. Their effect would be too uncertain. They are prescriptions of the abortionist. Isabella Bankes was in her second month of pregnancy when she died. Had she borne a child, Thomas Smethurst's bigamy would have been in great danger of discovery and his plans would have been at an end. Miss Bankes suffered from a degree of sickness beyond that found in most pregnancies. Combined with the substances used to bring on an abortion, she was subject to vomiting so severe that she could keep nothing in her stomach. She died of starvation. In her feeble state, the exhaustion of vomiting was enough to kill her. I reaffirm my conviction that Thomas Smethurst valued her more alive than dead. She stood, ultimately, to inherit thirty-five thousand pounds. That is the point where I first began, when I sought out her father's will.'

By the time that Sherlock Holmes stepped into the sunlight of a September evening, Sir George Lewis's private secretary had already drawn up copies of the letter of reprieve for immediate delivery to the High Sheriff of Surrey and the Governor of Horsemonger Lane Gaol. In his own hand, the Home Secretary himself began a more confidential memorandum. 'Sir George Lewis, with his humble duty to Your Majesty . . .' In the course of that memorandum, the name of the young Sherlock Holmes was first brought to the attention of the highest in the land.

VIII

The world knows the conclusion. Smethurst was reprieved from the gallows on the last day. The eminent toxicologist, Sir Benjamin Brodie, was appointed to inquire into the facts. He confirmed the findings of Sherlock Holmes in every particular.

Thomas Smethurst received a pardon, only to be arrested for bigamy and sent to prison for a year. On his release, he sued for compensation in respect of the murder trial. His effrontery failed. However, he then went to the Court of Probate and claimed the estate of Isabella Bankes, bequeathed to him under her dying will and testament. It went against the grain but, since the will was valid, the jury had no alternative than to find a verdict in his favour.

Holmes was later to remark to me, in the case of Grimesby Roylott of Stoke Moran, that, when a doctor does go wrong, he is the worst of criminals. In his determination to destroy the child of the woman he loved, even at the risk of her life, Smethurst had proved himself a standing example of this, whatever the law might determine. History does not record the last years of our bigamist. No doubt he returned to the life of Bayswater boarding-houses and the fluttering hearts of middle-aged spinsters. It was some years afterwards when Holmes first told me the story of the case.

'And the humour of it is, Watson,' he concluded, 'that a scoundrel such as he should owe his life to the laws of Sunday observance.'

'How so?'

'Why, if they had erected the gallows on Sunday, they would have hanged him at eight sharp on Monday morning. By observing the Sabbath, they had to respite him until Tuesday, the first morning when the platform could be ready. But for that, he might have been dead and buried before he could be reprieved.'

Then he lay back in his chair with that look of satisfaction for his youthful skill, which was perhaps the nearest he ever came to smugness.

The Case of the Crown Jewels

I

It is only now, with the death of the last public man involved in the scandal, that I feel easy enough in my mind to set down the truth of the strange affair of the Irish Crown Jewels. So long as Sir Arthur Vicars remained alive, Sherlock Holmes would permit nothing to be written that might revive the accusations against that unfortunate gentleman. Moreover, the manner of Sir Arthur's death is germane to the story. Since many of my readers will recall nothing of it, I shall give a brief summary of the events accompanying it.

On the morning of 14 April 1921, an early mist veiled the blue Atlantic sky over the hills behind Kilmorna House. Pleasantly situated in the far south-west of Ireland, Kilmorna was a Victorian country house built of brick in the Tudor style. Its tall chimneys and tower rose among well-kept lawns and trees. Latterly, it had been occupied by Sir Arthur Vicars and his wife, Lady Gertrude, who was considerably younger than her husband. Though my friend Sherlock Holmes spoke seldom and briefly of any relatives that he might possess, I have reason to suppose that he was distantly connected with Sir Arthur Vicars.

By the time of the tragedy, Sir Arthur's health was not robust and he made a habit of rising late after being brought his breakfast in bed. On that spring morning, when the maidservant had removed his tray, he lay propped on the pillows, discussing the business of the day with his estate manager. He saw nothing of the trap that now closed upon him.

From the trees that flanked the carriage-drive of Kilmorna, a group of men moved stealthily towards the house. There were about thirty of them, casually dressed, like a line of beaters with a gamekeeper. Some held revolvers and one, whose forehead was bandaged, carried a double-barrelled shotgun. The man with the shotgun smashed a pane of glass, reached through and entered the house by the main door.

At the sound of breaking glass, Sir Arthur got up and pulled on his dressing-gown, just as Lady Vicars ran into his room to tell him that the house was surrounded by armed men. As the couple and their estate manager went down the stairs, they smelled smoke and paraffin or petrol. Kilmorna had been free of the 'troubles' affecting other parts of Ireland and it was surely remarkable that such attacks should begin now. The Government of Ireland Act had been made law at Westminster and in five more days the independent Irish state was to come into being. Yet there was no doubt that the house had been set on fire by the intruders and that the lower panelling was already ablaze. Sir Arthur at once told the estate manager that they must save the most valuable paintings and furniture in the ground-floor rooms by passing them out of the library windows on to the terrace.

There was far too little time for that. In a few minutes more the flames were leaping and dancing on the interior woodwork. It was as much as the Lord of Kilmorna could do to save himself. He came out on to the terrace of the burning house and confronted 'Captain Moonlight', a ruffianly figure in cap and gaiters, the commander of the raiders. Thick clouds of smoke were floating across the lawns. Several men followed Sir Arthur as he turned away across the terrace, half hidden by a curtain of smoke. The estate manager lost sight of him but heard shouts and an argument. Sir Arthur said, 'You may shoot me first, but you won't get the key.' The man in cap and gaiters told him to prepare to meet his God. One of the other bandits began to count, 'One . . . two . . . three . . .' Sir Arthur said firmly, 'All right, fire away.' There was a brief silence and then several revolver shots cracked across the smoke-filled garden.

The servants huddled in fear of their lives at one end of the terrace but there was no further sound. It seemed that the raiders melted away behind the smokescreen, empty-handed. The estate manager went forward alone. He found Sir Arthur Vicars lying dead at the foot of the further terrace steps with bullet wounds in his body. Round his neck was a card bearing the legend: 'spy. informers beware. ira never forgets'.

How absurd it seems! I believe that the card and the legend were far more likely to have been the work of common thieves than of the IRA. Of what use was this death to the republicans when they had already gained the treaty they sought? Sir Arthur was a genealogist and historian, who had once held the office of Ulster King of Arms, presiding over the ceremonial of the Viceroy of Ireland's court at Dublin Castle. But that was fourteen years earlier. He was now an invalid with little interest in the politics of Ireland. In the columns of *The Times*, the senseless murder committed at a time when political differences had been resolved was condemned by the British Prime Minister, Mr David Lloyd George, as a cowardly and brutal crime against a man who had given no cause for offence.

There was, however, another explanation. Only a few of Sir Arthur's friends, including Sherlock Holmes, knew that Kilmorna House boasted a certain 'strong-room' or vault. 'Captain Moonlight' and his men had paid a previous visit, when they tried by brute force to smash their way into this strong-room through the ceiling above. Concrete and steel girders defeated the assault. You may be sure that their object was not Sir Arthur's modest collection of English silver or his library of genealogy. The raiders believed that in the vault at Kilmorna lay a treasure-house of diamonds, rubies, and emeralds, all set in gold, the regalia of St Patrick and the Crown Jewels of Ireland, which the world had not seen for fourteen years.

Such was the prize for which Sir Arthur Vicars died. His murderers were not patriots of any sort, but common robbers.

I could not hear of this outrage without recalling another death in the same family. Seven years earlier, when Sir Arthur's nephew, Peirce Mahony, was shot through the heart in the grounds of his father's house at Grange Con, south of Dublin, Captain Moonlight was nowhere to be found. But like his uncle, the young man had held office in the court of King Edward's Viceroy at Dublin, Lord Aberdeen.

The circumstances of his death were these. On Sunday, 27 July 1914, Peirce Mahony was with a family party at Grange Con. The talk was of the Austro-Hungarian ultimatum to Serbia, the mobilisation of the Austrian army on the Russian frontier, of what France and England would do. After lunch, Mahony took his gun and went out to shoot duck. By dusk he had not returned. A search of the grounds revealed the young man's body lying in the lake. Mahony had been shot twice through the heart by his own gun. There was very little spread of shot. The gun had been fired when the mouths of the barrels were more or less touching his chest, perhaps pressed against it.

Suicide was impossible, since Mahony would have been unable to reach the trigger if the muzzle was pressed above his heart. It was assumed that there had been an accident when he climbed over the wire fence to reach the lake. Perhaps he propped his gun against the fence. Perhaps he unwisely reached over to lift it by its muzzle with the mouths of the barrels pointing at his chest. A strand of wire caught in the trigger-guard and pressed the trigger back. The barrels were discharged simultaneously and he was knocked back into the water by the force of the impact.

Sherlock Holmes was far away from this tragedy but he later examined the trigger-guard of the shotgun with great care. There were no scratches on the metal, such as barbed wire might have made. All the same, why should anyone choose to murder a decent young fellow like Mahony? Holmes guessed that Mahony was a man who had learned some truth about the loss of King Edward's

Crown Jewels and was too honest to keep that truth to himself. My friend was of the opinion that the young man boldly threatened to unmask the thief who had stolen the regalia of St Patrick. If so, the thief had now murdered his accuser. If this version of events was correct then the killer, as Holmes judged him, escaped justice only for one more year before being seized after he had shot a policeman dead in a Hampstead street.

Of the three public figures involved in the 1907 scandal of the Crown Jewels, two had met violent deaths. Only one remained alive. Frank Shackleton. He was known to Mayfair society as the younger brother of the famous Antarctic explorer, Sir Ernest Shackleton. Sherlock Holmes described him to me more bluntly as 'a man of the worst reputation and a disgrace to a fine family'.

The deaths of Peirce Mahony and Sir Arthur Vicars were the last acts of the drama that had begun in the early summer of 1907 and involved Sherlock Holmes and myself in one of our most sensational cases. To that drama, I shall now return.

II

A reader of these sketches of the life of Sherlock Holmes would find it remarkable, perhaps incredible, had my friend's talents not been employed by the authorities in the more dangerous world of the new century. The long reign of Her Majesty had come to an end and she had been succeeded by the Prince of Wales as Edward VII. There was greater affluence and freer style at court. All the same, it was a world where political assassination and terrorist outrage had assumed menacing proportions.

Holmes had by now a reputation that stretched back over some decades. He was known to the mightiest in the land and was on close personal terms with men of influence. Among them, as young men, were two future Lord Chancellors, Halsbury and Birkenhead, as well as the great defender, Sir Edward Marshall Hall, KC. Once or twice in the earlier years of our friendship, when Holmes had rendered some private service or other, he would be absent afterwards to keep an engagement for lunch or tea 'in the neighbourhood of Windsor'. After his success in the matter of the Bruce-Partington plans in 1895, he returned from such a visit with a remarkably fine emerald tie-pin as a token of royal appreciation.

In a few more years, it was in the shadow world of such organisations as the 'Special Branch' of Scotland Yard or the new department of Military Intelligence at Queen Anne's Gate that Holmes was most often consulted. The 'Special Branch' of the CID had been created in 1884, in response to Fenian outrages by gun and bomb. Among the targets attacked by the dynamiters were the Houses of Parliament, the offices of *The Times*, the London railway stations, and Scotland Yard itself. From the first, Chief Inspector Littlechild, Assistant Commissioner Monro, and successive commanders of the Branch consulted Holmes in many of their most important cases.

From my notes, I see that it was in February 1907 when I accompanied my friend on a visit to Scotland Yard. At that time, our friend Lestrade had served more than thirty years in the Metropolitan Police. He had risen to the rank of Superintendent and there was no better commander within the higher echelons of the Special Branch.

He received us with that bluff courtesy which is his hallmark. We sat in leather chairs either side of the fireplace in his room, the curtains closed against a fusillade of rain on the windows that winter evening. Our host was plainly bursting with news of some kind and we did not keep him from it long.

'An announcement of importance will be made in the next few days, gentlemen. His Majesty the King is to pay an official visit to Ireland this summer. This is the year of the Irish National Exhibition in Dublin and it will not do to keep the King away. The world would think that he cannot safely set foot in that part of his dominions. It would never do, Mr Holmes. King Edward himself is determined on the arrangement and his officials are inclined to let him have his way. All the same, it poses a considerable risk.'

The impatient smile-like muscular spasm plucked at Holmes's mouth.

'Well, Lestrade, if the King will have it so, there is little you or I can do to stop him. In any case, His Majesty is quite right. If it seems that he dare not set foot in part of his dominions, there is an end of royal authority. You had better let the thing go ahead, my dear fellow.'

Lestrade looked uncomfortable at this and stroked his moustache.

'The King—or, rather, His Majesty's advisers—hoped that you might consent to play a part in the plans, Mr Holmes.'

This suggestion, made with some timidity, broke the tension in the room. Holmes threw back his head and uttered his dry sardonic laugh.

'My dear Lestrade! I have so many enemies in the world that I should merely draw fire upon the King. With me at his side, His Majesty would be twice as likely to be shot!'

'Not at his side,' Lestrade said quickly. 'You would have no objection to a visit beforehand to view the arrangements for his safety? Or to being there as an observer for the two days of the visit?'

Holmes sighed and stretched out his long thin legs towards the fire. 'I cannot say that I had included Dublin in my summer itinerary.' The superintendent paused and then came out with his trump. 'It was our late Lord Chancellor who suggested to His Majesty that your assistance might be called upon.'

My friend paused and the aquiline features assumed a look of dejection. His bohemian nature had given him a strong aversion to society and ceremonial, 'flummery', as he termed it. However, as soon as Lord Halsbury's name was invoked, I knew that the superintendent had won the day. Holmes looked a little despondent, as it seemed to me.

'You hit below the belt, Lestrade,' he said gloomily. 'Lord Halsbury knows I can refuse him nothing.'

So it was decided. We talked over a few matters and at length got up to leave. Holmes turned back to Lestrade.

'One thing, Lestrade. Where is His Majesty to be lodged in Dublin?'

'The Viceregal Lodge in Phoenix Park, as I understand.'

'Impossible.' Holmes brought his hand down flat and hard on the desk. 'It is the first place that would be made a target. Let him make the crossing on the royal yacht, anchor off Kingstown, and live on board. And let there be a cruiser either side of him. I cannot undertake this business if he multiplies the risks by living ashore.' I confess there had grown about my friend something of the prima donna in such matters. He must have his way. As the world knows, however, King Edward sailed on the *Victoria and Albert*, anchored off Kingstown, and lived aboard. The cruiser *Black Prince* was moored on one side, the *Antrim* on the other.

III

King Edward's visit was to take place on 10 and 11 July but the Irish International Exhibition opened in Herbert Park, Dublin, on 4 May. This was the occasion of our first glimpse. At eleven o'clock that morning, a grand procession set out from Dublin Castle for the official opening.

In the cool spring sunlight, the carriage of Lord Aberdeen, the Viceroy of Ireland, passed out through the triumphal arch of the castle gateway to the salute of sentries on either side. The glossy geldings turned down the short incline of Cork Hill into Dame Street, its cobbles ringing with the hollow hoofbeats of two squadrons of hussars, the upright plumes of their fur shakos stirring a little, their red tunics laced with gold and the sabres bumping against the dark blue thighs of their overalls. Behind the Viceroy and the Countess of Aberdeen came several more carriages, bearing officials of the viceregal household, including Sir Arthur Vicars, Ulster King of Arms. Holmes and I rode in the final carriage as guests of Lord Aberdeen.

Holmes longed to be anywhere but in the middle of such aimless pageantry. The familiar look of ineffable boredom on his sharp features was painful to behold.

'This will be the death of me, Watson,' he said from the corner of his mouth as we rattled along Dame Street, past the coloured glass arcade of the Empire Music Hall and the pillared elegance of the bank. He looked with complete incomprehension upon those who had turned out to clap and cheer the procession, as the Viceroy lifted the cocked hat of his court-dress in acknowledgement. The women waved and the men stood bareheaded, as if at the passing of a funeral.

Where the carriages and escort swung round College Green, the trams had been drawn up to allow the procession past the grey classical façade of Trinity College. There was a glimpse of lawns and chestnut trees. Then, behind the railings, rose a jeering outburst. The uniformed officers of the Dublin Metropolitan Constabulary moved quickly as clenched fists were raised at the King's Viceroy and his lady. Holmes brightened up at the promise of an affray.

Among the long residential avenues of south Dublin lay the exhibition grounds in Herbert Park with newly erected African villages and Canadian settlements, an Indian theatre and children's amusements. The cold May wind whipped and snapped at the flags of the nations on their poles. Each gust blew clouds of sand like stinging hail from the newly laid paths.

Inside the domed hall, as the procession formed up, rose the soaring chords of the *Tannhäuser* overture for organ and full orchestra. The dignitaries moved forward, led by the Knights of St Patrick in richly jewelled collars and the slim figure of Sir Arthur Vicars, Ulster King of Arms, in his herald's tunic bearing the royal lions in gold, like a figure from a Tudor court.

Sherlock Holmes stood in morning coat and trousers, still a picture of misery and boredom. I could not repress the thought that he would probably have been happier planning the assassination of the Viceroy's court than preventing it. Life returned to his dark brooding eyes only at the appearance of the two lesser functionaries, Peirce Mahony and Frank Shackleton, who walked behind the knights. Frank Shackleton, the Dublin Herald of the Viceroy's court, had about him that whiff of dark good looks and criminality which revived Holmes's spirits. He was a young man of no obvious fortune and considerable debts. Yet he contrived to run a household in San Remo, as well as a far more expensive London home in Park Lane. Each establishment had a separate mistress.

Holmes stared at the dark curls which gathered on the back of Shackleton's head as the music drew to its conclusion with Elgar's 'Pomp and Circumstance'. The procession halted. Cool sunlight caught the display of treasure that was borne slowly past us. I swear that my friend's thin and fastidious nostrils twitched, as though the golden horde gave off a fine and subtle perfume.

Glittering like broken flame, the Crown Jewels of the Irish kingdom shone in coloured fire on robes and tunics. The Viceroy's robe bore the Star of St Patrick. It seemed the size of a soup-plate, a shamrock of rubies and emeralds set in solid gold, bordered by Brazilian diamonds that blazed with flashes of white heat in the sun, every stone the size of a walnut. The eight points of the star were encrusted with Indian diamonds of smaller size.

Frank Shackleton bore on a black cushion the great Badge of Viceroyalty. Round its circumference was the motto *Quis separabit?* picked out in rose-tinted diamonds, looted by the British commanders from the Indian tombs of Golconda. With his dark curls and striking profile Shackleton looked every inch the part. Then the Knights of St Patrick walked by, each noble neck encompassed by a collar of finely wrought gold links, set with precious stones.

As the procession paused, emeralds, rubies, and clustered diamonds set in thick gold glowed and sparkled more richly in the shadows than in the sun. I saw Holmes's lips moving silently and mockingly for my benefit in the words that so often accompanied the music of Sir Edward Elgar, which now fairly deafened us.

'Truth and right and freedom, Each a holy gem, Stars of solemn brightness, Weave thy diadem.'

The look of misery was gone as he gazed upon the royal treasure, not for its beauty but for its eternal appeal to human greed and criminality.

'I think, Watson,' he said softly, as the orchestra fell silent, 'I think we must see how all this is managed.'

The safety of such treasures was no part of our business. However, there was no difficulty in arranging that we should accompany the jewels back to Dublin Castle. Our plain black carriage arrived immediately behind the police van containing the jewel cases, as it drew up outside the Bedford Tower, safely within the upper courtyard of the castle.

Apart from Ireland's Crown Jewels, the Bedford Tower contained the Irish Office of Arms with a fine collection of bound volumes and manuscripts on matters of genealogy and heraldry. It was not, strictly speaking, a tower but a classical pavilion with a fine portico of Italianate arches before the main door. An octagonal clock-tower with a cupola dome rose above. It faced the elegant viceregal apartments across the yard with the guard-room of the Dublin garrison next to it and the headquarters of the Dublin Metropolitan Police within a few yards. On the other side of it was the arch of the castle gate, where two sentries and a policeman were on duty day and night. If they could not between them secure such treasures, I was quite sure we should never do so.

'I think, Holmes, we might leave the matter there. Anyone might have read your face like a book just now but, surely, this is the safest place in the country for the regalia. Perhaps safer than the Tower of London itself.'

He chuckled but there was no laughter in his keen eyes.

'All the same,' he said, 'we must not disappoint Sir Arthur. He will die of chagrin unless we allow him to show us how well protected his treasures are.'

We got down into the sunlit courtyard and walked across to the figure of Ulster King of Arms in his Elizabethan tabard and breeches.

It will be as well if I say something of Sir Arthur Vicars, as he appeared to me then. He had held his office for fifteen years and lived much of his life at his Dublin town-house in St James's Terrace. At this time, he was still a bachelor, loyal to the English cause, and a ritualistically inclined member of the Established Church. He had a bland face and wistful air, the locks and whiskers of an

Elizabethan courtier. In his manner, he was apt to be pedantic, fussy and rather old-maidish.

On that afternoon, he appeared to have stepped out of a distant costumed past as he escorted us through the Bedford Tower to his office on the first floor. There were two rooms opening off the ground-floor vestibule. The library was to the right; ahead there was the clerk's cubby-hole office, which contained a steel door, the only way to the strong-room itself. Sir Arthur ushered us into the library, its shelves lined with handsomely bound volumes of genealogy and heraldry. Against the far wall, between two windows, stood a large 'Model A' Ratner safe, four feet wide and five feet tall. Sir Arthur walked across to it and then turned round to us.

'As you may see, gentlemen, we are pretty well provided for here. This is where the smaller items of the regalia are kept. The safe was installed by Ratner's four years ago. It has walls of two-inch steel and double locks of seven levers each. It is proof against any lock-picking or forcing. Nothing short of dynamite would blow it open and the amount required would bring down the entire Bedford Tower. For good measure, the gateway arch is outside. On the other side of this wall, there are two sentries and a policeman on guard day and night.'

'I congratulate you,' said Holmes with only the least trace of irony in his tone. 'How many keys are there and who holds them?'

Sir Arthur smiled. 'Two, Mr Holmes. One is always with me. The other is concealed in a place to which I alone have access and which is known only to me.'

'But would it not be better still to have the safe installed in the strong-room?'

A brief look of irritation disturbed Sir Arthur's self-confidence.

'After the strong-room was constructed, it was found that the safe was too wide to pass through the doorway. I have spoken several times to the Board of Works but nothing has been done.'

Holmes nodded and our heraldically costumed guide led us through the vestibule to the little office, which had just enough space for a chair and a desk.

'Our messenger and general factotum is here during working hours,' Sir Arthur said, 'William Stivey, formerly of the Royal Navy. He has been with us for six years. A conscientious worker of exemplary character.'

'Indeed?' said Holmes politely, but he was staring at the bonded steel of the strong-room door to one side, 'And this, I take it, is the work of Messrs Milner of Finsbury Pavement? The type is unmistakable. Double locked. Harveyed-Krupp steel plate of several inches, about half the thickness of a battleship's hull-armour and able to withstand a direct hit from a hundred-pound nickel-plated shell fired by a six-inch gun at a range of fifty yards.'

'You are admirably informed, Mr Holmes, I must say.' Sir Arthur spoke with the displeasure of a professional who finds himself outpaced by an amateur.

'Ah well,' said Holmes with a touch of insouciance, 'it comes only from inspecting such doors as these after they have been broken open.'

The wind left Sir Arthur's sails at this remark, for Holmes described the very thing our guide dreaded. It seemed as much as Sir Arthur could do to unlock the heavy steel door and draw it back on its smooth hinges. We entered the strong-room. The interior was about twelve feet square, like a library alcove with shelves and cupboards housing the more valuable genealogical volumes. Its window, looking on to the castle yard, was heavily and securely barred. Though most of the jewels were in the library safe, the strong-room contained within its locked cases several of the collars of knighthood, as well as the Irish sword of state, a gilt crown and sceptre, and two silver maces.

Immediately in front of us, as the door was drawn back, was a locked steel grille. I was surprised to see that the key to this interior grille was already in its lock and asked why.

'There is only one key,' Sir Arthur said. 'It would not do for it to be lost. It is as safe in here as anywhere. Therefore, we leave it in the lock at all times.'

Holmes nodded at me, exchanging a significant look.

'Besides,' said Sir Arthur quickly, 'beyond that wall is the headquarters of the Dublin Metropolitan Police and beyond the other is the guard-room of the military garrison.'

Though Holmes had teased him a little, there was little doubt that Sir Arthur had done his job well. Whatever might happen to King Edward himself, Ireland's Crown Jewels were surely as safe as if they had been in the Bank of England or the Tower of London. The strong-room door was closed and locked. We followed our guide up the spiral staircase to the other floor. There were two rooms at this level, one for Sir Arthur and the second for his secretary.

'And who has keys to the strong-room door?' Holmes inquired.

Sir Arthur stiffened at this renewed questioning.

'I have one,' he said. 'The other is with Stivey while he is on duty. It is returned to me when he leaves. While he is in his office, the strong-room is open so that the books and manuscripts may be consulted by me or my secretary. If he leaves the office, he locks the strong-room door and puts the key in a concealed drawer of his desk. We who are authorised to use it would know where to look, a stranger would not. There is a third key, which is not in use. It is kept in a drawer in the strong-room itself, oiled and wrapped.'

Holmes touched his fingers together. 'How many members of your staff use this building?'

Sir Arthur frowned with an effort of recollection. 'Stivey is one. My secretary George Burtchaell is another. There is Peirce Mahony as well. Stivey has the key to the strong-room while he is on duty. All three have a key to the front door. Detective Officer Kerr patrols the building from time to time when the office is closed. There is a key to the front door, which is kept in the Metropolitan Police office for his use. The only other person to use it is the cleaning woman, Mrs Farrell. She comes early in the morning and reports first to the police office.'

'It amounts to this, then,' Holmes said quietly. 'You, Burtchaell, Mahony, Stivey, Kerr, and Mrs Farrell have a key to the front door. You yourself have a key to the strong-room. Stivey and your staff have the use of one when the office is open. But you alone have a key to the safe in the library.'

'Precisely, Mr Holmes,' Sir Arthur said.

'And what of Mr Shackleton?'

'Mr Shackleton? He has no keys. He is Dublin Herald. Sometimes his letters are sent to him here. But he does not work here any longer. Indeed, he is rarely in Dublin. He has no key of any kind, nor has he need of one.'

'When he comes to Dublin, he is frequently a guest in your house, I believe.'

'Whether he is or not, Mr Holmes, can surely be no concern of yours. I repeat that Mr Shackleton has no access to a key nor any need of one.'

'Your keys to the safe and the strong-room—' Holmes began.

'Neither Mr Shackleton nor any other person, Mr Holmes, knows where they are kept.'

Holmes appeared to be satisfied by this but he walked across to the window above the courtyard only to return to the attack.

'I am a burglar, Sir Arthur. I approach the door of the Bedford Tower. What prevents me?'

'The policeman on duty or the guard commander will ask you your business.'

'And if I satisfy him that I have business?'

'Then you will still find the door locked against you until you ring the bell and Stivey opens it. If you have business, you will be attended every moment you are in here. I promise you, you will not be left alone. After the office has closed, you would be intercepted as soon as you came near it.'

I have several times remarked that Sherlock Holmes worked for love of his art rather than for the acquirement of wealth. So it was on this occasion. The jewels of the Order of St Patrick were nothing to him. So far as he had a duty in Dublin, it was the safety of the King. The contents of the safe and the strong-room in Dublin Castle were worth as many hundreds or thousands of pounds as you might care to name. Holmes would not have given a shilling for them. Yet the cleverness with which they were guarded intrigued him, and the means by which a thief might outwit such precautions occupied him for the rest of the day.

I wearied far more quickly of the topic and said so bluntly as we drank brandy and soda in our rooms that evening.

'I have always suspected that you have no soul, Watson,' he said jovially. 'Can you not imagine the effect of this morning's display of those gems on every dishonest mind in the hall?'

'I saw clearly enough that no one is likely to open those locks and doors except Sir Arthur Vicars himself.'

Holmes shook his head. 'By the time we left the Bedford Tower, I saw quite plainly the three separate methods by which the jewels and regalia might be removed from the safe and the strong-room without their guardians being able to lift a finger to prevent it.'

'Surely that cannot be,' said I.

He smiled. 'Then you did not notice the fatal flaw in Sir Arthur Vicars's self-confidence, while we were in his room?'

'Indeed I did not.'

'Why, my dear fellow, he told us that Shackleton did not know where the keys to the safe were hidden.'

'What of it?'

'A man may be certain of what he himself knows. He cannot tell what another may know or may find out. To think otherwise, my dear Watson, is a capital error when one deals with a first-class rogue. Who can tell what such a scoundrel knows?'

IV

It was more than another two months before the King's visit to Dublin was to begin, on 10 July. Holmes and I returned to England for the intervening period. So did Shackleton, whose visits to Ireland as Dublin Herald were now rare enough and whose business ventures kept him in London. Seven weeks passed. It was on the morning of 29 June, at about eight o'clock, that I woke from a deep sleep to find Holmes standing by my bed. My friend had never been an early riser but now he appeared in a large purple dressing-gown with a blue telegraph form in his hand.

'Wake up, Watson! We must be on our way. Events are moving in Dublin, as I expected. Sir Arthur has lost his key to the door of the Bedford Tower.'

I fear I was a little put out, since our planned departure for Ireland was still two days away.

'The tower? Is that all, Holmes? Half a dozen people have keys to it.'

'I should not knock you up without good reason,' he said a little sharply. 'Now, there is a boat-train from Euston at noon. We shall be in good time for the night boat from Holyhead and be in Dublin first thing tomorrow.'

I fear that I grumbled a good deal at this sudden change in our arrangements. All the same, I agreed to cancel my engagements for the next couple of days and accompany my friend. As the express of the Northwestern Railway carried us beyond Birmingham, I read the *Times* list of social engagements for the previous day. Among the guests at Lady Ormonde's luncheon party in Upper Brook Street was the name of Francis Richard Shackleton of the Royal Irish Fusiliers, the Dublin Herald. I handed the paper to Holmes.

'Whatever may have happened to Sir Arthur's key to the tower, Frank Shackleton cannot have taken it. He is here, in London.'

'I have no doubt of that, Watson. Shackleton has never left London since he returned from the opening of the exhibition in early May.'

'Are you so sure?'

I could almost swear that Holmes looked a little awkward.

'Our friend Lestrade has had officers keeping a watch. I think you may rest assured that Shackleton has scarcely been outside Mayfair, let alone London.'

He closed his eyes and never showed so much as the tremor of a lid until we pulled into Holyhead. I could think only of the inconvenience of having to wait more than a week in Dublin for the King's arrival. My displeasure was not diminished upon our arrival at the North Wall in Dublin early the following morning.

Detective Officer Kerr was on the quayside with a cab to take us to our lodgings.

'I fear, gentlemen,' he said sympathetically, 'that you have been disturbed without necessity. Sir Arthur mislaid his key to the Office of Arms two days ago. He could not find it on his dressing-table that morning. He came to me at once and reported this. I used my own key to let him in. Last night, however, I received a message from him. The key was on his dressing-table after all. It had slipped under the hollow base of a brass candlestick.'

'Hmm,' said Holmes, as the cab turned into the long elegant boulevard of Sackville Street. 'What of the strong-room and the safe?'

'All the keys are accounted for and the contents are secure, sir,' Kerr replied.

I was inclined to agree that the discovery of the missing key was the end of the matter. In any case, even a man who could enter the Bedford Tower was far from being able to open the strong-room or the safe. What more natural than that Sir Arthur had mislaid his copy of the door key?

Four days in Dublin passed without incident. On Wednesday, 3 July, a week before King Edward's arrival, Holmes and I had finished breakfast. We were sitting with the newspapers before us. Outside the handsome houses, there was a sound of children playing among the lawns and trees of the gardens at the centre of St Stephen's Green. I noticed in the *Morning Post* that Frank Shackleton had been at a reception in London the day before with the Duke of Argyll, husband of the Princess Louise and, hence, son-in-law of the late Queen and brother-in-law of King Edward VII. Scoundrel though he might be, Shackleton seemed to have little difficulty in securing social advancement. But he could not both be with the King's brother-in-law in London and making mischief in Dublin.

I had no sooner thought this to myself than there was a knock at the door and our landlady inquired whether it would be convenient for Mr Sherlock Holmes to receive Mrs Mary Farrell. We looked blankly at each other.

'Mrs Farrell from the castle,' the good woman explained.

Our looks changed and Holmes said, 'By all means send her in.' When the landlady had gone out, he added to me, 'No doubt this is some lady of the Viceroy's court. We had best see her.'

Imagine our surprise when there appeared in the doorway a gaunt and venerable figure dressed in black. Her clothes were the 'Sunday best' of the working-class widow-woman, the feather boa, the leg-of-mutton sleeves, the bonnet perched high on the tightly drawn hair, a handsome face hardened by toil and care. I do not think it had occurred to either of us that our visitor would be Mrs Farrell the cleaning-woman of the Bedford Tower. Now that we saw her, it seemed certain that she was the good woman whom Sir Arthur had mentioned in this connection. A look of concern contracted her features slightly and it deepened when she saw that Holmes was not alone. He rose, however, and received her with as much courtesy as if she had been a duchess or a *femme fatale*.

'Good morning, Mrs Farrell. This is an unexpected pleasure. My name is Sherlock Holmes. This is my intimate friend and associate, Dr Watson, before whom you may speak as freely as before myself.'

She looked a little awkwardly from one to the other of us.

'Pray take a seat, Mrs Farrell,' Holmes said gently.

Our visitor sat down, clutching her handbag on her lap.

'I must speak to someone about the tower,' she said in a tense quiet voice. 'I must speak, for I should not want to be thought any way dishonest.'

'Indeed, not,' Holmes said.

She looked at us both again.

'Well, sir, I came to clean as usual this morning, just on seven o'clock. The door of the tower was shut as it always is. When I put the key in the lock, it would not turn. I tried the handle and the door opened. It was unlocked all the time, Mr Holmes. For what I know it was unlocked all night. I cleaned as usual and could not see anything wrong with the building. Still, when I finished, I waited for Mr Stivey and told him I had found the door unlocked.

Mr Stivey told Sir Arthur, as soon as he came in. The strong-room was checked at once and they found everything in order. Nothing more is to be done.'

'Then you have no more to worry about, Mrs Farrell.'

She looked at him intently. 'If anything should be found amiss, sir, I would not have it come back on me. I cannot afford to lose work, Mr Holmes. I thought, if I spoke to you now, you might vouch I have been every way honest.'

Holmes smiled to reassure her. 'You need have no fear of that, Mrs Farrell. You have behaved as honestly as any woman might. Tell me, though, might not the door have been left accidentally unlocked?'

'It might,' she said doubtfully.

'And who would have been the last person to leave the tower before you?'

'Sir Arthur, Mr Holmes. He is always the last of the gentlemen to leave in the evening. But then Mr Kerr, the detective officer, makes his inspection, usually between seven and eight o'clock at night. Sir Arthur, Mr Mahony, Mr Burtchaell, and Mr Stivey all have keys. If any of them had come back later still, they might have left the door unlocked.'

Holmes assured her several times that she had done the proper and honest thing. Appearances may deceive, yet it was impossible to look at Mrs Farrell and think her anything but decent, loyal, and industrious.

'We ourselves will say nothing of this to Sir Arthur and his colleagues,' Holmes said to me, as soon as Mrs Farrell had left us. 'Nor to Detective Officer Kerr. Strictly speaking, the Bedford Tower is none of our concern.'

'And what of the jewels?' I protested, somewhat alarmed by my friend's apparent ease of mind.

'I think we may assume, my dear Watson, that St Patrick's regalia is as safe as it was yesterday—no more and no less.'

With this enigmatic comment he dismissed the topic, nor could he be persuaded to return to it.

V

Three more days passed and we came to the morning of Saturday, 6 July, four days before King Edward's arrival at Kingstown on the *Victoria and Albert*. There was no further explanation of the unlocked door, as Mrs Farrell described it, unless either Sir Arthur or Detective Officer Kerr had left it so. The matter was not mentioned to Holmes or myself by anyone but Mrs Farrell.

Holmes said with a shake of his head, 'By the nature of the thing a man cannot be sure of what he has forgotten. I think it would be safer to assume that the door was left accidentally unlocked and let us watch the consequences.'

What those consequences were to be became clear on Saturday morning. At about eleven o'clock, a boy in brass-buttoned livery arrived at St Stephen's Green with a regally embossed envelope. It was addressed to Sherlock Holmes in confidence by the Viceroy of Ireland, Lord Aberdeen, requesting him to go at once to Dublin Castle. There had been a discovery in the Bedford Tower which gave His Excellency cause for concern and materially affected the King's visit.

It was less than twenty minutes later when we entered the upper courtyard of Dublin Castle through the arched gateway on Cork Hill. Holmes rang the bell at the door of the Bedford Tower and we were admitted by William Stivey, a slightly built man of about fifty whose tanned face and somewhat rolling gait proclaimed his previous occupation.

'If you don't mind, sir,' he said to Holmes, 'you're to come straight to my office. Sir Arthur has a visitor with him just this minute but he'll see you as soon as he can.'

'Really?' said Holmes. Though he did not quite sniff, there was an air of scepticism about him. We followed Stivey to the little office and there found Mrs Farrell sitting in a chair with Detective Officer Kerr standing behind her. Kerr was a fine red-headed giant with the look of a man who has his career to make. Stivey announced Sherlock Holmes. Kerr, straightening up, at once told Mrs Farrell to tell us the story she had first told Stivey.

'It was like the other morning, sir,' the woman said, eyeing Holmes earnestly, 'but this time it was the steel door of the strong-room.'

'You mean it was unlocked?' Holmes asked quickly.

'I mean, sir, that when I came to work at about seven this morning, the door of the strong-room was partly open. I could see the grille inside it, which I never saw before, and there was a key in the lock of the grille. I took that key out and put it on Mr Stivey's desk, knowing he would be the first gentleman to arrive. Then I wrote a note, describing what I had found, and put it with the key. I closed the door to the strong-room but could not lock it, having no key.'

'You did right,' Holmes said. 'And what did Mr Stivey do?'

He swung round on the former naval rating who met his inquiry without flinching.

'As soon as Sir Arthur arrived, Mr Holmes, I went up to his room and told him that the strong-room door had been found unlocked and slightly ajar.'

'And what did Sir Arthur say?'

'He said, "Is that so?" '

Holmes stared at William Stivey.

'Did you not think that a curious thing to say?'

But William Stivey was loyal to his master. 'Sir Arthur had come in with a gentleman from West's the jewellers. He was much occupied, sir. The knight's collar intended for the investiture of Lord Castletown has been altered to bear his name and was returned this morning. Sir Arthur was preoccupied at that moment. I was able to tell him that I had checked the strong-room and that nothing was missing nor out of place. He was reassured by that.'

'Very well,' said Holmes, though he did not sound as if he thought it was very well. 'Then how comes it that the strong-room door was open?'

'It was not open at half-past seven last night,' Kerr said. 'I made my patrol then. As I turn the corner I always swing myself round by the handle of the strong-room door. I should have known at once if it was open or unfastened. If it was open this morning, someone unlocked it during the night. Apart from the key kept in the strong-room itself, there are two copies. Sir Arthur and Mr Stivey have one, though Mr Stivey's is handed to Sir Arthur when he leaves.'

'Do you say that Sir Arthur must have opened the strong-room door?'

Kerr shook his head. 'Sir Arthur was seen to leave at seven o'clock last night. He collected his mail from the Kildare Street Club at half past seven and was home at St James's Terrace when dinner was served at eight. To have returned here and then gone home again would have taken him almost an hour. He was seen constantly by his servants until after eleven o'clock last night. He retired to bed a little before midnight and, by his own account, did not leave the house again until nine o'clock this morning. Had he returned during the night, he would have been recognised at once by the guards on the castle gate.'

'Dear me,' said Holmes, as if to himself, 'how very singular. You are quite sure that you made a thorough patrol of the building last night?'

Detective Officer Kerr flushed a little, as fair-skinned redheads of his type are apt to do when falsely accused.

'So thorough, Mr Holmes, that I went through every room on both floors, even the coal cellars beneath. The one room I did not enter was the strong-room, to which I have never had a key. Only Sir Arthur has the keys to that.'

'The cellars,' said Holmes quickly. 'Do they have a coal-chute which might be used to enter the building?'

Kerr shook his head. 'There is a coal-hole but it is in the castle entrance. The military guard and the duty constable stand within a few feet of it, sometimes on top of it. In any case, it is fitted with a coal-stop, precisely to prevent an intruder getting in that way.'

Holmes nodded, as if he understood. Just then a bell rang on the floor above and Stivey, with a seaman's agility, went up the spiral staircase to answer Sir Arthur's summons. He returned a few minutes later with a leather box and a key.

'Sir Arthur presents his compliments, Mr Holmes, and will be down in a moment. If you will excuse me, I must return Lord Castletown's collar of knighthood to the library safe.'

You may be sure that Holmes and I followed the messenger as he walked into the next room where the Ratner safe stood between two windows. Stivey took the key, which Sir Arthur had just given him and which fitted each of the double locks. When he tried to turn it, the look of worry and irritation on his face told us that neither the key nor the lock would move.

'Turn it the other way, Mr Stivey,' said Holmes coolly.

Stivey did so. We heard the bolts move. He tried the handle but the steel door would not move.

'Ah,' said Holmes, 'now you have locked it. In other words, it seems that the safe as well as the strong-room door was unlocked this morning.'

Stivey backed away from the tall steel safe as if he feared it might explode. He turned to go back up the stairs and inform Sir Arthur Vicars but at that moment Sir Arthur was coming down. He nodded brusquely to us, like a man busy with the details of a royal visit four days in the future.

'Let me have the key,' he said impatiently, taking it from the messenger. Holmes, Stivey and I watched him. In his morning dress, Sir Arthur Vicars was no longer an Elizabethan courtier but every inch a modern official. He slid the key into the first lock, turned it and heard the bolts slide back. He repeated the process with the second lock and then drew open the safe door with something of a flourish.

We stood behind him, looking into the steel maw. There were shelves laid out with leather jewel cases, orderly and neat. As if he was in a hurry to get the matter over with, he drew out the first leather case and opened it. I could not see what it might contain. I heard only the hushed and tragic voice of Ulster King of Arms.

'My God! They are gone! The jewels are gone!'

VI

We stood in the sunlit library while Sir Arthur opened each box in turn and, at every discovery, the word 'Gone!' hung like the motes of dust in the summer air. Apart from two collars of knighthood in the strong-room and a third belonging to Lord Castletown, the entire Crown Jewels of the Irish Kingdom had vanished. Gold, diamonds, emeralds, rubies, sapphires had disappeared from a safe to which only Sir Arthur Vicars had the keys.

Holmes said nothing but watched Ulster King of Arms with sharp eyes, noting every nuance of his behaviour. Sir Arthur swung round on Detective Officer Kerr, as if to hold him to blame.

'Kerr!' he said in bitter panic. 'All the jewels are gone! Some of the smart boys that have been over for the King's visit have made a clean sweep of them!'

And still Holmes said nothing. Sir Arthur, in his misery, turned to him.

'The Board of Works are at fault in this,' he said pathetically, 'I have asked them for a good safe. I have correspondence to prove it. They refused it and did not give it to me. I have no confidence in this safe.'

To listen to him, you would never have thought that anything more was amiss than some trifling clerical error. Not that the entire regalia of Ireland's jewels had vanished into air. The sword of state, the orb and sceptre were still in the strong-room. But all that might most easily be sold for fifty thousand pounds had gone. He turned next to me.

'I would not be a bit surprised if they were returned to my house by parcel post tomorrow morning.'

Had he gone mad? Had the loss turned his mind? That was my first thought. Jewels are not stolen merely to be returned by parcel post next day! Sherlock Holmes said nothing.

'I must fetch Superintendent Lowe,' Kerr said. 'He must be told.'

'Indeed,' said Holmes at last, 'and someone will have to tell the King. I should not care to be that person. I do not suppose that His Majesty will be much amused.'

Then Sir Arthur Vicars was off again. 'My late mother's jewels, you know. I kept them in there for safety. They have gone too.'

There was, to say the least, something a little zany about his behaviour. In my own opinion, however, he betrayed shock rather than guilt. We went with Sir Arthur to his room on the next floor and awaited the arrival of John Lowe of the Dublin CID. Ulster King of Arms sat with his elbows on his desk and his head in his hands, a most abject study in self-pity as he bemoaned the loss. From below us we heard the sounds of a search beginning. Presently Superintendent Lowe arrived from the headquarters of the Dublin Metropolitan Police a few yards away. There were shouted commands. Detective Officer Kerr was given charge of three men who were to turn over every scrap of coal in the cellars.

I managed to get Holmes away from Sir Arthur.

'Are we to do nothing? I daresay the jewels were not our concern but yet—'

He shook his head and put his finger to his lips for silence. Presently he walked to the top of the spiral staircase and, leaning over the rail, called down, 'Mr Lowe! Before you trouble yourself any further in this matter, send for Cornelius Gallagher!'

'Who the devil is Cornelius Gallagher?' I asked.

'A locksmith, Watson. The finest in Dublin. He is employed by Ratner's as their leading man.'

In all my years with Sherlock Holmes, I had never before seen a smith take to pieces the lock of a safe. It recalled to me an experience of watching the most delicate surgical operation in my student days at Bart's. We stood over the bulky and breathless figure of Cornelius Gallagher as he dismantled the lock of the Ratner safe with his tiny screwdrivers, meticulous as a watchmaker. Within the lock were the seven slivers of metal, levers or mirrors as they call them. Each must be lifted by a segment of the key before the lock will open. Mr Gallagher unscrewed them one by one. Then he examined each through a small but powerful glass, turning the metal this way and that.

'Are they marked, Mr Gallagher?' Holmes inquired.

'Quite clean, sir. Not a scratch. They might be new.'

Holmes stood back. 'Then we may say, gentlemen, that this safe has never been opened except by the two keys which were made for it. A duplicate, however skilfully cut, is not perfect. Its tiny irregularities scratch the mirrors sufficiently for the marks to be seen with a jeweller's glass. A pick or a probe would do much worse. Is that not so, Mr Gallagher?'

Cornelius Gallagher twisted his head round.

'It is, Mr Holmes, sir. This safe was never tampered with, only opened in the usual way.'

A look amounting almost to terror seized Sir Arthur Vicars, though it was terror seen in farce rather than melodrama.

'Oh, no, Mr Holmes!' He seemed about to kneel and clutch my friend's legs. 'You cannot say it of me! It is unfair, unjust! You cannot say so, Mr Holmes!'

VII

That evening, after Lowe had left our rooms and we were sitting with brandy and soda, I said to my friend, 'Well, it cannot be Shackleton. He is still in London or still on his way to Dublin, and has not been in this city since the jewels were checked when the door of the Bedford Tower was found unlocked. You have Lestrade's word for it.'

Holmes said only, 'Hmm.'

'And if it was opened with the proper keys, both were in the possession of Sir Arthur Vicars and he alone knew where they were.'

'Does Sir Arthur Vicars look to you, Watson, like a man who would know how to sell the jewels even if he had them?'

'No,' I said, 'but I don't see how it could be Shackleton if he was never in Dublin.'

'Don't you?'

'If he was not here when it happened, which Scotland Yard itself confirms, it amounts to an alibi.'

'Does it?'

Conversation was impossible. Holmes had something in mind but no skill of mine would prise it forth. Next day there was worse news for Sir Arthur Vicars. Cornelius Gallagher examined the locks of the strong-room door, which had also been found open by Mrs

Farrell on that fateful Saturday morning. There was not a scratch nor a blemish on the polished steel mirrors of the lock. It had been opened with one of the proper keys. One of these was locked in the vault itself. The other two were in the possession of Sir Arthur and their whereabouts known only to him.

Of course, it was quite impossible that the scandal could be kept quiet for more than a few hours. The investiture of Lord Castletown was cancelled on the King's orders. How could the Knights of St Patrick parade shorn of all their splendour? It would have appeared ridiculous. By this time His Majesty was on the royal train, travelling to North Wales, where the *Victoria and Albert* lay at Holyhead, ready to carry him across the Irish Sea. His fury over the stupidity of the Viceroy's court for letting itself be robbed in this manner may be better imagined than described. In the meantime, the press burst upon us with headlines that stood inches tall. The value of the missing jewels was put at £50,000 and more. The stones represented the prize of empire in the eighteenth century and had been the gift of King William IV to the Viceroy's court in 1833.

Holmes seemed remarkably unperturbed by the disappearance of the jewels. Knowing his dislike of ceremonial occasions, I believe he took a secret pleasure in the discomfiture of the officials. He was present when Sir Arthur Vicars was questioned in his office by Superintendent Lowe two days after the robbery.

'I believe the jewels were taken by a man you know,' Sir Arthur began, 'a guest in my house. I am obliged to think he spied on me to find the safe key. I am sure that he must have taken impressions of my keys while I was in my bath. He sometimes came to this office on Sundays to collect his letters and he borrowed my key to the main door of the building.'

Superintendent Lowe, a sharp moustachio'd fellow, looked at Ulster King of Arms with pity.

'You forget, sir. The safe and the strong-room were opened with their proper keys. Impressions were not used.'

Poor devil! Sir Arthur was trapped, cornered, and there was an end of it.

'However it was done, it was he!' he cried.

Holmes sighed. 'I believe, Sir Arthur, that the jewels were last checked three weeks before. Frank Shackleton has not left England in the past month. I am informed that for the last two days, including that of the robbery, he has been a guest of Lord Ronald Sutherland-Gower at Penshurst in Kent. His travelling companion was the Duke of Argyll, the King's brother-in-law.'

'Then I do not know,' Sir Arthur said wretchedly. 'It cannot have been he. I have done him a great wrong by suggesting it. But the truth is that the young fellow has caused me a good deal of concern. I guaranteed two bills for him, fifteen hundred pounds owed to Wiltons the moneylenders in Piccadilly. And more for furniture bought from Wolff and Hollander. Wiltons charge steep for a loan, as much as fifty per cent in all. I hope I shan't be called on for it but I can't tell.'

The more one heard about Frank Shackleton's business ventures, the more unsavoury they sounded. Superintendent Lowe cleared his throat and flexed his moustaches. He unwrapped a sheet of paper and drew out two identical keys. They were the keys to the Ratner safe.

'These two keys, sir. This one was at all times worn round your neck? Day and night?'

'It was.'

'And this? As I understand it, this was wrapped and hidden in the spine of a certain volume on your study shelves.'

'It was.'

Holmes intervened. 'And did you check frequently to ensure that it was still there?'

'Every night, Mr Holmes, before I retired.'

'Then it would appear that the safe cannot have been opened by anyone but you,' Holmes said calmly.

Sir Arthur expostulated with an energy so nearly hysterical that I thought my professional assistance might be needed. There was a flaw in his temperament, as I saw it. He had become the most pitiable object. If logic meant anything at all, the innocent Sir Arthur had stolen the jewels and Shackleton the rogue could not have done so. Yet Holmes seemed entirely content to accept impossibilities. Shackleton was the thief and Sir Arthur Vicars his victim.

'It cannot be, Holmes!' I insisted that evening for the twentieth time. 'Vicars alone could have opened the safe and the strong-room. Shackleton could not have done it, even if he had travelled from London to Dublin and back at the speed of a bullet!'

My companion chuckled, lit his pipe from a coal in a pair of tongs, and said nothing.

'If you know the culprit, it is your plain duty to say so. It is the only means by which the jewels may be recovered!'

He looked at me with mild surprise and took the pipe from his mouth.

'My dear Watson,' he said gently. 'Do you not see? That is the means by which they would be irretrievably lost.'

VIII

There was a brief interruption, if it can be called so. King Edward arrived off Kingstown two days later. On Wednesday morning, 10 July, the early summer light revealed the graceful clipper hull and the twin buff funnels of the *Victoria and Albert* anchored off Kingstown Harbour, the royal standard at the mast flickering in a light breeze from the Irish Channel. To either side was anchored the more substantial bulk of a Royal Navy cruiser, *Black Prince* to port and *Antrim* to starboard.

Though the flagged streets of Kingstown were packed with sightseers by 10 A.M., they had to wait almost another two hours before the cruisers boomed out their royal salute and the steam pinnace puffed its way across the harbour to come alongside Victoria Wharf. It was a warm summer morning, the Royal Marine band playing and the welcoming dignitaries gathered expectantly in a closely guarded pavilion, hung with flags and bunting. King Edward and Queen Alexandra stepped ashore to the cheers of the crowd. Lord Aberdeen, minus certain items of the usual regalia, came forward to greet the King. The press assured us that King Edward was 'beaming with smiles and looking in splendid health . . . his hat raised in recognition of the kindly reception'. According to Lord Aberdeen, the royal gaze was fixed on the viceregal breast so intently that the King's representative wondered if he might be in some way improperly dressed. 'I was thinking of those jewels,' His Majesty said bleakly.

Another visitor had also landed at Kingstown, down the gangway of the *Black Prince*. He was a dark-suited nondescript figure, muscular and bowler-hatted. John Kane, Chief Inspector of the Special Branch, had been despatched by Lestrade to inquire into the matter of the missing gems. Kane described to us the King's fury at the incompetence of the Viceroy's court.

'And the worst of it is,' the Chief Inspector added, 'that Mr Shackleton was with His Majesty's brother-in-law when the robbery was discovered. And three days before, the young scoundrel was a guest at a luncheon party in Upper Brook Street. The Dublin visit and the jewels were mentioned. And do you know, Mr Holmes, what the young devil did? He smiled and told them that he would not be a bit surprised if the jewels were stolen one day!'

'Really?' Holmes replied with a yawn. 'You don't say.'

Kane became more earnest. 'It must have been Friday night they were stolen, Mr Holmes. Why else would the door of the strong-room have been open next morning?'

'Why else, indeed?'

'And it must have been Sir Arthur who opened the strong-room and the safe. That's what makes the King so mad, Mr Holmes. His Majesty knows as much now as you or I and the thought that a man in such a position of trust should betray it is beyond bearing.'

Holmes sat—or almost lay—in his chair, his eyelids drooping as if he could scarcely stay awake.

'King Edward himself is more likely to be the thief than Sir Arthur Vicars. Sir Arthur is one of the very few men who certainly could not have done it.'

Kane stared at him and Holmes raised his eyelids a little.

'If you know something, Mr Holmes . . .'

Holmes laughed. 'It is my profession to know something, my dear Kane. A week or so ago, there was a curious business of the Bedford Tower main door being found unlocked one morning. For several days before the robbery, I had arranged that a watch should be kept discreetly on Sir Arthur's house in St James's Terrace. Superintendent Lowe obliged me. In addition, when Sir Arthur left his office, I was in the habit of keeping an eye upon him until he was safely home. I followed him on Friday evening. He speaks the truth when he says that he left the Castle with his secretary and then went alone to Nassau Street, to the Kildare Street Club. He was there about ten minutes, perhaps collecting his post. From Nassau Street, he went directly home and was there for dinner at eight o'clock. He did not leave again until just before nine on the following morning, when he went to his office to find the strong-room door open and the safe empty.'

'And that was all?' Kane asked uneasily.

'Almost. A little after 10 P.M., a young woman who might have been a servant was admitted to the house. Her name is Molly Malony, or sometimes Molly Robinson, and she has a certain reputation. By that time, however, the light in the study had gone on and off as it did every night at the same time. In other words, Sir Arthur had checked that his key to the safe was in its hiding-place. The second key and the key to the strong-room were on his person. Even if the young woman could have got them, neither she nor anyone else left the house until the following morning.'

Kane looked at him soberly.

'Then, Mr Holmes, the robbery of the jewels can't have taken place on Friday night after all. Not if all the keys were in the right place. Friday can't have anything to do with it.'

'On the contrary, Mr Kane. It is the only night on which it can possibly have occurred. I'm surprised you don't see it.'

Sherlock Holmes had a greater capacity of infuriating his colleagues by these paradoxes than any other man I have known. He now appeared to lose all interest in the case. It seemed certain that the robbery must have occurred on Friday night. But the keys with which it had undoubtedly been committed could surely not have been used on Friday night. Chief Inspector Kane parted with us, not in the best of spirits. On the following afternoon, Holmes announced to me, 'I think I shall go back to London, my dear fellow. To speak frankly, Dublin has begun to weary me and I feel I shall do no good here.'

It was so contrary to his character to throw up a case like this—and one of such significance—that I wondered if he was quite well. I said as much.

'I was never better, Watson. All the same I shall go back. You must stay here, of course, and do exactly as I tell you without question.'

'But are the jewels lost for ever or not?'

'For all I know they may be,' he said with a casual shrug.

IX

I remained in Dublin alone. The case made little progress and it seemed to me that nothing of the least consequence happened. Whoever Molly Malony might have been, not the slightest interest was shown in her. The thieves had scattered such confusion in their wake that I felt sure we had seen the last of the gems.

Yet what had happened before was nothing to the madness that followed. First there was a message brought to Sir Arthur Vicars at St James's Terrace. A young woman who was a spiritualist medium had seen the missing jewels in a dream. They were hidden in a graveyard not far away. The Dublin police announced that this corresponded with a theory of their own and a search of several old and overgrown burial grounds was begun at Mulhuddart and Clonsilla. How any sane person, let alone a Special Branch officer, could sanction this hocus-pocus was beyond me.

Nothing was found. How could it be? Next, there was a message that the jewels would be found in a house at 9 Hadley Street. Of course, they were not. We had a week of this nonsense and then Sherlock Holmes summoned me back to London.

My first question, as we sat at last in our own rooms, was to ask him what the devil it all meant.

'Oh dear,' he said, 'I have kept you in the dark too long, Watson.'

'Seeing that you know neither how it was done nor by whom, that is hardly surprising.'

He looked at me with concern.

'My dear fellow, I have known from the beginning how it was done. Duplicate keys were used.'

'Why did they not scratch the mirrors of the locks?'

'They were not used on the mirrors of the locks. That is the goose chase which Kane and Lowe have followed.'

'You had better explain that,' I told him.

'Very well,' said Holmes. 'You recall that there was a spare key to the strong-room door locked in the strong-room itself? No one had looked at it for a year. There was also a second key to the safe hidden in Sir Arthur's bookshelves. He checked every night to make sure it was there. But he never used it to open the safe. Why should he, when he had one round his neck all the time? The great point of this crime, Watson, is that the duplicate keys were cut and were used. But they were not used to open the safe or the strong-room. Their task was merely to lie where the original keys had lain. By that means, all suspicion was cast upon Sir Arthur Vicars. He was, of course, entirely innocent, except perhaps of felonious and unlawful carnal knowledge of Molly Malony.'

'And the method?'

'Frank Shackleton, so often a guest of Sir Arthur's, must have discovered the second key to the safe hidden in the bookshelves. Perhaps it was accident, perhaps persistence. No doubt he saw Sir Arthur checking it one night. Shackleton had all day, after Sir Arthur left for Dublin Castle, in which to take that second key from the bookshelf to Sackville Street, have an impression cut, wrap the impression and slip it into the binding, keeping the genuine key for himself. That was probably done months ago. There was not the least danger of discovery. If Sir Arthur had ever examined the key closely and felt suspicious, he need only try it in the lock of the safe. It would have worked. But why should he? Each night, he felt a key wrapped in the binding of the book and was content.'

'So much for the key to the safe. And the strong-room?'

Holmes smiled. 'Shackleton was Dublin Herald. Nothing more natural than that he should visit the Office of Arms when he was staying with Sir Arthur. If Stivey was out of his office, Shackleton knew from experience where the strong-room key was hidden in the messenger's desk. He could open the strong-room and, even if Stivey came back, there would be nothing sinister in the Dublin Herald having gone into the strong-room to consult a volume of genealogy. The other strong-room key that was kept in the room itself had not been used for a year. Probably it was never looked at. Shackleton could safely pocket it, take it to Sackville Street, have a copy made, return the copy to the wrapping in the strong-room drawer and keep the original for himself. He now had the original keys to both strong-room and safe. He needed only a key to the door of the building. But that was a quite ordinary Yale. You recall he borrowed Sir Arthur's key to collect his letters? A copy would have been the easiest thing in the world to obtain. It could have been cut for him in a few minutes while he was on his way to collect his letters from the Bedford Tower.'

'And the door key that Sir Arthur mislaid for several days? And the fact that Mrs Farrell found the door to the Bedford Tower open several days before the theft?'

Holmes shrugged. 'Who knows? Perhaps Sir Arthur genuinely mislaid it. Perhaps it was stolen and copied then. It is of the highest importance in the art of detection to be able to recognise, out of a number of facts, which are incidental and which are vital. The mislaid key and the fact that the door to the tower was found open may be accident or coincidence. I am inclined to regard it as a coincidence but no matter. What signifies most is that our thief now had keys to open the main door, the safe, and the strong-room without leaving a single scratch on the mirrors of either the Ratner or the Milner lock. The most difficult part was no longer the robbery but returning the genuine keys of the safe and the strong-room to their proper places.'

'Yet it was done.'

Holmes gazed through the smoke from his pipe.

'The robbery began early, Watson, not during the night. I feel quite sure that when Detective Officer Kerr made his rounds at seven thirty that Friday evening, the thief was already there, locked in the strong-room. Kerr could not open that door and would not know of the intruder. When Kerr left, the thief let himself out and—if he had not already done so—emptied the safe of its jewels. He locked the safe. Then came the most important moment.'

'The key?'

'The genuine key to the safe must be returned to Sir Arthur's bookcase. The thief had a confederate. Molly Malony, I daresay. Perhaps she was with him in the building; more likely she was waiting outside. She slipped out with the key or, probably, she was already outside the tower. In that case he had only to drop it out through the letter-flap or a window. All you would see is a girl passing by, kneeling a moment to adjust the strap of her boot. A little later the key was in its proper place in the bookshelf at St James's Terrace.'

'What of the strong-room?'

'After the thief had emptied the safe, he waited until it was safely dark. About ten P.M. perhaps. He could then slip out of the door of the Bedford Tower into the shadows of the portico without being noticed. But when he left, there was one thing he could not do. One slight imperfection in a perfect plan. He must leave the genuine key to the strong-room wrapped in a drawer of the strong-room itself. He could not lock the strong-room door unless he used the duplicate key that had been cut. But that would scratch the mirrors of the lock. It would spoil the scheme by which all the evidence points to Sir Arthur. And so he chose to leave the strong-room door unlocked, as Mrs Farrell found it a few hours later on Saturday morning. With his carpet-bag in his hand, he let himself out into the shadows and slipped away. The duplicate keys were destroyed and there is an end of the matter. The original keys are all in their proper places once more and it seems that only Sir Arthur Vicars can have been the thief.'

'One thing remains,' I said quickly. 'It cannot be Shackleton. Who, then, is the thief?'

To my discomfiture, Holmes began to laugh, as if in sheer enjoyment of the tale he was telling.

'I think, Watson,' he said at last, 'it is as well that I have never tried on you my powers as a clairvoyant!'

X

'You?' The whole thing seemed preposterous. 'The message from the clairvoyante about the jewels in a graveyard? It was you who caused that to be sent?'

He was intent for a moment on recharging his pipe with coarse black tobacco.

'It was I, Watson,' he said with a sigh. 'Oh, I never doubted that Shackleton was the rogue but there was not a shred of evidence against him. If he was not in Dublin, he could not have taken the jewels himself. Therefore he had a confederate. But how to find that confederate among so many tens of thousands?' He put down his pipe. 'Imagine yourself in Shackleton's position. You have played your part. You suppose that the jewels are in the hands of your accomplice. But then you hear, or read in the newspapers, that they are to be found discarded in a graveyard. Worse still, you hear that the authorities are directed to Hadley Street, which you know to be the lodging of a young woman who assisted in the crime by seducing Ulster King of Arms. What will you do?'

I looked at Holmes. He lowered his eyelids and regarded me as a cat might study a mouse.

'I should want to know what the blazes was going on,' I said emphatically. 'But I should keep well clear of Dublin. I suppose I should send a letter—or better still a telegram. But if things are as bad as they seem, I should simply tell my confederate to bolt.'

His eyes opened and he beamed at me.

'Excellent, Watson! What a capital fellow you are.'

'I should tell him to bolt and lose no time about it, taking the young woman with him if need be.'

'Of course you would, Watson. I confess that when our friends at Scotland Yard convinced themselves that Shackleton could not be the thief, I took to watching him myself. I decided I would flush the game from cover. So I became the clairvoyante who wrote to say that her daughter, in a dream, had seen the jewels in a graveyard. I became the informer who wrote to direct Kane's attention to Hadley Street. I knew he would not find the jewels. But Shackleton would have been superhuman had he kept silent while such commotions were going on. My *pièce de résistance* was in knowing Sir Patrick Coll, a former law officer of the Crown. He and Shackleton belong to the same club and are known slightly to one another. Sir Patrick obliged me by saying in general conversation with Shackleton present that he had read a report of the jewels being recovered in Dublin.'

He smiled at this and continued.

'On top of the search in Clonsilla graveyard and the visit to Hadley Street, all in a few hours, it was too much for Shackleton to bear. He left Park Lane and walked quickly to the post office in Grosvenor Street. I watched him write his message on the pad of telegraph forms, tear off the page and go to the counter. I pretended to write on the next leaf, tore it off and followed him. He was agitated in the extreme and had therefore pressed hard with the pencil, as I expected he would. Even without dusting over the imprint, his indentation was easy enough to read. It was addressed to Captain Richard Gorges of the Royal Irish Fusiliers at Dublin Castle. It asked him to communicate at once with the sender.'

'Who the devil is Captain Gorges?'

'A greater scoundrel still, Watson, and the thief who worked to Shackleton's orders. My researches tell me that they served in the South African War together in a unit of irregulars. Gorges was a drinker, womaniser, and petty thief. Before the war was over, they drummed him out of the regiment. They did it in the proper style. Every man had a kick at him as he passed.'

'Then how comes he to be in the Royal Irish Fusiliers?'

'By the influence of Frank Shackleton, Dublin Herald. To speak the truth, he is not established in the regiment but serves it as a small-arms instructor. For all his faults, Gorges is a marksman. Who less likely to be stopped by the guard on the gate of Dublin Castle than an officer who passed that way regularly in the course of his duty?'

'Where is he now?'

'Gone, my dear Watson, no doubt with the jewels. Gone before he could receive Shackleton's telegram. Who knows where?'

'And Molly Malony?'

'Our friends in the Sûreté have traced her in Paris. She registered alone at the Hôtel Raspail in the Boulevard Montparnasse, forty-eight hours after the robbery, as Molly Robinson. I imagine she had been paid off.'

'And how is Captain Gorges to be found?'

'By Frank Shackleton,' Holmes said softly. 'Shackleton is in desperate straits. He must soon be revealed as a bankrupt and a man utterly disgraced. I am told that his debt to Cox's Bank in London alone exceeds forty thousand pounds. His business affairs have been gangrened by fraud. Prison is all that awaits him unless he has redeemed his position by robbery. The motive for the theft was as simple as that. Now we must wait. But he will answer, Watson, never fear.'

The fact that Gorges had escaped abroad with the jewels before he could be prevented might have soured Holmes's triumph. He had discovered to the last detail how the jewels were stolen and who had done it. But the evidence was not such as would secure a conviction in a court and the treasure seemed lost for ever. He remained philosophical.

'The jewels were stolen in the first place, Watson, by the British invaders from the tombs of their colonial subjects. At least they have very likely returned to those parts of the world whence they came.'

XI

In order that the story may be concluded, I must look forward a few years after the robbery. In Holmes's scrapbook is a cutting from the *London Mail* for 11 November 1912. It quotes a witness who saw Molly Malony leaving Dublin Castle at the time of the robbery and alleges that Sir Arthur Vicars himself provided the money to put her out of the way in Paris, as the scandal broke. For this last allegation, Sir Arthur recovered libel damages.

What of Frank Shackleton? For a year or two his fortunes improved surprisingly. He maintained a lavish *ménage* in Park Lane between the mansions of the Attorney-General, Sir Rufus Isaacs, and Lady Grosvenor. A few months after the robbery, he acquired a most expensive limousine for the sum of £850. Though he was the embarrassment of his brother, Sir Ernest, and the despair of his father, old Dr Shackleton, the law could not touch him. I did not doubt for one moment that he lived upon money remitted to him by the mysterious Captain Gorges, who was then disposing of the stolen gems in the secret markets of Africa or Asia.

But then the remittance of funds ceased. Shackleton returned to his old ways as a swindler. In desperation, he launched a succession of bogus companies, intending to fleece dupes, who were in many cases his wealthy friends. One after another, enterprises that existed on paper alone came to market. They gathered in the investors' funds, and failed. The Montevideo Public Works Corporation was followed by the North Mexican Land and Timber Company. This undertaking, upon its inevitable bankruptcy, was quickly succeeded by a series of Shackleton's commercial fictions.

As the storm broke about him, Frank Shackleton fled to Portuguese West Africa, beyond the reach of English law. From time to time, Holmes heard reports and complaints of Shackleton's conduct in Africa and Asia, usually in the safety of Portuguese colonies and enclaves. For all their chicanery, neither he nor Captain Gorges had the least aptitude for business or for dealing in gems. They themselves were robbed by more accomplished cheats among local traders and they had no grounds on which they dared to complain.

At length, Frank Shackleton fell foul of the laws of the Portuguese colonies and was held without trial in a festering gaol in Benguela. The conditions of this squalid and disease-ridden African prison were so atrocious that he volunteered to surrender himself to officers from Scotland Yard, if they would only take him back to England. To Inspector Cooper, who was sent to arrest him for fraud, he said, 'I will do anything to get out of this place. If I have to remain here much longer, I am sure I shall be dead.'

By the time that he stood his trial at the Central Criminal Court, Shackleton had no money and no jewels. He went to a long term in prison for fraud, having cheated his dupes of £84,000. Though there was still too little evidence to charge him with complicity in the jewel robbery, justice had him in her clutches. Though it is a platitude, he left prison many years later, a broken and dying man.

Captain Gorges, however, was to have a brief notoriety. As war threatened Europe, he slipped unnoticed into Ireland and then to England. Holmes had not the least doubt that, somewhere, Captain Gorges came face to face with Sir Arthur's nephew, young Peirce Mahony. I daresay by now Mahony had guessed the truth and threatened to unmask the scoundrel. Before he could do so, Mahony was found floating in the lake at Grange Con, his chest blasted open by the barrels of his own gun. That it was murder, rather than accident, was not proved.

Unknown to any of us and under an assumed name, Captain Gorges came to London, where he lodged with a professional boxer, Charles Thoroughgood, at Mount Vernon, Hampstead. Information had reached Special Branch independently that the house was an arsenal for the gunmen of Sinn Fein, for whom Gorges now acted as quartermaster. Two officers entered the house and searched it while it was unoccupied. They found only a revolver and two hundred rounds of ammunition.

That evening, after Gorges had returned to his basement room, the house was surrounded. The wanted man appeared on the area steps with his hands behind him. As the officers closed in and one of them seized him, it was evident that he was holding a gun behind his back. The first man, Sergeant Askew, struggled with him. During the scuffle, the gun went off and by an unhappy fluke shot dead Detective Constable Alfred Young, who was coming down the steps to assist his colleague.

Richard Gorges was taken to Cannon Row police station and charged with manslaughter, for which he later served twelve years' penal servitude. As the charge sheet was filled in, he said pathetically, 'Don't call me "Captain", for the honour of the regiment.'

No more than Shackleton would Gorges say what had become in the end of the Irish Crown Jewels. Those who knew no better assumed that Sir Arthur Vicars, the only man to possess the keys to the safe and the strong-room, had been the thief. He was dismissed from his post, though not for the theft. Later he paid with his life because a party of looters believed, as did others, that he had been the thief and that the treasure must still be in his strong-room at Kilmorna.

What of the stolen jewels? Their story was the strangest of all. There was no doubt that the thieves had sold them on the underworld market as best they could, though being cheated themselves in the process. Then, when the old King died in 1910 and preparations were made for the coronation of the present sovereign George V, a strange report began to circulate among those who would be first to hear such things. The jewels, or as many of them as could be found, had been 'ransomed'. The money had been paid by Baron William James Pirrie, Chairman of Harland and Wolff shipyards in Belfast. The story appeared only once in the press and was instantly denied on all sides. Great persuasion was used upon other editors to prevent its republication.

It was Sherlock Holmes, after all, who solved the mystery. I returned to his rooms in Baker Street one afternoon, not long after the coronation of George V and Queen Mary. Holmes had a picture paper spread on the table with several photographs beside it. It was not usual for him to take much notice of picture papers and more unusual for him to read Mr Bottomley's effusions in *John Bull*.

He had a magnifying-glass in his hand and was studying minutely the photographs of the royal couple and the princes and princesses. The article asserted that the Dublin jewels were once again in the possession of the royal family, having been sought and purchased from those who had them after Shackleton and Gorges lost them. Few men in England could rival Holmes in the particular knowledge of mineralogy required to identify precious stones.

'Even when they are recut, Watson, their shape cannot be entirely altered. A stone may only be cut along certain lines, as a triangle must always have three sides.'

He gazed again through the glass at the photograph of Queen Mary in the magazine and then at the photographic print on the table beside him.

'See here, Watson. If you will look at the stones in the Star of St Patrick, as I have marked them there, and the tiara of our gracious Queen there, I see no room for doubt. The jewellers have worked with the utmost discretion. The stones have been reset in new stars and badges for the new reign. After all, in the present political situation, it is hardly likely that His Majesty will require a set of Crown Jewels in Ireland much longer.'

Though I yield to no one in my estimation of Sherlock Holmes's forensic skills, I could not quite bring myself to believe him. Surely, the recovery of the Irish jewels would have been accompanied by some triumphal announcement. Surely he was mistaken. Surely sovereigns and governments do not deal in the dark like this. How wrong I was!

As I now look at his papers, I see a copy of a Home Office file, with the number 156, 610/16. By the time this account is published, the curious will be able to consult the document for themselves in the record office. It confirms that the Badge of the Order of St Patrick had survived intact, come into the hands of Sir Arthur Vicars, and had been returned to the King. The document was stamped, 'Most Secret'. Whether Lord Pirrie had paid a ransom and returned the jewels through the good offices of Sir Arthur, I cannot say. That some benefactor had done so, albeit anonymously, I could not doubt.

When I first read this secret file, not long after the death of Sherlock Holmes, I wondered why it should have been passed to him by the Home Office. After all, his name appeared nowhere in it. Why should it concern him? But, as I thought the matter over, I knew I had done my friend an injustice.

That afternoon many years before, he stood over the picture papers magnifying-glass in hand. He was so sure that Queen Mary's tiara, made for the coronation celebrations of 1911, contained lost gems of the Order of St Patrick. Could any man, however expert, be so certain of that when he had seen only a newspaper photograph? Perhaps, after all, even skill in mineralogy was not enough. Lord Pirrie may or may not have provided the ransom, that I cannot tell. But who more likely to have been the government's intermediary in those shadowy negotiations for the recovery of the precious stones than Sherlock Holmes himself? Who but government or monarchy would have the wealth to buy such a collection?

Of course Holmes had said nothing of all this. It was his usual habit, when the monarch was concerned in one of the investigations, to maintain a complete silence, even to me. But I swear that Holmes knew that King George and Queen Mary were in possession of the gems again long before he saw Mr Bottomley's picture paper! Alas, by the time I read the Home Office file on the subject, my friend was dead and I could not ask him.

As we sat in the firelight, on that evening long ago, I recall saying, 'So Shackleton and Gorges have escaped justice?'

He flung himself down in his chair and filled his pipe.

'I do not think they would agree with you upon that, Watson. A man who is in prison suffers. What more is there? He may commit two crimes but he cannot suffer twice at the same time. Those men are ruined beyond redemption and that is enough.'

He stared at the fire for a moment.

'All the same,' I protested, 'you seem to take the robbery rather lightly, for such a crime. Indeed, I find that you have never suggested that the theft itself was of great moral consequence.'

Holmes stared at the dancing flames.

'Perhaps I remember that there was another robbery, long before.'

'A theft of the jewels?'

He looked up at me. 'Of course, Watson. These were the holy treasures of the royal tombs at Golconda and elsewhere. Our imperial commanders ransacked those shrines to provide gew-gaws for the Kings and Queens of England. Theft compounded by sacrilege. A far worse crime, my dear fellow, than anything that Shackleton or Gorges could devise. If our sovereign or his subjects choose to buy back these stones from the very countries to whom they first belonged, so be it. I daresay the treasure could not safely go back to Golconda now. But if England took them without giving a single penny on the first occasion, I see no objection to her paying a fair price on the second. I call that true justice, my dear fellow. Don't you?'

The Case of the Unseen Hand

I

In that series of events which I call 'The Case of the Unseen Hand', everything appeared to turn against us from the outset. Yet, at its conclusion, Sherlock Holmes enjoyed a private success that was seldom matched in any of his other investigations.

Readers of 'The Golden Pince-Nez', a narrative made public in *The Return of Sherlock Holmes*, may recall my reference to the earlier triumph of the great detective in tracking and arresting Huret, the so-called 'Boulevard Assassin' of Paris, in 1894. Holmes was rewarded for his services with a handwritten letter from the President of France and by the Order of the Legion of Honour. The presidential letter was written in January 1895 by Félix Faure, who had just then succeeded to the leadership of his country at a most difficult moment, following the assassination of President Carnot and a few months of unhappy tenure by Casimir-Périer.

Holmes had a natural sympathy for Félix Faure, as a man who had risen from humble circumstances to the highest position in France. It was unfortunate for Monsieur Faure, however, that a month before he assumed office, Captain Alfred Dreyfus, a young probationary officer of the French General Staff, had been condemned by court martial to life imprisonment in the steaming and unbroken heat of Devil's Island for betraying his country's military secrets to Germany. In the aftermath of the trial there were rioting crowds in the streets of Paris, demanding the execution of Dreyfus. The President himself was attacked in public and spat upon for his leniency. The mob threatened death to any man courageous enough to doubt the guilt of 'the traitor'. Dreyfus was first 'degraded' on the parade ground of the École Militaire and then transported to that infamous penal colony off the French Guianan coast of South America. He was confined to a tiny stone hut, day and night, in the breathless heat of Cayenne Île du Diable. Though escape was impossible from such a place, his ankles were locked in double irons attached to a bar across the foot of his cot. His true punishment was not imprisonment for life but death by slow torture. A firing-squad would have been a more humane sentence.

The facts alleged against Alfred Dreyfus were that he had sold his country's secrets to Colonel Max von Schwartzkoppen, Military Attaché at the German Embassy in Paris. The court martial was held *in camera* but the details of the accusations were public knowledge. The paper, which his prosecutors insisted was in the hand of Dreyfus, conveyed to Colonel Schwartzkoppen specifications of the new and highly secret 120 mm gun, its performance and deployment; the reorganisation plan of the French Artillery, and the Field Artillery Firing Manual. Only an officer of the General Staff could have held such information.

Sherlock Holmes, like Émile Zola and a host of impartial men and women, never believed in the guilt of Captain Dreyfus. My friend's skill in graphology convinced him that the handwriting on the letter to Colonel Schwartzkoppen was not that of Alfred Dreyfus but, perhaps, a half-successful attempt at imitation. Like Monsieur Zola, Holmes also deplored the bigotry of the prosecution, the whole manner of the court martial and condemnation. Years later, our *Dreyfusards* were proved right. Colonel Hubert Henry of the Deuxième Bureau and Lemercier-Picard, who had both forged further 'evidence' to deepen the guilt of Dreyfus after his condemnation, committed suicide.

In the years that followed our adventure, the innocence of Dreyfus and the guilt of a certain Major Count Ferdinand Walsin-Esterhazy were to be established. Restored to his command, as a gallant officer of the Great War, Captain Dreyfus was to join Sherlock Holmes as a Chevalier of the Legion of Honour. The manner in which justice was done at last forms the background to my account of our own case.

II

In January 1899, when the presidency of Félix Faure and the imprisonment of Captain Dreyfus had already lasted for four years, Holmes and I travelled to Paris on behalf of the British government. Our confidential mission, which had been warmly supported by our friend Lestrade at Scotland Yard, was to meet the great Bertillon. Alphonse Bertillon was a former professor of anthropology, now head of the Identification Bureau at the Préfecture de Police. The 'Bertillon System' had enabled the French police to identify a man or woman uniquely by measuring certain bony structures of the body, notably those of the head. It was claimed in Paris that these measurements would render all criminal disguises and false identities futile. The objection at Scotland Yard was that such a system was far too complicated for general use. In England, Sherlock Holmes and Sir Francis Galton had been working upon the simpler method of identification by fingerprints, which Bertillon had also pioneered. They had been set upon the task by Mr Asquith, as Home Secretary in 1893. At first their opponents argued that no jury would be persuaded to convict a defendant upon such a whimsical theory. Twelve years later, however, the Stratton brothers were to be hanged for the Deptford Street murder on the evidence of a single thumbprint.

When we set off for Paris in January 1899, it was our mission to persuade Professor Bertillon to join his efforts with ours in championing this simpler method of criminal detection. One of Bertillon's original objections had been that a great many surfaces retain no visible fingerprint. Holmes had answered this when he devised in our Baker Street rooms a system for making these unseen or 'latent' fingerprints visible, by the use of silver nitrate powder or iodine fumes. Bertillon then demanded of him how such evidence was to be displayed in court. In reply, Holmes had painstakingly adapted a small Kodak camera by adding an open box to the front, so that the lens always looked down on the fingerprint from a uniform distance and was therefore permanently in focus. By this means, any number of photographs of a fingerprint might be made for a criminal trial. He had brought his prototype of the camera to display to the great French criminologist. All the same, there was no sign as yet that such advances would persuade Professor Bertillon to change his mind.

On a chill but windless January day, we crossed from Folkestone to Boulogne by the *Lord Warden* steamer. Holmes stood at the ship's rail, his sharp profile framed by his ear-flapped travelling-cap. As soon as we cast off from Folkestone harbour pier, it seemed that his interest in his French adversary underwent a significant change. Fingerprints and skull measurements were discarded from our conversation. He unfolded a sheet of paper and handed it to me.

'The affair of Captain Dreyfus, Watson. Read this. It is a private note from my disgraced friend Colonel Picquart, late of the Information Branch of the Deuxième Bureau. Even in this matter it seems that we cannot escape the shade of Bertillon. Picquart tells me that the professor is immoveable, convinced that the incriminating letter of 1894 is in the hand of Captain Dreyfus. For a man of Bertillon's capability to believe such a thing is quite beyond my comprehension. Unfortunately, however, his reputation as a criminal expert will count for far more in a courtroom than all Monsieur Zola's denunciations of injustice.'

He shook his head and gave a quiet sigh, staring across the Channel. The sea lay calm as wrinkled satin towards the sands of France, pale and chill on the horizon of that winter afternoon.

'Then what will you do?' I asked, handing back to him the sheet of paper.

'I shall pray, Watson. Not for a miracle—merely for an opportunity to demonstrate to Professor Bertillon the error of his methods in graphology and identification alike. There is a battle to be fought and won for Captain Dreyfus but it must be fought at the right time and in the right place.'

During the next few weeks our Baker Street quarters were exchanged for two bedrooms and a sitting-room at the Hôtel Lutétia in the Boulevard Raspail. It was an area of business and bustle, having more in common with the nearby railway terminus of the Gare Montparnasse than with the bohemian society of poets and artists which the name of that district more often suggests. The Hôtel Lutétia rose like the hull of an ocean liner above a quayside in this commercial avenue of tall houses with their grey mansard roofs, their elegant windows and balconies set in pale tide-washed stone. In front of many a grander building, a handsome *porte-cochère* entrance remained. Yet the days of Second Empire quiet had gone. As afternoon drew on, the winter sun threw up a dusty light from the constant traffic.

I was not present at the private discussions between Holmes and Professor Bertillon, which were concluded in a day or two. In truth, there was little to discuss so long as the two men remained immoveable. The silver nitrate, the iodine fumes, the special camera, were mere toys in Bertillon's view. To make matters worse, a further hostility arose in general conversation when the professor repeated his view that the incriminating message of 1894 to the German Military Attaché was written in the hand of Captain Dreyfus. The first day's meeting ended with ill temper on both sides. Next morning Bertillon returned to the debate over scientific detection, insisting that fingerprints might be disfigured or erased, or even prevented by the wearing of gloves. They were no substitute for the measurement of criminal heads, where counterfeiting was an impossibility. With that, he indicated that his exchange of views with his English visitor was at an end. Holmes returned from the Préfecture de Police in a filthy temper, his vanity bruised, and his appetite for battle with the French anthropologist all the keener. I could not help thinking—though I judged it best not to say so at the time—that the sooner we returned to Baker Street, the better.

I had begun to look forward to our return and was already picturing myself among the comforts of home, when I heard my companion in the lobby of the hotel, informing the manager that we should require our rooms for at least another fortnight.

'But why?' I demanded, as soon as we were alone.

'Because, Watson, an innocent man is condemned to suffer the nightmare of Devil's Island until he drops dead from exhaustion or the brutality of the regime. Bertillon, the one expert whose word might yet save him, refuses to say that word. As it happens, he also rejects, unexamined, the only infallible method of criminal identification upon which others have lavished years of toil. I do not greatly care for Alphonse Bertillon. I swear to you that these two issues may yet become a personal matter between us.'

'For God's sake, Holmes! You cannot fight a duel with the head of a French police bureau!'

'In my own way, Watson, that is just what I propose to do.'

After so much bluster, as I thought it, Holmes became inexplicably a pattern of idleness. So much for his threats against Professor Bertillon! Like a man who feels that the best of life is behind him, he began to describe our visit to Paris as a chance that 'might not come again'. Yet I could not believe that it was some premonition of mortality that determined him to spend two or three weeks longer in the city. More probably it was his usual mode of life, in which he alternated between intense periods of obsessional activity—when he would sleep little and eat less—and weeks when he seemed to do little more than stare from his armchair at the sky beyond the window, without a thought in his head.

The indolence that came upon him now was not quite of the usual sort. He tasted something of bohemian café society at the Closerie des Lilas with its trees and its statue of Marshal Ney. He spent an entire day reading the icy tombstones of Montparnasse cemetery, as he was to do next day at Père Lachaise. For the most part, we walked the cold streets and parks as we had never done in any other city.

A frosty morning was our time for the tree-lined vista of the Avenue de la Grande Armée, the lakes and woods of the Bois de Boulogne extending before us in a chill mist. Down the wide thoroughfare, the closed carriages of fashionable society rattled on frozen cobbles. The shrubbery gardens of the adjacent mansions lay silent and crisp beyond the snowcaps of tall wrought-iron railings.

'My dear Holmes,' I said that evening, 'it is surely better that we should go our separate ways for a little. There is no purpose in our remaining longer in Paris. At least, there is no purpose for me. Let me return to London and attend to business there. You may stay here and follow when you think the time is right. There can be no use in both of us remaining.'

'Oh, yes, Watson,' he said quietly, 'there is the greatest use in the world. It will require us both, of that I am sure.'

'May I know what the use is?'

'The question cannot be pressed,' he said vaguely. 'The purpose must mature in its own time.'

It matured at a snail's pace, as it seemed to me, for almost a week. During those days our morning rambles now took us through the red revolutionary *arrondissements* of the north-east. We crossed the little footbridges of the Canal Saint-Martin. Holmes studied the sidings and marshalling-yards of Aubervilliers with the rapt attention that other visitors might give to the *Mona Lisa* in the Louvre. A late sun of the winter morning rose like a red ball through the mist across the heroic distance of the Place de la République, where the statue of Marianne stands like a towering Amazon protecting the booths and shooting galleries. By evening we were in the wide lamplit spaces of the Place de la Concorde, the tall slate roofs of the Quai d'Orsay rising through a thin river mist on the far bank.

Five days passed in this manner, as if Holmes were mapping the city in his head, noting the alleys, culs-de-sac, escape routes, and short cuts. That evening, there were footsteps on the stairs. At the door of our rooms, there appeared briefly and dimly a visitor who brought an envelope of discreet and expensive design with the gold initials 'RF' interwoven. Holmes read the contents but said nothing.

Next morning, he came from his room in a costume more bizarre than any of his disguises as a tramp or a Lascar seaman. He was wearing the black swallow-tailed coat and white tie of court dress. Before I could ask what the devil this meant, there was a discreet tap at the door and our visitor of the previous evening reappeared, now similarly attired in formal dress. I caught a murmured exchange and the newcomer twice used the form of 'Monsieur le Président', when indicating that time pressed. Holmes accompanied him without a word. I turned to the window and saw them enter a closed carriage, its black coachwork immaculately polished but without a single crest or other emblem to indicate its origins. I could only suppose it was for this summons that Holmes had been waiting while we walked the streets of Paris.

III

In the hours that passed before I saw him again, I no longer doubted that the 'purpose' of our visit was working itself out. Holmes had used his influence, the Order of the Legion of Honour, as well as the reputation of a man who had rid Paris of the Boulevard Assassin, to obtain an audience with President Faure. The intention could only be to convince Félix Faure that Captain Dreyfus was no traitor and that the letter sent to Colonel Schwartzkoppen, the Military Attaché, would be shown on scientific examination to be the work of another hand.

It was late in the afternoon when my companion returned. He knew as well as I that there was no need for an explanation of his absence. He stood in the sitting-room of the hotel suite, a familiar figure in the unfamiliarity of his formal costume.

'Your patience may be rewarded, Watson,' he said with the quick movement of his mouth, which was sometimes a smile and sometimes a nervous quirk, 'I have put our case to President Faure.'

'Our case?'

He smiled more easily. 'Very well, then, the case of Alfred Dreyfus. The matter of the handwriting. We have, I believe, a chance to vanquish Professor Bertillon on both fronts. Who knows? If we succeed in this, there may be a path to victory over him in other matters. I have struck a bargain with Félix Faure. The evidence against Dreyfus will be reviewed. Indeed, though he still thinks the man guilty, in all probability, he has not set his face against a retrial.'

'Then you have succeeded?' I asked the question because, to anyone who had known him for a length of time, it was evident that Holmes was holding back some unwelcome detail.

'Not quite,' he said, another nervous movement plucking at his mouth, 'I fear, Watson, you will not like our side of the bargain. We are to remain in Paris for a few more months.'

'Months! What the devil for?'

'That, my dear friend, will be explained to you within the hour by President Faure's confidential secretary. It is not too much to say that the fate of France and the peace of Europe may depend upon the safety of the treasure we are to guard.'

'Treasure!' I exclaimed. 'What treasure?'

But Holmes waved his hand aside, recommending patience. He turned and went to his room, exchanging formal clothes for familiar tweeds and Norfolk jacket. Short of pursuing him and standing over him while he changed, there was little I could do. I walked about the tall corniced sitting-room on the first floor of the Hôtel Lutétia, folding a paper here and tidying a table there, in anticipation of a visit from the confidential secretary of the President of the Republic. Then I paused and stared down into the Boulevard Raspail with its busy traffic from the suburbs and markets. Would Félix Faure's confidential secretary really make a habit of visiting confidants in what was almost a public room? I thought of Sir Henry Ponsonby and Sir Arthur Bigge as Her Majesty's private secretaries, conducting confidential negotiations in the hotels of Bayswater or Pimlico. The idea was plainly absurd.

This was one of the rare occasions when I suspected that Holmes, on unfamiliar territory, was out of his depth. He had just reappeared in his tweed suiting, when there was a knock at the door. It was a hotel pageboy who had brought our visitor from the lobby. The stranger entered the sitting-room. As the page closed the door again, Holmes bowed, took the hand of the President's confidential secretary, and kissed it with instinctive gallantry. This newcomer was not the type of Sir Henry Ponsonby nor Sir Arthur Bigge, but one of the most striking young women upon whom I had ever set eyes.

IV

She might have been eighteen, though the truth was that she was thirty and already had a daughter who was ten years old. Yet there was such a soft round beauty in her face, a depth to her wide eyes, and a lustre in the elegant coiffure of her dark hair that she reminded one irresistibly of a London *débutante* in her first season. To describe her figure as elegant, narrow-waisted, and instinctively graceful in every movement is to resort to the commonplaces of portraiture. Yet Marguerite Steinheil was possessed of all these attributes and was never commonplace.

Such was Félix Faure's confidential secretary. Though I was struck by her beauty, even her modesty of demeanour on this occasion, the thought that preoccupied me was that no English politician's reputation could have withstood such an association with a young woman of so remarkable a presence as hers.

'Watson!' Holmes turned to me with a look of triumph. 'Let me introduce to you Madame Marguerite Steinheil, the emissary of President Faure. Madame, allow me to present my colleague, Dr John Watson, before whom you may speak as freely as to myself.'

Somehow, I scarcely recall how, I mumbled my way through the pleasantries of formal introduction in the next few minutes. If

I had thought before this that Sherlock Holmes had plunged into the Dreyfus affair beyond his depth, I was now utterly convinced of it. Madame Steinheil took her place on the chaise-longue, Holmes and I facing her from two upright gilded chairs. She spoke almost perfect English with an accent so light that it added to the charm of her voice.

'I believe,' she said, 'that I may soon be able to bring you good news of Captain Dreyfus, of whose innocence I have never myself entertained the least doubt. However, I may only help him, or help you, if you will assist me in return.'

'Then you must explain that, madame,' Holmes said quietly. 'I believe it is the President whom we are to serve, is it not?'

She smiled quickly at him and said, 'It is the same thing, Mr Holmes. More than four years ago, I became his friend because of his interest in art. My husband, Adolphe Steinheil, is a portrait painter. Our drawing-room has long been a meeting-place for men and women from literature, art, music, and public life. We have a house and a studio in the Impasse Ronsin, off the Rue de Vaugirard, near the Gare Montparnasse. Félix Faure was a guest at my *salons*, a friend before he became President. After his election, he bought one of Adolphe's paintings for the private rooms in the Élysée Palace. He is the President but he is also the greatest friend in the world to me. I must make this confidence to you. My own father is dead but Félix Faure has been, in his way, a father to me and I, perhaps, like a daughter to him.'

The more I heard of this, the less I liked it. I saw that Holmes's mouth tightened a little.

'Forgive me, Madame Steinheil, but you are not—are you?—a daughter. You are a confidential secretary and you will betray your trust if you seek to be anything more.'

She put her hands together and stared down at them. Then she looked up with the same smile, the same openness of her face and gaze, that would have softened any accusation in the world.

'Mr Holmes,' she said quietly, 'I need not tell you that the Third Republic of France was born from war and revolutionary bloodshed almost thirty years ago. Since then, there has been scandal, riot, and assassination. In England, I think, you have not known such things. Were you to see the secret papers of the past thirty years in our own country, you would be more deeply troubled still and perhaps a good deal more shocked than you have been even by the affair of Captain Dreyfus. These papers of which I speak are known to very few people. Naturally, they have been seen by fewer people still.'

'Of whom you are doubtless one, madame!'

The cold precision of his voice was a harsh contrast to the softer tones of Marguerite Steinheil. Yet she was a match for him.

'Of whom I am one,' she said, inclining her head. 'Since the President came to office, he has suffered abuse in the Chamber of Deputies, he has been physically attacked in public and spat at. Lesser men would have resigned the office, as his predecessor did, and France would go down in civil war. But he will not resign, Mr Holmes. He will fight. In order to fight, he must have a weapon. The pen, as you say, will prove mightier than the sword.'

'If it is used with discretion,' Holmes said gently.

She smiled again and then dropped her voice a little, as if fearing that even now she might be overheard.

'For the past three years, Félix Faure has been engaged upon his secret history of France since the Franco-Prussian War of 1870. It is to be his testament, his justification of steps that he must take, before the end of his *septennat*—his period of office.'

'And you, madame?' Holmes inquired coolly. 'What are you to him in such a crisis?'

There was no smile as she looked at him now.

'What am I in all this? Félix Faure saw in me a friend who would offer an undivided loyalty, a loyalty that is not to be found among the ministers and officials surrounding him. You have not lived in France during the past ten years, Mr Holmes. From your well-ordered life in London, it is hard to imagine the scandal and near-revolution that plagues this city.'

'One may deduce a little, even in London.'

'No,' she said, and shook her head with a whisper of disagreement, 'Félix Faure was called to office among the mortal injuries which France seemed determined to inflict on herself. The Boulangists would overthrow republicanism and restore the monarchy. The Anarchists would plunge us in blood. We had watched the *bourse*—the stock exchange—and the Quai d'Orsay brought to near-ruin by the Panama corruption scandals and the disappearance of two hundred and fifty million francs. We had seen governments created in hope, only to collapse in dishonour after a few months. Six months before my friend was called to the highest office, President Carnot himself was stabbed to death at Lyons by a terrorist. President Casimir-Périer was driven from office by libel and ridicule within a few weeks. During those weeks came the Dreyfus affair.'

Holmes was about to say something but seemed to think better of it.

'I watched that man's epaulettes torn from his tunic,' the young woman continued softly, 'on the parade ground of the École Militaire, his sword broken over the adjutant's knee. Mobs shouted for his death in the riots that followed. France had degenerated into such chaos that government itself seemed impossible. In our relations with the world, we had drifted from our alliance with Russia and were close to war with England over Fashoda and the Sudan. Félix Faure tried without success to persuade his ministers that a *rapprochement* with England and Russia was our sole salvation abroad. He failed to move them. How could he succeed when, as the secret papers confirm, his closest adviser in foreign affairs was a man whose mistress had for years been in the pay of the German Embassy? Four months ago, in October, matters were so grave that Monsieur Faure considered carrying out a military *coup d'état* as President, taking absolute power to impose order on the country by martial law.'

'And you, madame?' Holmes still pressed for an answer to the most important question of all. 'What were you to Félix Faure?'

'I was his eyes and ears throughout all this, as well as his amanuensis. I went privately to sittings of the Chamber of Deputies and the Senate, to certain receptions and parties. He is surrounded by enemies in government and now he knows it, through me. I was better able to identify certain men who might have destroyed him, had they been appointed to office. They are, Mr Holmes, without scruples or principles under their masks of public virtue. They are *arrivistes* ready to sell themselves to achieve their ambitions.'

Sherlock Holmes held her gaze dispassionately.

'As a woman, however, you were surely in greater danger of being compromised in your role of adviser than a man would have been?'

If Marguerite Steinheil blushed a little at the innuendo, I saw no sign of it.

'My sex was my advantage. No man is inscrutable to a woman, Mr Holmes, especially when that woman is devoted to one whom she has decided to help, and when she is supposed to care for nothing more essential than music, flowers, or dress.'

'But you do not play quite the same part now, I take it?'

'No,' she said softly. 'The dangers and the threats became so numerous that there could only be one answer—"The Secret History of France under the Third Republic". It is a weapon so powerful that our adversaries dare not provoke its use. Every afternoon, the President adds several pages to it, on foolscap paper which I buy for him myself. At first these pages were locked in an iron box at the Élysée Palace itself. Then, in the crisis of last October, Fèlix Faure asked me to take home the pages as he wrote them. Until this afternoon, three people in the world knew of this precaution: the President and I, of course, and Monsieur Hamard, Chief of the Sûreté, a man of honour to whom Félix Faure would entrust his very life. Dr Watson and yourself must now be admitted to the secret.'

'Then I trust, madame, you will use such a weapon as a shield, not as a sword.'

The young woman smiled at this. 'A shield is all we ask, Mr Holmes. The President's enemies cannot be sure what revelations drawn from the secret papers these chapters may contain. Yet he has taken good care that those from whom he has most to fear are aware of the consequences. If such pages were to be made public, the reputations of those men would be blasted. It would be impossible for them to hold office and they would be fortunate indeed to escape prosecution as common criminals. Perhaps you think such a threat unchivalrous? No doubt it is. I assure you, however, that there is nothing in those pages except what is the proven truth.'

She paused and Holmes said nothing for a moment. He took his pipe from the pocket of his Norfolk tweeds and then replaced it.

'It is on this account that you wish Dr Watson and myself to remain in Paris?'

'Only for a while,' she said gently. 'In a month—two months at the most—enough of the work will be done. A copy will be made and deposited elsewhere, to make the work safe for posterity. Meanwhile, new pages and documents will be taken back each night to a hiding-place in the Impasse Ronsin. In the past weeks, the President has been warned by Monsieur Hamard that visitors to the Élysée Palace are being watched by those who may be agents of foreign powers but more probably of our enemies within France. Some of our visitors are being followed. It would not do for a single page of the history or a single document to fall into the hands of those who would destroy us.'

Holmes spoke courteously but the scepticism in his eyes, as he regarded her, was inescapable to anyone who knew him.

'You have begun well, madame, by ensuring that the manuscript is removed from the Élysée Palace. You must surely have more enemies in that building than in the rest of the world. In a crisis, that is the first place where those whom you fear would search for it. As for the opinion of Monsieur Hamard, he and I have been acquainted ever since the case of the Boulevard Assassin. I hold him in the highest regard. If he warns you of a danger, you would be well advised to take heed.'

'Indeed,' she said, 'it is on Monsieur Hamard's suggestion that I am here this afternoon. Knowing that you were in Paris to confer with his colleague Professor Bertillon, he believed you might be prepared to assist. He advises that, for the future, any papers which

I take with me to the Impasse Ronsin each evening should be a decoy, documents of no importance. The pages of the manuscript itself will be entrusted to you. At a distance, you and Dr Watson will be my escort and courier. When you are satisfied that no one is watching or following, you may deliver the envelope through the letter-box of the Impasse Ronsin.'

Holmes looked unaccountably gloomy.

'Yes,' he said thoughtfully. 'Well, Madame Steinheil, I have had this put to me in similar terms by the President. It is hard for a humble ratepayer of Baker Street to oppose the will of a head of state. However, I shall ask you a question that I might not ask the President. What purpose is served by Dr Watson and myself remaining in Paris to do something that any well-trained policeman might do? Indeed, you might employ a different officer each evening, so that whoever attempted to shadow you would not recognise him. As for the papers, you scarcely need more than a porter to convey your luggage.'

There, I thought, he had tripped her. Marguerite Steinheil looked her prettiest at him.

'A President is surely entitled to ask for the best?'

'No, no, madame!' said Holmes with a flash of irritation. 'That really will not do for an answer!'

She flinched a little. 'Very well, then. Among the papers from which the narrative is drawn—in the pages of the narrative itself—will be found evidence to prove the innocence of Colonel Dreyfus beyond all argument.'

'Then let that evidence be published now,' Holmes said abruptly.

Again she shook her head. 'The man who might put the case beyond any further argument is in Berlin. He has been forbidden from speaking by the Chief of the German General Staff and by the Kaiser himself. If our plan succeeds, they will find in a month or two that they can command him no longer.'

There was a moment's silence. In that comfortable hotel sitting-room on the Boulevard Raspail, we pictured Dreyfus the innocent, the man of honour, riveted in his irons in the jungle mist of Cayenne Île du Diable, condemned to rot until death released him.

'Fiat justitia, ruat coelum', Holmes said at last, still with reluctance. 'Let justice be done, though the heavens fall. Madame, you shall have your way. God knows, it is a small enough price that we pay for the poor fellow's liberty.'

After she had taken her leave, he sat without speaking. Then, as he was apt to do when something of great weight was on his mind, he walked to the window and stared out into the street. It was dark by now and the scene was one that might have been painted by Pissarro or Manet. Each flickering gas-lamp threw out a misty halo, its shivering image reflected in pools of rain. The traffic of cabs and horse-buses dwindled from the brightly lit shops of the Rue de Rennes to the quiet elegance of the Boulevard St Germain. Men and women hurried homeward by the darkened skyline of the Luxembourg Gardens.

'So,' he said, turning at last, 'we are to remain here in order to guard a few sheets of paper every evening, to prevent them from being snatched away in the street! Can you believe a word of it, Watson? It reminds me of nothing so much as that other useless occupation, the Red-Headed League, whose history you were good enough to preserve in your memoirs! A man was paid handsomely for the aimless daily exercise of copying out the whole of the *Encyclopaedia Britannica* by hand. A pretty piece of villainy lay behind that!'

I was a little shocked by his tone.

'You do not call Madame Steinheil a villain?'

'Of course I do not!' he said impatiently. 'Wayward, perhaps. She has, I believe, the reputation of what is delicately called, among the fashionables of Rotten Row, a "Pretty Horse-Breaker".'

The vulgar phrase sounded oddly in his fastidious speech.

'Then you believe she has not told us the truth?'

'Not the whole truth! Of course not!' He looked at me in dismay, unable to see how I had missed the fact. 'It does not require the two of us to prevent an envelope being snatched from her hand or to see whether she is followed. She knows that as well as you or I!'

'What else is there to prevent?'

'After all that we have heard from her of *coups d'état* and treason, you still do not see why our services are preferred to those of the Sûreté or the Deuxième Bureau?'

'I do not see what else she hopes we may prevent,' I said with the least feeling of exasperation. 'What is it?'

Sherlock Holmes gave a fatalistic sigh.

'In all probability,' he said softly, 'the assassination of the President of France.'

V

During the next few days, the prediction seemed so preposterous that I had not the heart to remind him of it, even as a joke. Every afternoon, we took the same cab to the same drab stretch of the Rue de Vaugirard with its hospitals and public buildings. In the Impasse Ronsin, the tall house with its studio windows rose beyond a high street-wall and garden trees. As if at a signal, a second cab turned out on to the main thoroughfare and preceded us by way of the Boulevard des Invalides, the elegant span of the Pont Alexandre III, across the River Seine, and past the glass domes of the exhibition pavilions.

Sometimes, when the winter afternoon was sunny, the young woman would dismiss the cab at the river bridge and walk across the wide spaces of evergreen gardens with their regimented trees and little chairs, at the lower end of the Champs Élysées. This was done to give us a better opportunity of seeing whether she was shadowed. From time to time a man might look sidelong at the narrow-waisted beauty, the collar of her coat trimmed with fur that lay more sensuously against the bloom of her cheek, the coquettish hat with its net veil crowning her elegant coiffure. Many wistful and casual glances came in her direction yet no one followed her.

Quickly and unobtrusively, she was admitted by the little gate in the gold-tipped iron railings of the presidential palace, at the corner of the Champs-Élysées and the Avenue de Marigny. Not a soul took the least notice. Several times, on her return, she got down from the cab among the little streets of the Left Bank that run from the *grands quais* of the Seine, opposite the Louvre. In the early dusk, she paused at the shop-fronts of the Rue des Saints Pères in dark green or terracotta or black with gold. Curios and jewellery shone in the lamplit windows. The shelves of the *bibliothèques* glowed with the rich leather bindings of rare editions. Holmes and I knew from long experience that in such territory the hunter easily becomes the prey. The shadow must dawdle or feign interest or linger in his cab, while his quarry visits one shop after another. If there was such a man on these evenings, the trained eye of Sherlock Holmes failed to see him.

On several afternoons, Holmes and I were admitted by the same little gate to the grounds of the Élysée Palace, by the authority of the President's *chef de cabinet,* Monsieur Le Gall. The President's office was on the ground floor of the left wing of the palace, looking out upon a private garden. Beyond the presidential office and the private study, these quiet apartments ended in an elegant bedroom, used by Fèlix Faure on the frequent nights when he worked into the small hours, so that Madame Faure should not be disturbed by his late arrival.

On our occasional visits to Le Gall, neither Holmes nor I was admitted beyond an outer office, where the *chef de cabinet* guarded the entrance to the presidential suite. It was on 16 February that we were last there. Madame Steinheil was a little later than usual, arriving at about 5.30 P.M. to collect the papers that the President had been writing. We were received by Le Gall in his outer office a half-hour later. To that moment, there was no sign of anyone—man nor woman—shadowing the 'confidential secretary' who had been put under our care.

At the time of our arrival, Madame de Steinheil was already in the office or study of the presidential apartment, no doubt copying pages for the use of her patron. The President himself had just finished a conversation with a visitor who came out of the apartments, escorted by a chamberlain, taking his leave almost as soon as we had begun speaking to Le Gall. Even had I not seen his face in the newspaper photographs of the past few days, I should have guessed by his purple cassock and biretta that he was Cardinal Richard, Archbishop of Paris.

The purpose of the Cardinal's visit to the President was never revealed. As soon as His Eminence had left, however, Le Gall ushered Holmes and me to a waiting-room at one side. The door swung to but failed to catch, leaving us with a narrow aperture into the *chef de cabinet*'s office. A tall saturnine man in evening dress with a purple sash and the star of a royal order walked slowly past. On the far side of Le Gall's office, another door opened and closed. There was a murmur of voices. Holmes stretched in his arm-chair, took a pencil from his pocket and wrote something in his notebook.

'The Prince of Monaco,' he said quietly. 'This promises well, Watson. My information is that, for several months, His Serene Highness has been the go-between of the President and the Kaiser in the matter of Captain Dreyfus. Berlin is less threatened by the scandal than Paris but it would suit both parties to have the matter settled.'

Shortly after this, Le Gall or one of his assistants must have noticed that the waiting-room door was a little ajar. It was closed from outside, by whose hand we did not see. Whether the Prince of Monaco had left or the interview with the President continued was hidden from us.

In recollecting what followed, I believe it was about three-quarters of an hour that we had been waiting for our summons to escort Madame Steinheil back to the Impasse Ronsin. I was immersed in a Tauchnitz pocket-book and Holmes was reading the evening paper. Not a word passed between us until, without warning, Holmes threw the newspaper down and sprang to his feet.

'What in God's name was that, Watson?'

His face was drawn into an expression that mingled horror and dismay, a fearful look more intense than any other I can remember in the course of our friendship. The look in his eyes and the angle of his head assured me that Holmes, who had the most acute hearing of any man known to me, had caught something beyond my range.

'Do you not hear it, man? You must hear it!'

In two strides he was at the waiting-room door, which he flung open without ceremony. As he did so, I caught the shrill escalating screams of terror which rang through the private apartments of the President of France. They were a woman's screams.

Of Le Gall, there was no sign, though the fine double doors of white and gold that led to the President's office stood open. After so much talk of traitors and assassination, you may imagine what my thoughts were. The screams stopped for an instant, only to be resumed with greater urgency. They were not cries of pain but shrieks of unbridled fear. Perhaps, then, we should be in time to prevent whatever was threatened.

Holmes strode through the presidential office with the red buttoned leather of its chairs and the walnut veneer of the desk. Beyond that, the single door to the private study swung lightly in the draught. The curtains were still open. Outside, in the private garden, thin snow drifted down through the lamplight on to the lawns and formal paths. There was no one in the study itself but the far door opened into a small book-lined lobby. This lobby framed a further pair of doors—again in white and gold—which guarded the boudoir of the presidential suite. Those doors were closed and Le Gall stood facing them, pushing with his arms out and hands spread wide, as if seeking some means to force his way through. The shrieks, which now redoubled, were coming from the bedroom itself. I thought I heard the word 'Assassin!' with its French emphasis and pronunciation.

Holmes pushed the *chef de cabinet* aside, for had we left it to Le Gall he would never have broken open the locked doors. My friend's right foot rose and he crashed the heel of his boot into the ornamental lock. The double doors shuddered but held. Holmes took a pace back and again smashed the heel of his boot into the fastening. One of the two doors burst open and flew back against the inner wall with a crack. Holmes was first through the opening,

Le Gall after him. I brought up the rear with Holmes already calling out, 'Here, Watson! As quickly as ever you can!'

I stood in the doorway and saw before me such a sight as I hope never to see again.

VI

The tangled bodies in their nakedness were like nothing so much as a detail from some canvas depicting a massacre. Fèlix Faure was a well-built man of the heavily handsome type. Approaching sixty years of age, he had a head that was broad and tall, pale blue eyes, and a long moustache. He lay face down, naked as he was born, the gross bulk of him sprawling and slack in a manner that meant only one thing to me. Under him, trapped by his weight, without a shift or a stitch upon her, lay Marguerite Steinheil. There were spots of blood upon her face and shoulders which had come from his nose or mouth.

It was a horrible and yet, in its way, a commonplace tableau to a medical man. The tragedy of an old lover and a young mistress, cerebral congestion, apoplexy occurring in the excitement of some venereal spasm, is a textbook fact that needs no moral commentary here. I reached Fèlix Faure in time to detect a pulse that faded under my touch. In the moment of his seizure, the dying man had clenched his fingers in the young woman's hair, adding to her terror beyond measure. With some caution, I straightened the fingers one by one. Holmes and I turned the dead President on to his back. Le Gall snatched a dressing-gown from the closet and wrapped Madame Steinheil in it. She stood before us, still crying out hysterically, until there was a crack like a pistol as Holmes slapped her across the face.

Le Gall's hand was on the bell.

'No!' shouted Holmes. 'Wait!' Thereupon he took command of the situation while the *chef de cabinet* did his bidding. 'Get this young woman dressed!'

It was easier said than done. Without going to indelicate lengths of description, I can record that Madame Steinheil had been wearing a corset, which few women could put on again without the assistance of a ladies' maid. So it was that she was helped into her outer clothes, the rest being bundled into a valise.

'Touch nothing, Watson, until I get back! Nothing!'

With that, Holmes led the poor trembling courtesan out by a side entrance into the snow. I watched them cross the lawn to the little gate, with Le Gall following. On the *chef de cabinet*'s authority, the private gate at the Avenue de Marigny was opened and Madame Steinheil was put into the cab, which had been previously ordered to wait for her, with directions to the driver to proceed directly to the Impasse Ronsin.

In my friend's absence, I had found a nightshirt in the armoire. Between us, we managed to draw it over the head of the corpse and impart some decency to the mortal remains of the late Félix Faure.

'Monsieur!' Holmes spun round on Le Gall. 'Have the goodness to find a priest. Any priest! The Madeleine will be your nearest church.'

Le Gall was like a man in a stupor.

'No,' he said. 'There is no purpose. The President is dead and formalities must follow their course.'

'Formalities!' Holmes snapped at him, like a man waking a dreamer. 'Do you not see that there is enough scandal in all this to have a revolution on the streets of Paris before tomorrow night? That is where formalities will get you! Find the first priest that you can and tell him President Faure is dying!'

Badly shaken though he was, the *chef de cabinet* went out. In five minutes Holmes and I had drawn the sheets over the body and Félix Faure lay on his back, his head on the pillow and his eyes closed. Holmes paced the room, looking here and there, as if for some lost clue to explain the tragedy. But the explanation lay only in the medical textbooks.

'Here, I think!' he said presently, picking up a small ochre-coloured bottle from the dressing-table. 'What, my friend, do you make of this?'

As he held it before me, I could read only another parable of human frailty and old men's folly. There was little doubt that Félix Faure had taken a philtre of some kind which he hoped would aid his failing powers where women were concerned and which surely was the precipitating cause of his death. I thought, but did not say so, that he might have taken one of the capsules before the visit of the Prince of Monaco interrupted his intentions and had then taken another following it. For a man in his condition, it had been a most dangerous dose. Holmes took a small bag from his pocket and carefully dropped the bottle into it.

'It will not do, Watson, to leave such a thing where it may be found. The poor fellow is dead; let that be enough.'

Though little more than five minutes had passed, Le Gall was back with a young priest in a cassock, a prison chaplain who had been passing the main entrance of the palace on the Rue du Faubourg St Honoré as the *chef de cabinet* hurried towards the Madeleine. A little overawed by the magnificence of the death-chamber, the young chaplain murmured the phrases of absolution over the President's remains.

'Now,' said Holmes to Le Gall, 'you will have the goodness to send for a doctor and for Madame Faure, as quickly as possible. My colleague and I will take our leave by the gate into the Avenue de Marigny.'

Le Gall, in his confusion and grief, promised that no reward we might ask was too great for having averted a scandal that would surely have led to civil disturbance and bloodshed. Even as matters stood, the Paris newspapers were not long in circulating a rumour that the President had met his death through the murderous cunning of a Judith or a Delilah employed by the fanatics of Captain Dreyfus.

'I will take no fee and no reward,' said Holmes, 'unless it be a trivial souvenir of a great man.'

'Whatever you wish is yours,' Le Gall insisted.

With great delicacy, my friend lifted a little box of pale rose-coloured Sèvres *porcelaine tendre*, an exquisite thing no more than two inches square that might have been a snuff-box.

'Is that all?' the *chef de cabinet* asked, embarrassed by so slight a gift.

'Yes,' said Holmes quietly. 'That is all. And now I think it best that, so far as we are concerned, we should leave Paris and this matter should be at an end.'

VII

So it seemed to be. There were riots by an unthinking mob, encouraged in the right-wing press, who accused the *Dreyfusards* of murdering their President, but there was no revolution. Fèlix Faure was mourned and buried by the better part of his compatriots with a dignity befitting his rank. Dreyfus himself was still condemned to remain worse than a slave for life in the tropical hell of Devil's Island. Marguerite Steinheil and the 'Secret History of the Third Republic' were two subjects which Holmes swore he never wished to hear mentioned again.

We gave our notice to the Hôtel Lutétia next day. As Holmes said several times, we had been made fools of by Madame Steinheil and had wasted valuable words on Professor Bertillon. Worst of all, the death of Félix Faure in the arms of his young mistress had perhaps dashed all hope among those who sought justice for Dreyfus. As our last resort, Holmes swore that nothing would do but he must go to Berlin and confront Colonel Schwartzkoppen. He would have confronted Kaiser Wilhelm himself, in his present mood, had he been granted an audience.

Two days later, on a dull February morning, our train pulled out from the Gare de L'Est, among the departure boards for Vienna and Prague, Munich and Berlin, under the long span of the shabby Rue Lafayette with its workshops and warehouses. Holmes stared out at the open ironwork of bridges that carried the grey streets of La Chapelle and La Villette above the broad expanse of railway tracks. In the grey light of winter we entered a canyon below tall stone houses with peeling shutters and mansard roofs, the darkness of a tunnel enclosed us.

'And this,' said Holmes at last, 'is to be our reward. Let it take a place among our curios, Watson.'

He held lightly between his finger and thumb the little box of Sèvres porcelain. In his other hand lay several capsules, the contents of that box.

'The evil potion,' I said without thinking.

'Not the most evil, however,' Holmes remarked. 'Not evil enough, perhaps, to kill a man. Think how easy even that would be to someone who knew the weakness of Félix Faure and had the opportunity of access to him. Empty capsules may be bought from any pharmacy. They may be filled with anything, from stimulants for an old man's lust to the most deadly and instant poison. Dr Neill Cream, the Lambeth Poisoner seven years ago, was just such a killer.'

'You think she poisoned him?'

He shook his head. 'No, Watson. Not she. But what might not a man with evil in his mind do if he could fill one capsule with an instant poison and slip it among the others? Sooner or later his victim would take it. And when that victim was found dead with his mistress, as Félix Faure was found dead, would not his loyal servants act just as we have done? Who would demand an autopsy upon the body of a dead president in those circumstances? We believed that he had died from a foolish act of his own which would not bear the light of public scrutiny. Suppose it was worse—suppose it was poison. A murderer would scarcely need to cover his tracks, when we were eager to do it for him.'

'Then it truly was his assassination that she feared!'

Holmes shrugged. 'She had better fear for herself. If Félix Faure died by the hands of his enemies, the documents which those enemies feared are now in the hands of Marguerite Steinheil. I do not think, Watson, that I should care greatly to be in that young woman's shoes in the years to come.'

VIII

I thought that it was one of our worst defeats, complete as it was rare. We had lost both battles with Alphonse Bertillon. We had failed to save Félix Faure from destruction or self-destruction, whichever it might be. We had not been the triumphant saviours of Alfred Dreyfus. Even Colonel Schwartzkoppen returned the card of Sherlock Holmes with his pencilled regrets that official duties in Pomerania made a personal meeting impossible. Sometimes, in the months that followed, I wondered what had become of Félix Faure's 'Secret History of France under the Third Republic'. Did it ever exist? What did that matter now? The man to whom it would have been a shield was dead. His enemies might be uneasy at its existence but they would surely hesitate to commit murder as the price of its destruction. Though I read the daily news from Paris, I did not hear that Madame Steinheil had been murdered.

So we returned to London and I indulged Holmes so far as not to mention either Alphonse Bertillon or Marguerite Steinheil unless he did so first, which he did seldom and briefly. Yet the next twelve months saw a remarkable advance in the fortunes of Alfred Dreyfus. His persecutors had overreached themselves by arresting and imprisoning Colonel Picquart, Holmes's friend who was now head of counter-intelligence in the Deuxième Bureau. Picquart's crime had been to question the authorship of the treasonable letter to Colonel Schwartzkoppen.

Of the two men who had fabricated evidence against Captain Dreyfus, Colonel Hubert Henry cut his own throat with a razor on the day after his arrest. Lemercier-Picard anticipated his own arrest by hanging himself in his room. Among such events, the entire French civil judiciary demanded a retrial of Dreyfus, a call that the new President, Émile Loubet, dared not resist. At Rennes, to which he was brought haggard and white-haired from five years on Devil's Island, a military tribunal confirmed the guilt of Dreyfus but set him free. Frail but resolute, he promised to fight them until his innocence was recognised.

Time passed and Alfred Dreyfus won his last battle. His ally, Colonel Picquart, set free and vindicated, was about to become Minister of War in a new government led by Georges Clemenceau as Prime Minister, a man who had also demanded justice for Dreyfus.

'I fear,' said Holmes, laying down his morning *Times*, in which he had just read the news, 'that our friend Picquart will find nothing in the files to incriminate the persecutors of Alfred Dreyfus. The defeated party will have gone through the secret papers at the Élysée Palace and elsewhere with a fine comb to remove and destroy whatever might be used against them. More's the pity.'

Had he really not seen it?

'You forget the secret history,' I said gently. 'That is not in the Élysée Palace but, if it exists, in the Impasse Ronsin.'

He sighed, shook the paper out, and returned to it. The name of 'that young woman' was not mentioned after all.

'Yes,' he said quietly, 'I daresay you are right. Perhaps the Impasse Ronsin is where that strange concoction of fact and imagination had best remain.'

It was a matter of mere days before the wire came from Marguerite Steinheil, imploring the assistance of 'the great detective'. She was in the prison of St Lazare, awaiting trial for her life, on charges of having murdered both her mother and her husband on the night of 30 May. Had this been a fictional romance, I could not have believed such a thing. Next day, however, a brief report by the Paris correspondent of *The Times* assured us of its truth.

I quite expected that Holmes would decline to leave Baker Street. However, he withdrew to his room and I was presently serenaded by the sounds of cupboards and drawers being opened and closed, luggage being thrown about. I went to the door. Without question, he was packing all that he might need for Paris.

'You are going?' I said.

'We are going, Watson. By the night ferry.'

'After the manner in which she made fools of us?'

'She?' He straightened up and looked at me. 'She?'

'Marguerite Steinheil.'

'Madame Steinheil!' Holmes raised his voice loud enough to bring Mrs Hudson quite half-way up the stairs. 'I care nothing for Madame Steinheil! They may guillotine her tomorrow at dawn, so far as that goes!'

'Then why?'

He opened a drawer and took out a shirt, each movement tense with exasperation.

'Why?' he looked at me grimly. 'To seize an opportunity which will in all probability never present itself again. To settle a final account with Professor Alphonse Bertillon. That is why!'

With that he slammed shut the lid of the case and locked it.

IX

After all that, it was sweet as a nut, as the saying goes—one of the neatest of conclusions. Best of all, Holmes won the contest against Bertillon: game, set and match.

The Impasse Ronsin behind the shabby Rue de Vaugirard had changed by scarcely a brick or a pane of glass since we last saw it. The double murder had occurred on the night of 30–31 May. On the following morning, Rémy Couillard, the Steinheils' valet, entered the upper floor, where Marguerite Steinheil, her husband, and her mother—Madame Japy—slept in three separate rooms. The valet found the rooms silent and ransacked. Adolphe Steinheil lay dead in the doorway of his bathroom, kneeling forward as if he had died without a struggle as the cord was tightened round his throat. Madame Japy, the mother, had died upon her bed. The old woman had been gagged with such violence that a broken false tooth was found in the back of her throat. It was certain that she must have suffocated before the noose was drawn round her neck.

Marguerite Steinheil was found tied to her bed, bound and gagged but still alive. She told a confused story of having woken in the night to be confronted by three men and a woman in black ecclesiastical habits of some kind, the woman and one of the men having red hair.

'Where is your family's money?' they demanded. 'Where are your jewels? Tell us or we will kill you and them as well!'

Pleading with them not to harm her or the other members of her family, Madame Steinheil had told them. Until the valet came next morning, she lay on the bed with her wrists tethered above her head in such a way that at every attempt to move her hands the rope drew tighter about her throat. Her ankles were bound to the foot of the bed. Cotton wool had been forced into her mouth to silence her. Though she had heard Madame Japy's cries as the intruders gagged the old woman, she did not know until the morning that her mother and her husband were dead.

Madame Steinheil was not believed by the officers who investigated the crime. Her prosecutors insisted that she had first murdered her husband, then her mother, and had finally ransacked the house and tied herself up to support the story of a burglary. The motive was a wish to be rid of a weak-willed, improvident husband and to marry one of her numerous admirers.

Holmes glanced down the *résumé* of the evidence as we stood in the office of Gustave Hamard, Director of Criminal Investigations, opposite the monumental façade of the Palais de Justice, where Madame Steinheil appeared before her judges.

'The prosecution theory in that form may be disposed of at once,' Holmes said quietly to the French detective. 'I grant that Madame Steinheil might have strangled her husband, though the difference in their build and physical strength makes it unlikely. Why, though, would she first gag her mother, if her intention was to strangle the old lady?'

'Only the prisoner can tell us,' Hamard said sceptically.

Holmes shook his head. 'Consider this. The valet who released Madame Steinheil next morning did not undo the ropes. He cut them. The knots are still to be seen. She had been tied once or twice with a galley-knot. True, she might have tied herself to the bed but a galley-knot would be impossible in such places. It is, in any case, rarely used except among sailors or horse-dealers.'

'It would require a single accomplice,' Hamard said, 'who, in return for a reward, tied up the young woman and disposed of the other two. What better than to tie up Madame Japy and gag her, so that she might later be a witness to seeing a stranger in the house? Her suffocation appears to have been an accident.'

Again Holmes shook his head. 'It will not do, monsieur. If Madame Japy's death was not intended, why was the cord tightened round her throat? The poor old woman could not be permitted to live. It argues that at least one intruder was someone whom she might recognise and identify.'

For a week or two, the Steinheil murder case had threatened to cause almost as much disorder in Paris as the Dreyfus affair. One half of the city swore that Marguerite Steinheil was the victim of robbery, conspiracy, and worse. She had endured a night of terror, at the end of which the bodies of her husband and her mother were found lying in the other rooms. It was certainly true that four ecclesiastical costumes, identical to those in which she described her attackers, had been stolen from the property-room of the Théâtre Eden a few hours before the crime at the Impasse Ronsin. That in itself proved nothing.

The other half of Parisians thought her a notorious harlot who had paid villains as evil as herself to stage a make-believe robbery. The object was to murder her husband—of whom she was weary—so that she might make a better marriage. As for the pearls and other jewels, which Madame Steinheil claimed to have lost, they had never existed.

Holmes cared nothing for the jewels, whether they existed or not. There was another item which the valet and other servants testified to having seen in the house before the fatal night and never again after it. It was a package wrapped in brown paper and sealed. On its top was written the name of Marguerite Steinheil and the instruction, 'Private Papers. To be burnt unopened after my death'. Here and there the brown paper was torn and it was possible to see the corners of envelopes which the wrapping contained. This bundle of envelopes was, to all appearances, the secret history of the Third Republic and lay in a concealed wall-cupboard of Adolphe Steinheil's studio.

Madame Steinheil now swore that these were not the papers that might cause such embarrassment to the enemies of Félix Faure but a 'dummy' package to deceive burglars. The papers from the Élysée Palace were hidden in a secret drawer of her writing-desk.

There was never so inconclusive an investigation for the police. Dr Balthazard, forensic detective of the Sûreté, found nothing that would prove or disprove Madame Steinheil's story. Of the famous history of the Third Republic no more was said. As the judicial examination of Madame Steinheil began, it was widely doubted whether such a history existed—or had ever existed.

Professor Alphonse Bertillon used every means of scientific investigation at his disposal to identify those who had been at the Impasse Ronsin on the night of the crime. Despite his reservations over the technique, his assistants 'fingerprinted' every room and every article of furniture in the house. It was all to no effect. To be sure, there were fingerprints by the dozen in every room, and they were photographed and catalogued. Unfortunately, the system had been so neglected by the Sûreté, that it was impossible to check the identity of such prints without great difficulty.

Holmes was on better terms with Gustave Hamard, whose authority allowed my friend to tread where the great Bertillon had gone before, to examine the interior of the house in the Impasse Ronsin on behalf of his client. He had no wish to consult Madame Steinheil in prison. If ever there was a case to be decided on cold and precise points of evidence—away from the hysteria of the mob and the suspect—it was this. Hamard had shrugged his broad shoulders at the futility of further examination but granted the request.

By the time that Holmes finished his examination, the trial of Marguerite Steinheil on charges of murder had begun at the Palais de Justice. The final leaves of autumn fell from the birch trees of the Île de la Cité, which we had last seen breaking into a green haze of spring across the Boulevard du Palais.

A few days later, Sherlock Holmes and Alphonse Bertillon faced each other across the desk of Gustave Hamard. The duel that Holmes had promised was about to begin, with Hamard and myself as seconds. My companion took from his pocket a photographic card upon which the ridges and whorls of an index finger were plainly seen. He handed it to Bertillon, who shrugged and pulled a face.

'There were hundreds, Mr Holmes,' said the great anthropologist, taking off his glasses, brushing his eyes with the back of his hand, and replacing the spectacles. He took a page of fingerprints which was lying on the desk and ran his eye down it, looking aside from time to time at the image Holmes had given him.

'Try number eighty-four,' Holmes suggested whimsically.

Bertillon picked up another card and glanced down it.

'Indeed, monsieur,' he said affably, 'you are quite correct. The print of this finger was found a number of times, among many many others, in the studio of Adolphe Steinheil. It was not found, I see, in the rooms of the upper floor where the crimes were committed. The studio was entered by so many visitors that it can count for little, I fear.'

'Forgive me, monsieur,' said Holmes quietly, 'but the fingerprint upon the card I have handed you did not come from the studio of Adolphe Steinheil, nor from anywhere else in the Impasse Ronsin.'

'Then where?' asked Bertillon sharply.

The voice of Sherlock Holmes was almost a purr of satisfaction.

'From the presidential apartments of the Élysée Palace on the sixteenth of February 1899, at a time when the late Félix Faure had just received the last rites. You will recall that you and I were at that time exchanging views on the use, or otherwise, of such prints. Having received as a present from Monsieur Faure's family a small pill-box of Sèvres ware—a charming thing—I was boorish enough to subject it to dusting with silver nitrate and exposure to a fixed-range Kodak, a contraption of my own.'

Bertillon went pale. Hamard spoke first. 'Who do you say this print comes from?'

'The Comte de Balincourt,' said Holmes smoothly, 'alias Viscount Montmorency, alias the Margrave of Hesse, sometime assistant chamberlain at the Élysée Palace—under what name I know not, as yet. Dismissed after the passing of President Faure for some trivial dishonesty. A dozen witnesses will tell you that, not a few weeks before his murder, Adolphe Steinheil began a commission to paint in his studio a portrait of the Comte de Balincourt in hunting costume.'

Hamard's eyes narrowed. 'Do you say, Mr Holmes, that Steinheil knew such a man as Balincourt?'

'Not only knew him, Monsieur, but was heard in the studio discussing with him Félix Faure and the secret history of the Third Republic. There is a fingerprint, matching exactly the one I have shown you, on the door of a casually concealed wall-cupboard in the studio, where Balincourt was told that the papers of that secret history were kept. A package of papers remained there until the night of the two murders, inscribed with the name "Marguerite Steinheil" and with instructions that it was to be burned unopened upon her death. On the morning following the crimes, that cupboard was empty. The scratches on the mirror of its lock indicate that it was opened by a little force and a good deal of fraud.'

'Then the trial must be adjourned!' Hamard said. 'My God! What if all this were to come to light and she had already been condemned?'

'And where,' interrupted Bertillon, 'is the Comte de Balincourt?'

Holmes shrugged. 'At the bottom of the Seine, I imagine, or the bed of the River Spree, depending on whether his political masters are in Paris or Berlin. I do not think he will bother us again.'

'The papers!' Hamard said furiously. 'The manuscript! Where is that? Think of what it might do to the politics of France—to the peace of Europe!'

'The history of the Third Republic is quite safe,' Holmes said coolly.

Hamard looked at him with narrowed eyes. 'The cupboard was opened and the manuscript stolen, was it not?'

Holmes shook his head. 'Madame Steinheil trusted no one, least of all the discretion of her weak-willed and garrulous husband. She let it be known in the household that the wall-cupboard contained the manuscript and the secret drawer of her writing-desk held a dummy package. Alfred Steinheil did not know this when he boasted to the President's former chamberlain. In truth, it was the dummy package to which he unwittingly directed the man. After the blackest of crimes, the Comte de Balincourt handed his masters a bundle of old newspapers and blank pages. You may imagine how they will have rewarded him.'

If an Anarchist bomb had gone off in the tree-lined Boulevard du Palais and blown the windows out, Hamard and Bertillon could scarcely have looked more aghast.

'You say Balincourt is a murderer?' Bertillon demanded. 'Yet the same fingerprint was found nowhere upstairs.'

'Not for one moment did I suppose he had committed murder. I think it likely that he entered the upper rooms and that he was accidentally seen by Madame Japy. The poor old woman would have recognised him from his portrait sittings, for which reason she was put to death. Balincourt or his masters had hired men who would not scruple to take that precaution for their own safety as well as his.'

'A little convenient is it not?' said Hamard sceptically.

Holmes took from his pocket three more photographic prints.

'You will not know these fingerprints, for I believe they are unique to my own little collection. However, I shall be surprised if you do not find photographs of the three men in your Office of Judicial Identification. Baptistin is a young and violent criminal. Marius Longon, "The Gypsy", is a skilled and ruthless thief. Monstet de Fontpeyrine is a Cuban, a stage magician and a specialist in hotel robberies. He was seen last autumn, loitering in the Rue de Vaugirard, near the Impasse Ronsin. From there he was followed to the Metro station of Les Couronnes, where he met the other two men, a young woman with red hair, and a third man who is now identified as the Comte de Balincourt.'

'You know where these other men are?'

'In the same deep water as Balincourt, I should imagine,' said Holmes dismissively. 'I scarcely think you will hear from them either.'

'And the papers of the Third Republic?' Hamard persisted.

'Ah,' said Holmes with an air of false regret. 'They are where they will do no harm. I regret, however, that it is not in my power to produce them.'

'You will be ordered to produce them!' Hamard shouted.

Holmes was moved invariably by poverty, misfortune, desperation in others, never by browbeating.

'Those papers, monsieur, are essential to my client's defence. You have my word that, as yet, they have been seen by no other eyes than my own. After she is acquitted, which on the evidence I have produced to you is what justice must demand, I can promise you that these documents will trouble the world no more. If, after all that has been said in this room, she is condemned to execution—worse, if she *goes* to the guillotine—I will stop at nothing to see every word of them published in the leading newspapers of every capital.'

Gustave Hamard strode from the room and we heard his voice raised as he gave instructions to his subordinates. The trial of Madame Steinheil was adjourned early that day on the far side of the Boulevard du Palais. Two days later, its result was to be published across the world. After midnight, in the small hours of 14 November 1909, the jury that had retired to condemn Marguerite Steinheil was summoned into court again. De Valles, the president of the tribunal, imparted certain instructions to the jurors in the lamplit courtroom, his voice fraught with an anxiety that he had failed to show in the earlier stages of the proceedings. They retired and returned again to acquit Madame Steinheil of all the charges against her.

So much is history, as is the change in Professor Alphonse Bertillon's view on the usefulness of fingerprints. During the day or two left to us in Paris, he became almost a friend to Sherlock Holmes. The two men were now disposed to regard their past differences as something of a joke, each assuring the other that he had never really said the things that were reported—or that, if he had said them, he had never really meant them.

We came back to Baker Street by the night ferry to Charing Cross and arrived home in good time for lunch. That evening, as I watched Holmes arranging some experiment or other upon the familiar stained table, I brought up the subject that had lain between us for the last few days.

'If you are right about Balincourt, Holmes . . .'

'I am seldom wrong in such matters, Watson,' he said gently, without looking up.

'If that man tampered with the box of capsules in the Élysée Palace . . .'

'Quite.' He frowned and took a little brush to dust a surface with white powder.

'Then it was not an old man's lust that destroyed him, though it gave the opportunity.'

'Quite possibly.'

'Balincourt or one of their spies knew that Faure was about to change his policy—that he would turn to the *Dreyfusards!* That he would order a retrial! She had persuaded him.'

'I daresay,' he murmured, as if scarcely hearing me.

'It was not a love philtre but an instant poison, after all, disguised among the other capsules!'

He looked up, the aquiline features contracting in a frown of irritation.

'You will give me credit for something, I hope! My first analysis in Paris was confirmed by a more searching examination here. What was in the remaining capsules was a homoeopathic quantity of canthar. They call such pills "Diavolini". The truth is that their contents would not even stimulate passion in a man, let alone kill him. Their effect, if any, is entirely upon the mind.'

He returned to his studies.

'Then we witnessed it, after all!' I exclaimed.

'Witnessed what, my dear fellow?'

'The assassination of the President of France by those who had most to fear if Dreyfus were found innocent!'

'Oh, yes,' said Holmes, as if it were the most ordinary thing in the world. 'I had never supposed otherwise. However, it would not do for you to give that to the world as yet, Watson, in one of your little romances. Sleep on it a little, my old friend. Speaking of romances, there is one that requires our attention without delay.'

He took a bundle of papers from a Gladstone bag and broke it open. A pile of well-filled foolscap envelopes slithered out randomly across the table.

'I have made my promise to Gustave Hamard,' he said. 'Madame Steinheil has paid me in kind. All debts are now discharged.'

He took the first sheaf of papers, on which I just had time to catch sight of a few names and phrases in a neat plain hand. 'General Georges Boulanger . . . Colonel Max von Schwartzkoppen, Königgrätzstrasse, Berlin . . . Pensées sur le suicide du Colonel Hubert Henry . . . Les crimes financières de Panama . . . L'affaire de Fashoda . . . Colonel Picquart et le tribunal . . .' An envelope lay addressed in black ink to Major Count Ferdinand Walsin-Esterhazy, Rue de la Bienfaisance, 27, Paris 8°.

The fire in the grate blazed whiter as the first pages burned. Holmes turned to take another envelope and emptied it. There fluttered down to the floor a note on the stationery of the Italian Embassy in the Rue de Varenne, inviting Colonel Schwartzkoppen to dine with Colonel Panizzardi. He scooped it up and dropped it into the flames. The fire blazed again and a shoal of sparks swept up the chimney. For half an hour, the secret ashes of the Third Republic dissolved in smoke against the frosty starlight above the chimney-pots of Baker Street.

The Case of the Blood Royal

I

The adventure of 'The Final Problem' formed a concluding narrative to *The Memoirs of Sherlock Holmes*. In the following case, its readers may find a prologue to that fateful and famous death-struggle at the Reichenbach Falls. They will also find an epilogue, twenty years later, with which I now begin.

Sherlock Holmes was not present on 1 February 1911 to see justice done. His part in the investigation had ended at the Falls of Reichenbach and it was judged best that he should now remain concealed from public scrutiny. We were assembled in the Lord Chief Justice's Court at the Royal Courts of Justice, a large wainscotted chamber of oak carved in the Gothic fashion with curtains and hangings in dark green, the Royal Arms in bold relief. Even had Holmes wished to observe the trial of Edward Mylius, he might have found himself too busy at that moment with another matter. He was so greatly trusted by Lord Stamfordham and the Royal Household that he was more urgently engaged in an attempt to obtain from Daisy, Countess of Warwick, the love letters of the late King Edward VII, written to her ladyship when that monarch was still Prince of Wales. It was a delicate and expensive negotiation but my friend succeeded in averting another palace scandal.

Upon the judicial bench, in wig and scarlet robe, sat the Lord Chief Justice, Lord Alverstone. Below him the Attorney-General, Sir Rufus Isaacs, was in attendance for the Crown. On the bench behind Sir Rufus was the Home Secretary, Mr Winston Churchill, accompanied by Sir John Simon, then Solicitor-General and our future Lord Chancellor. Mrs Churchill and a number of other ladies sat in the Judge's Gallery. I was one of the few on the public benches, such was the success of the government in preventing advance information about the nature of this hearing. No indictment was laid before a magistrate or presented to a grand jury. The case was brought directly by the Attorney-General, whose office requires no such preliminaries in charges of this sort.

We were gathered almost *in camera* for a Special Jury to determine an issue of the gravest consequence. Whether Our Sovereign Lord, King George the Fifth of Great Britain and Ireland, Defender of the Faith, Emperor of India, had been guilty of the wilful crime of bigamy on the island of Malta in the year 1890, as defined by the Offences Against the Person Act 1861.

Few people who lived during the years from 1890 until 1911 escaped some rumour of this scandal. Until 1892, when his elder brother the Duke of Clarence died suddenly at the age of twenty-eight, Prince George had not been in the most direct line of succession to the British throne. It was still occupied by his grandmother, Queen Victoria. After her, Prince George's father was to succeed as Edward VII. Then it was supposed that the Duke of Clarence would succeed as elder son and after him any children he might have. These last hopes were cruelly ended on 14 January 1892 by the death of the young Duke of Clarence. George, 'The Sailor Prince', who had looked forward only to the life of a naval officer, became heir apparent to his father.

In the following year, 1893, Prince George was betrothed to his dead brother's fiancée, Princess May of Teck, and the couple were married a few weeks later. Yet even before the day of the betrothal passed, on 3 May, the *Star* newspaper reported that the future King had already contracted a morganatic marriage in 1890 or thereabouts with the daughter of a British naval officer. The *Star* was a mere rag of a newspaper which had risen to fame by its salacious reporting of the Whitechapel Murders in 1888 and its invention of the vulgar sobriquet 'Jack the Ripper'. However, its charges against the future King had been made and were not to be ignored by the gossips.

Prince George himself had been twenty-five years old in 1890, if that was the year alleged, and commander of the first-class gunboat HMS *Thrush*, sailing via Gibraltar to the West Indies. The ship was laid up at Gibraltar for more than two weeks, awaiting the torpedo boat that she was to tow across the Atlantic. It can do no harm now to reveal that the unnamed naval officer whose daughter's name was associated with the future king's was Admiral Sir Michael Culme-Seymour, who commanded the Mediterranean Squadron. Sir Michael had also been Naval Aide-de-Camp to Queen Victoria for five years while Prince George was a child. There were two Culme-Seymour daughters, Laura who was to die in 1895, and Mary, who married Captain Trevelyan Napier in 1899.

The story was taken up by the press and aired from time to time in *Reynolds News*, the Brisbane *Telegraph*, and the *Review of Reviews*. Worse still, however, was the allegation arising from the reports that, before Prince George's betrothal to Princess May, two children were born of this former union.

Upon the death of King Edward in 1910 and Prince George's accession to the throne as King George V, it might have been hoped that such gossip would die of repetition. Quite the contrary. The embers were fanned again in the very weeks preceding the opening of the new King George's first parliament and the coronation ceremony itself. Holmes later showed me His Majesty's comment upon the allegation of a morganatic marriage. 'The whole thing is a damnable lie,' King George wrote in his forthright quarter-deck manner, 'and has been in existence now for over twenty years!'

The accused, who was called up to the dock on that winter morning in 1911, was one of many to repeat the story. However, he was surely the most deserving of the law's attention. Edward

Mylius was a thin saturnine man of thirty, dressed in black, who lived in Courtnell Street, Bayswater. He was the English editor of a republican magazine, the *Liberator*, published in the Rue St Dominique, Paris, by Mr Edward Holden James, a cousin of the famous American novelist. Mylius had denounced King George's coronation in an article entitled 'Sanctified Bigamy', which condemned the Church of England for its complicity in having knowingly wed a married man to Princess May and for preparing to crown the bigamist. A copy of the article was sent by its author to every Member of Parliament and the unsavoury matter was even raised in the House of Commons by Mr Keir Hardie and others. Mylius assured his readers that after a few years of his first secret marriage and the birth of two children, Prince George 'foully abandoned his true wife and entered into a sham and shameful marriage with a daughter of the Duke of Teck'.

During the winter of 1910 there had been much discussion among members of the government of Mr Asquith as to the advisability of prosecuting Mylius for a criminal libel on the monarch, this being by far the most scurrilous version of the story to be published. Mr Churchill, as Home Secretary, was most anxious to proceed against the 'buffoon', as he called him. Yet a prosecution for a criminal libel on the sovereign had not been brought since the worst days of King George IV in 1823. The Law Officers of the Crown advised the cabinet on 23 November of the danger that lay in giving courtroom publicity to Mylius and his story. If it were to be done none the less, they said, it had best be done quickly and quietly. He was arrested on 26 December, held to bail for £20,000, which he could not possibly find, and kept in strict confinement, allowing him no opportunity of communicating with the press before his trial.

The first that the public knew of the case was when they read in the newspapers of 2 February that the trial was over. It was stated in court and in the papers that neither King George nor the Culme-Seymour daughters had been in Malta in 1890. Sir Michael, though by now elderly and in poor health, gave evidence of this, as did his surviving daughter.

There was one moment when a chill touched my spine. Sir Rufus Isaacs, like a handsome dark-eyed eagle in wig and gown, was examining Mary Culme-Seymour—as I still call Mrs Napier. In answer to his question, she replied that she had never so much as met Prince George from 1879, when she was eight, until 1898, five years after his marriage to Princess Mary. It was not the truth and there was public proof of that! As Holmes and I had reason to know, not only had she met him but on one occasion she and Prince George had opened the dancing at a grand ball in Portsmouth Town Hall on 21 August 1891. Worse still, the fact had been reported at length in the *Hampshire Telegraph and Sussex Chronicle* at the time, for anyone who cared to read it! Happily for Sir Rufus Isaacs, this was not a newspaper that Mylius had seen. This untruth or slip of memory did not, of course, make Mary Culme-Seymour the wife of Prince George. At the same time, it might have opened the way for the accused man to dismiss her evidence, if only he had known of the error.

Mylius had refused to be represented by counsel. Instead he issued a most impudent subpoena which summoned King George to give evidence and to be cross-examined upon it! This device would have been outrageous, had it not been so foolish. The Attorney-General knew the law of the constitution, if Mylius did not. The sovereign cannot be summoned as witness in a court where he is the source of justice. It is true that Edward VII before coming to the throne gave evidence in the Mordaunt divorce case and in the Tranby Croft libel action, when one of his friends had cheated at baccarat in his presence. He did so as Prince of Wales, however, and not as monarch.

As the cold February evening drew in, Mylius endeavoured to justify the truth of his libel. He could not do so to the satisfaction of the jury, which took against him from the start. All day, Mr Churchill had sat behind Sir Rufus Isaacs, murmuring to him the questions that should be put to witnesses and, more importantly from the view of Holmes and myself, warning him of the answers that were not to be pursued. Mylius, of course, stuck to his story.

Thank God that, in one or two essentials, the scoundrel had got it wrong!

In that marble temple, which forms the lobby of the Central Criminal Court, I afterwards overheard Mr Churchill's comment to Sir Rufus Isaacs. A few minutes earlier, Edward Mylius had been taken down the steps of the Old Bailey dock, after the Lord Chief Justice had sentenced him to a year's imprisonment and a substantial fine. The smile of a portly cherub lit the Home Secretary's face.

'A man of that sort cannot resist the temptation to fight to the last ditch,' he said. 'It was as well for you, my dear Rufus, that the guttersnipe did not plead guilty and say he was only repeating what a dozen other newspapers had written already. Then you might have had to indict 'em all and we should have had the gravest constitutional crisis on our hands for the last fifty years.'

Sir Rufus Isaacs with his dark dignity stared unsmiling at his companion.

'The scoundrel has gone to prison, Winston,' he said suavely. 'That will be the end of him. To the people of this country, a man who goes to prison on a jury's verdict is a liar. He might publish the marriage certificate itself and they would not believe him now.'

'Well,' growled the Home Secretary cheerfully, 'we may all thank God for that!'

As the world knows, there was spite enough to come but the worst damage had been avoided. No incriminating papers of any kind could be produced by Mylius and his gang. The libeller served his year in prison and was released. He made his way to New York and there, beyond the reach of English law, he published his booklet, *The Morganatic Marriage of George V.* In these pages he described, as he had not done in court, how Prince George had been at Gibraltar from 9 June until 25 June 1890, with ample time to reach Malta and return, and how a Miss Culme-Seymour was at Marseilles at the same time.

By then, of course, it was too late. The wretched fellow had been branded as a liar and a criminal. Sir Rufus Isaacs was quite right in predicting that no one would listen to him now, even with the marriage certificate in his hand. I believe that only Holmes and I knew the entire truth of why that certificate could not be produced, even had it existed. Now the whole disagreeable business was to be eclipsed by the splendour of the coronation of King George V and Queen Mary in Westminster Abbey, by the spontaneous affection and loyalty shown all along the route by their subjects. That was answer enough to the libel.

On the February evening of the trial I took a cab back through the damp streets of Holborn and Marylebone to Baker Street. Sherlock Holmes had retired in 1903 to Fulworth, near Cuckmere Haven on the Sussex coast. I never thought it would last. After six months, he had wearied sufficiently of his bee-keeping to spend two or three days of almost every week in our old haunts at 221B Baker Street. Though I had been married for nine years, Mrs Watson's occasional absences from London on family matters, and the discovery of a most efficient *locum*, had led me increasingly to spend a few days at a time in our old diggings. Indeed, I had been a regular visitor ever since the mystery of the Irish Crown Jewels.

There had been little news of the Mylius case in the evening papers, for they were scarcely prepared for it. Holmes had spent the day in tedious negotiation with the representatives of Lady Warwick but he was impatient to hear the outcome of the trial. He stood with his pipe in his hand and nodded at every sentence in my account, looking up only when I described Mary Culme-Seymour's slip in the witness-box. When I revealed how it had all ended with the removal of Mylius to begin his sentence in Wormwood Scrubs, he let out a long sigh.

'It would not do for the truth to come out now, after all this time.'

'The truth of the marriage or the lack of it?'

He drew his pipe from his lips and shook his head.

'No, Watson. The truth of the part which you and I played in that intimate drama. I should not care for that to be known during the lifetime of either of us.'

In that observation, of course, he was quite right.

II

Such was the end of the story, the least sensational part of it. When this scandal of a bigamous marriage first threatened the British throne, we had confronted far worse men than Mylius, including one to whose existence I have only alluded obliquely in the past, under his alias of 'Charles Augustus Milverton'. Our adventure began soon after breakfast on a sunny morning more than twenty years before during one of my residences at Baker Street. All one's instincts were to chuck work for the day and walk under the elms and chestnuts of Regent's Park. For Holmes, of course, that would not do. I do not believe that my friend ever chucked work for a single day of his life.

We had come home late the previous evening from a Joachim recital at the St James's Hall, where Holmes had sat with his eyes closed and a faint smile upon his lips as the great virtuoso filled the concert room with the plaintive melodies of Beethoven's Violin Concerto. As we entered the sitting-room and I turned up the lamp upon the table, the light fell upon a card. It had been left by Sir Arthur Bigge, who had scribbled in pencil on the reverse his intention of returning at 11 A.M. next day. If it was impossible for us to receive him then, we should find him at the Army and Navy Club in St James's Square. The matter was of such urgency that he would not leave London until he had laid the facts of it before Sherlock Holmes. He did not need to be more precise, for all England knew that Sir Arthur Bigge, later Lord Stamfordham, was Assistant Private Secretary to Her Majesty the Queen.

Neither of us had the least idea what had brought the young courtier from Windsor. He was by then in his thirties, a man of good family with a distinguished career as a young subaltern in the Zulu Wars of 1879–80. Slight of build and unassuming in manner, his fair-haired military moustache betraying his former profession, he was to serve loyally as Assistant Private Secretary until 1901, when he became Private Secretary to the late Queen's grandson, first as Prince of Wales and then as King George V. He seemed to me always to have about him an inbred air of anxiety. It was particularly marked on the following morning when we received him in Baker Street. Sir Arthur looked from one to the other of us, as he sat forward in the fireside arm-chair, where we had installed him.

'Gentlemen,' he said quietly, 'what I have to say must be said to you both, though it is repugnant to talk of such things at all. I know something of our antagonists and I am sure that this is not a commission to be undertaken by any one man. Before you ask me why I have not gone to your friend Lestrade at Scotland Yard, let me tell you simply that a prince of the blood is threatened with blackmail—not without reason, if one can use that term for such a loathsome crime. I will also tell you that neither the Prime Minister, the Attorney-General, nor any member of the government has been approached.'

Holmes stood at the window, looking down at the immaculately polished coachwork of the waiting carriage with its two glossy bay geldings. Unlike Sir Arthur, he spoke without the least trace of astonishment that such a crime should now threaten the stability of the British throne.

'I assume you will not object, Sir Arthur, to telling us the name of the blackmailer. Will you also tell us the name of his intended victim? You have our word, of course, that neither will go beyond the walls of this room.'

Sir Arthur shrugged. 'You will have to know both, Mr Holmes. From my presence here, it will not surprise you to know that Her Majesty's grandson, Prince George, is the object of this villainy, though it touches his elder brother, the Duke of Clarence.'

'And your blackmailer?'

'I cannot tell you the name of the plot's contriver, Mr Holmes. I know only of the man who presents himself as the agent of it.'

'The agent?'

'The agent of one who says that he wishes well to Her Majesty. One who has in his—or her—hands stolen papers that would infallibly bring disgrace on the royal house. Letters from two royal sons to women of a certain kind. Part of Prince George's private diary.

The letters were easy to steal from their recipients—the diary easier than it should have been from a ship of the fleet. The client professes to be one who seeks only to ensure that the documents are never disclosed. To this end, he proposes to name a price!'

'A loyal subject!' Holmes exclaimed sardonically. 'Who represents this anonymous patriot?'

'You have perhaps heard of the name of Charles Augustus Howell?'

'Ah!' said Holmes reminiscently. 'I know of him well enough, Sir Arthur. I have yet to meet him privately but his name occurs frequently in my files.'

'What do you know of him, Mr Holmes?' For the first time there was a light of hope in Sir Arthur's eyes.

Holmes assumed a grimace of distaste. 'You might call him an interesting subject, in his way. He has been a diver for pearls and sheikh of a North African tribe. He is Anglo-Portuguese by birth and escaped from criminal vengeance in Portugal after a card-sharping scandal when he was just sixteen years old. Since then he has followed a career of dishonour with dedication. As a young man, he was implicated in Orsini's plot to assassinate the French Emperor. He defrauded Mr Ruskin, as a secretary, and endeavoured to facilitate the great man's meetings with very young girls.'

The lines of Sir Arthur Bigge's face relaxed and he said thankfully, 'Then you know the worst of him, Mr Holmes.'

'Indeed, Sir Arthur. Howell is known in artistic circles, in the pawnbroking trade, and in houses of ill fame, whether they be the stews of Seven Dials or the more genteel mansions of Regent's Park and St John's Wood. He is provider of pleasures to the dissolute, though he does not spare the innocent. Some time ago, he was Mr Rossetti's agent and marketed pictures ascribed to that artist which were rank forgeries. Among poets, he facilitated Mr Swinburne's perverse enjoyments at a house in Circus Road, St John's Wood, and then blackmailed Admiral and Lady Swinburne as the price of his silence. He defrauded Mr Whistler in the matter of a valuable Japanese cabinet, which he "borrowed" and then sold simultaneously to two different dealers, leaving the artist to reimburse them both. I could tell you more, Sir Arthur, but I trust that will suffice to assure you that my files contain a number of facts about Mr Howell that are otherwise known only to the criminal and his victims.'

Though our visitor breathed more freely, a look of concern betrayed his unease at the extent of such depravity.

'And what do you find his methods to be, Mr Holmes?'

Holmes walked from the window, sat in the opposite chair and chuckled.

'His methods are not subtle but they are apt to succeed. Mr Rossetti was unfortunate enough to lose his wife, the beautiful Elizabeth Siddal, from an overdose of chloral. He was so distraught that he buried a notebook—the only copy of his poems—in his dead wife's coffin. After several years, Howell insisted that the gesture was quixotic, a ruinous loss to literature. He persuaded Mr Rossetti to have his wife exhumed from Highgate Cemetery at night and the poems retrieved. It was not the least improper. The Home Secretary signed an exhumation order. Yet, to the grieving husband, it was a necessity at which he shuddered. Within weeks he heard from Mr Howell—'

'Did he?' Sir Arthur sat forward again, his face tight with anger. 'Did he, by any chance, hear that certain sensitive letters and documents had been pasted into Howell's album? Did he hear that his friend Howell had fallen on hard times and been obliged to pawn his possessions—including that album? Did he hear that Howell was unable to redeem the album for lack of funds? Was he told by this blackguard that he would be best advised to go to the pawnbroker and negotiate before the album went to auction? And when he did so, did the pawnbroker demand a king's ransom to prevent these confidential papers being sold at an auction without reserve?'

'It was the case in every detail,' Holmes said quietly. 'Howell works hand in glove with one or two villains in the pawnbroking trade. Mr Rossetti's letters contained nothing dishonourable, yet he would have died rather than see his private feelings about the woman he loved held up to public auction and the curiosity of the multitude. Six hundred pounds was, I believe, the price.'

Sir Arthur looked pale, though he was thinking of Prince George rather than Mr Rossetti.

'Could nothing be done to bring such a criminal to justice?'

Holmes spread out his bony fingers and studied them.

'I beg you will not underestimate him, Sir Arthur. He shows a practised cunning. No law is broken. A man who writes a letter to another makes that other the owner of the letter. The other may not, of course, publish it without the consent of its author. In this case, publication was unnecessary to Howell's scheme. Possession by whomsoever he chose to buy the letters was sufficient threat. Had Howell attempted blackmail, he would have gone to prison for fourteen years. But he might claim that urging his victim to go quickly to the confederate pawnbroker and purchase the letters was a friendly act, designed to forestall embarrassment.'

'Nothing was done?' Sir Arthur inquired fearfully.

'No,' said Holmes abruptly. 'Nor was anything done when the same trick was played upon Admiral and Lady Swinburne. Their son fell into a bohemian set and, among women at such houses as that in Circus Road, indulged passions that belong to the alienist rather than the moral censor. You have perhaps, Sir Arthur, noticed the works of the Baron von Krafft-Ebing in the past three or four years? The treatises on psycho-pathology of Cesare Lombroso or Démétrius Zambaco?'

Sir Arthur Bigge shook his head. It was evident from his expression that he had not the least idea what Holmes was talking about. The most arcane rituals of the Zulu tribes against whom he had fought as a young officer would have meant more to him than the great alienists whose works my friend had at his fingertips.

'No matter,' Holmes said casually. 'Suffice it to say that Admiral and Lady Swinburne paid a considerable sum for the album of letters describing Circus Road pleasures, which their conceited young son had addressed to his friend Howell. Howell pleaded again that poverty had forced him to pawn the correspondence and that he had not the money to redeem it before the sale must take place.'

There was a silence. Sir Arthur could scarcely bring himself to the point. At last he looked up and said, 'It is the same, and yet it is worse.'

'Because it is Prince George?'

Our visitor stared at the carpet and shook his head. 'Because Prince George will one day be King George.'

I interrupted and said, 'But surely his elder brother, the Duke of Clarence, will be king?'

'He would be,' Sir Arthur said quietly, 'if he lived. I shall have to tell you so much that I must add this as well. The Duke of Clarence suffers from a wasting disease. I would give all I possess to be proved wrong, gentlemen. Yet I doubt that the Duke will even outlive his own father. The plot against Prince George is a plot against our future king.'

History was to prove Sir Arthur right, for the Duke of Clarence died not long afterwards, while his grandmother was still queen. I did not dare ask what the wasting disease might be for so often, even in the case of great leaders like Lord Randolph Churchill, it proves to be syphilis contracted through youthful folly.

'I believe, Sir Arthur,' Holmes said gently, 'you must trust us with the nature of the plot.'

The royal secretary nodded. 'It is this, Mr Holmes. Howell claims first to have letters and documents which establish a marriage, contracted upon the island of Malta, between Prince George and the daughter of Admiral Sir Michael Culme-Seymour of the Mediterranean Fleet.'

To my astonishment, Holmes threw back his head and laughed in the heartiest manner that I had heard from him for a long time.

'Oh, he does, does he? I believe I know a little of the British constitution, Sir Arthur. In the first place, the Royal Marriages Act of 1772 would make such a union unlawful. Prince George may not marry without consent of the monarch until he is twenty-five. When he is over twenty-five, he may marry by giving a year's notice to the Privy Council and there being no objection from the Houses of Parliament within that period. Prince George is scarcely of an age to dispense with royal consent for a lawful marriage.'

Sir Arthur was briefly but gravely displeased.

'Had that been all, Mr Holmes, I should not have bothered to come to Baker Street or to trouble you in any way. Of course, Prince George denies that, having met Miss Laura or Miss Mary Culme-Seymour on the island of Malta, he eloped with her. Yet if this story is made public and believed—even half believed—how could he make a royal marriage later in the face of all mankind? If he did so, could he be crowned with the rest of the world believing that he had taken his solemn oath to Miss Culme-Seymour and fathered children by her? It will not do to talk of the Royal Marriages Act! That has no validity to the common sense of the human race. If this story were believed, he could not be crowned. That much is certain. If he were not crowned, under such circumstances, the very foundations of the monarchy and the state must tremble. Do you not see that?'

There was a slight, scarcely perceptible movement of Holmes's eyes and the laughter went out of them.

'You must forgive me, Sir Arthur, if I do not follow you in seeing why those foundations must tremble. Howell claims to have documents which would establish the existence of a morganatic marriage between Prince George and the daughter of Sir Michael Culme-Seymour. Whether there are grounds for believing this to be so is something I will not ask. Whatever the outcome, would you not be wise to call Howell's bluff without delay, to let him do his worst? The nation will forgive a young man who makes a romantic marriage. Let him abdicate his claim to the throne, if necessary. If neither Prince George nor the Duke of Clarence should be king, there are three sisters. Any one of them might be queen in her own right.'

'If it were as simple as that, Mr Holmes, I should not be here.' Again Sir Arthur gazed at the carpet. 'The lie of a secret marriage is but one of the items with which Howell or his client threatens us.

The others are not lies. Forgive me, I do not find this easy. Might I have a glass of water?'

The water was poured and our visitor continued.

'Prince George is at sea a good deal. When he returns to Portsmouth, there has been a young woman to whom he goes. One with whom he lives and one whom he knows, in the biblical sense. Howell's client has her name, the address of the house, the stolen letters, the times of the prince's arrivals and departures.'

'Indeed,' said Holmes thoughtfully. 'Yet Howell is a mere collector of documents, Sir Arthur, not the midnight spy.'

Sir Arthur brushed the objection aside. 'Whatever the prince's dealings with Miss Culme-Seymour may be or may not be, she is a respectable young woman of good family. It is not the case in Portsmouth, where he has chosen for himself and indiscreetly. Howell has the details from his client.'

'I think I should like to meet this client,' Holmes murmured.

'There is worse,' Sir Arthur continued. 'Prince George and the Duke of Clarence are named in another matter. It concerns a girl in St John's Wood whom they share between them. I cannot put it more delicately.'

'One moment, Sir Arthur!' Holmes raised his hand more gently than his voice. 'This sounds such a *canard* that I must break a rule I made for myself just now and ask you whether this is true—and how you know it can be true.'

'Because Prince George himself told me,' our courtier said sadly. 'He called her a clipper or some such name from yachting.'

'And Howell or his client knows all this? That the young woman in St John's Wood is shared by the royal brothers?'

'Yes, Mr Holmes, he knows it. And even if the story of the royal marriage is a *canard*, as you use the word, the other stories are true. If there is a public scandal and those are proved to be accurate, will not the world also believe the marriage story which cannot be so easily proved?'

I sat in my chair and listened to such things said and discussed calmly in the familiar surroundings of the Baker Street rooms. It was as if someone would come in presently and tell me it was all a joke or a misunderstanding. The heir to the throne, who was indeed king twenty years later, had confessed to having a paid woman with whom he slept in Portsmouth—where Miss Culme-Seymour was also to be found!—and to sharing the bed of a girl in St John's Wood with his own brother, which had more than a hint of incest. In all the time I had known Sherlock Holmes and in all the cases of crime and infamy whose details had been paraded before us, I had heard nothing to equal it.

This was far worse, however, because the sin of lust had opened the way to the crime of blackmail.

'There is another matter,' Sir Arthur said sadly, 'which touches the Duke of Clarence, though it does not involve Prince George.'

He sipped his water and seemed scarcely able to continue.

'You had best tell us all, Sir Arthur,' Holmes said kindly.

'Very well, Mr Holmes. You recall that the courts dealt lately with certain cases arising from a house in Cleveland Street, where unnatural vices had been practised. It touched both Lord Arthur Somerset of the royal stables and Lord Euston, though the latter was quite innocently associated with the place.'

'Something was reported by the papers,' Holmes said vaguely.

'It was not reported, Mr Holmes, that the Duke of Clarence was innocently at that place and was seen by witnesses. At the first hint of impropriety he left, as did Lord Euston. Indeed, Euston threatened to knock down the first man who spoke to him.'

'Then Howell knows all this?'

'A number of people know of it, Mr Holmes, but only Howell seeks to make something of it. The scandal that he threatens over the so-called marriage may come to nothing. Yet when he talks of the girl in Portsmouth, another in St John's Wood shared by the royal brothers, the fact that the Duke of Clarence—however innocently—was in that house in Cleveland Street, he talks of what is true.'

Holmes shrugged. 'Then you had better buy from the scoundrel whatever papers he possesses at whatever price he asks.'

Sir Arthur Bigge shook his head. 'It is not so simple, Mr Holmes. He will not sell them. His client's documents are in a bank vault, as he calls it. They will remain there in confidence so long as he is paid on behalf of that client. If the client were to come to any harm, those documents would be published to the world. They are, you might say, his form of life insurance. Set aside the business of the Culme-Seymours and think what the rest of the scandal might do.'

'So you are to pay him—and pay him again whenever he asks—and in exchange for that the papers remain where they are?'

'Unless you can find means to outwit him, Mr Holmes.'

For a moment Holmes said nothing. Then he looked directly at our visitor.

'I have no doubt I shall. However, if you will take my advice, Sir Arthur, you will put Mr Howell from your mind for the present.'

'Ignore him?'

'Ignore him, if you prefer to put it that way. I will tell you, here and now, that none of this is the work of Charles Augustus Howell. Oh yes, he is party to it in a small way. But behind him there is a far stronger and more devious mind. The client. If I am right, the client is a man who might crush Mr Howell—or any one of us—in a single clenching of his hand. If I am right again, this is a man who has not so far demanded money because his true reward would be power beyond price. He holds this threat over you in order that he may be your equal—beyond the law, above the law, perhaps above the Crown itself. That is not Howell, Sir Arthur. That is a man whose shadow falls on his victim with an unearthly chill. I almost seem to know his name.'

'Yet the name is not Howell's?'

Holmes shrugged. 'I am probably wrong in my guess. Yet to blackmail our poets and artists is work for soft hands and men like Howell, whose crimes are those of weakness rather than strength. To attempt such a thing against the greatest power in the realm—the greatest in the world—requires a man with a will of steel and a heart proof against fear. That man is not Howell.'

'Then you will not meet him or negotiate with Mr Howell?'

Holmes sighed. 'I will meet him if you wish, Sir Arthur, since one must begin somewhere. But it will not be for the purpose that Mr Howell supposes.'

III

Such was the unwelcome commission that came our way. There was nothing for it but to arrange a meeting between Holmes and the man whom Sir Arthur Bigge took to be our enemy. It was less easy than I had imagined. Mr Howell was apprehensive, with good reason, of traps that might be set for him. There was not a room in London where he would consent to be alone with Sherlock Holmes. So it was that this most secret of negotiations occurred in the most public of places.

The two men sat side by side in steamer-chairs, hired by the hour along that stretch of Hyde Park that slopes down towards the waters of the Serpentine. They might have been taken for genial companions, but for their looks. The soft lines and shallow honesty of Howell's face was made a contrast to the sharp intelligence of Sherlock Holmes's profile that it was hard to imagine they had anything in common. Far off the riders moved in a light cloud of dust along Rotten Row, beyond the glittering waters of the boating-lake. The trees sighed in a light breeze and on the bandstand the musicians of the Coldstream Guards enlivened the sunny afternoon with the overture to *The Marriage of Figaro.*

Holmes and I had laid our plan. For the moment I sat at a little distance reading the *Morning Post* and was, I believed, unrecognised by Mr Howell. Much of the time, I could not catch the words that passed between the two men. Only at intervals, as the breeze dropped or the band fell silent, did I hear a few isolated exchanges.

'My dear sir,' said Howell, in his whimsical insinuating manner, 'it is a little curious, is it not?'

Holmes gazed at the spring sunlight among the trees of the park but his voice was as cold as the Himalayan snows.

'You must forgive me, sir, but I am not here to discuss curiosities.'

'All the same,' Howell said languidly, 'it remains one. There is such a bother about a marriage which, arrived at unofficially or even by elopement, is an honourable estate among men, as the liturgy has it. Yet much less is said about common whoredom, even where the woman is shared between two brothers.'

'You will do me the courtesy,' Holmes said acidly, 'of confining our conversation to the issue.'

There was almost a lisp in Howell's voice as he said, 'It is necessary, Mr Holmes, that those who have sent you here should understand one thing. I am no republican—indeed, I wish well to Her Majesty—but nor am I a sycophant. When a woman is bought and sold, it is whoredom, whether it be on the Ratcliffe Highway or in St John's Wood, whether the purchaser be a crossing-sweeper or a prince of the blood.'

Holmes said something but I could not catch it. They talked a little longer and I supposed that my friend might be trying to negotiate an outright purchase of the stolen documents, to put an end to the matter. At any rate, what I next heard, several minutes later, was Howell saying more loudly, 'They lie in a bank vault, sir, let that suffice. That they should do so is my insurance against chicanery on your part or on the part of those who instruct you. Times, dates, documents are all there. Even if you could destroy those papers, you could not destroy the knowledge. Instructions have been given to those whom it may concern. If some misfortune should befall me or my client, the contents of those papers will be public knowledge within the week.'

Holmes muttered something else, which I could not quite hear. I caught Howell's answer.

'Quarterly, Mr Holmes, is the suggestion. Each quarter day by banker's draught to an account which I shall open. It will then be forwarded to my client.'

Holmes spoke again and Howell replied.

'My client allows me a little elbow-room,' he said suavely. 'If you wish, you shall see a *résumé* of the contents of the documents—a bill of lading, as it were—which will entirely convince you of the necessity of our coming to an understanding. Better still, I shall bring you, within forty-five minutes, a page of a letter in Prince George's handwriting. You shall have sight of either—or both—if that will settle your doubts.'

'Within forty-five minutes.' That would surely put the repository of the stolen papers within a mile or two of the Serpentine. It was little enough to go on but, as I thought then, it limited somewhat the area of the search.

'I will wait forty-five minutes and not a moment longer,' Holmes answered coldly.

'You would do well not to be so impatient, Mr Holmes,' said Howell with a soft chuckle. 'I cannot make it too plain that, if our little negotiation should fail, there will be no lack of other bidders. Though I may regret it personally, two foreign governments and a number of less reputable organisations have shown a lively interest in the Windsor papers, as I call them. It is provoking to hear fornication, adultery, sodomy, and the like mentioned in the same breath as the illustrious personages against whom the accusations are levelled—often levelled against themselves in their own words.'

Holmes said something which I heard only as a growl and his companion laughed again.

'Mr Holmes, your interests and mine are indivisible. I am, in a most unusual way, your friend. You have every reason to wish me health and prosperity. If, for any reason, misfortune overcame me, you would not be offered the same chance a second time. You would not hear of these Windsor papers again until they shamed publicly those who were indiscreet enough to pen them.'

To those strollers who passed them, these were men of affairs sitting and discussing the terms of the most innocent commercial contract. As they did so, I wondered what darker and more powerful figure stood behind the slippery and evasive presence of Mr Howell. I could see that Sir Arthur Bigge did not believe in such a master criminal. For myself, I doubted whether the blackmailer of Mr Rossetti or Mr Swinburne was a match for the present crime without a more resolute figure behind him.

It was Holmes who later repeated to me Howell's parting remark to him.

'Forty-five minutes will suffice, Mr Holmes. Please do not think of following me or communicating with your friends. You are watched at this moment and I shall know if you have left this place for a single instant during my absence. If that is reported, you will never see me again and your employers know what the consequence will be.'

Even without this warning, it would have been quite impossible for Holmes to follow Howell as the other man left the park. The long paths, even with the trees to either side, are poor cover for the hunter. For that reason, my friend and I had agreed that any tracking of our adversary must be left to me. I did not walk straight after Howell but cut down to Rotten Row, at a right angle from him, and then turned so that our paths would converge near Hyde Park Corner. It was a weakness in their scheme that because they watched Holmes, they could scarcely keep track of me at the same time, or so I thought.

As soon as I was clear of any possible observation, I began to stride out, looking behind me from time to time to make sure that no one matched my pace. Either a pursuer must do so or lose me and I saw no sign of pursuit. As I came out of the park near Apsley House and the start of Piccadilly, Howell was ahead of me on the far side of the busy street that runs by Green Park. It suited me well. Suddenly he turned into a side-street and I dodged between the cabs and twopenny buses to keep him in sight. The side-street turned again and brought me out into the busy thoroughfare of St James's Street, the sunlight golden on the clock-face of the palace at the far end.

By now I felt sure that the destination was one of those old banking families whose premises are ranged along Pall Mall. So it proved to be. Howell looked hastily about him, seemed to scent no danger, and walked swiftly up the steps of Drummonds Bank.

I could hardly believe it would be so easy. In my mind's eye, I saw a police cordon thrown about the bank, Lestrade in his uniform presenting a search-warrant to Henry Drummond, the papers seized and returned to Sir Arthur Bigge at Windsor, where Prince George or the Prince of Wales himself would entertain us to tea as a token of gratitude.

Walking back a little down the broad street, I stood concealed by the ancient brick archway of St James's Palace itself. I kept no count of time but it was surely no more than five minutes later that Howell reappeared with an attaché case in his hand. This time I allowed him to get far ahead of me, for I knew his route.

I kept my distance, pretending to watch the riders on Rotten Row. What I saw of the encounter was Holmes, Howell, and the attaché case on a park bench. A sheet of paper was handed to my friend, presumably for verification. By accident or design, Holmes seemed to let go of it. The light breeze carried it several feet into the air and then let it drift slowly to the grass a yard or two further off. Howell was after it, like a greyhound from a trap. He seized it, came back, and picked up the attaché case to restore the document. Soon after this the meeting ended and the two men went their separate ways. Holmes walked in my direction. I waited at the edge of the riders' avenue, so that he passed behind me. As he did so, there was no slackening of his pace and no movement of recognition. I heard only the crisp tone of his voice.

'Get after him, Watson! See where he goes!'

You may be sure that I did so, as unobtrusively as I could, Holmes striding away in the other direction. I was certain that, if we were spied upon, no one would guess that there had been any communication between us.

I knew quite well what would happen next. Charles Augustus Howell walked back the way he had come, a somewhat overweight figure with his soft face and wavy hair. He carried the attaché case up the steps of Drummonds Bank and I waited for him to reappear. He did so a few minutes later, still carrying the attaché case. Had he deposited the papers in the bank vault already—or was he still carrying them?

What made his reappearance the more curious was that he came down the steps into Pall Mall at almost the same moment as a second man, who carried an identical case. Picture a tall and stooping figure, a gaunt spectre, clean-shaven and pale, his forehead forming a white dome-like curve and his eyes appearing all the more sunken for that. I had no idea who this might be. Yet he and Howell carried attaché cases so alike that it was impossible to say which of them had been taken into the bank a moment before.

This appearance might have been a coincidence but I was sure it was not. At the foot of the steps, the stranger turned right towards Charing Cross and Howell turned left towards St James's Palace. It was impossible to follow them both. If Howell had reappeared without an attaché case, I should now have shadowed the stranger. As it was, I heard in my mind the last instruction of Sherlock Holmes and obeyed it. 'Get after him, Watson! See where he goes!'

He went smartly under the brick archway of the palace towards the Mall. I knew I must not lose him now and so I cared little if he saw me or not. Across the Mall he went, Buckingham Palace quiet in the sunlight at the far end. He dived into St James's Park and began to cut across towards the ducks on the lake, as if he was making for Birdcage Walk. He was hurrying but not sufficiently for me to lose sight of him. Then he paused. I stepped aside behind a chestnut trunk. Howell looked about him, as if to see whether he was alone. Then he thrust the attaché case into a box at the edge of the path, a green wooden receptacle in which the gardeners deposit grass clippings and fallen leaves.

What the purpose of this could be, I had no idea. As he strode off, I made my way as quickly as I could to the box and took out the leather case. It was not even locked. I opened it, expecting a bomb or a bundle of state papers, I know not what. It was empty. I might have followed either of the two men who came out of Drummonds Bank into Pall Mall. I knew now that I had followed the wrong one.

IV

'Let it be a consolation to you, my dear fellow, that they have made fools of us both.'

Holmes was examining the empty attaché case by the morning light that filled the sitting-room windows from above the Baker Street chimney-pots.

'Then who is he?' I asked. 'Which is the other man?'

'The client, I should say.' Holmes frowned and threw down the leather case as yielding no further clue. 'I know you will forgive the deception, friend Watson, but as you followed Howell back to Pall Mall, I followed you. When Howell came out again, I watched you shadow him and I went after the other man. The same trick was played in the Strand. My man went into Grindlays and two men with cases came out. By instinct, I followed the new man. He led me east to Cheapside, to the City and Suburban Bank. Our opponents were playing a game and did not care if I knew it. Two of them came out again into Cheapside but the second one was that same tall stooping man whom I had lost the last time in the Strand. I followed him again and lost him at the Banque Indo Suez in King William Street. That is how they play it and they can play it until doomsday. One man goes in and two come out. It would take Lestrade and fifty of his officers to keep track of them all. They are playing the game because they believe they hold every card in the pack. A dangerous folly.'

At this point, several days had passed since the meeting between Holmes and Howell. If there had been progress, I had seen none.

'Then it is all a wild-goose chase?' I said.

'So it would seem.' Holmes spoke as if he did not greatly care. 'Matters cannot be left as they are, however. I must invite Mr Howell to ask his client to name his terms. Howell may bring them to me tomorrow night. I will communicate them to Sir Arthur Bigge and leave the issue there.'

'Then we are not to get the better of these scoundrels?' I asked incredulously.

Holmes nodded at the empty attaché case. 'As the score stands now, Watson, it seems that we are not.'

This indifference was so unlike him that I wondered if Holmes might be unwell. I decided to test him.

'Then you will not require my further services? If not, I have a practice to attend to and preparations to make for Mrs Watson's return.'

He nodded, as if he quite understood. Then he looked up at me.

'One more thing,' he said, 'I should be grateful for. If Howell comes tomorrow night, I should prefer these rooms to be under observation. If it will not inconvenience your practice and Mrs Watson, perhaps you would keep Lestrade company.'

'Keep Lestrade company? Where?'

He gestured at the window. 'I have taken a room in Camden House across the street. It will give you a good view of these apartments. Should anything untoward take place, my signal for assistance will be the turning down of the gas.'

He was not himself, I now felt sure of it. That the great Sherlock Holmes did not dare be alone in his rooms with a spineless wretch like Howell, unless I and a Scotland Yard man were within call, was quite out of character.

'Has Lestrade agreed?'

'Yes,' said Holmes quietly, 'Lestrade has agreed. He knows only that it is a confidential matter.'

'Then I shall keep him company.'

'Thank you, my dear old friend,' he said in the same quiet voice. 'I never doubted that I could count upon you.'

V

The next evening it was dusk at about seven o'clock. Lestrade and I found ourselves in a first-floor room, which looked directly across to the Baker Street lodgings. Camden House was between 'lets' and this room contained little more than two chairs with a plain table. Holmes had pulled down the cream blinds and put up the gas.

He was sitting in his chair, the shadow of his sharp features and square shoulders thrown upon the blind by the gaslight. Indeed, if Howell or one of his confederates intended some desperate act, Holmes might have made a perfect target from one of the buildings opposite or from the street itself. Presently he got up and moved about the room beyond our vision. A light rain began to fall in the long street, and the people on the busy pavements wore coats and cravats, collars turned up and umbrellas open.

'Tell me,' I said to Lestrade, 'do you find anything unusual in Holmes's behaviour of late?'

Our Scotland Yard man sat in the twilight, puffing at his cigar, his pea-jacket and cravat giving him a somewhat nautical air.

'There's no use denying that,' Dr Watson. It's not like him to want protection from me against whatever twopenny-halfpenny scoundrel that calls on him.'

'Indeed it is not!'

'Nor to have these fancy ideas about spoiling the paintwork of the London banks.'

'Oh?'

'Seems to have some bee in his bonnet about a man going round London defacing the paintwork and the fittings of the banks. I've not seen such a thing, sir. Have you?'

I assured him I had not. Before I could say more, the hooves of a cab horse slowed and stopped as a hansom drew up outside 221B Baker Street. Holmes's visitor had arrived. We could see little of him beyond the door opening and closing again as he was admitted. Holmes himself was still upstairs, turning in his fireside chair as he heard the footsteps. The cab moved off, to return again at its appointed time. Someone, Holmes presumably, now drew the curtain part-way across the window.

There was very little more to be seen. From time to time Holmes or his visitor threw a partial shadow on the blind. It was, I suppose, an hour later when the cab returned and the visitor left. As if in salute to the departing guest, there was the faint but unmistakable sound of Holmes striking a little Mendelssohn from his violin.

We waited twenty minutes more and then, as I had expected, the gas was turned down in the opposite room. Lestrade picked up his black canvas bag.

'Well, Dr Watson, I can make neither head nor tail of the business, nor shall I try.'

We crossed the street and Holmes greeted us—or rather met us—at the door. He was subdued and pale as a ghost. Lestrade refused his invitation to brandy and water. I remained for no more than an hour.

'The matter is concluded,' he said, 'so far as Howell is concerned.'

'Concluded?'

'Concluded,' Holmes said and closed his eyes. I thought it best to let it go at that.

VI

I had almost finished my surgery on the following evening. At any rate, I was told that there remained only one patient still waiting to see me. I looked up as he came through the doorway of the consulting room.

'Lestrade? What brings you to Paddington? Surely not a need of medical advice from me, of all people?'

He sat down across the desk from me, an unfamiliar sight among the bottles and sterilising dishes. His face expressed a mingled anxiety and anger.

'What's going on, Dr Watson? That's what I want to know. What the devil's up?'

'Nothing so far as I know. What should there be?'

'Mr Charles Augustus Howell!'

My heart sank at the revelation that Lestrade so much as knew of the man.

'What of him?'

'He wouldn't have been Mr Holmes's visitor last night, would he?'

'I have not the least idea. You must ask Mr Holmes.'

'Oh!' Lestrade's eyebrows shot up, almost humorously. 'I'll be asking Mr Holmes that, all right, the first chance I get. What concerns me just now is whether you and I might not have been used as an alibi.'

'An alibi for what?'

'You haven't heard then? An hour after Mr Holmes's visitor left last night, Charles Augustus Howell was found in the gutter outside the Green Man public house in Chelsea. His throat had been cut and a half-sovereign was wedged between his teeth.'

'The sign of vengeance on a slanderer . . .'

'The sign of something that has to do with Mr Holmes,' Lestrade said fiercely. 'They think a soldier did it, a Colonel Sebastian Moran who wrote letters to a young woman—letters that Howell was trying to sell back to him, for what that matters now. There's a tale from two informants that Mr Holmes put Colonel Moran on Howell's track last night, even that he was there. That's as much murder as if he did it himself! I'll tell you something worse, doctor! They took Howell to St Thomas's Hospital. He was dead by the time he got there, if not before. A murder inquiry was to begin this morning. Then I'm told, Dr Watson, there's to be no inquiry. Not a question to Colonel Moran! Someone very important—friend of Mr Holmes, I daresay—put a stop to a Scotland Yard investigation. I wasn't going to hold for that, so I inquired at the hospital. I asked what was on his death certificate. Do you know what it says? It says he died of pneumonia! Pneumonia! Did you ever hear the like?'

'No,' I said, half to myself. 'No, Lestrade, I don't think I ever did.'

'Pneumonia!' Lestrade said self-pityingly. 'That leaves nothing to investigate. But he didn't have time to die of pneumonia, Dr Watson. I saw him with my own eyes, lying there with his windpipe slit and looking like a real Robin Redbreast, if ever a man did. I'd like to know what's going on, that's all.'

But poor Lestrade was never to learn the half of that.

VII

'But if Howell is dead, we have lost the scent!' I repeated with greater exasperation. What was the matter with him? Could he not see it? Holmes lit his pipe with a spill from the fire of the Baker Street sitting-room. He shook the flame out in a flick of his wrist and puffed smoke over the room.

'I have observed several times of late, Watson, your tendency to over-dramatise the commonplaces of life. Even making allowances for the burdens that fall upon you as a married man, I cannot applaud it.'

I cut him short. 'This is not a common event. The heir to the throne is blackmailed. Howell is the one man who might have led us to the heart of the conspiracy. Howell is dead and so is the scent. Where shall we begin again? There is a good chance now that we shall never know where the documents concerning Prince George and his brother have been secured.'

He looked at me in genuine surprise, unable to believe I could be so dull.

'But, my dear fellow, since the day after I met Howell by the Serpentine I have known where they are. According to my best information, they have not been moved since.'

'But you cannot have known.'

'They are in Walkers Repository, the Cornhill Vaults at 63, Cornhill. I have been occupied with other matters or I should have had them out before now. Your new life has softened—blunted—your detective instinct. Did you suppose that I should go to meet Howell unprepared? Did you truly believe that I might not prove a match for such a petty trickster as he?'

'That does not explain it,' I said with some little asperity.

'Very well,' said Holmes in a more conciliatory manner. 'I will only say that I expected something of what happened. Suppose a man has goods to sell, stolen goods in this case. He must prove that he has them. I did not know whether Howell would bring them or fetch them. I thought he would fetch them in order that he and his friends might see if he was followed. His accomplice spotted you from the start, I fear.'

'I saw no one!'

Holmes waved his hand generously.

'It matters nothing, Watson. They were seduced by their own cleverness. When Howell returned with the paper in the attaché case, you were standing at a little distance. Perhaps you noticed a paper slip from my hand—a *résumé* of the stolen documents? It was carried several yards by the breeze in the park. As I hoped, Howell went after it like a hungry pigeon after a breadcrumb. It was only for a few seconds but his back was, necessarily, turned to me.'

'Of what use was that?'

Holmes stood up, walked to the table and picked up a small and tightly sealed bottle.

'It is a modest preparation of my own, slow-drying, colourless when wet, setting like a semi-luminous coat of white paint. Like many albumens it forms a white layer as it coagulates. Seen through a magnifying glass, it appears speckled with silver and aluminium grey from its other constituents. I do not think I would mistake even the smallest spot of it for any other compound. It was the easiest thing in the world to daub the bottom corners of the attaché case before Howell turned to me again. The back of the seat and my own coat concealed the movement of my hand from any other observation. The white smudges would not show on the leather until it dried hours later. Even if it was remarked, it would seem like some accidental blemish imparted during their use of the case.'

'So that was it!'

'I quite believed Howell when he told me that he and his confederate would keep the stolen documents in a strong-room—and that only he and the other man knew the contents of those documents. When one enters a bank, there is generally a special booth to one side of the counter at which to apply for access to such a vault, partitioned from the other clerks for privacy. It would be the most natural thing in the world for Howell or his confederate to lay an attaché case upon that counter, while his business was attended to. Of course, in those banks where they merely played their little game of one man going in and two men coming out, there would be no trace of my patent compound on the varnished wood. They would not go to the counter in such a place for they had no business there. Sooner or later, however, they would reach their destination. I flattered myself that, as it lay upon that counter, the attaché case would leave a mark that would be visible at once to the trained eye.'

'You could not be certain.'

Holmes sighed philosophically.

'Nothing, Watson, is certain. If it were, I should find it impossible to earn my bread. Let me say I thought it inconceivable that it should not be so. The following day I visited every counter of every bank vault and safe repository in the City of London that I thought at all likely. I was an inquirer after the facilities that they offered. At Walkers Vaults in Cornhill, there was a blemish on the polished wood, as if a brush loaded with white paint had touched it carelessly. Under the pretence of imperfect sight, I was able to examine it through my glass as I glanced at a paper. The characteristic specks of silver and aluminium grey were unmistakable.'

I shook my head.

'It will not do, Holmes. Even if you are right so far, you do not know where, in an entire bank vault, the papers are to be found.'

He did not reply directly.

'Do you recall, Watson, that two men came out of Drummonds Bank, when you followed Howell there a second time?'

'Distinctly.'

'Do you recall the second man, tall and thin, stooping as if from long hours of study, pale and sunken-eyed, a head so heavy with intelligence that it hangs—or lolls—as if it were too heavy for his neck to carry?'

'I should know him again at once.'

'I hope you will, Watson. That is Professor James Moriarty of mathematical celebrity, the man I describe in my notes as the Napoleon of Crime. When I told Sir Arthur Bigge that I felt I almost knew the name of our blackmailer, I already thought it was he. This plot bears the hallmark of his demented genius—for genius he is, in his way. He uses no alias and employs no disguise, believing that the brilliance of his mind alone is proof against all detection or arrest. Scotland Yard might find him at any time, for what good that would do them. His appearance on the steps of Drummonds Bank proves me right. Professor Moriarty is the "client" of the late Charles Augustus Howell, a man who might hold Howell in the palm of his hand and crush him with a clenching of his fingers, as I picturesquely described it to Sir Arthur.'

'But who is he? How can he be a professor of anything?'

'Oh, he is, Watson, or rather he was until proceedings for moral turpitude put an end to his career. The ruin of that poor young woman walks the *pavé* of the Haymarket to this day. Moriarty had won international fame at twenty-one for his paper on the binomial theorem. He is the first man in two centuries to prove Fermat's Last Theorem, the first in a hundred years to demonstrate the truth of the Goldbach Conjecture. He has no scruples, no morals, no pity. He is a genius, Watson, a criminal genius, and without doubt the most dangerous man in all Europe. Nothing would please him better than the prestige of having laid low a great royal house and a great nation. Think what his threats might command after that!'

'How do you connect him so positively with the Cornhill Vaults?'

Holmes smiled rather wanly. 'I did not trust to a smudge of paint alone, my dear fellow. When I made my inquiry as to the possibility of renting a strong-room drawer, I assured them that I could provide whatever references they needed. I offered your name, Watson, and I fear they shook their heads, for they had never heard of you as a healer of the sick in Paddington Green. I then offered the name of Professor James Moriarty and their faces radiated confidence. He is, they tell me, one of their most valued customers.'

'Then you will compromise with him? If you know where the papers are, you surely have him cornered.'

'I would shoot him like a rabid dog before I compromised with him,' Holmes said with some little heat.

'Then what are we to do?'

'This morning is Friday,' Holmes said. 'By Monday, our adversary may have discovered that his agent did not die of pneumonia, after all. Therefore, Watson, you will spend Saturday with a tray round your neck, selling matches for the benefit of a truly charitable cause. What shall we say—what heroes shall we commemorate? I have it! You shall sell matches for a group of old and forgotten soldiers. The Last of the Light Brigade, as Mr Kipling has it in the verses which he kindly read at our recent meeting.'

'And you, Holmes? What of you?'

He took the pipe from his mouth. 'Dear me,' he said. 'I see nothing for it but to turn safe-breaker and visit the Cornhill Vaults.'

VIII

A madcap scheme if ever there was, or so it seemed. However, as readers of our other narratives will recall, Sherlock Holmes had the arts of the cracksman at his fingertips and was not averse to using them when justice required it.

The Cornhill Vaults stood on one of the busiest streets in London, until the traffic dwindled at noon on Saturday and the city lay quiet over the weekend. The premises were equipped with a series of safes, Milner's Quadruple Patent, described as 'Violence, Robbery, and Fraud-Resisting', and steel drawers for documents. These were also fire-resisting chambers, the safe doors of half-inch wrought iron and the bodies quarter-inch. The stacked document drawers and the safes themselves were ranged against the iron-lined walls of the room.

A curiosity of the room was that it was on constant display to the public. Iron shutters were drawn down to the pavement whenever the premises were unoccupied but these shutters were pierced by holes, whereby pedestrians, including policemen on the beat, might look through narrow apertures into the strong-room. The interior was brightly lit by gas, day and night. It was a novel form of security, simple as it was ingenious, and was coupled with a reward of £500 to any member of the public who provided information of an attempt upon the safes. To facilitate this, several mirrors had been arranged in the vaults by which every approach to the safes and the stacks of steel document drawers would be visible through the holes in the iron shutters.

From 2 P.M. on Saturday afternoon, it was my duty to stand by the iron shutter with my tray of matches and wooden collecting box. By then the business of the week was over for the banks and offices of the City of London. Cornhill would lie as empty as a country road until Monday morning. At the approach of a pedestrian, I was to rattle my collecting-box loudly enough for Holmes to hear on the other side of the aperture, also calling out, 'Last of the Light Brigade!' When the pedestrian had passed, I was to rattle the box again but without speaking.

From the start, I feared that it would go wrong. Next to the Cornhill Vaults, at street level, was a tailor's shop. There were other business premises on the upper floors—a watch-maker, an insurance agent, a re-coverer of umbrellas—which were reached by going through a narrow arch to the rear of the building and up the courtyard stairs. All the premises, like the tailor's shop, closed for the weekend at 1 P.M. on Saturday or before. Holmes had reconnoitred the building the previous day by taking an umbrella for repair.

At about noon on Saturday, the elderly woman who kept watch on the door in the little court was surprised by the arrival of the gasman. He was a rather stooping grey-haired figure who had seen his best days, his moustache straggling and his eyes owl-like behind rimless spectacles. Someone had reported a smell of gas. The good woman had not herself noticed it. On being invited out of her cubby-hole, however, she found a distinct smell of gas on the stairs. Holmes the Gasman had prepared a tin of coal-tar, adding to it such ingredients as would enhance the smell of gas, when the lid was surreptitiously removed.

It was almost 1 P.M., while the woman was on the top floor making her final tour of the building, when the gasman found his leak and noisily tightened the joint of a pipe with a spanner, which he took from his leather bag of tools. He shouted up to her and ambled off down the stairs. She heard him close the courtyard door as he went out. Holmes, of course, had closed the door and remained in the building. On his first visit, he had noticed a cupboard under the stairway with a sloping ceiling, where the cleaners deposited brooms and buckets. It had a little bolt on the outside, just sufficient to serve as a catch and held in place by tacks. There was no reason for the female guardian to look in there but, to make assurance doubly sure, my part was to enter the courtyard door with my tray of matches and push the little bolt across. If the good woman glanced at all, she would think it quite impossible that anyone could be in there while it was bolted from the outside. To distract her a little further, I shouted up the stairs from the doorway to inquire whether any of the tradesmen on the floor above might care to support a worthy cause. She replied abruptly that they had all left for the weekend.

Within ten minutes, she had gone, locking Holmes alone in the building, the safe-breaker's tools in his gasman's bag. To force open the cupboard door which concealed him, wrenching out the slot of the little bolt, was the work of a moment. Then, for appearance's sake, he had tacked the metal fitting back into place.

He made his way to the work-room at the back of the tailor's shop, secure in the knowledge that he would scarcely be disturbed before Monday. Freeing the carpet at the rear wall, he folded it back, taking up two short lengths of board. Lowering himself through the gap, he was in the unlit foundations, rubble underfoot and boards above, divided from the Cornhill Vaults by a rough stone wall.

This wall was a crude division rather than a load-bearing support. There was even a ventilation grille between the two premises. In the next hour, Holmes was able to tap out the grille and two stones adjoining, which gave a sufficient space to slither through. By two o'clock, as I took up my sentry-go with the collecting box and the matches, he was in the space that served as foundations for the Cornhill Vaults.

From his previous visit to the Vaults, Holmes told me that he had a good idea of where the attack must be made. To try the strong-room floor above him was out of the question. The floor, like the walls, would surely be reinforced by iron. Behind the strong-room, however, was an office with a carpet at its centre, stretching almost to the walls, where varnished boards formed a surround a few inches broad. It was possible, from underneath, to use the old jack-in-the-box safe-breaker's tool which lay in his gasman's bag. The jack could bring pressure of a quarter of a ton against a safe and as its iron thread extended upwards the nails holding down the floorboards burst from the joists. By half-past two, Holmes was in the rear office of the Cornhill Vaults.

I could picture him as he confronted the strong-room door. His long experience and the sensitivity of his tools would put a locksmith to shame. I had watched him practise his skill on the latest locks, laying them on the table in Baker Street. Once, as his accomplice, I had seen him tackle a safe that was almost identical to the strong-room lock of the Cornhill Vaults. I pictured him now, as then, unrolling his case of instruments and choosing each one with the calm scientific accuracy of a surgeon who performs a delicate operation. He would work with concentrated energy, laying down one tool, picking up another, handling each with the strength and unhurried delicacy of the trained mechanic. You might have exploded a bomb outside and he would not have heard it. Yet he could read in his mind, as if it were the softest music, the tiny whisper of steel touching steel in the mechanism. One after another, he patiently guided five metal probes into the lock, each covered with lamp-black and each designed to show the position of one of the levers as the probe was turned and the lamp-black scraped off by contact with the metal.

Caution, as well as skill, brought him his reward on these occasions. Taking the measurements, Holmes would adjust a skeleton key, until its five teeth met exactly with the five levers in the lock.

After a few minutes, the steel skeleton turned freely and the lock of the door rolled back.

The Cornhill Vaults provided another obstacle. Within the next few paces, Holmes would be revealed to the spy-holes of the iron shutter by the mirrors that covered the approaches to the safes and stacks of steel document drawers. Outside, the street of banks and commercial premises was clear, except for an elderly man and a middle-aged couple strolling on the far pavement. I could not help turning and caught the reflection of the 'gasman' standing by a tall stack of deep metal drawers, each locked by its own key. They were not, of course, identified by the names of the customers but only by their numbers. However, each drawer contained a little frame with a card, which indicated when the drawer had been opened by its tenant, the initials of the visitor verifying this. Holmes first eliminated all those that had not been opened at least twice on the previous Tuesday, once to take the 'specimen document' out and once to return it. There were two drawers remaining. He would have broken open both, had not one card borne the initials 'J. M.'

'The Last of the Light Brigade!'

I shouted the warning even before I rattled the collecting box, which as yet held only the coins I had put in at the start. The policeman on his beat was walking slowly along this side of the street, glancing at doors and windows, sometimes testing the handle of a door. Prudently, I moved a little away down the pavement from the iron shutter of the Cornhill Vaults so that I might not appear to be concealing anything. It seemed an age before he reached the spot where I had been standing. He stooped a little and put his eyes to the holes in the iron shutter. Then he straightened up, saluted as he passed me, and walked slowly on with his rolling gait. I let him get twenty or thirty yards away before I shook the box once more. Holmes, who had moved out of range of the mirrors, stepped back and resumed his task.

To break open a document drawer, as to break open a safe, two implements are used. The first is a metal wedge known as an 'alderman'. It is heavy and will widen the gap between the door and the frame of almost any safe that has ever been built, provided there is time enough and power enough behind the hammer-blows that are struck. It may take six or seven hours where the safe is of the strongest kind but the gap will open in the end. To avoid more damage and more labour than is necessary, several smaller wedges, known as 'citizens', are employed second to force clear the tongue of the lock.

Holmes used the 'alderman' once and with great delicacy. He followed this with three 'citizens' spaced along the top aperture between the drawer and the frame. Twice more I had to interrupt him but at last, doing as little damage as possible, he felt the drawer move. The documents that had threatened so much now lay before him in the depth of the metal drawer. There was a slim journal-volume, two packets of letters in their envelopes, tied with ribbon, and several papers in a folder.

The hardest part, he told me, was to manipulate the lock of the drawer so that it gave some semblance of being fastened again. A bank official or a locksmith would know at once that it was not working properly. So would our adversary but he dared not say so. He would find the drawer empty and would know that he had got the worst of the battle, hoist by his own petard.

For the next few hours, as the afternoon mellowed into sunset and evening came, Holmes retraced his steps. He could not, he told me, leave everything perfectly in order. His aim was to leave such an *appearance* of order that he would cause no alarm nor even curiosity among the guardians of these premises. His greatest concern was for the steel document drawer. Yet if its tenant did not complain that it had been tampered with or that its contents were missing, what reason had the guardians of the vault to suggest it?

The closing of the strong-room door was as meticulously effected as the opening of it. Holmes then wrapped a probe with lint soaked in surgical spirit. Using this, he wiped away as much of the lamp black as was possible. Regaining the office behind the vault, he dropped down through the gap in the floorboards, drew the edge of the carpet into place and slid the two boards into the gap. He could not force the nails of the last board into the joist but trusted to the first man who walked across the carpet to do that for him. At the worst, it would merely be taken for a loose board.

At the rough wall, dividing the foundations from those of the tailor's, he replaced the two stones and the grille. By the time he had finished, it appeared that the mortar holding them might have crumbled but without giving cause for suspicion. Then it was simple enough to pull himself up through the gap and into the work-room behind the tailor's shop, replacing the boards and treading them down. The lamps had scarcely begun to glimmer down the length of Cornhill when he let himself out quietly into the darkness of the courtyard at the back of the building. The skeleton key was adjusted to three simple levers and the door was locked after him.

Next day, Sherlock Holmes begged an appointment with Sir Arthur Bigge at Windsor. He reported that the plot consisted of Howell and his 'client', the professor. There had been other men hired by them to carry attaché cases here and there—but without knowing why. Yet Holmes was sure that only those two conspirators had known the secrets of the stolen papers. Howell had met a sudden death. Professor Moriarty, in the next few days, discovered that the documents by which he set such store were no longer in his possession. He did not complain of this, for he dared not. If our information was correct, our adversary paid his final bill for rent at the Cornhill Vaults and fled.

IX

Our adversary had fled! Would that he had! Months passed and then a dreadful ordeal, what I have called elsewhere 'The Final Problem', was upon us. One meeting of Holmes and his adversary was described in that narrative as a mere report. In truth, I witnessed it but could scarcely bear to think so.

A week or so after the visit to the Cornhill Vaults, I was with Holmes in the Baker Street sitting-room when a cab stopped outside. My friend stood up.

'That voice!' he said, as the passenger dismissed the cab. 'It is he, Watson. You had better leave. No! You had better stay. Go into the bedroom and wait. He will not, I think, try violence here but it is as well to be prepared.'

I did as he said. Holmes had been lounging at ease in his dressing-gown and now made no attempt to change for there was scarcely time. As I went into the next room, I heard him call out to Mrs Hudson to show the visitor up. Then I heard him open a drawer and there was the bump of metal against wood. This guest, then, was the professor of reptilian face, as Holmes described him, who had won his youthful laurels by a commentary upon the binomial theorem. I heard the new arrival say, 'It is a dangerous habit, Mr Holmes, to finger loaded firearms in the pocket of one's dressing-gown.'

There was a sound of the pistol being laid on a table.

'Pray take a seat,' said Holmes coldly. 'I can spare you five minutes, if you have anything to say.'

'All that I have to say has already crossed your mind,' the visitor remarked.

'Then possibly my answer has crossed yours,' Holmes replied equably.

'You stand fast?'

'Absolutely.'

Through the crack in the door I saw that the other man, whom I first set eyes upon walking down the steps of Drummonds Bank with Howell, had clapped his hand into his pocket and Holmes raised the pistol from the table. But his guest merely drew out a memorandum-book in which he had scribbled some dates.

'You crossed my path on the fourth of January, Mr Holmes. On the twenty-third of January you incommoded me. By the middle of February I was seriously inconvenienced by you. At the end of March I was absolutely hampered in my plans. Now I find myself placed in such a position through your continual persecution that I am in danger of losing my liberty. You must drop it, Mr Holmes, you really must, you know.'

Holmes said something which I did not quite catch.

'It is necessary that you should withdraw,' the other insisted. 'It has been an intellectual treat to me to see the way in which you have grappled with this affair of Prince George's marriage—for I am assured he really was married, you know—and it would be a grief to me to take any extreme measure. I anticipated that you must surely be the one man to whom Sir Arthur Bigge would turn. It was my hope that such a design as mine would draw you out and that we should meet at last—that we should meet upon equal terms and perhaps become partners in some great enterprise. My mistake, I confess, was in allowing Mr Howell to impose himself upon me.'

'A mistake on his part too,' Holmes said drily, 'though certainly a far greater mistake on yours. There is a world of mathematics where you might enjoy such fame and such respect as you never will among common criminals.'

'I had hoped,' the professor said, 'that our recent test of skills might bring us into harmony. Come, now, do not play the outraged subject of the Queen! You care no more for flummery and majesty than I do! Confess it!'

'I care nothing for flummery,' Holmes said, his fingers never more than a few inches from the pistol, 'nothing at all. I care, however, a good deal for honour and, in general, for truth.'

'But evidently not for the truth which I have revealed!'

'No, sir.'

'I did not do it for money,' Professor Moriarty insisted, his eyes staring and his large head rolling a little. 'I have more than I need. I hoped you and I, in sympathy, might forge a revolution that would change the world. There will be such a revolution, you may be sure. Why should it not be ours, the work of men who stand above the vulgar herd, the hero whom Nietzsche promises?'

'If you know the least thing about me,' Holmes said brusquely, 'you will be aware that such a suggestion can hold no charms for me.'

The stranger sighed with a regret that seemed entirely genuine.

'Then I must tell you that you will stand in the way not merely of an individual, Mr Holmes, but of a mighty organisation. Within it, you might have untold influence. If that is not for you, however, you must stand clear or be trodden underfoot.'

Holmes stood up and spoke with the coldest insolence he could muster. 'I regret, Professor Moriarty, that in the pleasure of this conversation I am neglecting business of importance which awaits me elsewhere.'

Moriarty now stood as well.

'It has been a duel between us, Mr Holmes, this matter of the royal papers. As yet, however, we have exchanged but the first shots. You hope to place me in the dock. I tell you I will never stand in the dock. If you are clever enough to bring destruction upon me, rest assured that I shall do as much to you.'

How those words were to echo, after the two men met on that dreadful day at the Reichenbach Falls. All ended well, I suppose, though the missing years of Sherlock Holmes were like missing years in my own life too. When, three weeks after that day on which I last saw him, an invitation to Sandringham arrived in the hand of Sir Arthur Bigge, my own state was such that I was obliged to present my humble duty to His Royal Highness and decline, on a card that was edged with black. Three years were to pass before death gave back my friend and Holmes was able to collect his diamond tie-pin after all. His return to London was final confirmation that Professor Moriarty, the second man who sought to blemish the reputation of our royal house, was dead. What secrets there might be were now safe for as long as it should matter.

In those three years of separation, when I believed my friend dead, not a day passed without my thinking that he had gone willingly to his death to ensure the simultaneous destruction and silence of Professor Moriarty. The secrets of the stolen papers could not be safe again until both men who had known them were dust. The documents might be recovered but the knowledge was stolen for ever. Did Holmes take a secret vow that both Moriarty and Howell must die—so that the knowledge should die with them—even at the cost of his own life?

I thought that was why he had gone without protest to his fate at the Falls of Reichenbach. But what of Charles Augustus Howell?

Was Lestrade right, after all in his suspicion that he and I had been tricked to provide an alibi for Sherlock Holmes? It would be hard to imagine a better witness than a Scotland Yarder!

Night after night I lay awake and thought. Could Holmes have left the rooms at 221B Baker Street, while Lestrade and I watched them? Could he have been absent for an hour while we thought him there, so that he might track down Howell in Chelsea as a matter of cold necessity, cut the man's throat, wedge the half-sovereign between his teeth, and return home? I would get up from my bed, light the lamp, and examine for the hundredth time how such a trick might be performed. We had seen Holmes's outline against the blind. But my friend had once shown me that perfect bust made of him by Oscar Meunier of Grenoble, a masterpiece of reality if ever there was. And then we had heard the snatch of Holmes playing Mendelssohn upon the fiddle at a time when he must have been several miles away slitting Howell's windpipe, if he were the murderer. But Holmes was an enthusiast of the American phonograph and had acquired a machine as early as 1889. I later watched as he recorded Joachim's music for *Hamlet* by playing into the mouth of the great horn on to the cylinder of wax. What had we heard? The music of Holmes or his ghost?

Sitting in my chair on such sleepless nights, I pictured to myself a scene in which Mycroft Holmes was the muffled figure who arrived by cab, responding to his brother's most pressing request. While Mycroft Holmes from time to time adjusted the shadow of the bust against the blind, adjusted the wax cylinder upon its spindle and wound the phonograph, his brother slipped out by the back door of Baker Street, met the cab by appointment, kept the fatal rendezvous and returned. Was it an absurd midnight imagining or the truth? After so much of his cleverness with locks and strong-rooms, was not the simple truth that two men knew the secrets of royal scandal in all their facts and all their truth—and that those two men must die to ensure silence? Colonel Sebastian Moran, a bad enough man indeed, was merely a name thrown in to confuse Lestrade. If all this was true, Holmes had gone to the Reichenbach Falls to meet destiny in the only way that would put an end to the case, as a soldier will sacrifice himself in battle to save his comrades.

He would never discuss it after his return, or rather he laughed it off. Meantime, the removal of Professor Moriarty had happier consequences than that of Howell. Even before Sherlock Holmes's triumphant reappearance, Prince George was betrothed to Princess May of Teck. Two months later, the future King and Queen were married in the Chapel Royal of St James's Palace. Charles Augustus Howell lies in Brompton Cemetery, a victim of 'pneumonia'. I did not hear that the body of Professor James Moriarty was ever recovered.

The Case of the Camden Town Murder

I

In the course of his professional career, Sherlock Holmes seldom worked in collaboration with the great legal names of his day. Yet on the few occasions when his advice was sought, he owed the recommendation to a famous barrister whom he once helped as a young man and never met again.

The encounter took place late one evening, in the very last months of the nineteenth century. I was about to wish Holmes goodnight and turn in when there was a clang of the bell at the street door of our rooms. It was repeated almost at once with a note of greater urgency. In a few moments, the housekeeper, who had been roused from bed herself, announced that a young gentleman of the most respectable appearance insisted upon seeing Mr Sherlock Holmes at once and would take no refusal. I quite expected my friend to make some protest at the lateness of the hour, but he said only, 'Dear me, Mrs Hudson. Then, if he is so very insistent and respectable, I suppose we must grant him an audience.'

The good lady showed up a tall and thin-faced young man, a saturnine and somewhat satanic-looking figure in a Norfolk jacket and knickerbockers. A handsome dark-haired young devil he looked, with eyes that were black in an intensity of natural passion. He appeared, Holmes afterwards remarked, as if immaculately shaved and barbered not an hour before. Only when the housekeeper had withdrawn and the door was closed did he tell us that he was Mr Frederick Edwin Smith, a junior barrister on the Northern Circuit, and that he had killed a man in Liverpool the night before.

Holmes seemed little surprised but insisted that Mr Smith should tell us his story carefully and calmly from an armchair with a glass of brandy and soda in his hand.

For fifteen minutes my friend and I listened without interrupting to the man whom the world later knew in succession as F. E. Smith, Member of Parliament, Attorney-General, Earl of Birkenhead and Lord Chancellor of England in the government of Mr Lloyd George. His tale that evening was dramatic and yet curiously commonplace. This young man, not long called to the Bar at Gray's Inn, had been on a municipal tram-car in Liverpool late the previous night. A ruffianly fellow had attempted to get on at a stop near the centre of the city, just as a young lady was getting off. He had thrust her aside so hard that she stumbled. Mr Smith's chivalry brought him to his feet and he struck the ruffian hard on the jaw. To his dismay, he saw the man fall backwards from the boarding platform of the tram. The poor devil dropped heavily into the street and hit the back of his head with terrible force on the stone kerb of the pavement.

Our visitor knew at once that the man was dead, as the next day's newspapers confirmed. At the time of the accident, with instinctive panic or great presence of mind, our young client had leapt from the tram and had run as fast as his legs would carry him from the scene. In a torment of indecision, which was quite out of character, he had come from Liverpool to London to consult Sherlock Holmes, the one man in England whose discretion and resource he trusted. Money was no object and, as to his immediate course of action, he put himself entirely in our hands. Holmes showed not the least hesitation.

'I have no doubt, Mr Smith, as to what you must do. First, tell no one else of this event. I make it a habit to read a little of the *Law Quarterly Review* from time to time and have seen some excellent pieces of yours on Maritime Law. It is a sphere of commerce in which you seem admirably informed. I assume from this that you have certain business connections thereabouts. Go to a friend whom you can trust implicitly, preferably a man in the shipping trade. Arrange to travel as secretly as you can and as far as you can—and stay away for as long as you can. I should say that six months would probably be sufficient. I concede that you are more expert in law than I, but I believe I may claim an advantage in knowledge of the police and their methods. If nothing is discovered in six months about this mishap—for one can scarcely call it a crime—the Liverpool police will have lost interest in the investigation. I think you may return then without risk of being called to account for it.'

The young Frederick Smith did as Holmes advised and found his confidence in my friend well placed. In the years that followed, several cases of greater interest came our way, most of them I believe on the recommendation of the famous barrister to whom Holmes was a good friend and counsellor on that evening in his youth.

These occasional investigations were usually in cases over which Sherlock Holmes was approached by solicitors whose clients faced the gallows or long prison sentences. Among the most famous defenders of innocent and guilty alike, he had known very few. It was not until 1907 that he first met the great Sir Edward Marshall Hall, though the two men had been equally celebrated in their respective fields for almost twenty years by that time.

Holmes and Sir Edward shared that curious balance of a passionate temperament and a cold dedication to forensic analysis. Both were expert in the mysteries of firearms and medical curiosities. Yet there was a deeper sympathy between them. Holmes was one of the few men to know the details of the great private tragedy that had made Sir Edward Marshall Hall turn his back upon hopes of domestic happiness for many years and throw all his energies into a public career. As a young barrister, Sir Edward had married a beautiful wife, a match that was the envy of the world of London society. Within hours of the wedding ceremony, his young bride told him that she never had and never could care for him. She would be his wife in name only. Why she should have married him at all was a mystery that only a physician might resolve.

On their honeymoon in Paris, the poor deranged young woman disappeared for days or nights at a time. She sought in the habits of the street-walker some solace for her dark cravings. After a few years of unutterable misery for them both, she died at the hands of an abortionist and in the presence of a young lover whose child she feared to bear. To those who knew him professionally, Holmes had a mind that was cold and precise to the point of seeming pitiless. Yet I had seen him moved to tears by human tragedy, never more profoundly so than in the secret agony of Sir Edward Marshall Hall.

Their first meeting was the result of a few paragraphs in the morning papers on 13 September 1907. Like the death of the ruffian who had fallen from the Liverpool tram, the story was dramatic but commonplace in the twilit world where it had occurred.

A young London prostitute, Emily Dimmock, who went by the name of Phyllis Shaw, had been found with her throat cut in shabby lodgings, in the little streets of Camden Town. The wound was so deep that her head was almost severed from her body. The police surgeon's examination suggested that she had been murdered in the small hours of the morning of 12 September. Her body was not found until her common-law husband returned a little before noon from his overnight duty as Midland Railway cook on the express between King's Cross and Sheffield. He, at any rate, was innocent of her death. The poor girl's naked body lay face-down on the bed. In the other room were several empty beer bottles and the remains of a meal set for two, the sole evidence that she had had a companion with her that previous night.

Several days passed and little was added to the reports of the crime. There were no arrests, despite the appeals of the police and the offer of a £500 reward. It was three weeks later when Holmes folded his morning paper and leaned back in his chair. This was the hour after breakfast when he was accustomed to deliver his opinions on the news of the day. He handed me the paper.

'From the point of view of the criminal investigator, Watson, the Camden Town murder promises a most interesting suspect. They have charged an artist, a *protégé* of the late Mr William Morris, with cutting the throat of that unfortunate young woman.'

'An artist?'

He leaned forward and tapped the newspaper report with the stem of his pipe.

'Mr Robert Wood, twenty-eight years old. A painter of designs on glass for the Sand and Blast Manufacturing Company of Gray's Inn Road. A young man whose talent was praised by no less a patron than the last of the great Pre-Raphaelites. You see? When an artist turns to murder, Watson, it augurs well for the student of unusual psychiatric syndromes. You should read again De Quincey's "On Murder Considered One of the Fine Arts", if you have not done so of late.'

I thought my friend's view of the sordid crime in Camden Town a little grandiose and absurd. Yet Holmes was wont to pass frivolous comments on the blackest of crimes, for the fun of seeing if I would rise to the bait. I had grown accustomed to letting such sallies pass without comment.

Unfortunately, it was plain that my friend was not prepared to let the matter drop. We returned from our ramble that afternoon, during which it had taken all my persuasion to prevent him from setting out across the autumn lawns of Regent's Park to examine the back-street of Camden Town, where the murder had been committed. After tea he took a glowing cinder with the fire-tongs and lit the long cherrywood pipe, which he preferred to a clay pipe when he was in an argumentative mood. It was a relief to me, just then, to hear the jangle of the doorbell and the housekeeper's steps on the stairs before he could begin. Mrs Hudson entered with a card on a tray. Holmes took it up.

'Mr Arthur Newton,' he read out, 'Attorney of Lincoln's Inn. By all means, Mrs Hudson. Show Mr Newton up!'

He looked happier than I had seen him all week. Our visitor was a dapper man of forty with an old-fashioned collar, a round and rather sallow face, dark hair that was a little curly, and the general air of an Italian baritone. He made his apologies for intruding, was reassured by Holmes, and then came to the point as we seated him by the fireplace.

'I daresay, gentleman, you will have read by now something of the death of a young woman in St Paul's Road—'

Holmes shot forward to the edge of his chair.

'The Camden Town Murder!'

'No murder has been proved, Mr Holmes. Nor do I intend that it shall be. Not against Mr Wood, at least.'

I intervened at this point. 'All the same, Mr Newton, a coroner's jury has found murder and Mr Wood is named by them as the perpetrator.'

I thought, as the saying goes, that my reply took a little of the starch out of Mr Newton. He seemed ready to make peace.

'Very well, gentlemen. I believe in his innocence but I must concede that matters look black for Mr Wood. For that reason it is the more imperative, even before we brief counsel, that we should endeavour to build a secure defence. There we have a great difficulty. Because of it, and because I fear an innocent man may go to the gallows, I have asked leave to retain your services in the matter of gathering evidence.'

'Quite so.' Holmes sat back and studied the end of his pipe. 'And what, pray, is your great difficulty, Mr Newton?'

'Mr Robert Wood himself. He is a young man of respectable family who, unknown to his father, has for some time kept company with those prostitutes frequenting the public houses of Camden Town and the Euston Road. He was with Miss Emily Dimmock on the three nights preceding her murder. Indeed, at the police station after his arrest, he was pointed out on the identification parade as the last person to be seen with her. It was a few hours before her throat was cut, gentlemen. Worst of all, he was picked out by a witness as the man seen leaving the house in St Paul's Road where the dead woman was found. It was a few minutes before five o'clock in the morning, at just the time she met her death, on the evidence of *rigor mortis* and the digestion of her last meal. He has also been identified, by the peculiarity of his gait, as a man seen walking away from the house at the same time. This last suspect was seen to hold the left arm bent awkwardly as he swung it and the right shoulder forward. The Crown has a witness or two who will swear that Robert Wood used to walk in that manner, even if he can prevent himself from ever doing so again.'

Holmes got up and went across to the window. He stood between the parted blinds, gazing down into the dull neutral-tinted London street as the October afternoon thickened into twilight.

'A strong case in circumstantial evidence, Mr Newton. Apart from the fact that your client was identified as the man seen leaving the house in the early morning, it might be plainly answered. Even with that identification, I hardly think a jury will convict on the uncorroborated statement of a single witness who has never seen Mr Wood on any other occasion. There is little in such evidence which might not be countered by his apparent lack of motive for the murder and the good character of the accused. Your client is a *protégé* of Mr William Morris, is he not? That may stand him in good stead.'

Mr Newton turned in his chair to face Holmes.

'There is more to it, Mr Holmes. A postcard to Miss Dimmock, signed "Alice" but in my client's handwriting, was found in the dead woman's room. In the fireplace were fragments of a burnt letter, the unburnt pieces in his handwriting.'

'Hmmm!' said Holmes. 'Not so good.'

'Furthermore, Mr Holmes, my client behaved unfortunately after the murder.'

'In what manner?'

'He asked a friend, a young bookseller in the Charing Cross Road by the name of Joseph Lambert, to keep secret the fact of seeing him with Dimmock in the bar of the Eagle public house opposite Camden Town station at ten thirty on the night of her death. Worse still, he persuaded his own mistress, an artist's model known as Ruby Young, to concoct an alibi with him for the whole evening.

Both Lambert and Miss Young have informed the police of these collusions, for fear of being charged as accessories to the murder.'

'Is that all?' Holmes inquired.

'No, Mr Holmes. The worst of it, as I say, is Wood himself. He is vain as a peacock and sure of his own cleverness. He makes the worst possible witness.'

'Then you must not call him,' I said, intervening again.

Mr Newton looked at me sadly.

'Until the Criminal Evidence Act became law in 1898, Dr Watson, the accused was not permitted to give evidence in a murder trial. Now that he is permitted, it is also expected. The worst conclusions are drawn if the defendant in a murder trial fails to tell his story and be examined upon it. True, prosecuting counsel is forbidden from commenting on a refusal to give evidence. The judge, however, may say what he pleases to the jury—and usually does.'

Holmes turned to me.

'Mr Newton is correct, Watson. If Wood refuses to appear in the witness-box, he will hang as high as Haman.'

Our visitor spread out his hands. 'So you see, gentlemen, our one hope is to ensure that the case can be won upon the facts, despite all that young Mr Wood may do to destroy himself.'

'Just so,' said Holmes thoughtfully, puffing at his pipe and gazing down into the fire. 'If you have so difficult a client as this young man, the facts are the only things that may save him—if they do not hang him first.'

Half an hour later, Mr Arthur Newton took his leave. In the middle of that night as it seemed, I was woken by Holmes shaking me briskly by the shoulder. He was holding a lantern and its light showed him to be fully dressed.

'We must hurry, Watson. It is very nearly four o'clock and it will not do to be in St Paul's Road later than a quarter to five.'

Holmes was habitually a late riser and, until that moment, I had no idea that we were to visit the scene of the murder at the same hour as the crime was committed. With some grumbling to this effect, I dressed and was ready a little before twenty past four. Dawn remained a good way off and the weather seemed the worst that autumn. In the tempestuous October morning, the wind screamed and rattled against our windows as we drank black coffee which Holmes had prepared. Presently we battled our way to the all-night cab-stand in the Euston Road, where the drivers lounged against the counter of the stall with its steaming urns.

Ten minutes later, in the lamplight, our cab turned into the Hampstead Road and then into the huddled streets of Camden Town. It is that area where the great railway lines run north in cuttings or on arches from Euston and King's Cross, the night air torn by the scream of engine-whistles and the rush of steam. St Paul's Road was a vista of houses in soot-crusted yellow brick, behind them on one side a blank railway wall. Below that wall, the engines of the London and North-Eastern snorted, goods wagons shunted and clattered, the red eyes of the signal gantries glowed in the dark as the night express rattled and hooted its way across the steel points of the tracks to Edinburgh and the north.

The house where the young woman had met her death stood tall and shabby at the end of a terrace. A long flight of stone steps led up to the front door. A man leaving these premises would be on full view to passers-by while he closed the front door and came down the steps to the street. Had it been any other house in the row, he might have been less plainly visible. However, number 29 was illuminated from both sides by street-lamps, as plainly as a spot-lit stage. As if to prove this point, the witness MacCowan had picked out Robert Wood at once from the men lined up in the police station yard.

Holmes said nothing. We stood with the collars of our coats turned up, the wind too strong to allow an umbrella. Five o'clock came. Half past five followed it. There was no sign of a man on his way to work with his left arm bent and his right shoulder hunched forward. It seemed a fruitless vigil. We walked back to Camden Town station and took another cab to Baker Street. Holmes sat silent in his chair, the morning papers unread. The plain truth was that Robert Wood had behaved with every sign of guilt in asking two friends to lie on his behalf. He had been picked out as the man who stood in the lamplight, and as he who walked in the unusual manner. He was the last person to be seen with Emily Dimmock. Mr Wood, it now seemed to me, was likely to become our first client to be hanged.

II

I quite expected Holmes to be anxious or subdued by this confirmation of Mr Newton's fears. Instead, he appeared to behave in a most frivolous and unaccountable manner. In the evenings of the following week, he was seldom at home. Nor, indeed, did he return until the small hours of the morning. He had not been near Camden Town. Most of his time was spent at the Café Royal or, more often, at Romano's with its famous upstairs bar and tables, its oysters and champagne, its fish-tank in the bright first-floor window that blazed across the Strand.

I had not the least idea, nor would he say, what purpose there could be in so much time spent with sporting swells like 'Flash Fred' Valere or 'Little Jack' Shepherd, with rowdy guardsmen and Gaiety girls. Robert Wood was certainly no part of their world. When it was not the Café Royal or Romano's, Holmes's steps took him to the Criterion Bar, always among much the same company. In my anxiety, I lay awake and listened for his return. I would hear his footsteps on the stairs, then Holmes moving about the sitting-room, murmuring to himself the tune of the latest ditty from his new companions.

O, Jemima! O, Jemima! Your poor old mother's heard
All about our little games—she has upon my word . . .

He no longer read *The Times* after breakfast, preferring the tinted racing columns of the *Sporting Times* or the *Pink 'Un*, whose editor John Corlett was one of his new friends. I bit my tongue and kept silent.

Then he was gone for two entire days and nights. Mr Newton called, anxious for news of our progress in the inquiry. I could tell him nothing and feared the lawyer's apprehension might soon turn to anger at the lackadaisical manner in which Holmes seemed to be treating the investigation.

This anxiety was nothing compared with the callers at our street door. There were quite a dozen in the course of those two days and more to follow. They were an evil and violent-looking procession of ruffians, some with 'cauliflower' ears, a picturesque variety of broken noses, burly and crop-haired for the most part, a few of them smaller in build but all the more malicious in their attitude.

By the time that those two days were at an end, I had confronted a goodly number of such visitors, many of whose photographs no doubt adorned the rogues gallery at Scotland Yard. One and all of them had called to see Captain O'Malley. They had been told that, if the gallant officer was not at home, they were to leave an address at which they might be contacted. I was used to receiving such inquiries for 'Captain O'Malley' or 'Captain Basil' when Holmes was away on business. I took their messages but nothing would have persuaded me to allow a single one of these savage-looking fellows across the threshold.

There was one who left no address. Though he looked less of a villain than the others, his manner was more threatening.

'Cap'n O'Malley live 'ere, does 'e?'

'I regret that Captain O'Malley is not at home.'

'Well, p'raps that's jist as well for 'im. You tell him, with my compliments, I ain't no bloody liar and 'f he says again that I am, I'll be round to smash his face for him. All right? Understood?'

I had had more than enough of this 'prank' but it was not quite over. The last to arrive was somewhat different in appearance but I cannot say that I liked the look of him much better. He was a rakish young workman with a goatee beard and a self-confident swagger.

'Cap'n O'Malley?' he said, as if I might be he. Before I could reply, he struck a match on the sole of his boot and lit a clay pipe with a gesture of insolence. Then, with an audacity beyond belief, he blew a cloud of foul-smelling tobacco-smoke in my direction and began to elbow his way past me into the hall.

'What the devil—'

Before I could go further, the apparition threw back its head and laughed.

'Excellent, my dear Watson! My thespian labours are rewarded indeed!'

I fear I was abrupt with him as we reached our rooms.

'There are a dozen messages left for you by the most lawless ruffians to whom I have ever opened our door. Happily, I was able to keep watch and reach them before Mrs Hudson.'

'Good!' he said enthusiastically. 'Capital!'

'Another of them says that you have told lies about him.'

'So I have, Watson. One after another.'

'Then you had better know that he proposes to call here again to smash your face.'

Holmes turned and, despite his disguise, his features were a study in triumph as he put down the scraps of paper left for him and heard of the threat that had been made.

'Splendid, Watson!' he said. 'That will be Mr MacCowan, I expect. A most estimable man. To smash my face? That shows true feeling. And these slips of paper too! I had scarcely dared to hope for so many replies and such complete success.'

As he stood beaming at the scraps of paper in his hand, I had not the least idea what his outburst meant.

'Do you mean, Holmes, that young Mr Wood is no longer in danger of being hanged?'

He looked at me with an air of surprise. 'I should say, Watson, that he is in very great danger of being hanged. But that will be because he plays the conceited young ass in the witness-box and the jury takes against him. I think I can promise you that he will no longer be hanged on the evidence. He will have to do the job for himself.'

With that he turned to his bedroom to remove the goatee beard and the rest of his impersonation. Before leaving the room, however, he took a large sheet of paper which had been folded in his pocket. He threw it on the table and said, 'Here, Watson. See what you can make of that.'

I saw columns of figures with dates beside them and the name 'ELSIE' scrawled in pencil at the top. By now I was in something of an ill temper and decided that I would let Holmes explain the matter himself.

On his return, he rang for Mrs Hudson and warned her that we should receive a number of visitors in the next few days. The good lady was not to be alarmed if they included a desperate-looking man, who was in truth as amiable as an old family dog. There might also be a man who wished to smash the face of one or other of us, but he was really a most respectable fellow. There might also be a young lady of great presence and poise but with a certain past to live down. All were to be admitted at any hour.

III

For the first day we heard nothing. On the second, in response to a letter which Holmes or 'Captain O'Malley' had written, there arrived at noon one of the ruffians whom I had encountered on our doorstep. He now strode into our presence with a great air of self-confidence. Holmes treated him like a Crown Prince.

'Mr William Westcott? My name is Sherlock Holmes. May I introduce my colleague, the medical examiner Dr Watson? We are here on behalf of Captain O'Malley, who is abroad at this moment, as I explained in my card to you. What is your occupation, Mr Westcott?'

Our visitor lowered himself into a chair and the wooden frame of it creaked a little ominously under his bulk.

'I'm a ticket-collector, Mr Holmes. Midland Railway at King's Cross.'

'And the fact that you received my card and came here presumably means that you still live at 25 St Paul's Road? Is that not very close to where the Camden Town Murder happened?'

Our visitor was only too glad to share his moment of fame with us.

'That's right, Mr Holmes. I must have left that morning about the same time as the murderer was seen leaving the house two doors down, being on the early turn that week.'

'The early turn, Mr Westcott?'

'At half past five. I always allow thirty minutes for the walk and five minutes for clocking in. It means I leave home at five to five on the dot.'

'Just as well that you avoided the murderer,' said Holmes with a pleasant laugh, 'though they say there was a policeman standing opposite the house.'

Mr Westcott's pouched and rubbery face creased in a grimace of indifference.

'No policeman that I could see. And certainly no one leaving 29 just then. There was a cove coming down the road from the far end, same way as me. He walked after me but he wasn't a bit like the chap they arrested for cutting her throat.'

Holmes laughed again. 'So you suffer no nightmares from the memory of the man who was following you.'

Mr Westcott's grin revealed gums that lacked most of the usual set of teeth.

'I can look after myself, Mr Holmes. It'd take a mighty fine murderer to give Bill Westcott nightmares.'

There was laughter all round.

'No,' said Holmes pleasantly. 'And Mr Westcott didn't get a broken nose and a cauliflower ear from being a ticket-collector.'

Westcott joined in the laughter again.

'Well now, Mr Westcott,' said Holmes more earnestly, 'before we go further, perhaps you wouldn't mind just walking up and down the room a few times so that Dr Watson can make a note of your mobility.'

The chair creaked again as our visitor heaved himself up and began to pace between the fireplace and the door. He moved as if gathering energy for some great effort. The big man walked with his left arm swinging and crooked a little, his right shoulder hunched forward as if to protect his jaw. No one who saw him could sensibly doubt that this was the fellow whom one witness had seen, going about his innocent business in St Paul's Road at the time of the murder.

We had a pleasant discussion of the prospects of Mr Westcott, ticket-collector and amateur boxer. Holmes was as good as his word. 'Captain O'Malley' had spoken to several of his new friends at Romano's, from whom he had obtained the names of likely contenders for an amateur knock-out contest at the National Sporting Club in Regent Street. Before the eyes of wealthy connoisseurs of the noble art, Bill Westcott became the Camden Conqueror before the year was out.

'How the devil did you find him?' I asked, when Holmes and I were alone again.

'My dear fellow,' he said quietly, 'that you of all people should ask that! When Mr Newton described the gait of the man whom the witness had seen, it could only be a boxer. You recall the shoulder hunched forward, the left arm crooked?'

'Then MacCowan saw Mr Westcott come down the steps from 25 and not Wood from 29!'

Holmes shook his head.

'We may even doubt that Mr MacCowan saw Mr Westcott or anyone else on the morning of the murder. He says there was a policeman standing on the far side of the road and Mr Westcott tells us there was not. Perhaps Mr MacCowan remembers the wrong morning. That is something we cannot prove. Yet I was sure that one witness had described a boxer. I judged it imperative to discover where that boxer had come from and who he might be.'

'Romano's and the *Pink 'un*!'

'Precisely, Watson. I spent several agreeable evenings among sporting entrepreneurs who live on the art of such men as Mr Westcott. As Captain O'Malley, I passed as one of them. I advertised by word of mouth and in the *Sporting Times* for men to compete at the National Sporting Club. My informants had told me of such a contest yet to be announced, so I deceived no one. He could only have been a boxer, Watson. I am still amazed you did not see it from the start. Young Mr Robert Wood may have his genteel talents, but he would not last two minutes in the ring with Mr Westcott.'

For the rest of that day, Holmes divided his time between lounging in his chair, staring at papers which I swear he did not read, and pacing before the window.

'Damn it, Watson!' he said several times. 'Where is the fellow?'

'You mean MacCowan?'

'Of course I mean MacCowan. He is a witness in the case and I may not approach him. That would be contempt of court. I must make him come to me. If he does not, Mr Wood may still be lost.'

Despite Holmes's anxiety, the doorbell on the following morning announced the arrival of this second visitor. Mr Robert MacCowan was not, in truth, the type to go about smashing faces. When the door was opened to him by the redoubtable Mrs Hudson, the wind quite left his sails and he murmured no more than a wish to see Mr Sherlock Holmes, for 'Captain O'Malley' had been kept exclusively for practitioners of the noble art.

Indeed, when Mr MacCowan was shown up, he proved to be a tall and rather thin fellow with a shock of fair hair and a face haggard beyond his years. I placed his voice as that of a Norfolk man, though Holmes afterwards assured me it was Suffolk.

'Mr Holmes?' he said plaintively. 'I have a bone to pick with you.'

'Indeed?' said Holmes. 'I understand that my face was to be smashed.'

'So it ought to be,' said MacCowan. 'So it should be for what you have done. You were in the Eagle at Camden Town station. You were in the Rising Sun in the Euston Road. Where else you might have been I can't say. But everywhere that you were, you put about the story that I had lied as a witness to the police, and to the justices, and to the coroner's jury. I'm a man that hasn't had regular work the last eight months and if such stories are told about me I may never work again.'

Holmes motioned the tall, sad man to a chair.

'Come, Mr MacCowan, please sit down. If it is in my power, as I believe it is, to procure employment for you, rest assured that I shall do so. I have never called you a liar. I have simply offered a harmless wager or two that events referred to in your witness statements did not take place.'

MacCowan, who had half sat down, stood up again and was not yet mollified.

'That's as good as to call me a liar.'

Holmes stood as well.

'We may all of us be mistaken or confused in our recollections, Mr MacCowan. It does not make us liars, I hope.'

'You had no business, Mr Holmes. None whatever to say such things in a public place.'

The amiability went from Holmes's eyes and there was the faintest suggestion of a hiss in his breath. His hand, half-way to his pipe with a spill from the fire, froze in mid-gesture.

'I have business indeed, Mr MacCowan. I have such business when an innocent young man stands in the shadow of the gallows, that I will stop at nothing to see that business completed.'

He lit his pipe, tossed the spill into the grate, and continued.

'Moreover, Mr MacCowan, I do you a service if I save you from making a fool of yourself in the witness-box.'

'I don't need saving, Mr Holmes. I know what I saw. I saw that man!'

'If you will not sit down, Mr MacCowan, I shall. Which man was that?'

'Which man? The man I picked out in the police station yard. The man I saw standing on those steps of the house with two lights shining down on him. Robert Wood.'

'And what about the second man, Mr MacCowan? The one who was standing opposite the house when you passed at five minutes to five on the morning of the twelfth of September?'

MacCowan's shoulders moved in a pretence at laughter. 'The policeman? You don't think he cut her throat!'

Holmes put his pipe down. 'I am quite sure that he did not. How was this policeman dressed?'

MacCowan scowled at him. 'Same as they all are. And he'd got his cape on, it being a wet morning.'

Only those who knew Sherlock Holmes well would have noticed the slight dropping away of tension in his body as he felt the prey within his grasp.

'And yet, Mr MacCowan, on this wet morning as you call it, from midnight until the next midnight, the reports tell us that not a single drop of rain fell upon the whole of London.'

MacCowan was first disconcerted, then scornful.

'I never said it was raining, Mr Holmes. It was damp, murky.'

'Ah,' said Holmes, taking up his pipe again. 'Quite so. Murky and misty. Poor visibility. Without the lights, you might scarcely see across the road.'

He stood up and handed his visitor the sheet of paper headed 'ELSIE' with its columns of dates and figures.

'What's this?' MacCowan asked. 'Who's Elsie?'

'The goddess of light,' said Holmes quietly, 'EL . . . C . . . The Electric Company. Those, my dear sir, are the times at which street lights all over London were turned off automatically on the morning of the twelfth of September when Emily Dimmock met her death. If you will look just down here, you will see that the lamps in St Paul's Road, Camden Town, were turned off at five thirty-nine A.M., sixteen minutes before you claim that two of them shone brightly enough to identify Mr Robert Wood, despite the distance and the murk of the morning.'

MacCowan blinked, like a man hit hard but still on his feet.

'Then I was earlier than I thought. I was at the Bread Company in Brewery Road to look for work at five o'clock. I must have passed down St Paul's Road earlier. I come from home, Hawley Road in Chalk Farm.'

'Indeed,' said Holmes coldly. 'It is noted by the gatekeeper that you arrived at the V. V. Bread Company in time to be one of the first group of workers taken on that morning at five o'clock precisely. I have checked that for myself. You may also care to know that the distance from Hawley Road to Brewery Road is half a mile—29 St Paul's Road is at the mid-point. I grant that a man may take a little longer than he first thinks to walk such a distance. I am a little puzzled, however, as to how a man in possession of full health and who says he was not delayed in any manner could take almost twenty minutes to walk a quarter of a mile—half the distance from Hawley Road to Brewery Road.'

MacCowan sat in silence, looking at his hands.

'Come,' said Holmes a little more kindly. 'Either you passed the house at five minutes to the hour, when you cannot have seen the man who left because there was no light to see him by. Or else you passed no later than twenty minutes to the hour, when the lights were on and when you cannot have seen him because, according to this evidence, he did not come out for another fifteen minutes.'

MacCowan caught at a straw. 'There were other lights, Mr Holmes, that's what you'd know, if you weren't so bloomin' clever. Lights from the railway that runs by the street. I didn't just exactly notice at the time where the light was from. There's lights all along that railway and they keep 'em on.'

Holmes nodded. 'So they do, Mr MacCowan, and those lights may have been on at five minutes to five. If you were to measure, however, you would find that the railway line on to which the lights shine is forty feet below the level of the road. Moreover, there is an unbroken line of houses opposite the one we are discussing, shielding it from any reflection. There cannot possibly have been any light of any kind shining upon 29 St Paul's Road by which you could identify any man leaving the house.'

Robert MacCowan left our rooms still blustering yet with a dreadful light of fear in his eyes. He had nailed his colours to the mast before the coroner's jury and the magistrates. Nothing could save him, in a few weeks' time, from a public martyrdom at the hands of Edward Marshall Hall in the witness-box of the Central Criminal Court. Yet Sherlock Holmes was as good as his word. Captain O'Malley retained sufficient influence among his sporting friends to obtain for Mr MacCowan a place as table-waiter at Romano's, through whose famous window we once or twice glimpsed him in the years that followed.

We had one other visitor, the saddest of all. She was a dark-haired young woman of delicate beauty and moral frailty, the artist's model, Ruby Young, who had been Robert Wood's mistress. She came because, in her fear, she believed that she had now betrayed her lover to the gallows. As soon as the murder was reported in the press, Wood had asked her to swear a false alibi that they were together the night of Emily Dimmock's death and had not parted until 10.30 near Brompton Oratory.

Uncertain what to do, dreading that the false alibi she had given might make her an accomplice in murder, she had confessed to the police. With tears, she now pleaded with Holmes to assure her that she had not done a terrible wrong.

'Not in the least,' Holmes said airily. 'You have done Mr Wood a great service.'

She looked up at him. 'But it was I who asked him to meet me and led the police to him!'

'Madam,' said Holmes, 'consider this. Emily Dimmock was seen alive at ten thirty P.M. by Joseph Lambert the bookseller, and by others in the bar of the Eagle, in the company of Mr Wood. She ate a meal soon afterwards and met her death three hours after consuming it, to judge by the state of digestion of the food found in her stomach. She cannot have died before 2 A.M. at the earliest. The degree of *rigor mortis* in her body when it was first examined suggests that she more probably died at about 5 A.M.'

'I did not know,' she said simply.

'Nor could Robert Wood have known anything about the medical evidence when he asked you for an alibi,' said Holmes firmly. 'It was not public knowledge until the coroner's inquest. Consider his dilemma beforehand. He was a young man who knew that questions would be asked by the police of all those who had been seen with Emily Dimmock on the last evening of her life. He was also a young man who dreaded that his family, with whom he still lived, would hear that he kept the company of prostitutes in the public houses of Camden Town and the Euston Road. That was the reason why he wanted an alibi for Wednesday evening. Not murder! Do you not see it, Miss Young? The alibi for which he asked you, covering the evening until half past ten, was useless to him as a defence against a charge of murdering Miss Dimmock in the small hours of the morning. But only the murderer himself would have known that at the time when you were asked for a false alibi. Therefore, the murderer was not Robert Wood.'

The world knows the conclusion of the story. The case against Robert Wood was not dropped, despite Mr Arthur Newton's best efforts. Our young artist went on trial at the Central Criminal Court in December 1907, where the great defender, Edward Marshall Hall, cut up the witnesses for the Crown into very thin slices, as the saying goes. Robert Wood was acquitted and left the court to the cheers of the crowds outside. The unfortunate Ruby Young was jeered and chased down the street for her betrayal of her lover, as the London mob believed.

The name of Sherlock Holmes was not mentioned directly at the trial. Yet his shadow fell upon it in consequence of the visits we had received from the belligerent Mr MacCowan and the tearful Miss Ruby Young. Those who care to read the proceedings in the Notable British Trials volume that contains the case of Robert Wood will find a comment by Mr Justice Grantham at page 149, with reference to a complaint by MacCowan.

> I learn now that MacCowan was a witness before the magistrates. If the persons who are guilty of causing the annoyance are brought before me, they will not forget it in a hurry—that is all I can say. It is intolerable that witnesses should be subjected to attack and abuse for giving evidence, and if the person responsible is brought into this Court, it will be some time probably before he goes free.

Holmes insisted that he had not interfered with the witnesses in the case. One and all had come to him of their own free will, even

MacCowan. He had not obliged them to seek him out. Perhaps my friend was a little disingenuous. They walked into a trap, which he had baited with great care. So far as the courts of law acknowledged his existence, Mr Justice Grantham's comments on my friend's investigation of the murder of Emily Dimmock was as close to the wind as Sherlock Holmes ever sailed.

IV

After the acquittal of Robert Wood, no other person was brought to trial for the Camden Town murder. Detective Inspector Arthur Neil and his assistant, Sergeant Page, had gathered all the evidence available to them. If it did not point to Wood, it seemed to point to no one. Yet there was a curious epilogue, if one may use the word for so bizarre a conclusion.

In the attic of our Baker Street diggings, the first lumber-room alone remained orderly enough to have been a work-room. Holmes had a horror of destroying documents, especially those connected with his past cases. Yet it was only once in every year or two that he would muster energy to docket and arrange them. From time to time one or other of us had occasion to go up to this first room. On the wall hung a painting, which was curtained in red velvet, as if to protect it from the light. I had once seen what lay beneath and had no wish to repeat the experience.

Thereafter, Holmes was the only person who ever drew that curtain back. It veiled a painting by a friend of Robert Wood and was the only token of thanks that Holmes ever received from the young man. The artist was the impressionist painter Walter Sickert, more famous in later years than he was at the time for his studies of low life. This canvas was a horror. It showed Emily Dimmock as she was found with her throat cut on 12 September 1912. Other studies from Sickert's *Camden Town Murder* series have long received public display and general interest. Holmes judged that this item had best remain curtained from innocent eyes. On his visits to that lumber-room, he once told me, he would stand with the curtain drawn back, smoking his pipe as he gazed at the image on the canvas and pondered what manner of man was, in truth, the Camden Town murderer.

Several years after the case was concluded, Holmes met Walter Sickert for the first time during an artists' dinner of some kind at the Café Royal. There was a good deal of boastful talk, which led Sickert to assert that 'a painter cannot paint something of which he has no experience'.

My friend was struck by this remark. A few weeks later, he secured an invitation to the artist's studio in Camden Town. It was there that he saw a portfolio of drawings on the same subject and purchased one inscribed *Persuasion,* in which a man sits on a bed, a woman lying across his lap and his hands obscurely round her throat, either in a caress or an act of strangulation. The painter afterwards became sensitive to questions about his 'Camden Town murders' and changed the title of the series to 'What Shall we Do for the Rent?'

Holmes sought occasion over some other matter to invite Inspector Neil to our rooms. In the course of the visit, he displayed a few souvenirs including the snuffbox of Sèvres porcelain which had belonged to President Faure and the diamond tie-pin which he had brought home with him after a visit to Windsor in 1890. Then the two men went up to the lumber-room.

I did not accompany them but noticed that Inspector Neil came down a good deal paler than he went up. Guessing the cause of this, I poured him a glass of brandy and soda, setting it on the little table by his chair.

'A nasty daub, that painting,' I said reassuringly, 'and all the worse for being in a blotchy impressionist style. If it were mine, I should burn it.'

Sherlock Holmes intervened. 'Robert Wood, after he was released, acted as the model,' he said.

Neil looked up at him. 'That's not it. I saw Wood's likeness clear enough. That's not it.'

'What is it, then?' I asked.

'That room of hers, where she died!' he said. 'It's as we found it, in every detail! I'm no artist, Dr Watson, and I know little enough about the ways of art. But he has got that room and the girl herself as plain as if it were a photograph!'

'Do you say,' asked Holmes innocently, 'that a painter cannot paint something of which he has no experience?'

Neil stared into his glass.

'I can't say that, Mr Holmes. You might, if you understand art. I know little enough of such things—and where's the evidence now? Wood never denied he'd been to her room on earlier nights—and he might have described it to anyone. But Dr Watson is right. If that thing were mine, I should take it off its hook and burn it before I looked at it again.'

Holmes made a sympathetic sound but, from his eyes, I could see that for him Walter Sickert's daub now took on the quality of a true work of art.

The Case of the Missing Rifleman

I

In order that the reader may understand more readily the investigation that follows, it may be as well if I say something of the origin of the inquiry. It was the second case in which the path of Sherlock Holmes crossed that of Sir Edward Marshall Hall, thirteen years after the trial of Robert Wood for the Camden Town Murder. On this later occasion, however, there was to be a certain bruising of vanity in both parties.

The mystery dated from the summer of 1919, the first after the Great War, a time when a good number of young men and their officers were returning to civilian life from the army and the trenches of the Western Front.

A few miles to the east of the town of Leicester lie a number of little villages connected by a network of small country roads or lanes. Once these were farming communities—now they supply labour to the factories and industries of Leicester itself. Annie Bella Wright was a respectable young woman of twenty-one who worked in a rubber factory and was engaged to a naval stoker. On 5 July 1919, she came off the night shift and cycled home the few miles to the little village of Stoughton, where she lived with her parents. She went to bed and, after several hours' sleep, got up to finish writing some letters. She posted these at about 4 P.M.

At 6.30 that evening, she took her bicycle and set off for the hamlet of Gaulby, three miles away, to visit her uncle, Mr Measures, and his son-in-law, Mr Evans. By the time that she arrived at their cottage in the centre of Gaulby, Bella Wright had a companion, a young man riding a green BSA bicycle. Safely inside the cottage, she assured her uncle that this young man was a perfect stranger, who had overtaken her as she was cycling from Stoughton and had engaged her in conversation on the remainder of the short journey. Mr Measures clearly remembered that his niece had said to him, 'Perhaps if I wait a while he will be gone.'

When Bella Wright left her uncle's house, however, the young man had returned, as if he had been waiting for her. 'Bella, you *have* been a long time,' he said pleasantly. 'I thought you had gone the other way.' The two of them rode off together, the time being about a quarter to nine and the summer evening still light. Half an hour later, Bella Wright was found lying dead less than two miles away in the Gartree Road, which was not her direct route home. Her head had been badly injured and the first doctor who was called thought she had died as a result of a bad fall from her bicycle. Next day, a policeman who searched the narrow country road at the point of the incident found a spent .455 cartridge on the ground, seventeen feet from where her body had been lying. A post-mortem revealed the entry wound of a bullet in her left cheek, just below the eye, and a larger exit wound at the top of her head.

A curiosity near the scene of the crime was the discovery of a carrion crow, lying dead in the adjoining field, about sixty feet away. It was described at first as being gorged with blood, which was presumed to have come from the dead girl's wound. The amount that the bird had consumed was said to have caused a surfeit from which it had died. There was a field gate on to the road a few yards from where the girl's body lay. Between the white-painted gate and the body were what appeared to be twelve bloody claw-tracks, six in each direction, as if the bird had moved to and fro between the gate and the corpse.

A description of the man on the green bicycle and of the machine itself was issued by the police. A reward was offered for information.

Many months passed and nothing more was heard, except from two girls of twelve and fourteen, who had been cycling in the lanes nearby. They agreed that, earlier on 5 July, a man riding a bicycle came towards them, smiled and spoke to them as he passed. Having gone by, he stopped, turned his bicycle and began to follow them. The girls, feeling uneasy at his interest in them, reversed their own direction and rode home towards Leicester.

It was little enough to go on. The summer ended. Winter came and went. The investigation got nowhere and the Leicestershire county police were not helped by a complete lack of any apparent motive for the killing. Bella Wright had been neither robbed nor assaulted in any way. Why should any individual, the rider of the green bicycle or not, shoot dead a blameless and industrious young woman?

Holmes had followed the scanty newspaper reports with a vague interest but, in truth, there seemed little that even he could have done with such disjointed scraps of evidence. His attention was caught at last when he read, in March 1920, that a man had been arrested and charged with the murder of Bella Wright. The accused was an assistant master at a school in Cheltenham, a former engineer who had been an officer of the Honourable Artillery Company, invalided out of the service with shell shock at the end of the late war. Until his appointment to the school two months earlier, he had lived with his widowed mother in Leicester. Yet even this information was nothing to the expectation that glinted in Holmes's eyes when he saw that the young man, Ronald Light, was to be defended by Sir Edward Marshall Hall.

Neither Holmes nor I supposed at the outset that there was anything likely to involve us in the investigation. Since the acquittal of Robert Wood in the Camden Town murder case, thirteen years had passed during which both Sherlock Holmes and I had admired the skill of Sir Edward from a distance. The newspapers of those days were filled with the triumphs of his advocacy and, no less, with reports of sensational trials in which even he had not been able to save his client's neck. Dr Crippen, George Joseph Smith of the 'Brides in the Bath' murders, and Seddon the poisoner were among his clients who had gone to the gallows. In the most famous of his cases, Holmes was of the opinion that Sir Edward could have saved Dr Crippen, had not the defendant's chivalry forbidden the calling of any evidence that might implicate his young mistress, Ethel Le Neve.

It was the more surprising that, within a few days of Ronald Light's arrest, my friend should have received a wire from Sir Edward's clerk, Mr Archibald Bowker, asking us as a matter of urgency to attend a conference at his chambers in Temple Gardens on the following Monday. Sir Edward was at that moment conducting the defence of Eric Holt at Manchester Assizes, where this other young officer of the late war was accused of having shot his mistress. Holmes had shown himself increasingly reluctant to act as Mahomet summoned to the mountain by his clients, but even he could scarcely decline an invitation from a man of such public reputation.

To enter the presence of Sir Edward Marshall Hall in his middle years was a little like sharing the company of a great actor. It was well said that he had a head of Roman nobility on shoulders of Saxon power. By now his hair was silver and his profile a little sharper. Yet his voice retained a characteristic resonance and range, a depth of passion that would have been the envy of Henry Irving or Beerbohm Tree. The effect of his performance upon a jury was such as to make him the despair of even the most eminent of prosecuting counsel. Add to this the acuity of his mind, the speed and drama of his response, a knowledge of forensic science unparalleled at the English bar, and you will have some idea of the power of the great defender, as he was called. He could no longer enter a courtroom without every head turning in his direction, with a stir of excitement and a murmur running from floor to gallery.

Sir Edward stood in the window of his room at 3, Temple Gardens, as we entered. To either side, the break-front walnut bookcases housed maroon leather volumes of case reports, their green labels stamped in gold. Behind him, the lawns and trees fell away to the glitter of the Thames below Westminster Bridge, the smoke of steamers and the sails of barges along the Surrey shore. He shook our hands with a powerful grip, rang for tea and cakes, then motioned us to leather chairs. His desk was piled with briefs tied in pink tape and marked for his attention. I could not help noticing that one of these was inscribed 'Rex v. Light' and endorsed with the words 'Special 50 Guineas'. Sir Edward was not a member of the Midland Circuit and the etiquette of the Bar required that he could not appear there unless he was briefed 'special' in addition to his usual fee and daily refreshers. He looked at us a little forlornly, as it seemed to me.

'Gentlemen, I regret that I have had to bring you here but I must be at Manchester again tomorrow and had not the time to come even as far as Baker Street on this visit. Let me get to the point at once. It will not surprise you, I daresay, to know that the matter at issue is what is called the Green Bicycle case. You have no doubt read something of it.'

'A little,' said Holmes cautiously. 'Enough, at any rate, to follow the story as far as your client's arrest. May I ask how it was that he became a suspect, after so many months?'

Sir Edward's mouth tightened.

'Nemesis, Mr Holmes. There is no other word for it. Last month, on the twenty-third of February to be precise, a boatman was taking a load of coal into Leicester by the canal. Close to the town gas-works, the tow-rope from the horse ran slack and dipped under the surface. When it tightened and came up, it lifted from the water the frame of a bicycle. The man was able to see it for a moment before it slipped from the rope and fell back into the water. He returned next day, no doubt remembering the rewards that had been offered in the case of Bella Wright. A canal dredger dragged the water until the bicycle was found again. It was the frame of a green bicycle, a BSA De Luxe model, without the rear wheel. The individual number of the bicycle had been filed away. However, the owner evidently did not know that the De Luxe models have a further number-stamp on the handlebar pillar. From this it was established that the machine was made in 1910, ordered by a wholesaler in Derby, and sold to Ronald Light. Mr Light has also been paraded by the police and identified by Mr Measures and Mr Evans as the last person seen with Miss Wright before her death.'

I could not restrain my feelings after this last revelation. 'Well, sir, this looks even blacker than the Camden Town murder did for Mr Robert Wood!'

'Blacker yet,' Sir Edward said. 'Valeria Craven and Muriel Nunney, the two schoolgirls who were followed by a man on a bicycle, also identify Ronald Light as that man. Bella Wright's uncle and another member of the family who was in the cottage at Gaulby identify him by his appearance and by his voice as the man who waited outside for Miss Wright, while she remained indoors and hoped he would go away. They are quite sure that it was his voice which said, "Bella, you *have* been a long time," when she left them.'

'Curious,' said Holmes to himself, but the advocate held up his hand, entreating a further explanation.

'There is worse, Mr Holmes. When the police dragged that same stretch of the canal a few days ago to see what else might be found, they retrieved the holster of a Webley Scott .455 service revolver, such as Mr Light was issued with during the war. It was filled with .455 ammunition, identical to the bullet which killed Miss Wright.'

'And the revolver?' Holmes inquired.

Sir Edward shook his splendid head. 'It was not found.'

Holmes gave a sceptical sniff. 'He throws away the holster and the ammunition but not the gun, the very article that might hang him!'

'Perhaps it is there but not found, Mr Holmes. I scarcely want to encourage a further search.'

'Would it not be found in a canal, Sir Edward? It is little more than dragging a pond. Smaller items like a holster or cartridges are found but the revolver is not? Singular, to be sure. And does your client offer any explanation for his extraordinary conduct?'

Sir Edward looked grim but resolute.

'He insists that he met Bella Wright for the first time that evening as she was riding to her uncle's cottage. She was standing by the side of the road. The front wheel of her bicycle was loose in the fork and she asked him if he had a spanner to tighten the nuts. He had not. They rode carefully to her uncle's cottage. Ronald Light claims that he had a slow puncture in his front tyre and could not ride for very long at a time without stopping to pump up the tyre. He met her again as she left her uncle's cottage and kept company with her for about ten minutes until their routes parted. With his slow puncture, the short distance took some time. He then rode on back to Leicester. That was the last he knew of her.'

'He has told you all this himself?' Holmes asked quickly.

'No, Mr Holmes. I have not met Light and I shall not do so until the day of the trial. To speak frankly, his character was not of the best during his military service. Moreover, when he was arrested he first intimated that he had an alibi for the evening on which Bella Wright met her death. Then he threw that defence away, admitted his ownership of the bicycle and his meeting with her, but insisted that she was alive and well when he last saw her at about five minutes before nine P.M. Twenty minutes later she was dead.'

'And will you not probe him further?'

'Mr Holmes, I fear that if I were to discuss the case with Light, he would either blurt out some half-confession of guilt or solicit my advice as to the best story he might invent. I should have to withdraw from the case, if anything of the sort were to happen. There are clients whom it is best to represent at a distance. We must put Mr Light aside and concentrate upon the evidence, the facts in the case. If you are prepared to assist in the matter, I should consider it an honour to retain your services and those of your colleague, Dr Watson.'

There was no delay in agreeing this, since Holmes was intrigued beyond measure by the mystery of the case. Before we left, however, he returned to two points which seemed to Sir Edward of little significance, by comparison with the evidence of firearms and bullets.

'Strange, is it not?' Holmes said. 'They have only known one another for fifteen or twenty minutes at the most, according to what the poor girl said to her uncle. Yet as she left the cottage, Light called her "Bella". The exact words were, "Bella, you *have* been a long time." Hardly a familiarity that a stranger would use. Is it not more likely that he said "Hello"? "Hello, you *have* been a long time"? It would be easy enough to mistake the two words. "Hello" might sound like "Bella" if spoken rather softly or heard at some distance.'

'Mr Measures insists that the man with the bicycle called her "Bella".'

Holmes sighed. 'Well, Sir Edward, that is as nothing compared to the difficulty of the bird, the carrion crow, as the newspapers describe it. I assume its cadaver has not been preserved as evidence?'

'There was no apparent reason to do so, Mr Holmes. It was dissected but nothing was found. No shot and no bullet.'

'With the greatest respect, Sir Edward, there was every reason to preserve evidence in this matter. Take, for example, the matter of the tracks.'

'Which tracks, Mr Holmes?'

'The twelve little tracks of blood that we are told ran to and fro between the gate of the field and the body of the unfortunate young woman,' Holmes said thoughtfully. 'The police recorded those tracks with their usual meticulous care. We are invited to believe that this evil bird sat upon the gate. I have no doubt that it did. We are further invited to believe that it then flew to and fro, gathering blood from its victim and returning to the gate to consume it.'

'Well, Mr Holmes?' It was impossible not to see that Sir Edward Marshall Hall's expression had darkened a little with displeasure. He had staked everything on firearms or ballistics and was in no mood for a lecture on ornithology.

'Well, Sir Edward, if you observe a carrion crow or any other bird of its sort, you will see that it does not fly to and fro. Unless it is disturbed, it stands over its loathsome feast and continues to feed there until it has finished. But, of course, there is a far greater objection to the tracks of blood.'

'Indeed?' said Sir Edward coolly.

'There are twelve!' Holmes said. 'I am surprised that even the local constabulary did not notice the absurdity of it. Twelve! I ask you, Sir Edward!'

He sat back with a flourish of his hand as if in despair at all human intelligence.

'You think them too many?'

'Not the least,' said Holmes reassuringly. 'Thirteen, if you like. Or twenty-three, or thirty-three. But not twelve or fourteen or sixteen or eighteen or any other even number. If the bird went to and fro from the gate, be it flying or hopping, it would not have had blood upon it when it first made towards the body. Therefore the number of tracks surely cannot be twelve or any other even number, if we are to believe the story we have been told. You had not noticed that, Sir Edward?'

It seemed that Sir Edward had not, nor was he best pleased by having it drawn to his attention in this casual manner. However, we got through the remainder of the interview without further damage to vanity on either side. A few days later, in the sunlight of an early spring morning, Holmes and I took the London and North-Eastern Railway from St Pancras to Leicester.

II

Holmes spent the greater part of the journey reading again those statements of evidence which Sir Edward Marshall Hall had had copied for him. I had read them the previous evening but could add little to my friend's remarks at our meeting in Temple Gardens. At the same time Ronald Light, like Robert Wood in the Camden Town case, had made the task of defending him infinitely more difficult by his foolish or guilty conduct. Instead of coming forward at the time of Bella Wright's death to tell the police what he knew, Ronald Light—like Robert Wood—had behaved as a murderer might have done. In Light's case, he had got rid of his green bicycle in the canal, throwing his revolver-pouch and ammunition after it. Had these items never been discovered, he might have lived undisturbed for the rest of his life as a teacher of mathematics in Cheltenham. Yet the boatman's tow-rope on the Leicester canal might now prove to be the very rope that hanged him.

We were almost at Northampton before Holmes put the papers down and lit his pipe.

'The story will not do, Watson,' he said. 'It will not do at all. I do not care for this case in the least. Sir Edward's brief is to fight for his client at all costs and win whatever it may take. As a dispassionate investigator, I find that uncongenial.'

'You think Ronald Light guilty?'

He stared at the flat fields in which the winter rain still lay like a lake.

'I think him very foolish. At the moment, I think no more.'

I gave a laugh and said, 'Then you must be the only man in England who thinks no more than that. Even Sir Edward will not go near him, for fear of being compromised.'

Holmes thought for a moment.

'I do not say a jury will find him guilty, Watson. Sir Edward will find a good deal to say in his defence. Consider this. We are to believe that Light went out on his bicycle to meet, or seduce, or rape, girls or young women. There is no evidence that he had ever done so in the past but set that aside. We are also to believe that he took with him a Webley Scott service revolver for the purpose. He is a professional man of some intelligence and must have known that he dared not use the gun without the probability of being hanged, as the last man seen with the poor girl. There again, the sound of a shot carries a good distance on a quiet summer evening in the country and would surely be heard. Even to threaten a young woman with a gun in broad daylight on a public road would be his downfall. Surely it would be reported. If it is true that he behaved in such a manner none the less, Watson, it falls in the area of mania. That subject belongs to your profession rather than to mine.'

'Yet he may have had such a purpose, gun or no gun, since two girls were followed by him on the same day.'

'Were they?' asked Holmes laconically. 'They did not make statements to the police about it until some months later. One of them picked out Light on an identity parade but only after first seeing his description. Moreover, they were not asked by the police on which day the incident happened but whether it happened on the fifth of July! A leading question, if ever there was! I fancy Sir Edward will make short work of all that in court.'

And, on that last point, Holmes was to be proved right.

'It leaves us with the gun, then,' I said.

'And the bird, Watson. We must not forget the bird.'

It seemed that the bird was to prove more important in this case than anyone had imagined.

III

For several days we rode from Leicester round the five or ten miles of country lanes with their undulating fields showing the first green shoots of spring. We passed through villages that were hardly more than clusters of cottages and handsome churches. Flat hunting land stretched as far as the eye could see from every crest of the road.

Seldom had the time and place of a murder been so precisely defined. Bella Wright was alive at quarter to nine in the evening when she rode from Gaulby in company with Ronald Light. It would have taken her some fifteen minutes to cycle to the spot where her body was found by Farmer Cowell. She had died at that spot between nine o'clock and quarter past, to take the period at its longest. Though she cannot long have been dead, Farmer Cowell heard no shot, except perhaps the pop of a rook rifle, and saw no one. Perhaps, then, Miss Wright was shot at nine or a few minutes afterwards—not with a rook rifle.

Holmes and I stood at the scene. The hedgerows of the narrow road were already high and would grow to almost eight feet by midsummer, the season of Bella Wright's death. They would screen the narrow road and the fields from one another. To one side was the white-painted field gate on which the crow had sat and beyond it was the field in which the bird's body had been found. There was the stretch of road rising towards a junction and the spot where Farmer Cowell had found her. Seventeen feet beyond that the spent bullet had been discovered next day by Constable Hall. The bullet had been greatly deformed, as it was thought, by being trodden under a horse's hoof.

'Watson,' said my companion presently, standing astride the saddle of his bicycle. 'Be good enough to imagine that you have a gun in your hand. You are to shoot me from at least five feet. We are told the old wives' tale that the distance was not less, since the victim showed no burned powder on her skin. Let that stand for a moment. The bullet is to enter below my left eye and exit from the crown of my head. I am standing here and we are arguing.'

I flatter myself that I handle a service revolver pretty well and know a good deal about the wounds inflicted by one. I tried to imagine the line that Holmes described and could do so only by going down on one knee immediately in front of him. It was not a position from which Sir Edward's client would have been likely to threaten or murder Bella Wright.

'Now,' said Holmes, 'try again, as if I were riding along with my head a little down as I pedal harder and approach the crest of the rise.'

I did my best and then gave up.

'It is quite impossible, Holmes,' I said at last. 'I should almost have to lie under the wheels of the bicycle.'

'Interesting, is it not?'

He took some measurements and presently I said, 'You would never hold your head back far enough while you were cycling for that wound to be made. Suppose, however, that she did not fall from the bicycle as a result of being shot, but was shot when she was already lying on her back in the road. That would perfectly explain the angle of the wound.'

'My dear Watson, I do not understand why he would shoot her when she was lying in the road, if he had not done so when she was upright. You are quite correct, however. It is a possible line. Unfortunately, there was no sign of injury before death to suggest such a fall. An accident, however, would be a quite different matter. Imagine a young fool playing about with a gun—perhaps to threaten her. The barrel is pointing down but the gun goes off. The bullet hits the road and comes up at a ricochet. Bella Wright falls dead and Ronald Light flees in panic. Let us look further.'

He propped his bicycle against the white-painted gate and entered the field. After about thirty feet, we came to a stone sheep-trough.

'Hmmm,' he said to himself, 'it is rather as I supposed. Convenient, if mundane.'

Without further explanation, he took his magnifying glass and examined the stonework of the trough along its upper edges, touching the masonry here and there where it seemed a little brighter from some abrasion or other.

'Someone has used this often as a firing-post,' he said presently. 'We had best go and present our findings to Sir Edward.'

'It seems to me, Holmes, that we have found very little of use to him.'

'Precisely,' he said cryptically. 'In that case we had better go and tell him so. I feel, however, we may assure him on the matter of the unfortunate crow.'

'The crow?'

'Yes, Watson. I confess that the crow has been the biggest impediment to this investigation. There have been only two exhibits of significance in this case so far: the blood of the crow and the bullet that was found flattened on the roadway the day after the girl's death. It is most unsatisfactory.'

On the evening of our return to London, Holmes withdrew after dinner to the cellar that we had leased as part of our premises, and which extended a little under the pavement of Baker Street, where there was a coal-chute. Soon after our arrival as tenants, Holmes had filled one end of the underground tunnel with rubble and masked it with iron plating, so that it was even possible to test heavy-calibre big-game rifles without danger. For some time he had been investigating the possibility, yet to be demonstrated at that time, that he might be able to identify the individual gun from which a particular bullet had been fired, as well as the type of weapon. To retrieve the bullet, he fired into a row of fifteen twelve-bore cartridge boxes stuffed tight with cotton wool. A Webley Scott service revolver would penetrate six and a Mauser twice that number. His method was so precise that he knew without fail in which box a spent bullet might be found. Once it had been retrieved, he would go to work with his comparison microscope.

On that spring night of our return from Leicester, homeward-bound pedestrians might have been a little puzzled by a series of powerful but muffled thuds from below the paving stones. Until long after midnight, the cellar was brightly lit.

On the following afternoon, we took a cab to Temple Gardens to report the extent of our progress. It was not the happiest of occasions as we sat once again in the bay-fronted room overlooking the quiet lawns and trees. Our findings were meagre enough. There was also an air of rivalry, for Sir Edward Marshall Hall, no less than Sherlock Holmes, regarded himself as an expert in the matter of firearms and ballistics, which Sir Edward was eager to discuss. Holmes preferred the dead carrion crow.

'I believe, Sir Edward, that we may now be certain the bird was shot either as it sat upon the top bar of the gate or, more likely, a moment after it had taken off.'

Sir Edward passed a hand over his noble jaw. 'We are told that it died because it was gorged with the girl's blood.'

'Such a thing would be quite impossible,' said Holmes. 'Look at the proposition for one moment. We are invited to believe that it died of apoplexy, the result of consuming a surfeit of blood. The annals of ornithology will show that birds do not die in such circumstances, or very rarely so. If there is a surfeit, they regurgitate. In this case, the interval between her death and the finding of the body was a matter of minutes. It scarcely allows time for our bird to gorge itself. Then we have the bloody tracks between the gate and the young woman's body, the impossible number upon which the theory of surfeit relies. It is surely plain that the bird was shot, and that its blood sprayed or splashed from it in the direction of Bella Wright's body. That gives the direction of the bullet. It was shot by someone in the field, not far from the gate.'

'Yet the body of the bird was found fifty or sixty feet away from the gate.'

'Precisely,' said Holmes, 'Forgive me, Sir Edward, but I have made a little study of how birds and other creatures die when they are shot. A bird that is shot while in the air, assuming that our crow had just taken off, will "tower" upwards immediately after the impact, rather than dropping straight down. It gains height for a moment and then falls dead. Yet it still does not fall in a straight line. The consequence is that it will very probably hit the ground at a little distance away. Sixty feet would be nothing.'

'At what range do you say was it shot?'

'Twenty-two feet,' Holmes said without hesitation.

The lawyer's eyes narrowed. 'You can be so precise?'

'I can, Sir Edward. There is a stone sheep-trough in the field, twenty-two feet from the gate. A man or boy hunting crows or other vermin might kneel behind it for cover, no doubt waiting for his prey to show itself. A shot fired at the gate from such cover would travel upwards at an angle of about twenty degrees. It would pass through the body of the bird, which the splashes of blood suggest, and continue upwards with its force somewhat reduced.'

There was no mistaking the excitement in Sir Edward's eyes. He got up and walked to and fro across the window, illustrating by his movements what he believed to have happened to the dead girl.

'Just so, Mr Holmes. Bella Wright is cycling on the near side of the road. Her attention is caught by the bird or the presence of the man. She turns her face in that direction, however briefly. This happens in the interval of her passing the gap in the tall hedge, where the gate stands. The unlucky shot is fired by the man, who has tightened his finger on the trigger before seeing her. The bullet passes through the bird and by the most dreadful chance continues upwards, entering Miss Wright's left cheek just under the eye. Still travelling upwards, it makes its exit wound at the crown of her head. She falls dead from the bicycle. The second impact robs the bullet of most of its force and it strikes the ground seventeen feet away, where it was found next day. There we have it, Mr Holmes.'

He sat down again.

'Not quite,' said Holmes coolly. 'There are two items of evidence missing in your defence, Sir Edward. There is the identity of the man who fired such a shot and there is the gun that might have been used. Moreover, as the Attorney-General will point out to you, your client is the last person to be seen with the dead girl. He concealed evidence from the police. He lied to them when arrested, and he threw his bicycle into the canal. Worst of all, he possessed cartridges identical to that found on the road and which he threw away immediately after the murder. We have only his word for it that he no longer possessed the Webley Scott service revolver for which ammunition of that calibre was designed.'

Sir Edward stood up, reached across the wide desk for a folder and opened it.

'You would agree, Mr Holmes, that if Light shot this young woman, he must have done so at close range and that, presumably, he would have used the Webley Scott revolver?'

'I think it probable.'

Sir Edward displayed a gruesome post-mortem photograph.

'Mr Holmes, have you never seen someone shot in the head at close range by such a weapon? Look for yourself. The bullet not only makes an entry wound and an exit wound. It is hardly too much to say that the victim's head is almost blown apart by the velocity of the bullet. Moreover at such close range, the skin would be marked by the discharge of powder from the barrel.'

'Indeed,' said Holmes sceptically. 'Indeed, Sir Edward, what you say of the head being blown apart might be true if the ammunition were in good condition. Where, however, cartridges have been kept as souvenirs and are of indeterminate age, the results are quite different. A bullet will go off rather like a damp squib. It would have power enough to pass through the victim's head at close range. Yet the powder blast would be relatively slight and the force of the bullet insufficient to do more than make the wounds of entry and exit. It would not be remarkable that it should drop to earth seventeen feet further on. As to the scorching of the skin, I have myself tried experiments with portions of a cadaver. Small-calibre ammunition does not scorch the skin greatly. Even when it is of larger calibre, as in this case, the powder may be washed away by something as simple as a flow of blood.'

Sir Edward Marshall Hall sat back in his chair and met his adversary's gaze with a long stare. It was impossible not to see that he was thanking whatever gods might be that the services of Sherlock Holmes had been retained on behalf of his client and had not been put at the disposal of the Crown.

'Then what, Mr Holmes, are we to think? The bullet that was found has been misshapen by some such impact as a horse's hoof while it lay unnoticed in the road. However, you will not deny that it has been fired by a rifled barrel and that such rifling indicates a rifle.'

'It may indicate that,' said Holmes smoothly, 'but it does not prove it. I must warn you, Sir Edward, that if you ask such a question in cross-examination, you will be told that a Webley Scott revolver has a rifled barrel, though it is not a rifle, and that it leaves seven narrow rifling grooves on any bullet fired from it.'

For the first time in our dealings with him, a shadow of alarm crossed the great lawyer's handsome countenance.

'Do you say, Mr Holmes, that this bullet could not have been fired from a rifle?'

Holmes shook his head. 'No one can say for certain that it was not fired by a rifle. However, a .455 cartridge would suggest a rifle of unusual power. An elephant rifle, perhaps.'

Sir Edward sat upright. 'An elephant rifle?'

'Quite so,' said Holmes, 'and you will no doubt be asked how many of the good folk in these charming villages go out in the evenings to shoot crows with an elephant rifle.'

'This will not do, Mr Holmes!'

'Very well,' said Holmes, 'I will give you an argument, though it is not one I should care to use myself. Let us take a military rifle made by thousands and used by cadets or volunteer companies. The Martini-Henry is frequently of .452 bore, some were rebarrelled to various bores when the Lee-Enfield was brought in. It would be hard to prove that a Martini-Henry or any other particular gun had not fired a bullet as badly deformed as this one. The fact that the rifling is so defaced by a horse's hoof in this instance might suggest a badly worn Martini-Henry. Since the war, a Martini-Henry is the most common rifle to be found, as .455 is the most common calibre of ammunition.'

It was all the comfort that Sir Edward seemed likely to get. He walked with us to the door and Sherlock Holmes turned to him with fastidious courtesy.

'I hope you will not think me precipitate, Sir Edward, if I tell you that I have now done almost everything that I can on behalf of your client and that I positively must withdraw from the case. I shall, of course, accept no fee.'

There was no doubt from his face that Sir Edward felt a dread that his defence of Ronald Light would prove to be built upon sand.

'Withdraw, Mr Holmes? For God's sake why?'

'It will be better if I keep my reasons to myself,' Holmes said quietly. 'However, if I may offer a last piece of advice it is this. Mr Robert Churchill, the gunsmith of Agar Street in the Strand, has given evidence in many cases of this kind. His knowledge and skill are unparalleled. I must urge you to retain his services at once, unless you wish your client to be hanged.'

For all his forensic brilliance, Sir Edward Marshall Hall was baffled—and exasperated.

'What can Mr Robert Churchill tell me that you cannot?'

'I will only repeat,' said Holmes quietly, 'that unless you retain his services at once, you are likely to see Mr Light hanged.'

At that moment, I thought I saw a glimmer of comprehension in the grey eyes of Sir Edward Marshall Hall. Whatever it was that he comprehended was quite beyond me.

As we stood outside in the sunlight of Temple Gardens, I was almost dumbfounded. Never, in all our acquaintanceship, had Sherlock Holmes ever behaved in such a manner towards a client.

'You have abandoned him!' I said incredulously. 'Indeed, you have abandoned them both, Sir Edward and Ronald Light!'

He looked at me without expression. 'On the contrary, Watson. I believe I may just have saved Mr Light from the gallows and Sir Edward from a terrible defeat.'

IV

As was too often the case when Holmes appeared to play the prima donna, he refused positively to discuss the matter with me. All the same, we attended the days of drama in the courtroom of Leicester Castle when Ronald Light stood trial for his life, charged with the murder of Annie Bella Wright.

Sir Edward Marshall Hall played a desperate game but he never played one with greater skill. The two young girls who claimed that Light had followed them were dismissed from the case. In their stupidity, the police had not asked them when they were followed but *whether* it had been on 5 July. That leading question was an end of their evidence. Worse still, the two girls had picked out Light from the men at the police station only after having first been given his description.

When it was known by the prosecution that Mr Robert Churchill was for the defence in the matter of the guns, it was supposed that Sir Edward had an ace up his sleeve. The Crown was content to call a local gunsmith of Leicester, Mr Henry Clarke. He was no match for the forensic power of Sir Edward Marshall Hall. In cross-examination, he agreed that the .455 bullet had been standard ammunition for at least thirty years past and had been made in thousands of millions. He agreed that the rifling marks on the bullet that killed Bella Wright were consistent with its having been fired either from a revolver or a rifle. He still maintained that it might have been fired from close range, passed through the young woman's head, hit the road, then risen and landed further on. He was not, however, able to find the mark on the bullet that would have been caused by the first of two such impacts with the road.

Having got so far in the matter of the gun, Sir Edward Marshall Hall did not call evidence for the defence on this point from Mr Robert Churchill or anyone else. Nor was this surprising. Ronald Light had escaped the gallows by a whisker. Later, Holmes handed me a summary of the report that Mr Churchill had made to Sir Edward, a document that the lawyer passed to my friend with a brief note of gratitude for his advice in retaining the famous gunsmith.

In Robert Churchill's opinion, the bullet that killed Bella Wright had been fired from a Webley Scott service revolver and no other weapon. Not only had the victim been shot by a revolver of the type for which Ronald Light possessed holster and ammunition, she had been shot from such close range that the bullet had scarcely begun to gather speed. No hunter shooting crows with a rifle had killed her. If Mr Churchill had given such evidence in court for the Crown, Ronald Light would surely have been hanged.

'My dear Watson,' said Holmes equably, the night after Light's acquittal on the grounds that the lingering effects of shell shock had unnerved him from going to the police when first suspected, 'I quite thought you had grasped my reasons at once.'

'Your reasons for what?'

'I withdrew from the case in order that Sir Edward might retain the services of Mr Robert Churchill. It is a simple matter of legal procedure. Mr Churchill is perhaps the greatest expert on firearms this country has ever known. If the defence retained him, the Director of Public Prosecutions could not. Sir Edward was good enough to suggest that my expertise might equal Mr Churchill's and it would be ungracious to argue over that. By my withdrawal, he was able to ensure that neither of us gave evidence for the Crown. He dared not put Mr Churchill in the witness-box once he had read his report. Yet he had deprived the other side of that advantage.'

'For God's sake, Holmes! You have saved the girl's murderer from the gallows?'

He stretched out his legs and laughed.

'There is no murderer, Watson! Why do all of you fail to grasp that essential point? Somewhere in the Leicester canal or a similar hiding-place lies the Webley Scott revolver once issued to Lieutenant Ronald Light. It is not the weapon of a murderer, though it killed Bella Wright. He was, I imagine, playing the fool with it to impress or amuse her. To his horror, it went off, the bullet hitting the stone-work of the road, glancing upwards and passing through her head. It is the only angle consistent with the wound and therefore the only likely explanation. Light knew that his record in the army had not been of the best. His conduct with young women was much the same. It was a dreadful accident, not a murder, but who would believe him now?'

'And the carrion crow?' I asked sardonically. 'Did he shoot that before he killed Bella Wright—or afterwards?'

Holmes smiled to himself.

'Not far away, under those same muddy waters that hide the revolver, there lies a rifle. Not an elephant-gun to be sure. Not even a gun of .455 calibre. Perhaps an old Martini-Henry used by lads or even their fathers to take pot-shots at crows and the like. Far more likely a rook rifle. It belonged to some other young man who fled from the scene of the tragedy in terror. Imagine him concealed behind the sheep-trough as the crow lands on the gate. He sights the bird and shoots it. Then he gets up and continues on his way to the gate itself. Looking over, he sees the most dreadful sight, the poor girl dead upon the ground, the bicycle beside her.'

'And where is Ronald Light?'

'There is no one to be seen, Watson. For this young woman was shot at about nine o'clock and it is now ten minutes later. The fellow with the gun thinks what Sir Edward made the jury think. The bullet from his rifle passed through the crow, hit the road and glanced up, passed through the girl's head and came to rest. A .455 bullet! It would have blown a crow to pieces.'

'It is what Sir Edward himself thinks, as well as the jury,' I said firmly.

'Then he really is quite mistaken, Watson. The lad—for rook-shooting is a game for lads—saw what he had done. Or, rather, what he thought he had done. He did not stop but took to his heels in terror with the phantom of the hangman at his back. For how was he to prove that it was an accident and no murder?'

'Two shots at once? Something of a coincidence, surely?'

'Two shots, Watson, at an interval of ten or fifteen minutes. Not so much of a coincidence in such splendid hunting country on a fine summer evening.'

In what was to become known as 'The Green Bicycle Case', the explanation that Holmes expounded was the only one to explain the features of the case. For five or ten minutes we sat either side of the fireplace, smoking and thinking.

'Then what do you think of Ronald Light in the end, Holmes? What judgment will you pass on your former client?'

'I only think, Watson, that he is one of the luckiest young men alive. Lucky to be alive and not hanged by the neck in Leicester gaol.'

He added a little brandy to his soda. Half an hour later, he yawned and stretched.

'I believe you have found our little adventure in Leicestershire one too many for you, Watson. Just now you thought I had protected a murderer. I assure you, I have done no more than to save a fool. If you should ever include the case in those romantic fictions of yours, you will find it easier to compose if you first hit upon a good title. I will give you one. You will not talk of bicycles, nor revolvers and cartridges, nor the habits of the carrion crow. You will call it simply, "The Case of the Missing Rifleman". That will explain it completely.'

He puffed at his pipe and said no more. The rest of the world speculated on whether the single bullet that killed Bella Wright passed first through the body of the carrion crow. To Holmes, it was far simpler. There were two bullets. The coincidence of two guns being fired in hunting country within fifteen minutes on a summer evening was trivial compared with the coincidence of a single bullet passing through such a remarkable trajectory. The perversity of his opponents in the debate produced only a shrug from Holmes at the hopelessness of arguing with frailer intellects, who were driven to suggest that the deed must have been done by a lad shooting rooks with an elephant gun! As for Sir Edward Marshall Hall, it seemed a certain awkwardness had been generated between us by this disagreement, for he never communicated with either Holmes or myself again.

The Case of the Yokohama Club

I

Looking back on the career of Sherlock Holmes, it is plain that the years from 1894 to 1901 were those during which his services were in the most constant demand. Each new case of public importance or private investigation came close on the heels of the last. Gone were the easy-going days of the eighties, when he would lean back in his chair after breakfast, unfold his morning paper at leisure, and fold it again ten minutes later with a lament that it presented few possibilities to the mind of the criminal expert.

Our rooms in Baker Street now received visits from the great and the humble alike. One week our inquirer might be an emissary from Windsor, Downing Street, or one of the chancelleries of Europe. Next week it would be a poor widow-woman or an old soldier with nowhere else to turn. Holmes worked, as he said often, for the love of his art. Yet his instincts and his sympathies were with the weak rather than the mighty. Distress was never turned away from his door.

During these busy years, the manner of his life was everything that a healthy man's should not be. The needle and the cocaine, his chosen implements of self-poisoning, lay conveniently to hand in their drawer. He would spend such hours of recreation as his engagements allowed shut away from sunshine and fresh air, breathing the fumes of some chemical experiment or playing his favourite Haydn and Mendelssohn on the violin. That was all the solace he knew, apart from his pipe. So great was the burden of work that even his rivals in the detective profession were concerned for him.

'Mr Holmes will run himself into the ground, if he keeps up this rate,' said our Scotland Yard friend Lestrade to me after one of our shared adventures. From observation, I was bound to agree. Yet I knew from experience that nothing was more useless than to offer advice to Holmes in medical matters.

With such calls upon his energies, it might seem remarkable to those who knew him only by reputation that he should have given so many weeks of his time in 1897 to an investigation that took him to the other side of the world. Perhaps he was moved by the plight of a young woman—little more than a schoolgirl—facing death at the hands of an arcane and unjust law. Perhaps he also saw from the first how easily a private wrong of this sort might become a scandal and a public disgrace to the British Crown, if her execution were to take place. Whatever the reason, his interest in the story began, as so many of our inquiries did, in the familiar surroundings of Baker Street. For convenience, I have gathered the disparate events that followed under the title of 'The Case of the Yokohama Club'.

Those who remember the London autumn of 1896 may recall that it rained as if it never meant to stop. It did not wash away the city fog but reduced it to an oppressive mist. As the days shortened, the lowering skies in the west seemed to bring perpetual twilight and it was dusk by three in the afternoon.

On such an afternoon towards the end of the year, as the sunset faded before tea-time, Holmes was sitting at the table with a large folio pharmacopoeia open before him and a test-tube of malodorous green liquid in the rack to one side. His long thin back was curved and his head was sunk upon his breast in the attitude that had always suggested to my mind a large and gloomy bird of grey plumage with a black top-knot. I was about to break in upon his thoughts when the sudden clang of the doorbell forestalled me.

Holmes appeared not to hear it as he turned another page of his folio and settled morosely upon the next paragraph. Standing by the window, I moved the curtain a little and looked down into the street. An empty cab was just moving off with the driver's 'Yah-yah-poop!' to the horse and a flick of the reins. From what I could see, the man who stood awaiting an answer to his summons was a stranger to us. The gas had already been lit in the house, so that the fanlight of the door beat full upon the gleaming shoulders of his waterproof, which ran with steady rain. There came an exchange of voices in the hall and the light knock of Mrs Hudson at our door.

'A gentleman, Mr Holmes,' the good lady said unnecessarily. 'Mr Jacob has no appointment but begs you will see him on a matter of the greatest urgency.'

How many times had I heard these words, or their like? Holmes looked up from his calculations and his face seemed brighter.

'Very well, Mrs Hudson. If Mr Jacob takes no more than half an hour of my time, I will listen to what ails him.'

Our housekeeper closed the door and presently, after our visitor had been relieved of his waterproof in the hall, we heard a heavy tread upon the stairs. A broad-shouldered fair-haired man of thirty or so entered the room, well built but with a wan, sensitive, clear-cut face. His blue eyes seemed the brighter for the dark shadows round them.

Holmes watched him cross the room and then stood up to take the visitor's hand.

'Please,' he said, indicating the vacant chair by the fireplace. 'Please take a seat, Dr Jacob, and tell me how I may be of service to you.'

Our visitor went, if that were possible, a little paler on being addressed as 'Doctor'.

'You know me, Mr Holmes?'

'I had never heard of you until a few minutes ago,' Holmes said reassuringly. 'That you are a doctor is, I fear, betrayed by the double deformation which the side pocket of a jacket acquires from carrying the two metal tubes of a stethoscope with the ear-pieces overlapping the edge of the cloth. This is my colleague, Dr Watson, before whom you may speak freely. I have had ample opportunity of observing the ill effects of that medical instrument upon his tailoring.'

Dr Jacob seemed relieved by this simple explanation. He sat down.

'All the same, Mr Holmes, it is disconcerting to be seen through so easily.'

Holmes stood before the fireplace with legs astride, arms folded, one elbow cupped in the other hand.

'Come now, Dr Jacob. I mean you no harm. It is a matter of inference only. I cannot be sure of everything. I am very probably wrong. I should say, however, that you had not long moved to the house in which you live and that it is conveniently near to the railway station. You travel up to Victoria or, possibly, Waterloo. Victoria, I think, is more likely. I am already persuaded that the matter on which you have come to see me is indeed of great urgency. It evidently involves someone dear to you who is far away. The worst news of her reached you yesterday, somewhen following lunch. After a night that was passed in waking rather than sleeping, you decided this morning that you must come here in person and ask me to undertake a long journey on behalf of this lady. I regret that I cannot promise I shall be able to oblige you.'

It would scarcely be too much to use the cliché and say that our visitor's mouth fell open with astonishment and the poor devil's eyes started.

'You cannot know, Mr Holmes! Someone has surely been here before me. One of the Carews!'

Holmes sat down on the sofa and crossed his long legs comfortably, as if this would reassure Dr Jacob.

'No one, I promise you,' he said kindly. 'I know nothing of any Carews. I observe only that you came by cab to our door, so that your shoes are scarcely wet. Yet they show that you have walked a little in the rain earlier today. They have dried since then, so it cannot be in the last fifteen or twenty minutes. If you went on foot from your own house to the station, the condition of your shoes suggests that the distance cannot have been great. However, the wet has caused particles of stone or shingle to adhere to the uppers as they dried. Some are little more than husks. I have experience of those and I recognise them as sea-dredged aggregates. They are used very commonly on roads of new houses in Surrey and Sussex, conveniently close to the channel dredging. One finds them on byways not yet adopted by the local council and not yet treated with tarmac. Therefore, I assume you cannot have lived long in your present home, and that it is in Surrey or Sussex, near the station.'

'That at least is correct,' Dr Jacob said. He seemed relieved to discover that scientific deduction, rather than witchcraft, had revealed so much of him.

'Furthermore,' Holmes said quietly, 'you came here by cab. The square of pasteboard shaped by the cloth of your waistcoat pocket is, I believe, a railway ticket, but not a metropolitan one. It is in any case merely a return half. The underground railway line from Waterloo to Baker Street is very convenient and generally faster than a cab. Not so from Victoria. I am inclined to think you came from Victoria Station. As for your purpose, I suppose it merely by the weight and size of the notecase in your inner breast pocket, which appears—once again by the deformation of the suiting—to be more than amply filled. I beg you will take care, Dr Jacob. It is an invitation to thieves and footpads to carry so much money with so little concealment. I observe from your face that you slept badly last night and that, though perfectly clean-shaven yesterday, the hand that held your razor has been less certain today. I infer that whatever ill news you received reached you yesterday, too late to bring you here at once.'

Dr Jacob stared at him bright-eyed but said nothing. He seemed mesmerised, or perhaps a little fearful, at the performance which Holmes was giving for his benefit.

'I do not wish to be presumptuous,' Holmes concluded, 'but I should be surprised if you had not come here today in the expectation of paying in advance a large sum in cash. That a cheque will not suffice and that the sum is so large suggests to me both that the matter is urgent and the expenses far greater than would be justified unless the investigation involved foreign travel of some kind. Put all these things together and I infer that only some person dear to you and now in great peril would explain them in their entirety. That the person is a lady is, I confess, mere conjecture. Yet nine times out of ten, in such circumstances as these, it is so. She is not your wife, I think. Either you would be with her or you would be on your way to her before now. A daughter, at your time of life, would be too young. A sister, shall we say? Or perhaps a cousin? A sister, I think, is the more probable.'

For the hundredth time, as it seemed to me, I saw emotions of astonishment and relief cross the face of a client, like clouds driven in succession over a windy sky. For a moment, Dr Jacob seemed too overwrought to speak. At last he said, 'It is my sister, Mr Holmes. She is the youngest of us, as I am the eldest. You are correct in every detail of your account. In the last few minutes you have convinced me that everything said about you is true. You alone can save her, if any man may.'

'And where is your sister, Dr Jacob?'

'She is in Yokohama, where she is very likely to be hanged.'

The name of Yokohama fell like a thunderbolt into the room. In my mind I had thought of Paris, Berlin, perhaps even Rome or New York, as the probable scene of the drama. But Yokohama! It was impossible, surely, that Holmes would contemplate such a commission?

My friend got up and walked to the window, the curtains still open, and stared out into the street.

'Yokohama!' he said at last, very softly but with an excitement that was unmistakable. He gazed out into the dismal London night, deeper in thought than I had seen him for a long time. 'And very likely to be hanged!'

It was raining more heavily now and the gaslight of the room shone dimly out through the streaked and dripping glass, falling upon the pavements and the black ribbon of the wet street. Holmes kept his thoughts to himself a moment longer. In the silence, the air was full of the sounds of rain, the thin swish of its fall, the heavier drip from the eaves, and the swirl and gurgle down the steep gutters and through the sewer grating. At last he turned round.

'Dr Jacob, before we go further, I should be very glad if you would tell us slowly and quietly of your sister's difficulty and how it is that you think we might help her. I must tell you, however, that I am a criminal investigator and not a worker of miracles.'

So we heard the story of Mary Esther Jacob and the late Walter Raymond Hallowell Carew. In brief, Carew was a married man and Miss Jacob was thought to have been his mistress, one of many in the course of his colonial career. The man had led a rackety sort of life in the Malay Straits Settlement, Hong Kong, and last of all in the English colony at Yokohama. For some time before his death in October 1896, he had been Secretary and Manager of the Yokohama United Club, where English and American officers and businessmen were wont to gather. Seven years ago, he had married Edith Mary Porch in England and taken her to the Straits Settlement. There he spent several years as a Treasurer in the Colonial Service. Brandy and soda had very nearly killed him in such a climate. Then both he and his bride had fallen ill with malarial fever and, after a spell in Australia, they had come to Yokohama. Neither was ever in perfect health and medication was regularly prescribed for them.

There was no disputing Carew's vices. He had begotten children by a number of women before his marriage. One was even supported afterwards out of his wife's money. The couple also had two children of their own and Miss Mary Jacob, previously living with her brother, had gone out to Yokohama as nursery governess. Another infection from which Carew suffered was of the venereal type, a case of gonorrhoea known only privately until the report of the inquest upon him at the Royal Naval Hospital at Yokohama in October last.

Mrs Carew was little better than her husband, he playing the part *of mari complaisant,* so long as his own pleasures were not interfered with. Edith Carew had found lovers easily in the foreign settlement area of Yokohama. Her husband shrugged at this. The couple even gave such men the nicknames of 'The Ferret' or 'The Organ Grinder'. The latest young man prepared to give his life for her was Harry Vansittart Dickinson, a clerk at the Yokohama branch of the Hong Kong and Shanghai Banking Corporation. Letters of a compromising kind had passed between Dickinson and Mrs Carew for several months, in which the young man urged the errant wife to seek a divorce and become his own bride.

The story of Mary Jacob in such a flashy and sickly household was one of the oldest in the world. It was not long before the inexperienced young governess believed herself in love and became Carew's mistress. This adulterous *ménage* was broken up several months later by the death of the man himself. He had been ailing for several years, since the venereal infection had occasioned a stricture. Far worse, his drinking had brought on symptoms of an incipient cirrhosis of the liver. He could no more resist brandy and soda than he could ignore a pretty servant. With the easy credit and bonhomie of the Yokohama Club, those who sent him on colonial service to cure his drinking had better have sent him to Hades as an escape from summer heat. The state of his liver grew worse and the doctors in Yokohama threatened him with acute jaundice. Carew ignored them. He preferred to put his faith in self-prescribed 'tonics' containing a homoeopathic dose of arsenic as well as sugar of lead.

After his death, Miss Jacob fled the house, as if on suspicion of poisoning a lover who had spurned her. It was certain that during the last weeks of her residence Carew's health grew rapidly worse and he lapsed into delirium. He had died on 22 October, having been taken to the British Naval Hospital at Yokohama a few hours previously. His final illness had lasted for about a fortnight but he had grown suddenly worse in the last twenty-four hours.

The inquest found that Carew had died from arsenical poisoning. What motive was there for murder? Mrs Carew enjoyed freedom in her married life to do as she pleased and had little reason to murder her husband. However, Mary Jacob had far greater cause for vengeance when she discovered that the lover who had cast her off might also have infected her with a dreadful disease.

The suspicions of Carew's doctors had been roused very late. In the last two days they forbad any member of the household to be alone with the invalid. They appointed nurses of high character, one of whom was always in attendance. Yet as late as the last night, when the nurse was away from the room for a few minutes, two servants had seen Mary Jacob standing before the medicine cabinet in the sick man's room. The bedroom door had been locked to prevent this very thing. Miss Jacob must surely have kept or copied a key given her by her lover in happier days. Next day he was dead from a final and fatal dose of arsenic, the equivalent of a one-ounce bottle of Fowler's Solution of Arsenic. Three such bottles were found almost empty in the house. Miss Jacob alone, it seemed, had found the opportunity and motive to do away with him.

'It is most unfortunate, Mr Holmes,' Dr Jacob added, 'that after Carew died, my sister went to the chemist to ask for the return of the order-form for the last bottle of Fowler's Solution. It was written in her own hand, you see. She swears that Carew ordered it and that she merely wrote his instructions.'

Unfortunate! If anything further were needed to put the noose round young Miss Jacob's neck, she had surely provided it by going to beg back this paper written in her own hand! Holmes seemed unperturbed, however, and asked about the behaviour of Carew himself during these last weeks, so far as Dr Jacob knew of it. The dead man's final words offered little comfort to our client.

'I have taken a whole chemist's shop today,' the witnesses heard Carew gasp as he waved away the glass, despite the pain that consumed his entrails. 'I do not want more medicine. I want a brandy and soda.'

That brandy and soda was the last the poor fellow ever drank for by some means the murderer had evidently added the entire bottle of Fowler's Solution to it. By the next morning, the last of his life, he was in such agony and sickness that it was necessary to give him a morphine injection, as well as tablets of cocaine. Carew was in a pitiful state, swearing in his delirium that he could feel worms crawling under his skin and driving him to madness. He also murmured of Mary Jacob and her secret visit to him on that final night. He blessed her as the angel who had poured brandy and soda and held it to his lips in his fever. Had she not been seen by the servants, that might be thought mere delusion. He was in such a state that, in the darkened room that last night, he would believe anyone to be his sweetheart who said she was.

'There is no question, Mr Holmes, that my sister bought Fowler's Solution of Arsenic from the chemist,' said Dr Jacob with a sigh. 'But she swears that she did so on Carew's orders. It was poured into the brandy and soda or into the tonic he took against the state of his liver. Now he is dead and cannot speak for her. It is said that she made evil use of the tonic, for one single-ounce bottle of Fowler's Solution contains twice the fatal dose. The other witnesses, one and all, agree that in those last days there hung about her a scent of lavender. It does not grow in Yokohama, Mr Holmes.'

Holmes's features contracted in a frown.

'Indeed not,' he said softly.

'But all the world knows that Fowler's Solution of Arsenic is strongly scented with lavender to make it more palatable. Dr Watson will bear me out.'

I was about to do so, but Holmes intervened before I could agree. 'I can bear you out, Dr Jacob. I have made a little study of such matters.'

There was worse news that came to our visitor. It was discovered that Mary Jacob had been in the habit of going through the waste-paper baskets to find fragments of letters sent to her employers, especially to Mrs Carew. She took these to a friend, another nursery governess in Yokohama by the name of Elsa Christoffel, who pasted and stitched them together. Mary Jacob was later seen by a witness practising Mrs Carew's signature on a sheet of paper, also marked by the initials 'A. L.' Indeed, Miss Jacob had shown this to the witness as proof of her skill in forgery or imitation.

The foolish young woman seemed determined to wear the rope and spring the trap. Before and after Carew's death there were letters from 'A. L.' and 'Annie Luke', suspected of being written by Mary Jacob. 'Annie Luke' had been Carew's mistress, according to her claims in these letters. In the last one, written to Mrs Carew's lawyer, Mr John Frederick Lowder, the writer confessed in every detail her wicked murder of Carew. Though the letters were signed by Annie Luke, the hand was still said to be that of Mary Jacob.

Dr Jacob's sister now faced trial for murder on the far side of the world by a British consular court, whose like would never have been permitted in our own country. Any jury chosen from the few hundred members of the British community at Yokohama must already know of Miss Jacob and the Carews. They would very likely hold her guilty before the case was opened. She would be held in the British Naval Prison at Yokohama and hanged there by a military executioner, if the verdict went against her, as it now seemed that it must.

'Mr Holmes,' said Dr Jacob softly, 'it is a nightmare. She is beyond help, condemned by a system that I do not begin to understand. Can it be justice?'

Holmes put down his pipe.

'It is the law,' he said quietly, 'whether or not it be justice. Law is what concerns us, Dr Jacob. Law and evidence. The system dates from the treaty with Japan in 1858. Great Britain may exercise consular jurisdiction over her citizens in the five Treaty Ports. They live in foreign settlements within these ports. In return, they are forbidden from travelling more than a few miles from the settlements. In such cases as this, they are tried before the consul's court and acquitted or convicted there. In a conviction for murder, the trial and the execution are to be carried out by British officials in Japan.'

'But that is not justice!' he exclaimed. 'Can she not be brought to England?'

'The law does not provide for that,' said Holmes in the same quiet voice. 'It deals with such a crime in the place where it was perpetrated.'

'How can it be dealt with?' the poor fellow asked in despair. 'How can there be an impartial jury chosen from the few British residents in a port like Yokohama, where all know one another? They will all have taken sides by now. I fear they will listen to the doctors and the other witnesses that the Carew family will put forward, rather than to a seduced and vengeful nursery governess. Forgive me, Mr Holmes, but that is what she will be called!'

'Then we must see to it, Dr Jacob, that, if your sister is innocent, she is acquitted on the evidence, rather than convicted on prejudice.'

'Acquitted, Mr Holmes? I beg you will not mock her.'

Holmes stood up.

'I was never more serious in my life, Dr Jacob. If the facts are as you have described them, I begin to have hopes.'

But I looked at Dr Jacob and, for a moment, I thought the poor fellow might break down in tears. There was such agitation in his face as he thought of the helplessness of this poor girl—for his sister was quite ten years his junior—facing her doom alone on the far side of the world. By the fastest route, Yokohama was almost four weeks away from London. Events there were moving with a terrible speed, while he was trapped so far away. He seemed like a sleeper in a fearful dream, the course of which he could neither alter nor even influence. If Holmes could see a way through the case against the girl, I could not.

'Someone must go to her, Mr Holmes!' Dr Jacob began again. 'She has no family there, no friends that I can call upon. She must have help!'

Holmes stared at the stem of his pipe, his mind further away than Yokohama. A moment later he was the cold and practical thinker once more.

'From what you tell me, Dr Jacob, there would seem little to persuade a jury that your sister is innocent. Fortunately for you, I am not that jury. I find one or two points in the evidence a little curious. I daresay they are nothing but I should like to probe them further. One, at least, has a certain air of fabrication. While

Carew was dying, your sister was seen in his room alone with him. Standing before the medicine cabinet. How many witnesses are there to that?'

'Two. Both are servants of good character. They are girls from the Tokyo Mission School, employed by the Carews.'

'At this time, no other person, not even Mrs Carew, was permitted to be with him unsupervised?'

'No. And I cannot tell you, Mr Holmes, how my sister came to be with him in the few minutes the nurse was absent. The windows of the room were inaccessible. The door was locked and two witnesses on guard outside it. She could neither get in nor out, unless she had a key given her by Carew when he was her lover—or she had stolen one. My sister is no magician, Mr Holmes.'

Holmes stared at him, long and steadily. At last he said, 'I daresay she is not. However, it is not your sister who concerns me, Dr Jacob. I should like to know how these two estimable young witnesses from the Mission School saw your sister standing before the medicine cabinet, if she was alone.'

Dr Jacob shook his head. 'There was a sound in the room, as if someone had banged the window to. They looked through the keyhole of the locked door and saw her. She was standing before the medicine cabinet on which was a triple table-mirror for dressing.'

The faintest smile of triumph touched my friend's fastidious mouth.

'Were I intent upon being locked in with my victim, Dr Jacob, I should take care to leave the key in the lock after I fastened the door behind me. It is convenient if one needs to leave quickly and it prevents any intrusion. It also blocks the view. No one, however morally estimable, even from a Mission School, would see me through the keyhole with the key in the lock. A little curious is it not? Pray, continue.'

Just then, for the first time, I knew that Holmes was set upon Yokohama. It was a madcap adventure but he had never resisted an adventure of any sort.

'The smell of lavender,' Holmes said quietly, 'how was that noticed?'

Dr Jacob shook his head, as if to clear it. 'In the days before the man's death, Mr Holmes, there was a scent of lavender that seemed to cling to my sister's clothes, to her hair. The very same smell was noticed in the sick room.'

'Lavender water is a common enough perfume, Dr Jacob. What matter if your sister chose it—or if someone gave her a present of it to use?'

Dr Jacob looked at Holmes with the faintest suggestion of disappointment in my friend's abilities.

'You are well informed in the pharmacopeia, Mr Holmes, as I infer from the copy at present on your table. You know, perhaps better than I, the extent to which Fowler's Solution of Arsenic is perfumed with spirits of lavender to make it more palatable.'

'Hmmm,' said Holmes drily. 'From where did your sister buy the Fowler's Solution that she was sent to get?'

'Maruya's Pharmacy in the town. She went there rather than Schedel's European Pharmacy because it also sold books and stationery.'

'Mrs Carew was a customer of Schedel, I take it?'

'I daresay she was,' Dr Jacob looked up a little sharply. 'But spirits of lavender are a characteristic ingredient of Fowler's Solution of Arsenic.'

'In England,' Holmes said, as if finishing the sentence for him.

'But Fowler's Solution is universal, Mr Holmes.'

'Indeed, it is, Dr Jacob but the British Pharmacopeia is not.'

He stood up, pulled a pamphlet from the shelf, and handed it to our visitor.

'You would perhaps care to consult this most interesting monograph by Professor Edwin Divers of the Chemistry Department of the Imperial University of Tokyo—late of the Medical School of Middlesex Hospital. Dr Divers, being expert in the toxicology of tropical medicine, is something of an inspector-general of pharmacies in the Far East. His analysis establishes beyond question that neither spirits of lavender nor sandalwood tincture are used in Japanese Fowler's Solution, such as Maruya's would sell. You will find the comment on page eighteen at the end of the second paragraph.'

He handed the open pamphlet to our guest. Dr Jacob looked up.

'I had no idea, Mr Holmes, that Fowler's Solution from a Japanese pharmacy would be differently constituted, nor would most of my profession.'

'No,' said Holmes languidly. 'Nor did the person who sought to incriminate your sister by so foolish a trick. That alone does not acquit her nor incriminate Mrs Carew. From what you tell me, much of the evidence and motivation is still against Miss Jacob. Yet this point has a certain interest, does it not?'

Dr Jacob drew a handkerchief from his pocket and blew his nose bravely.

'Then you cannot promise anything, Mr Holmes?' he asked, standing up like a man of courage to face his executioners. Holmes remained seated.

'I did not say that, Dr Jacob. I said that much of the evidence and the motivation appears to be against your sister. Appearances, however, invite investigation. I must urge you not to entertain false hopes but, if you wish, I will see what can be done for Miss Jacob.'

'You will go to Yokohama?' It was plain that Dr Jacob could not credit this. Nor could I. Holmes, however, inclined his head.

'If that is what you wish.'

'To Yokohama, Holmes?' I could not restrain my interruption. 'To Japan?'

'I understand that it is where the port of Yokohama is to be found.'

Dr Jacob still stared at him, as if he thought my friend would qualify such a promise. Then he saw the truth.

'Mr Holmes, I did not dare to believe that you would—or could! That you would do this for a stranger, whom you never saw until today!'

Holmes laid down his pipe. 'I ask no thanks, Dr Jacob, and I make no promises. I would not go at all if it were only to please you. I confess, however, that the case against your sister intrigues me. It is so strong—almost too strong—and yet the matter of the keyhole and the impeccable Mission School witnesses, like the perfume of lavender and the irreproachable nurse, possesses a certain undeniable attraction.'

The continuation of the analysis was lost upon our visitor, weary with grief and bewildered as he was. He reached into his pocket and drew out the amply filled note-case. Holmes held up a hand.

'If you please, Dr Jacob, we will have no payment and no discussion of fees as yet. When I bring your sister safely home, you may repay me. If I do not, then I fear I should be unable to accept anything for my services.'

II

'What the devil is this, Holmes?' It was ten minutes later and we had parted with our visitor until the next day. 'We are to set out for Yokohama, with all that remains to be done here? We are to chase after a foolish girl, who from everything we are told is probably guilty of the crime with which she is charged? We are to do all this without any certainty of having so much as our expenses paid?'

'We are to do all that, Watson, just as you say.'

'But why?'

'My dear Watson,' he said smiling, 'have you learned nothing of the criminal mind in all these years of our acquaintance? In this case, all my instincts are one way and almost all the facts are the other. Yet there are one or two curiosities. Did you ever hear of a devious poisoner, who calculates dosages and times with such care, but deliberately takes the key from inside the door so that she may be broken in upon at the moment that will reveal her guilt?'

'That means nothing, Holmes. It may happen all too easily in the stress of the moment, when the crime is so monstrous and the criminal lacks experience or thought.'

'Does it not strike you, Watson, as a little too convenient?'

'I can't say that it does,' I answered in some little pique.

'Very well, then. Did you ever hear of a murderer who writes a confession of the crime, disguising her name as another but writing in a hand obviously or even probably known as her own to all involved in the investigation?'

'She may be a lunatic.'

'She may be indeed,' he said philosophically. 'She may be mad—or bad—or both—or neither.'

'And for that we are to go to Yokohama? To the far side of the planet?'

Holmes sat down and closed his eyes.

'It is more than enough, Watson. Who knows when such a chance will come again? Never, perhaps! Neither of us is immortal, my dear fellow. Think of Yokohama and the Orient! You have no soul, Watson! No, that is too harsh. You have a soul without an ounce of romance, if you cannot see that we must go. We are meant to go. And there may be a glorious victory in store.'

It was impossible to argue with him in this mood. I could not help feeling, however, that he might find the reality of Yokohama and the Orient something less alluring than his pipe-dream.

III

A man cannot decide to go to the other side of the world one evening and set off next morning. Days passed before our departure from Euston Station for Liverpool and the liner *Parisian*, the pride of the Allan Line, that would take us to Montreal. On our last two days, Holmes disappeared from breakfast until late afternoon, ferreting in the registers of Somerset House. When I asked why, he shrugged and said, 'My dear Watson, we are about to travel to the far side of the Pacific on the assumption that Mary Jacob has a brother and that the brother was our visitor. A little confirmation from records of births, marriages and deaths is in order before we commit ourselves further.'

I could not dispute the wisdom of the precaution. Then, that last evening, he announced that we should take our ease at the Egyptian Hall, London's temple of magic, which looks as if it had been lifted by a genie from Abu Simbel and set down among the mansions of Piccadilly.

'Have you entirely forgotten, Holmes, that we leave for Japan tomorrow morning?'

'Just so, Watson. Then let us make our farewells to Egypt tonight.'

Mad though it seemed to me, we sat through the entire programme of Maskelyne and Cooke, Hercules carrying a pyramid of seven burly men round the stage on his shoulders, Mazeppa in tights and spangles locked in the Indian Basket to be run through with pitiless swords, only for the opened basket to be empty and the houri to enter with a smile from the far side of the stage, the disembodied head of Socrates answering the magician's questions. Holmes chuckled and applauded like a schoolboy. When it was over, he slipped backstage for a moment to congratulate the performers.

'One forgets, Watson,' he remarked as the cab bore us homewards, 'that no theatrical feat can equal the perfection of well-practised illusion. Not Shakespeare, not the opera nor the ballet can ever have quite that absolute success—for absolute success or failure it must be. The least hitch means utter disaster, as it never would for Miss Ellen Terry or Sir Henry Irving. Magnificent, was it not?'

I agreed that I supposed it was, in its way. Next day our journey began and Dr Jacob was at Euston to see us on our way. He brought little presents and messages for his sister but it was the sight of his anxious face, so drawn and newly marked by distress, even since our first meeting, that made it impossible to begrudge the journey after all.

The first part of our voyage was familiar to us from previous expeditions. A few days later we anchored in the mouth of the St Lawrence River. The waterway was crowded with tiny brown rocks and great islands, the majestic Laurentian mountain range beyond and French-Canadian villages on the shore. By the next night we were at Montreal, whence the long and heavily laden train of the Canadian Pacific Railway would take us to Vancouver in a few days. Our travelling companions, who were American, Chinese, and Japanese, as well as Canadian and English, broke their journeys for a day at the modern cities of Winnipeg or Banff. Holmes, however, would not delay longer than necessary. For three hours, our powerful engine climbed slowly up the great backbone of the American continent until the train reached the Kicking-Horse Pass, where streams flow down one slope to the Atlantic and down the other side to the Pacific. Before us lay flimsy-looking trestle bridges and miles of snow-sheds. High above, domes and spires of ice towered to the sky over the hard sheen of glaciers. Deep gorges lay below, with foaming streams and great cataracts.

Two days later we joined the liner *Empress of India* at Vancouver, a fine new city entirely lit by electricity and served by electric tramcars, the wharves of its harbour lined by ships from China and Japan, Australia and the South Seas. Our Pacific crossing was long and lonely, the horizon broken only once by a sail and once by a view of the bleak and barren rocks that are the Aleutian Islands. The long sea voyage was not to Holmes's taste and he seemed to care little for either the scenery or the miracles of nature. More than once he invoked the comment of Dr Johnson to Boswell on the Giant's Causeway. 'Worth seeing, but not worth going to see,' as Holmes phrased it.

My great concern had been that we might not reach Yokohama before the trial of Mary Jacob opened in the British Consul's Court. Holmes had wired Miss Jacob's counsel, Mr Scidmore, to this effect. An adjournment was sought. As our white-painted liner with its three buff funnels entered Tokyo Bay, we had several days to spare.

Yokohama was the end of the liner's voyage, just short of the Japanese capital but in the same picturesque bay, with little fishing villages, shrines and pagodas along its shores. At anchor off the harbour were warships and merchantmen, sampans that might have been mistaken for gondolas crowding round our hull. The entrance to the fairway is marked by a lightship and a pair of buoys. Our white liner came in close to shore and let go her anchor. Holmes at last shrugged off the *ennui* of the voyage and his eyes were keen with excitement at the sights and scenes around us. Half an hour later we were ferried ashore to the granite breakwater within the harbour light. A further half-hour was enough to bring us through the Customs House, where we were met by Mary Jacob's attorney, Mr Scidmore.

Mr Scidmore was a man of impressive appearance, well suited to that of counsel in court or an opera singer on the stage. He was about fifty, tall and portly, with imposing features and an air of command. He scorned the white ducks and tropical uniform of his compatriots. His taste ran to a sombre and rich style, black frock-coat, shining hat, neat brown gaiters and well-cut pearly-grey trousers.

His first concern was not with the case but with which hotel should accommodate us.

'You might stay at Wright's,' he said cautiously, 'but Lowder the prosecutor has put up there, so that would never do. You will find the Grand Hotel and the Club Hotel facing the Bund, as they call the sea wall. Mr Dickinson, a prosecution witness, is at the Grand so that would scarcely be advisable. There is the Oriental at the back of the Grand on Main Street, near the Consulate. Mrs Carew has connections with both so you had best not stay there. Perhaps, after all, it would be best if you were to stay at the Yokohama United Club. A man may keep himself much more easily to himself there than in any of the hotels.'

The Yokohama United Club, like the English villas and bungalows, stands on what is called The Bluff, looking out across Tokyo Bay. This is the English compound. Like the other four Treaty Ports, Yokohama has its area of 'Foreign Settlement' where the national laws of the inhabitants are applied.

The road from the port to The Bluff is steep and like all journeys within the town is accomplished by a 'ricksha', something like a bath-chair with shafts, pulled by a runner. Among the public buildings at this upper level we passed the Club Germania, a Masonic Temple, and a public hall for plays and other entertainments. Just then, an exhibition of wonders was advertised, including the performance of the Indian Rope Trick. The English villas were newly built and had the handsome four-square look of Bournemouth or Cheltenham. Some of the English shops were on the quiet Bluff and many more lay below in the streets of the busy town. The Yokohama Club itself was a recent building that might not have seemed out of place in St James's Street or Pall Mall.

Until one lives a week or two in one of these enclaves, it is impossible to imagine the power that lies in the hands of Her Britannic Majesty's Consul. James Troupe, whom we met next day, was Consul, Magistrate, Governor of the Prison, Superintendent of the Hospital, Judge of the Criminal Court and, in all but the literal sense, Executioner. Dr Jacob had never seen the place but his worst fears of injustice in his sister's case seemed well founded.

Holmes was not one who cared greatly for gentlemen's clubs. Indeed, he loathed fashionable society with his whole bohemian mind. The Yokohama United Club was imposing in appearance but less so in its ambience. Holmes found himself among strangers who knew one another but to whom he was a man of no great significance. He did not want their company but it would have pleased him had they sought his. Such was the egotism which I more than once observed to be a strong factor in my friend's singular character.

A change for the worse came over him as he looked about him at the well-appointed club house. The loud talk and fatuous laughter, the guzzling and swilling, the shallow pleasantries of his compatriots, were contemptible to his fastidious sensibility. Far from being the exotic adventure he had pictured, the case of Miss Mary Jacob seemed, on that first evening, one that he was anxious to have done with, so that he might book the next passage home.

'From such people as this,' he hissed to me, 'they will choose twelve men to decide whether that unfortunate girl shall live or die! It is intolerable!'

Matters were not improved by our being hailed on our way into dinner by Mr Rentiers of the British Consulate. He was an arrogant young buck in his white mess-jacket but the story he had to tell improved neither Mary Jacob's chances nor the temper of Sherlock Holmes. He had been put 'in charge' of us by Mr Troupe, the Consul, as if to see that we came to no harm. There was no easy or courteous way of getting rid of this young flunkey. He sat us down in the spacious dining-room under the slow ceiling-fan, the portrait of Her Majesty looking down at us from the far end of the room. Mr Rentiers ordered largely and confidently from the Chinese waiter who came in answer to his snapped fingers.

'We don't think a lot of the old-fashioned ways out here,' he said airily. 'I daresay Carew wasn't a saint, but then most aren't.'

Holmes broke off a small piece of bread. 'Really?' The tone of his voice encouraged the conceited young ass to continue.

'Waste of time, you know, it really is,' Rentiers said dispassionately.

'What is?'

'Trying to stir up mud about the Carews. Granted he'd had the pox but that was bad luck. Walter Carew took the bad luck for most men of his age out here alone. As for his liver, you can't drink in the Malay Straits or Yokohama as freely as you can at home. Most find that out too late. So did he.'

Holmes stared at Rentiers as if considering him for dissection.

'And Mrs Carew?'

The thin lip under the wispy moustache lifted a little in a smile of appreciation.

'Edith Carew's a sport. A real old sport. Race Course, Regatta Day, tennis, cricket, everything. Part of it all.'

'And Mary Jacob?'

Rentiers tasted the wine and pulled a face.

'A thieving nursery governess, she and her little friend Elsa Christoffel. Two of the same. Blackmailers the pair of 'em. If Mary

Jacob wasn't to be tried for murder, she might get fourteen years for blackmail anyway. So might her conniving little friend. The evidence is laid before the Consul already. Two other servants saw Jacob fetching scraps of torn-up letters from the wastepaper baskets in the Carews' villa. Christoffel sewed the scraps together. Mostly letters from Harry Dickinson to Edith Carew. Letters of a compromising kind. What do you suppose the two little sluts were going to do with them unless it was blackmail?'

'I have not the least idea,' said Holmes expressionlessly.

'What's more, the servants saw Jacob practising Edith Carew's handwriting. Forging it, in other words. Even before Carew died there were letters coming to him and his wife from Annie Luke, a woman he'd had before he married. A woman in a black veil called at the house when he was out. Harry Dickinson saw her crying on the street corner by the Water Street entrance of the club on the day of Carew's funeral. Almost the last time that Carew left his house, he went round Yokohama trying to find her. We've got witnesses to that.'

'And was Annie Luke here, in Yokohama?' Holmes asked gently.

Rentiers leaned back and laughed at him. 'Not she! It was a stunt by Christoffel and Jacob. Like the other letters.'

'What other letters?' asked Holmes casually.

'They both wrote other anonymous letters to men in Yokohama. Christoffel admits in her witness statement that she did it. Jacob denies it but she was the one who wrote the "Annie Luke" letters. A pound to a penny. Christoffel was Edith Carew's rival for Harry Dickinson. She admits she wrote anonymous letters, begging him to leave Edith Carew for her, talked about humiliating herself in front of him. She admitted it, when they examined her at the committal proceedings. The little bitch actually laughed about it in the witness-box! Laughed in our faces!'

Holmes reached for the pepper. 'Indeed? And Miss Jacob?'

Rentiers grinned. 'That's the best bit. She must have thought the tricks with the letters would never be found out. In the last one, Annie Luke confessed to the murder of Carew. But Annie Luke isn't in Yokohama. Never was. So if Mary Jacob wrote those letters from so-called Annie Luke, as will be proved, then Mary Jacob has already confessed to the murder of Carew. There's a naval prison here and that's where Miss Jacob is now. There's a naval hangman too—petty officer with two ratings to assist. So if this goes wrong for Miss Jacob, she'll be six foot under by the prison wall in a few weeks' time. And good riddance.'

Rentiers opened his mouth in a large silent grin of appreciation at his own cleverness. How Holmes kept his composure in the face of this insolent young scapegrace, I did not know. Rentiers took another spoonful of soup. Then he said, 'Anything else you wanted to know?'

'Yes,' said Holmes courteously, 'Why did Mr and Mrs Carew refer to you in their conversations and letters as "The Organ Grinder"?'

It was a pistol-shot through a bullseye. Rentiers put his spoon down. From his shaven neck to the roots of his hair, his young face went the shade of ripe raspberries. He said not a word but rose from his chair, and walked from the dining-room without a glance to either side. We never saw him again.

'Holmes! How the devil did you know?'

Holmes stared after him.

'I have not the least idea, Watson. No more than an instinctive sense of human frailty. But you, of all people, my dear fellow, will acknowledge that in such matters I am very seldom wrong. Now, at least, we may finish our meal unmolested by the chatter of that young jackanapes.'

In that, he was right. No one but the Chinese waiter came near us for the rest of the evening. After Holmes's casual insult to a consular official, we had advertised ourselves as lepers.

IV

The name of Sherlock Holmes meant little to the English colony of Yokohama, an isolated and inward-looking community of adventurers and younger sons who had been despatched to the East so that they should not incur scandal or expense at home. The Consul and his officers presided over them for all the world like schoolmasters trying to manage unruly boys.

It suited Holmes that he and I should be regarded as nothing but two more 'griffins', as new arrivals are contemptuously called. He would not have given two-pence for the entire English settlement. When he drew my attention, it was to admire the natural beauty of the Japanese girls with the blue-black *bandeaux* of their *coiffure* immaculately dressed so that not a single hair was out of place, the piled tresses revealing the prettiness of each face and the ivory perfection of the nape and ears. Or else he would be struck by the reality of Japanese life and how perfectly its scenes resembled the decorations on fan, ornamental tray, or screen. He watched the jugglers in the street, many of them children, and the skill with which a spinning top seemed to move as if by wizardry.

Our first encounter with the members of the Carew household was when Holmes interviewed Rachel Greer, a Eurasian girl who had assisted Mary Jacob in the nursery, and Hanauye Asa. They were brought to the secretary's office in the club and left with us. These were the two who had been Mission School pupils before entering service and neither of them faltered in her story. Their honesty was so palpable that I confess my heart sank a little for Mary Jacob. Rachel Greer spoke for both of them, interpreting many of Hanauye Asa's replies. Yet even to judge by her expression and manner, Hanauye Asa spoke the entire truth of what she had seen.

'Be kind enough to explain,' said Holmes gently to Rachel Greer who stood before the desk like a naughty child, 'how it was that you saw Mary Jacob in Mr Carew's room the evening before his death. I am correct, I believe, in saying that the only door to the room was locked at that moment during the few minutes the nurse was away and that the nurse had posted the two of you to see that no one came near, while she was absent?'

'Yes,' said the girl earnestly. 'No one passed.'

'No one?' asked Holmes gently. 'But Mary Jacob passed, did she not?'

Rachel Greer shook her head. 'Not while we were there. We heard a sound, while the nurse was out of the room. The window banged. We knew it could not be Mr Carew, for he was too ill to get out of bed. We looked through the keyhole and saw Mary Jacob standing in front of the mirror.'

'Which mirror?'

'The triple-mirror on top of the cabinet, where the medicines were kept.'

'Just standing there?'

Rachel Greer nodded. 'She stood for a moment, looking at it. Then she looked down at something in her hands. Then I think she moved away and we could not see her.'

'What else happened?'

'Someone in the opposite room downstairs, on the far side of the courtyard, shone a bright light to see what had made the noise. It was Mrs Carew who shone the light from the nursery window opposite when she heard the window bang. But she swore she saw nothing in the garden or the house. Almost at once, we heard the nurse coming back and Mrs Carew calling us down. She asked what the noise was but we could not tell her. We told her that Miss Jacob was in the room.'

'And what did Mrs Carew say?'

'She said it was impossible for Mary Jacob to be in the room unless she had passed us. Just after that, Mary Jacob was in the nursery.'

Not by a single facial movement did Holmes suggest that Rachel Greer might not be telling the truth. Yet if she was, then Mary Jacob was the last person to be alone with Carew on the final night of his life except his nurse. Rachel Greer and Hanauye Asa stood guard outside the door all night, on Mrs Carew's insistence, so that even when the nurse was absent for a few minutes no one could enter. From the time that the two servants had looked through the keyhole until the moment of Carew's death, no one but Mary Jacob or the nurse could have administered the three grains of arsenic that had killed him. The nurse had already been acquitted of all suspicion.

'Had you ever seen Mary Jacob in Mr Carew's bedroom at any other time?' Holmes asked. The girl stared at her hands with an air of modesty.

'Before he was ill, yes.'

'Did she take the children in there to see their father?'

Something rather like a smirk of embarrassment touched Rachel Greer's lips.

'She went to him alone. When Mrs Carew was out, playing cards or riding.'

The point was so hopeless that Holmes seemed to give it up.

'And what of the letters belonging to Mrs Carew that Mary Jacob took?'

'Mrs Carew used to tear up letters after she read them and throw the pieces in the basket. Miss Jacob would take the pieces and put them together. She and Miss Christoffel. She showed them to me. I saw her take them from the basket.'

'Why did she take them?'

Rachel Greer shrugged. 'To find out what Mrs Carew was doing. Things that she should not do. Some of the letters were from a gentleman.'

'And what else did you see?'

The girl looked up at him, direct and sincere in her emphasis.

'She used to copy Mrs Carew's writing. Her signature. I saw a paper where she had written Mrs Carew's signature. She copied other writing as well. She copied Annie Luke.'

There seemed no more to be done. Holmes thanked the two girls and then paused.

'One moment,' he said quietly. 'Mr Carew's bedroom faced the nursery, did it not? Across the little lawn?'

'Yes,' said Rachel Greer simply.

'How many other rooms were there to either side of his?'

'None on one side. On the other side there was Mrs Carew's room.'

'So they slept in the two adjoining rooms on that last night. Was there a door from one to the other?'

'There was a door but it was locked. On Mr Carew's side, it was bolted at the top and bottom by the nurse who was with him.'

'Did you see Mrs Carew go into her own room that last night?'

'Yes. She went in at eleven o'clock and she did not come out until the morning. It was just before they sent for the doctor and the ambulance to take Mr Carew to the hospital. But it was impossible for Mrs Carew to go through the other door between the rooms. She must come out on to the landing.'

'No one was with Mr Carew when the nurse was away for a few minutes during the night?'

Rachel Greer shook her head again. 'Mr Carew was alone then. No one could go to him. We stayed outside the door all the time, on the landing. Mrs Carew did not come out of her room and she could not get through the other door. The Consul's men examined that door between the rooms to see if it had been tried.'

Later that evening I could not forbear saying to Holmes that our client had cooked her own goose. She was Carew's lover, either spurned by him or infected by his dreadful disease. She had ordered and bought 'plenty poison', as the chemist called it, for Carew's tonic. The three bottles of Fowler's Solution of Arsenic had been found in the house after the man's death. All three were nearly empty. A lethal dose of it had found its way into him. Much as Edith Carew might have hated her husband in secret, it was impossible to see how she could have got near him during the night when the fatal dose was administered. Short of believing that the doctors or nurses had poisoned the poor devil, Mary Jacob was the only suspect. If she had been in the room alone with him the evening before his death, she had only to empty an entire ounce of Fowler's Solution into his brandy and soda. By then he was delirious and calling for his drink. Fowler's Solution in Japanese pharmacies contains no lavender. It is intended to be tasteless and would certainly be so in a stiff brandy of the kind Carew drank. Who but Mary Jacob could have done it?

Holmes sat in his chair, eyes closed and fingertips pressed together under his chin, as I listed the evidence that would hang Mary Jacob. Then he said lightly, 'You have something still to learn about circumstantial evidence, Watson. It is never more suspect than when there is too much of it. There is too much of it in this case. Far too much. If the wind should shift to another quarter, the accusation will lie in quite a different direction.'

Next morning we were taken by appointment to interview Miss Mary Jacob at the British Naval Prison. It was a beautiful winter morning on The Bluff, milder by far than anything in England, the elegant villas and bungalows commanding a fine view of Tokyo Bay. At the prison, they had made a cell for her from a room in the commandant's quarters. It was bare enough with its bed, chairs, a table under its barred window, a smaller one by the bed. Whatever passion Walter Carew may have felt for her, Mary Jacob was not a beauty but more of a simple village lass. Small wonder if her elder brother took her under his wing. Her dark hair was rather scragged back just then and the strong lines of her face reminded me a little of Kate Webster, who had gone to the gallows twenty years earlier for killing her mistress with an axe. Mary Jacob's face had an air of resentment, even towards those who had come to help her. There was resolve in the line of her chin and a natural anger burned at the corners of her wide cheekbones. When she turned her brown eyes upon us, there was the look of fear and hate that one sees in a cornered animal.

She sat at the table, Holmes sat opposite her, and I at the end.

'Miss Jacob,' said Holmes after we had introduced ourselves, 'I do not conceal from you that your case is one of the most difficult that has lately come my way.'

She scowled at him and said belligerently, 'They are all against me. Because of him.' The sullen accusation would do little to help her.

'That may be so,' Holmes said persistently, never once raising his voice. 'What concerns me more than the people you say are against you is the amount of evidence which is undoubtedly against you. It is more than enough to hang you, unless you pull yourself together. Now, if you please, we will have truthful answers to questions.'

She looked up in astonishment, as if her defender had just slapped her face, when he dealt with her in this manner.

'First,' said Holmes, 'you bought enough arsenic from Maruya's Pharmacy in Yokohama to kill Mr Carew several times over.'

'Because they told me to. He asked me to get it.'

'At Maruya's?'

'No, not at any place in particular, only to get it.'

'Miss Jacob,' he said quietly, 'there is incontrovertible evidence that you bought that poison. There is no evidence whatever, apart from your own assertion, that you were ever asked to get it.'

'I didn't even know what it was!'

'Come!' said Holmes gently. 'The order was in your own handwriting.'

'Fowler's Solution? I didn't know what Fowler's Solution was! Only a tonic. I wrote down what he told me.'

'But when he died, you went to the chemist and asked for that writing back, did you not? Is that the action of an innocent person?'

'I was frightened!' At last there was something that sounded like a cry.

'So you might well be,' said Holmes in the same quiet voice, 'but more frightened, perhaps, if you were guilty than if you were innocent. The truth might protect innocence but never guilt.'

From time to time, I could not help reflecting upon the worldly success that might have awaited Holmes in a career of cross-examination at the Criminal Bar. Yet I was more than a little anxious at the tone of scepticism that he continued to employ upon Mary Jacob. With the weariness of an unbeliever, he turned to the next topic.

'You were seen by two independent witnesses taking the torn fragments of Mrs Carew's letters from the wastepaper basket. Why?'

'I thought they were mine!'

'How could Mrs Carew's letters be yours?'

The tears began to sparkle as the poor young nursery governess spoke of her home and her family.

'She kept my letters from home and never let me have them. I never received my mother's letters to me all the time I was in that house. Never an answer to mine. Perhaps she stopped my letters as well. Only she wrote to my home and told them how happy I was and how well treated. Well treated, Mr Holmes? She used me like a slave! I thought perhaps they were my letters from home torn up and thrown in the basket, so that I should not see nor answer them.'

'Perhaps your mother had not written to you.'

'I'm not a fool.' The anger burned again at the points of her cheekbones. 'Even Mrs Carew's brother, when he came out from England, said I'd been written to.'

Holmes looked her in the eye.

'I think you had better explain why Mrs Carew should stop your mother's letters.'

The tears had dried and there was a look of triumph on the girl's face.

'They never told you? Mrs Carew lived in Somerset, near Glastonbury, before she married. My people were at Langport in those days, a little way off. She didn't know where I came from until after I arrived out here because I wrote from my brother's in Surrey. I was a doctor's sister, that's all she knew. Now she's frightened that I'll hear about her from home, how she's never been any better than she should be. I might have told Mr Carew. I might have told all her precious friends on The Bluff and at the Club, as well as the ones at the Race Course and the tennis courts. Oh yes, I was her servant right enough. But I had a mother who knew who my father was, which hers never did!'

'Quite,' said Holmes coolly, 'but why stick the fragments of the torn letters together?'

'To show to Mr Carew, if Mrs Carew went on treating me as she did. Perhaps then he would love me and not her. Let him see what a fool she and Mr Dickinson were making of him. He'd turned a blind eye before, but this time he was ready to divorce her.'

'Really?' said Holmes, with the least flicker of interest. 'Why, then, did you practise writing Mrs Carew's hand and her signature? And the writing of Annie Luke?'

'Annie Luke was just a name I heard from Mr Carew. A young lady from Devonshire that he knew once in the days before he was married.'

'And Mrs Carew's writing?'

'I was going to pay her out,' the girl said miserably. 'He was never going to love me, after all, was he? And then I found out about the disease he had and how I'd been deceived by him. I was going to pay them both out. I thought I could write to Mr Dickinson, pretending to be Mrs Carew. I should tell him that I couldn't see him again because I knew about the disease Mr Carew had. Let them show their faces on The Bluff after that!'

Holmes sat back and stared at her for a moment. Then he said, 'I much fear, Miss Jacob, that you have just supplied almost all the motivation necessary for the Crown to establish a case of murder against you.'

There was horror in her eyes as the trap seemed to open under her. 'You won't tell them? Oh, God, you won't!'

'I am not retained, Miss Jacob, to supply the deficiencies of the Consul's investigators. I shall not repeat so foolish a story as the one you have just told me. However, it is now plain that our only hope is to attack the circumstantial evidence. I have but one question to ask you.' She watched him, half doubting and half hoping. 'Were you in Mr Carew's room at about eight thirty on the last evening of his life?' Holmes demanded simply. 'Think carefully before you answer. Two reputable and independent witnesses swear that they saw you standing before the medicine cabinet.'

'No!' It was a shout rather than a cry. 'I was in the garden.'

'Alone, no doubt?'

'I was reading a book!'

'Reading a book in the dark?'

'No. I was sitting on the verandah seat, under Mr Carew's window, where the seat and the lantern is. I liked to sit there alone and read.'

Holmes stood up and walked across to the window-ledge as the girl watched him. He picked up two novels. *The Play Actress* and *A Romance of Two Worlds* by Marie Corelli.

'A book like these?'

Mary Jacob seemed puzzled. 'No,' she said. 'Those were left here for me, from the Club library.'

Holmes rippled the pages, sniffed, and put them down.

'What happened while you were sitting there, reading your book, at about eight thirty?'

'I was asked that,' she said. 'There was a bang from up above, in Mr Carew's room, like someone pulling the window shut. Something fell on the grass. A piece of wood or stone, even loose paint perhaps. It was too dark to tell.'

'What did you do?'

'I just looked up, I suppose.'

'And what else?'

'Mrs Carew must have heard the bang as well. She opened the curtain facing across the little lawn from the nursery side and shone the big lantern to see what was happening. Then I heard her call Rachel and the other girl.'

'You know that Mrs Carew has deposed that when she shone the light out, you were not sitting on that seat, nor were you anywhere else to be seen until five or ten minutes later when you were in the nursery?'

'But I was there!' the girl cried, the tied length of dark hair swishing on the back of her dress as she looked from one to the other of us.

'And you know that Rachel and her companion both swear that they heard the window bang and saw you in Mr Carew's room at the very same moment?'

'They're lying!' she cried again. 'Mrs Carew gave him poison in the night!'

Holmes looked at her coolly.

'You also know that one or other of the nurses was with Mr Carew the last two days before he was taken to hospital, except for occasional intervals of a few minutes each? Mrs Carew could not have come out on to the landing to go into his room without being seen by the two servants. The other door in the wall between the two rooms was locked and bolted on Mr Carew's side. No attempt was made to force it. The only arsenic in the house was in his room, in the medicine cabinet. You were the only person seen there, apart from the nurses.'

Mary Jacob sat before us, abject and exhausted.

'I was never in that room,' the poor girl said helplessly, 'not that night, not that day, not the night nor the day before that!'

'I fear that will not answer in the court,' Holmes said, though his voice was not unkindly. 'We must see what better can be done.'

'And the nursery amah and the other girl who say that they saw me? What of them?'

'Well,' said Holmes drily, 'I imagine they are very likely to be believed.'

At this she bowed her head over the table and began to weep, arms hanging down in dejection, not attempting even to cover her face.

'I beg you will not cry,' said Holmes irritably. 'Listen to me! I shall return this evening. It will be quite late. Until then, you are to leave every article in this room where it is at the moment. Do you understand?'

The poor girl looked up, not understanding in the slightest, but she nodded.

'Do as I say,' he said more gently. 'The next hours are of great importance.'

I was used to the insouciance of my friend on such occasions but as the cell door closed behind us on the picture of fear and dejection that Mary Jacob presented, I could curb my feelings no longer.

'Is that all?' I asked him, as we walked away towards The Bluff.

'Naturally,' he said, with a shrug of his thin shoulders. 'What else can there be? If Miss Jacob was not in the room on that last night, she could scarcely have put three grains of arsenic in Carew's brandy and soda. If she was in the room, then she was quite certainly the person who did so. I imagine the case hinges on that.'

'For God's sake, Holmes! How could you? You might as well have told the poor child that she was going to the gallows and have done with it!'

He was not the least put out. 'Left to your detective skills at present, Watson, that is precisely where she would be going.'

'Stop a minute,' I said with malign satisfaction. 'While you were busy browbeating that poor girl, you quite missed the most important clue in her defence.'

'I daresay,' he murmured, walking on, but I stood still and made him stop, turn and listen to me.

'When the window banged and something fell, Mrs Carew drew back the curtain of the opposite room in a second or two and shone the big lantern out. Even the servants agree.'

'Well?' he asked quietly. 'And what if she did?'

'Don't you see it, Holmes? For that to have happened in a second or two, the lantern must have been already lit. No woman sitting in a nursery or in any such room keeps a big outdoor lantern lit. It would take fifteen or twenty seconds at least for her to prepare it, light it and shine it out, not two or three. Surely she must have known beforehand that the window of the upper room would bang at that moment. But how could she know? What would be the purpose in knowing?'

He looked at me kindly. 'My dear Watson, I owe you a most profound apology. I had quite begun to think that the enervating air of Yokohama had sapped your powers of observation and deduction. And now, if you please, we will try the luncheon at Wright's Hotel in the town. I am a little weary of the Club and Her Britannic Majesty's Consular Kingdom. The prospect of meeting counsel for the prosecution would be more agreeable than another encounter with Mr Rentiers. Indeed, though Mr Lowder is the prosecutor, he has agreed with Mr Scidmore that we may inspect the scene of the crime this evening. I think it probable that your questions about Mrs Carew's curious conduct will then be answered.'

'Would it not be better to go in full daylight?'

'I think not,' said Holmes firmly. 'This was a crime of darkness and had better be examined under such conditions.'

V

That afternoon saw Holmes in one of the queer humours that overtook him unpredictably from time to time. He seemed to lose all interest in the investigation, quite indifferent to the fate of Mary Jacob, and took himself off to the library of the Yokohama Club. He sat in the depths of a green leather chair, absorbed in the trashier type of fiction that graces such colonial outposts as this one. He flipped through volumes of games and sports which, under normal circumstances, would not have lightened his most jaded mood. Even the bound volumes of the *Japan Gazette*, as the English paper is called, occupied him for some time.

After all this, I found him in a better mood than at any time since our arrival. He had spent a pleasant hour interrogating the librarian on the excellence of George Meredith's fiction, the fine intellectual cruelties of the great novelist. It was evident that the club librarian had never read *The Ordeal of Richard Feverel* or any other of the author's works but he committed the unwise sin of pride in pretending at first that he had done so. Holmes found him out at once but never revealed the discovery to his victim, enjoying fine sport at the poor fellow's expense. Before long, the guardian of literature was only too happy to discuss any other topic under the sun than the works of Holmes's favourite novelist. I left my friend to his amusements until the time when we were to collect the keys that Mr Lowder had left for us. We made our way on foot to 160 The Bluff, part-way down the hill.

Since the death of her husband, Mrs Carew had taken rooms at the Continental Hotel, as if the memories of the final ghastly days at the villa were too much for her. The Carew villa was a modest house in a garden of trees and lawn, befitting the Secretary and Manager of the Yokohama United Club. It was built on three sides round a narrow lawn. Carew's room was on the second level, at the end of one of these narrowly separated 'wings'. It looked across to the rooms of the other wing, one of which was the nursery.

In the past few years, there had been minor structural alterations to the building. The two adjoining bedrooms of Carew and his wife had once been a large single room but a substantial partition wall with a communicating door had been inserted. The verandah of each bedroom had been glassed in to form a dressing-room area, though at ground level the verandahs of the lower rooms had been retained. The metal-framed windows of the dressing-rooms above could not be opened, except for a fanlight at the top, some two feet square. Under Carew's room was the wooden seat where Mary Jacob claimed she had sat when the window banged and when his wife had shone her light across the strip of garden to see what the noise might be. She had not seen Mary Jacob sitting there, nor had the other witnesses.

Holmes and I stood on the narrow lawn between the two wings of the house, looking at the wooden seat and at Carew's window on the floor above.

'However else our client entered Carew's bedroom, she did not pass through the door from the landing while it was guarded by the two angels of truth from the Mission School.'

'Could she have reached it from the garden?'

'I think we may say, Watson, that for Mary Jacob to have entered the room from the garden, she must have had a ladder or, at least, a rope. Picture her climbing up and finding no way in but by the fanlight of the dressing-room window. I daresay she could get through an opening of that size, though she must have fallen to the floor. Perhaps, as she did so, the fanlight banged after her. The sound was heard. A light was shone. But where was the ladder or the rope? And how can she be one moment half-way through the fanlight with nothing to aid her descent into the room, and within a split second—as long as it takes to crouch and look through a keyhole—she has fallen or dived silently from the opening, tumbled on to the floor without making a further sound, picked herself up, rearranged her dress, and is standing before the medicine cabinet without a hair out of place.'

He betrayed his feelings no more than by a certain twitch of the mouth.

'It could not be done,' I said with a little irritation. 'If there was a rope she must also draw that up or kick away a ladder. Far more likely that she got into the room earlier and hid there, waiting her chance until the nurse was away for a few minutes. She might take her bottle of poison and pour it into his drink or his water-bottle then.'

'Admirable, Watson,' he said, leading the way into the house as dusk deepened in the garden, 'and how did our cunning murderess get out of the room again? A bright light was shining on its exterior. Mrs Carew and the other servants were hurrying up the stairs by this time. The nurse was coming back, for Rachel Greer and her companion heard her as they were going down the stairs in answer to Mrs Carew's summons. Yet Mary Jacob must have got out, for she was seen in the nursery a few minutes later. Could she have scrambled up five feet of window-glass unaided, gone feet-first through the fanlight, got down eighteen feet to the garden in the glare of the light, unseen and without making a sound? She was not seen doing so, and no sound was heard by any of the witnesses, therefore she was invisible and inaudible.'

The answer came to me at once, as I thought.

'She had a key, not to the landing door but for the communicating door directly into Mrs Carew's room. If the nurse saw her coming out of Mrs Carew's room, she would suspect nothing.'

Holmes paused on the staircase.

'Unfortunately, Watson, she would be suspected at once. She might unbolt and unlock the party-door to the other bedroom and she might lock it after her. But there is no means known to criminal science by which she might fasten the bolts on the far side of the door. No means, either, by which she could have got out of Mrs Carew's room unseen in order to be in the nursery a few minutes later. It will not do, my dear fellow. Perhaps we shall have better luck if we examine the scene.'

It was a chill sensation to enter the bedroom where Carew had endured the agony and delirium of his last days. There was the bed, as if it had scarcely been re-made. There was the table beside it and the dressing-room area made out of what had once been the verandah. There was the fatal medicine cabinet with its mirror on top. To see the wall of glass, which the window formed, with its fanlight at the very top, was to see the impossibility that Mary Jacob could ever have come or gone by that route. A professional burglar would not have given it a second glance.

Holmes spent a little while examining the window and the medicine cabinet with its wooden-framed triple-mirror on top, his fingers delicately turning and adjusting the glass as he did so. I gave my attention to the communicating door in the partition wall between the two bedrooms. It remained locked and bolted. Door and frame had been painted long before Carew's death and there was no sign of any chip or blemish that indicated an attempt to tamper with the fastenings.

Holmes seemed content with all that he had found.

'Be so good, Watson, as to stand on the landing with the bedroom door locked and the key in your pocket. When you hear the window bang, look through the keyhole and see what you may see. Do not, on any account, unlock the door.'

'And you, Holmes? What of you?'

'I shall go down to the garden and smoke a pipe.'

'What if the window should not bang?'

'As to that,' he said with a smile to himself, 'I think I may promise you that it will.'

Before I could register a further protest, he had made his way down the stairs and vanished. The house was silent and in almost complete darkness as all light faded from the garden. I waited for what seemed an interminable time but was perhaps no more than five minutes. I was about to give up and go down to the garden when there was the unmistakable rattle or bang of the bedroom window, so unexpected by now that it made me jump. If I hesitated, it was no more than two or three seconds before I was down on one knee and peering through the keyhole of Carew's room. There, standing before the mirror of the medicine cabinet and smoking his pipe was the figure of Sherlock Holmes.

VI

I twisted my head and tried to see through the tiny aperture how the devil he could have done it. Then he moved from my field of vision, for the keyhole gave a very imperfect prospect of the room as a whole. Then he came back, and then he went for good. I waited several minutes like this, kneeling and trying to see where he might be, until my heart jumped as a voice behind me said, 'My apologies for startling you, Watson. I can scarcely believe, though, that this is your first encounter with Professor Pepper's ghost. I flatter myself that they would hardly have done it better at the Egyptian Hall.'

Holmes, whom I had just seen through the keyhole of the locked door, was now standing behind me. I struggled to my feet and turned upon him.

'Who the blazes is Professor Pepper?'

Ignoring my question, he took the key from me, unlocked the door, and laughed.

'To tell the truth, I half suspected something of the sort when Dr Jacob first told the story in Baker Street. Then I thought perhaps they lacked the expertise. It was the window banging and something being thrown out that convinced me.'

We stood in Carew's room once more and now Holmes lit the lamps.

'Picture yourself, Watson, sitting on that garden bench. Above you, the window bangs and something is thrown out. What is your natural reaction?'

'To wonder what the devil is going on.'

'Be more precise.'

'Well,' I said, half suspecting a trick, 'I should look up to see who it was and what had happened. Then I might look for what had fallen, if I could find it.'

'Excellent!' Holmes said, rubbing his hands. 'It is what any sensible person would do. How long would you look up?'

'A minute or two, until I could see what the matter was.'

'And if you saw nothing—or nothing that signified?'

'I should go on with what I had been doing, if all I had heard was a window banging.'

'Just as Mary Jacob did. Suppose now that you are guarding a room with the door locked. Inside is a man alone, lying asleep, between life and death, his very existence in peril from assassins. The nurse is absent. Inside the room the window bangs. What would you do?'

'I should try at once to see what was going on in there.'

'But how? You cannot open the door and you have no means of seeing through the window itself.'

'The keyhole, of course.'

'Precisely.'

'But what if I were to run for help without bothering to look?'

'You might, Watson. But if there were two of you, the chances that one at least would look through that keyhole are doubled. It is well-nigh inconceivable that one of you would not do so before running for assistance. Is it not the instinctive thing to do, just as Mary Jacob's instinct would have been to look upwards?'

This was all very fine but I was getting a little weary of the joke and I knew nothing of Professor Pepper or his ghost. Holmes took from his capacious pocket a copy of a book which he had purloined, apparently, from the library of the Yokohama Club. *Secrets of Stage Conjuring* by J. E. Robert-Houdin, published by George Routledge at London in 1881. He pointed to a page which appeared full of geometrical figures and a tribute to Professor Pepper of the London Polytechnic.

The principle of the stage illusion was simple enough. A figure stood below the stage at the level of the orchestra pit, concealed from the audience and looking upwards. Also at that level, hidden from the audience, a bright light shone directly upon the figure's face. The face looked up at a sheet of glass, angled as a fanlight might be. The result, in the darkness of the surroundings, was to produce a perfect replica of the face. The darker the surroundings, the more vivid the image.

'The principle is simple, Watson, but the art is making the image perfect. It is as you see your own ghost outside the window of a railway carriage when you travel at night.'

He opened Robert-Houdin's book again. In its pages was a slip of paper, which recorded that the volume had been borrowed from the club library on 8 September last by Edith Mary Hallowell Carew.

'I am a little surprised that she should have needed it,' said Holmes quietly, 'for Edith Mary Hallowell Porch, as she was then, was a devotee of the magic arts. A witness at her wedding was Miss Julia Ferret of the Recreations Japonaises, as that performance of wizardry is known in England. She assisted at a famous performance in Yokohama by Josef Vanek, the Professor of Physics at Budapest, who forsook his laboratory for the stage.'

Holmes had constructed his own geometrical plan of the trap laid for Mary Jacob. He had drawn it up with the precision of Euclid or Pythagoras. The pebble, stone, or other object, had hit the window quite gently above Mary Jacob's head, and fallen on the ground. The sound, as the glass and frame vibrated, had caused the girl to look up, where the fanlight was open at an angle. What more natural than that Edith Carew might draw the curtain back at the noise and a stream of electric brightness be directed across the narrow lawn?

As Mary Jacob tried to discern what had happened in the room of the man who had once been her lover, her face was reflected in the square of fanlight glass, clear as day in the darkness. From the glass it was caught in one side of the triple mirror and caught again in that other side, which had been carefully angled so that it filled the view from the keyhole of the door. That Mrs Carew should 'put the mirror straight' when she visited her husband would cause the nurse no unease whatever.

'Stop a minute, Holmes,' I said insistently. 'I grant you Professor Pepper's illusion works well enough, for I have seen it myself just now. I daresay Edith Carew had the skill to attempt it. But this is not a theatre. She could not be sure that Mary Jacob would sit on that bench at that time or that she would look up at the sound. She could not know that the nurse would leave the room or that the two servant girls would look through the keyhole.'

I thought that my friend looked at me in a little disappointment.

'My dear Watson, you have not grasped it, after all. The solution to this mystery depends very little on Professor Pepper's ghost and almost entirely on the operation of the criminal mind. Edith Carew is a cold-blooded poisoner. I have thought so from the first. The arsenic was obtained well in advance, through Mary Jacob as an innocent messenger. This was no crime of passion but a calculated act of cruelty. What if the ghost illusion had failed? It was probably one of a dozen stratagems. Perhaps some had already been tried and had failed. If this one had not succeeded, there would have been others. Sooner or later, by whatever means, she would rid herself of the husband who stood between her and a guilty liaison with a younger man—Henry Vansittart Dickinson. A husband, Watson, who had not only possessed himself of her money for his own pleasures and his vices but also threatened her with a vile and incurable disease.'

So far I could follow him. The rest was sheer impossibility.

'What you say, Holmes, may acquit Mary Jacob. It cannot convict Edith Carew. When she knew that she had trapped Miss Jacob, she must have acted at once to commit murder. Yet it is impossible that she could ever have got near Carew again. That last night she went into her own room. The nurse was alone with Carew, absent once or twice for only a few minutes. Edith Carew could not come out on to the landing because Rachel Greer and Hanauye Asa would have seen her. She could not have gone through the communicating door between the two rooms because it was locked and bolted on Carew's side. How, then, could she have put three grains of arsenic into Carew's brandy and soda or anything else he drank?'

'I should say, Watson, that she put three grains into each vessel, so that whether it was his brandy and soda, his drinking water or his medicine, he was done for. She had ample time to wash out the glasses and bottles next day, after they had removed him to hospital but before arsenic was suspected.'

'But how could she do it, if there was neither door nor window by which she could enter the room?'

Holmes stared at the partition wall. 'By doing what Professor Vanek used to do every night in front of several hundred people,' he said. 'In a house as casually constructed as this, a child might almost do it.'

VII

In my mind's eye, I can still see the wall with its communicating door as it had been built between those two rooms. The rooms had a common floor of planking, which ran lengthwise, parallel with the windows. Where it formed the floor of the dressing-room area it ran over the verandah at ground level. To install the partition wall, they had first laid a strip of stout rubberised felt across the boards of the dressing-rooms to insulate the carpets from the winter damp or cold of the verandah beneath. Then they had laid a heavy beam across the boards, wall to window, and constructed a lath and plaster wall upon this. It might not be the way of building in London but it was solid enough in such a climate as this.

It was impossible that Edith Carew or an accomplice could have passed through that wall or the communicating door while the nurse was absent. Nor could there have been a way over the wall without breaking through the ceiling. There was a tiny gap between the supporting beam and the floorboards with their insulating felt which it traversed. That gap was not half an inch. It would have been possible, of course, to have taken up the floorboards, climbed down to the verandah and climbed up into the other room through a gap on the far side. To reach the floorboards, however, would have required cutting through the felt, which ran in a single length across both dressing-room floors under the beam.

'If it was done,' I said a little morosely, 'I'll be hanged if I can see how. Edith Carew or her accomplice could not have gone through that wall, over it, or under it without leaving traces of the damage they caused. And there are none.'

'But then, my dear fellow,' said Holmes gently, 'you are no physicist—and Professor Vanek was. Once Mary Jacob was compromised, Edith Carew knew that she must strike her blow that night.'

'How?'

He beckoned me from the room and we went down the stairs. Holmes took a lantern from the hall and lit it. We stood in the verandah that ran along the narrow lawn, just under the dressing areas of the bedrooms. The ceiling of the verandah, if one can call it that, consisted of what were now the floorboards of those dressing-rooms, nailed down on several joists. The lower surface of the boards, like the rest of the verandah, had been painted white.

Holmes stood on the bench where Mary Jacob had sat. He stretched his thin arms upwards and the boards under the partition wall of the two rooms shifted a little.

'I thought as much,' he said, screwing his face up and looking at them more closely. 'Edith Carew could not risk being seen to tamper with them afterwards or even asking someone else to do so. The floorboards at the centre have been prised up from the joists. There are no nails holding them down.'

He moved one a little and there was a fall of tiny debris. Wood scraped on wood as he drew one end of the first board down at an angle.

'Hold the lantern up, Watson, there's a good fellow.'

It was, I suppose, a four-foot length of board, several inches wide, that came clear. He handed it down. Five more of the same size followed until, as we looked up, only the waterproof felt separated us from the room above and the beam supporting the new partition wall.

'She could not have done it from here, of course,' he said. 'That felt is complete and uncut from one end of the two rooms to the other. We had best go back up.'

Back in the dressing area of Mrs Carew's bedroom was evidence enough to indict her, if not to convict her. It was as if, under the heavy waterproof felt, a stage trap-door had been opened. Though strong and thick in itself, the material sagged all the more for being at the centre of the flooring. The gap of half an inch under the supporting beam of the partition wall was now half a foot. By moving one or two pieces of furniture from the dressing area to the main bedroom, it was possible to make the felt sag further as the weight holding it in place was lessened.

'I had supposed,' Holmes said, 'that she must have had an accomplice. Her lover Harry Dickinson, for example. Yet she might have done it for herself. There is a gap under the partition beam that even I might get through.'

He took off his jacket, folded it, and eased himself under the beam, head-first and on his back. The bony knuckles whitened as the strong fingers gripped the beam from underneath as a support. Then his long legs were drawn after him and Holmes stood in the other room on the far side of the partition wall.

'There was surely an accomplice,' I said, as we prepared to leave the house half an hour later. 'Someone to see Edith Carew's signal that the nurse had gone, to draw the boards clear from underneath and to replace them when a second signal was given.'

'Perhaps,' he said thoughtfully. 'Yet it needed only the edge of a carpet on the other side to conceal the way in which the felt was sagging. In that case, she could have drawn the boards out much earlier, before she came up to her room for the night. I daresay we shall never know.'

'Could a woman undertake so much?' I asked.

He chuckled in the darkness of the driveway as we made for the lights of The Bluff.

'My dear fellow, your incredulity as to the resolve of the fair sex on these occasions never ceases to amaze me! Mrs Edith Carew was about to prepare a fatal dose of arsenic for her husband and chance the gallows for it. It was that night or never, if she was to let Mary Jacob hang in her place. Compared to such a gamble, I do not suppose that removing a few boards from the verandah or turning back a carpet and wriggling under a beam caused her the least hesitation.'

I had no doubt that he was, as always, correct.

We went at once to the British Naval Prison, where Holmes demanded—rather than asked—to see Mary Jacob. The poor little soul was, if anything, paler than before. I swear she was more frightened of Holmes than of those who would hang her.

'Very well,' he said, as we sat at the bare table. 'I see you have done as I asked and left everything in this room as it was. Before we go further, be so good as to fetch me the birthday present Mrs Carew gave you in September.'

Mary Jacob looked astonished.

'How could you know that my birthday was in September or that she gave me a present?'

'Never mind that,' he said gently. 'Fetch it and show it to me.'

Mary Jacob got up and went to the little table by her bedside.

'For God's sake, Holmes!' I said under my breath. 'How do you know there was a birthday present?'

'Because, my dear Watson, Edith Carew loathed her far too much to risk giving her a present on any other occasion. Even she could hardly ignore the girl's birthday. It fell, most conveniently, in September. The records of Somerset House confirm her date of birth. You must give me credit for sometimes following the strait and narrow path of the obvious.'

Miss Jacob returned and set down before us the bottle of Yardley's Lavender Water. Holmes unscrewed the top and sniffed at it, then he held it up to the light.

'They have made it almost too easy for me,' he said wistfully to himself, then turned to his client again. 'If I may say so, Miss Jacob, you have used a good deal of spirits of lavender in the few weeks since your birthday.'

She looked a little abashed.

'There was an accident. It was upset on the dressing-table when the Chinese boy, Ah Kwong, was cleaning the room.'

'Poor boy! No doubt the perfume seeped into all the drawers and among their contents,' Holmes said sympathetically. 'And were you there when this unfortunate accident happened in the first week or so of October, Miss Jacob?'

'No,' she said, seeming surprised. 'Mrs Carew told me when I came back from running her errands down the town.'

'And even before you returned, poor Ah Kwong was dismissed for an act of clumsiness that was by no means his first.'

'Yes,' she said earnestly. 'But how could you possibly know that it was not the poor boy's first clumsiness or that it happened in the first week of October, unless someone else has told you?'

Holmes laughed, this time to reassure her.

'You give me too much credit, Miss Jacob. I do not know such things: I merely guess them. Very often I am wrong. I hope, however, that you will keep the empty lavender-water bottle in a place where you may always see it, to remind you of a very narrow squeak.'

He got up and left the little room. Through the open door I heard him demanding—rather than requesting—the immediate release of his innocent client.

VIII

'You knew from the first, Holmes!' I said as we left the building. 'This whole business might have been cleared up without our having to leave Baker Street!'

'Not quite,' he said with a sigh. 'I was pretty sure from the second day after Dr Jacob visited us. The date of Mary Jacob's birthday, of course, I got from Somerset House. Then I went to pay a call on brother Mycroft at the Diogenes Club. Remarkable place for the *recherché,* Watson. I suppose you would scarcely credit that their reading room takes the *Japan Gazette.* The latest issues are a little delayed but they had the report in full of the inquest on Walter Carew. I had to be sure that Dr Jacob's information was correct—and so it was. Mrs Carew gave evidence that she had once bought

Fowler's Solution from Schedel's European Pharmacy on The Bluff. Mary Jacob, as we have seen for ourselves, had a penchant for the more sensational type of fiction. Naturally she went to Maruya's in the town, a bookshop as well as a pharmacy. If only Mrs Carew had known that, when Fowler's Solution is prepared in Japanese pharmacies, spirits of lavender are not added, I doubt if I should ever have left Baker Street at all.'

The true financial cost of the investigation would have taken all the money from Dr Jacob's note-case and a good deal more. Holmes preferred to regard his expedition to Japan as a voyage of experience. He positively refused to take a fee of any kind from our client. His last meeting with Mary Jacob, however, was no more comfortable than the others.

'You would do well to remember, Miss Jacob,' he said dispassionately, 'that taking letters addressed to others and practising their signatures is a game in children and a crime in adults. I hope that you have learned that lesson thoroughly.'

The world knows the conclusion of the story. The case against Mary Jacob collapsed and the prosecution in Her Britannic Majesty's Consular Court at Yokohama was withdrawn. In that same court, Mrs Edith Carew was afterwards convicted of the murder of her husband. On a day of winter rain driving in from the Pacific Ocean, Mr Justice Mowat, who had sat beside Consul Troupe throughout the trial, placed the black cap upon his head and pronounced a sentence of such unusual jurisdiction that Holmes positively would not leave Yokohama until he had heard it.

'The sentence is that you Edith Mary Hallowell Carew, be forthwith taken from the place where you now stand and be taken to the British Consular Gaol in Yokohama, and therein interned. And that on a day appointed by the proper authority, you be taken to the place of execution, and there be hanged by the neck until you are dead . . .'

The sentence of death on Edith Carew, to be carried out at the British Naval Prison in the presence of the Consul, was forwarded to the Ambassador in Tokyo for confirmation. The Ambassador recalled, however, that on the day before her conviction, the Japanese Emperor had proclaimed a remission to all his subjects who were under sentence that day. It was accordingly ordered that Mrs Carew should be reprieved and sent to penal servitude with hard labour for life. She was brought home to Aylesbury prison to serve her sentence, from which she was released fourteen years later.

In the sunshine of what seemed like a spring afternoon, Holmes stared across the sparkling water of the natural harbour.

'You see, Watson? It is just as I told you. The true mystery after all was not Professor Pepper's ghost nor the tensile strength and elasticity of materials as Professor Vanek of Budapest and other physicists had studied them. Our interest must be the mind that can purchase and measure death by spoonfuls day after day with a kindly smile and without the least remorse for the martyrdom of pain. Not death by a single blow, my dear friend, but by slow and deliberate torture. I confess that I find the new science of psychopathology deficient in its study of this most interesting of all states of the human mind. Our experience here ought not to pass without some commemoration of it. I wonder whether I might not spend the leisure of our homeward journey in writing a short monograph on so deserving a topic.'

Author's Note

The stories in this volume are based upon historical events, over which the shadow of the Great Detective is allowed to pass. Apart from Sherlock Holmes and John Watson, almost all the other figures in the stories played the parts ascribed to them here, except where minor characters have been invented to give continuity to the narratives.

'The Ghost in the Machine' alters little except for the introduction of Sherlock Holmes, as the scientific detective who saved Dr Smethurst from the gallows. The near-fatal error of the forensic investigators occurred in fact, as it does here in fiction.

In 'The Case of the Crown Jewels', the explanation of the robbery is based upon the characters and activities of two gentlemen-crooks of the Edwardian period, Frank Shackleton and Richard Gorges. Gorges survived his imprisonment for shooting a policeman and died as a pauper in an institution in the 1950s. Sir Arthur Vicars and Peirce Mahony died in the circumstances described here. The Crown Jewels of Ireland have never been found.

'The Case of the Unseen Hand' is based upon events in the history of the Third Republic, between 1894 and 1909. The main story is taken from Marguerite Steinheil, *My Memoirs*, Eveleigh Nash, 1912, which describes President Faure's 'Secret History'. The account of the President's death, in bed with Madame Steinheil, was given by President Casimir-Périer to the French Ambassador to St Petersburg, Maurice Georges Paléologue. It was suppressed until the publication of Paléologue's *Journal de l'Affaire Dreyfus*, Librairie Plon, 1955. Gustave Hamard and Alphonse Bertillon were prominent figures in their respective branches of the Súreté. The criminal activities of the Comte de Balincourt and his three associates are described in Marguerite Steinheil's memoirs. There exists a heroic painting, *The Deathbed of President Faure*, in which the great statesman expires decorously with his ministers, family, and priests standing round. Madame Steinheil triumphed over the scandal and the double-murder prosecution. She was to die in England, at the seaside town of Hove in 1954, as the sixth Baroness Abinger.

Rumours of a morganatic marriage between the future George V and the daughter of Admiral Sir Michael Culme-Seymour at Malta in 1890 circulated in the press until the specific allegations by Edward Mylius brought the case to court in 1911. The allegations referred to in 'The Case of the Blood Royal' are in the Public Record Office at PRO KB28/704/1. The manuscript of the Prince's diary for 1888, cited in Kenneth Rose, *King George V*, Weidenfeld & Nicolson, 1983, and James Lees-Milne, *Harold Nicolson: A Biography 1930–1968*, Chatto & Windus, 1981, refers to the unnamed girl with whom he used to sleep at Portsmouth and another in St John's Wood, whom he shared with his elder brother, the Duke of Clarence. 'She is a ripper,' he added. The death of the blackmailer Charles Augustus Howell—whom Conan Doyle presented as 'Charles Augustus Milverton'—was reported by Oscar Wilde and by Thomas James Wise in *A Bibliography of the Writings of Algernon Charles Swinburne*, 1919–20. His death certificate more tactfully describes the victim as dying of 'pneumonia'.

The defence of Robert Wood and the Green Bicycle Case were among the greatest triumphs of Sir Edward Marshall Hall as a defence lawyer. 'The Case of the Camden Town Murder' and 'The Case of the Missing Rifleman' make Sherlock Holmes the colleague of the great defender. Each criminal investigation took the form and had the outcome described in the two stories. The Camden

Town killer was never caught. However, Walter Sickert's obsession with painting and drawing the subject led to suggestions of his involvement. Sickert (1860–1942) was a friend of the young artist, Robert Wood, who stood trial for the murder, and helped to raise money for Wood's defence. In Stephen Knight, *Jack the Ripper: The Final Solution*, Harrap, 1976, it is suggested that Sickert's dedication to the Camden Town Murder extended to an involvement in the Whitechapel murders of 1888.

The murderer of Bella Wright was never brought to justice. Marshall Hall's attitude to Ronald Light, before and after the trial, suggests that he believed Light had killed the girl, probably by accident. As counsel, he appears never to have discussed the case directly with his client except for a few minutes after Light had already entered the dock. A short story in the *Strand* magazine described how a single bullet from a hunter's rifle, intended to shoot the crow on the gate, might pass through the bird and kill Bella Wright. The story did not explain why the hunter would shoot crows with ammunition of .455 calibre or what weapon could be used for this.

'The Case of the Yokohama Club' involved criminal proceedings little reported in England but carried verbatim in the *Japan Gazette* in 1896–7. Mary Esther Jacob was prosecuted at the instigation of Edith Carew before the Court of the British Consul at Yokohama, on a charge of having murdered her employer, Walter Carew. The evidence against her was such as the story describes. The case collapsed suddenly when further evidence was uncovered against Mrs Carew. Edith Carew was tried and sentenced to death by the same court in Yokohama but reprieved as a result of the intervention of the British Ambassador in Tokyo. She was brought back to England and was released from life imprisonment in Aylesbury gaol in 1911. The stage-magicians described in the story were well-known figures of Victorian entertainment. The ghost illusion is described at length in Chapter 6 of J. E. Robert-Houdin's *Secrets of Stage Conjuring* (1881).

Some further light is shed on the lives of Holmes and Watson. It has long been known that Holmes retired in 1903 to a life of bee-keeping on the southern slopes of the Sussex Downs, near the coast at Cuckmere Haven, taking with him Mrs Hudson as housekeeper. It is not surprising that, after a while, he should have missed his old acquaintances and the stimulus of criminal investigation. His services to the nation also required his presence in London. As several of these stories indicate, he took on the Baker Street rooms again when they fell vacant, alternating professional work in London and retirement in Sussex until after the First World War.

Dr Watson's first two marriages interrupted his residence in Baker Street, which ended at last with his third marriage in 1902. He was, however, the guest of Sherlock Holmes during weeks when the third Mrs Watson was absent from London 'on family business' and when the two men were engaged in such matters of national importance as the disappearance of the Irish Crown Jewels.